MINERVA'S
TURN

MINERVA'S TURN

HELEN FAYE ROSENBLUM

G · P · PUTNAM'S · SONS NEW YORK

Published simultaneously in Canada by Academic Press Canada
Limited, Toronto.

Library of Congress Cataloging in Publication Data

Rosenblum, Helen Faye.
  Minerva's turn.

  I. Title.
PZ4.R81159Mi   [PS3568.07887]   813'.54   80-13073
ISBN 0-399-12532-9

Ray
Joshua
Steven
Charles
. . . their book

MINERVA'S
TURN

Hawk Simon tenderly pulls shut the half-glassed back door of the farmhouse, then carelessly allows the screen door to crash closed on its narrow, archaic spring. The noise will not touch Cara, who is sleeping the sweet and heavy sleep of the recently stoned. It will, however, arouse Lucy, the cantankerous old watchdog. His clamor will in turn beget the wrath of five rapidly maturing part-Siamese kittens. Paul the Parrot, understanding that he has somehow been betrayed by his cage cover, will announce, "Joseph Heller! Joseph Heller! Something Happened! Something Happened!" until Radiant, who has been asleep or pretending to be asleep in his Snoopy sleeping bag on the kitchen floor since last Thursday, shouts, "For Christ's sake, Caravelle, can't you do something about this goddamn menagerie?"

Hawk, inculpable, leaves it all behind.

He pulls his antiquated Austin-Healey, acquired in what he considers the trade of a lifetime after the accident, backward off the gravel drive onto the grass. It swings around a hundred eighty full degrees in one compact loop. Then Hawk heads it down the long, meandering driveway toward the road, glad to be out of it. He feels clean and tangentially virtuous, having spent an inordinately long time under the caress of the telephone shower in the claw-footed bathtub. Precious little hot water remains for Cara, which doesn't matter too much, since she doesn't have to report to work at the state hospital until the afternoon shift today anyway. She can shower later, he grudges, in the wake of an evening where their tacit mutual exuberances at dinner had progressed from banter to bed. Ambivalently Hawk had allowed himself to succumb. In the reflective morning, his typewriter every bit as untaxed as it was last night, Hawk's sense of charity has outreached its limits. Oh, he is in love with Cara. He just isn't sure that he likes her very much.

She goes off in a semiregular pattern of recurring shifts, but Hawk can hardly believe that someone so selectively slovenly can be a nurse. He hardly knows what to think, in spite of her trim little cap, her proud velvet band. When she wore white stockings, it seemed to Hawk that they were discarded and replaced more often than laundered. When her hospital bowed to modernity and converted the entire clinical staff to street clothes in the space of one memorable day, Hawk wondered whether the whole uniform business had been his psychotic illusion.

No more can he credit her claim that she was named Caravelle because she was conceived in the rest room of a jet-prop airplane. If that's the family legend she's been alluding to, she can have it.

She leaves, she returns. She contributes to the financing of their odd ménage, if not to its sense of order. Hawk doesn't intend to spend much more of his life with her anyway. He would rather embroider mentally upon the true origins of her name—all such fine headwork becoming grist for his creative mill, perhaps—than pay too much heed to anything she actually says.

State Route 600, snaking along the river northward to the capital and southward into Saint Kathareen's, dramatically terminates the gravelly run of his access road. It used to be called Highway 60. In the natural way of such matters, thousands of dollars were spent to reprint thousands of maps, for which project thousands of trees were somewhere felled, pulped, forgotten. Hawk hates it. At the same time, every local resident along the length of the route continues to refer to it as "Old 60," retaining the dignity of a double-digit designation. Hawk feels both spurned by the downgrading of his favorite thoroughfare, and bravely, stoutly, farther from his native suburban New Jersey soil than ever before. He is not dissatisfied with the balance.

He waits at the end of the drive for a growling tractor to clank past. He has pulled up just far enough to be certain of clear visibility beyond the stand of sassafras, but not too far, lest he impede the passage of the slow, wide vehicles heading northward. Finally the tractor clears, and he wheels in expertly behind it.

He has chosen the follower's place this morning, rear guard to the smelly exhaust and muddy tread. He wants to follow the farmer's eye as far as it goes, to project himself into the special dignity of dirty fingernails and snakeproof boots. He wants to imagine all the things beyond suburban imagining. Then gun his engine into its fourth forward gear as the old man turns off, gliding up the terraced side of the hill across the river in plenty of time to get a good segment of conversation on tape to show for the day. Hawk wants to be sure that there is plenty of time for everything. Particularly for Minerva, his fascination, his . . . might he say, love?

Hawk notices the clean, bluish beginnings of early cabbages in rows along the highway, and the smallest tracings of the first beans. A few reckless souls have dared their tomatoes into the earth as well. The low foliage is verdant, but the neat, vertical poles look strangely naked. Irrigation sprinklers worry the ground where the road curves in toward the loamy black bottomland. Hawk annually thinks of this particular watering ritual as favoring the favored, but he has not shared his homely little insight with anybody.

He can't bring himself to go that far into domestic confidence with Cara. He never knows what might cause her to take offense, move out on an impulse as impenetrable as the one with which she first moved in. He talks about his concerns for pulp and water only with Lucy when they happen to stroll together of an evening. But Lucy, an old farm hound, has his own notions of timing and direction. Although they begin together and end together as a rule, he and Hawk rarely share more than a fraction of the circumnavigation. Hawk ends up talking to himself.

On this shimmering morning, Hawk keeps his own counsel. He reads no omen in the fragrant sky. The earth is untainted. The farmer in front of him finally nods and waves in a gesture of rural solidarity as he turns off to the left. Hawk returns the signal, a willing compatriot.

The town of Saint Kathareen's appears around a sharp turn to the right. Hawk thinks for the thousandth time how he cherishes the virginity of this place. He wonders how the violation will come—with a Holiday Inn? a Taco Bell? some more unimaginable horror, signaling the end of a tradition, the beginning of a Strip? God forbid.

Another side of Hawk Simon pulls at him, centers him in the middle of a tug of thoughts, yearns toward the freedoms and the horrors of the urban conglomerations he has left behind, the cities to which he imagines he is destined to return after he has outworn the bucolic elegances of Saint Kathareen's.

As the hour of parting becomes something Hawk feels impelled to consider, the tensions mount. He is smoking a little too much grass in the effort to keep his perspectives sharp. He thinks about what he is doing as a problem only when Radiant shouts from the kitchen floor, "Hey, man, a person can hardly sleep with all the fumes from the pot-smokin' goin' on in there."

[9]

Cara says that that is Radiant's way of asking for a toke.

Hawk says, "Shit, let him ask, like everyone else." And, reluctant to give up without proper ceremony what he has hoarded, Hawk shifts the burden back to Radiant. He returns his concentration to the quality of the grass, keeping his excuses for using it, or the protocols of the situation, at bay.

It's home-grown grass, hilltop grass, and very good. The stand of plants hidden strategically in the ruins of an old brick-tile silo have kept many such an unlikely family unit as Hawk's warm through the Valley winters. He had thought his good fortune in finding it there was unique, until Miss Minerva had apprised him otherwise. Even after hearing her out on the subject more than once, he refuses to take this aspect of his good fortune for granted, continues to demand formality and ritual as surely as if he were copping scarce and costly reefer on the street.

In the mornings after his indulgences, Hawk awakens clear-eyed, energetic. He emerges from the fairly orderly tangle of Wamsutta sheets feeling slightly guilty because he knows he should be involved in some kind of ideological boycott against their manufacturer. However, son of a Jewish mother, he enjoys the meticulousness of their corners. He allows her to send them to him semiannually, with the relentless regularity of White Sales. He has more linens than a trousseau, about which he is defensively embarrassed. Yet, to enter a fray of denial with his mother could, in his estimate, end more disastrously than any conceivable violent demonstration of social consciousness. Hawk understands a great deal about the varieties of human violence. He steers as clear as possible.

Turning at last into the familiar driveway, Hawk maneuvers into a position where the shadow of the ancient water maple, old when Foothill House was young, will shelter the Healey until he reclaims it. Thinks momentarily of Cara, then flees to other pastures. Still he feels no portents in the day. But an incipient, mild unease, coming from nowhere.

He wonders, picking up a notebook, when Professor Robley will have the short fiction papers back, but reminds himself that the decision is already made somewhere in the recesses of Robley's reasoning. Let Robley take all the time that he needs. All the better for Hawk to stay on top of the Oral History. It is not Hawk's policy to create anxieties where none need exist.

He cradles his tape recorder and the College Spiral carefully in his left arm as he closes the door with his right. He uses just enough force to make the catch tumble into security, not enough to jar the element of balance in the atmosphere. A fondness for balance, for symmetry, has always marked Hawk's personality. It is thus that he admires his own magnanimity for sharing his house with so oddly assembled a lot of people and animals. He floats in a delicate state of limited grace, generosity being the coin of his exchange.

He does not see any phase of his present condition as permanent or perpetual. He imagines that, upon graduating from Saint Kathareen's College, he will embark upon some kind of literary life, sharing his brains, his lusts, his stash, with a more orderly, less residential series of fulfilling women. Certainly no animals but Lucy. He has begun to discriminate between his follies and his serious quests. He can, in fact, at certain sober times envision the future as a place where he can't wait to be. Nor does he labor majestically to shed his current infatuation with history. He doesn't want to be trammeled forever by this kind of thing, but he assumes that when the time comes he will shake it off as easily as Lucy shakes would-be marauders from his coat. Easy Hawk.

 ONE

I

Her parents had named her Minerva Kathareen Robley Niesenwandering. She couldn't shed the baggage fast enough. She married Hammond Kettering Bolton, dry-goods merchant and occasional rider to hounds, primarily to acquire the use of his name. She would have had serious second thoughts had she realized that most of his acquaintances called him "Ham," sneering.

By nineteen, Minerva Kathareen Robley Niesenwandering Bolton had matured. The part she liked best about marriage to stodgy old Hammond, who was already showing indications that he would become porcine as if to round out his name, was shocking the daylights out of him in bed. Not that the enterprise required much effort. All that Goodwife Bolton had to do was await Hammond in the feather bed, lights extinguished, counterpane pulled up to her subtly dimpled chin, stark naked. Hammond invariably protested righteously. Minerva invariably ignored his *pro forma* resistance. She chucked him under the chin, fumbled expertly with the elaborate corsetry he affected beneath his copious nightshirt, and nuzzled in. Usually Hammond unbent sufficiently to make the romp worthwhile for all concerned. But far from him ever to condone her behavior by so much as a secret wink or a squeeze of the hand.

The occasions on which he wouldn't, or couldn't, uncoil past his posture as his wife's keeper and arbiter of her morals occurred infrequently. Once, however, was more than enough for Minerva. Before her twenty-first birthday, she examined her marriage from the critical viewpoint of a twentieth-century woman, and found it wanting. Carefully she considered the remedies that seemed applicable—philanthrophy, children, whist—and rejected them one by one. To Minerva, they all seemed to treat symptoms, where only a clean excision would do.

On her own, then, without fanfare or moral support, she walked out of Hammond Bolton's bedroom one cold but sunny morning in February of 1906. She left no tears, no regrets. She further declined to leave even a minor bauble of the heirloom jewelry which the family Bolton had acquired through various forms of chicanery, highway robbery, and honest sweat through the centuries. The pieces had found their way with varying degrees of honor from Ireland to Massachusetts. Minerva, sensible to the core, had no pragmatic attachment to Massachusetts as a place where an article of potential usefulness needed to make its eternal home.

Hammond Bolton had dreamed many a hopeful dream, he once told his wife in unprecedented intimacy, of graceful Bolton daughters flashing emeralds and garnets as they waltzed their way through life and cotillions. Never at his creative best could he have imagined the zesty Minnie pawning her way across the Alleghenies, leaving most of the Bolton birthright behind her in petty increments, keeping her personal honor and incidentally her own modest family principal equally intact. Nor could he have envisioned her ending up unadorned, crusty, and optimistic, as she arrived at the remote outpost of Saint Kathareen's in the first flush of false spring in the year 1906.

Minerva was exhilarated. Her sense of independent accomplishment eclipsed every insecure quaver she had harbored during the terrifying darkness along the way. She carried not a swatch of regret among her baggage. If she had done anything questionable, it had been in the matter of the jewelry. That, however, couldn't be helped. At the rate Hammond was amassing money, he would be able to replace it many times over before the end of summer, if he so chose. She would not believe that sentiment could enter into consideration for a man with Hammond's paucity of wit.

The other item which niggled temporarily at her brain was her failure to have done anything about securing a legal divorce. Well, Hammond would see to that, no doubt. He would arrange that the taint of the present circumstances be eradicated from his life fully and forever. He'd probably revoke her birth certificate if he could, cleanly efface the specter of something flawed from his universe. Well, let him. Let the dead bury their dead. Minerva Bolton had other things to do.

She arrived at Saint Kathareen's with no intention of trying to cash in on her Robley connections. Although the tales of fresh waters and verdant valleys that had drawn her ancestors to settlement had equally magnetized her, Minerva had decided not to make claim to the founding and reportedly still dominant fathers of the compact little metropolis. She had spent her twenty-odd years of life so far content that her namesake, Kathareen Robley, lay well buried at the center of her own name. Minerva, Massachusetts-bred herself, knew too much about the departed lady to be inclined to disinter her. She possessed, in fact, far more data than most current residents of the river valley would have taken comfort in knowing, steeped as they were in the local sentimentalities. For her part, Minerva originally assumed that the town had been named with local ironies sophisticatedly in place. When she discovered the grossness of her error, her hilarity redoubled.

Thus, exuberant, very nearly penniless, and on the verge of lusty laughter, Minerva first viewed Saint Kathareen's. Her breath caught just as she rounded the last turn, at the sight of the Valley before her. The landscape rolled, lush and green, away from the hill at whose crest her exhausted team stopped to recover its collective wind. She was glad for the time, the moment's respite. Minerva gaped in wonder.

At the confluence of the rivers nestled a Lilliputian accumulation of buildings, extraordinarily uniform in color and spirit, but dissimilar in size and presumably in purpose. Terra-cotta predominantly, they modulated through tones of rose to buff to blood as the sun followed the course of the river toward late afternoon. The unwavering, unifying slate of the somber roofs stabilized the picture. Minerva thought the scene was rhapsodic. The stones of Florence, she would later decide, had nothing on the native brick of Saint Kathareen's.

Fleetingly she hungered to endow the moment with the special permanence that accompanies experiences shared. She nearly turned, cried, "Hammond! Look!" Her hand almost strained for a hand to hold, an arm to clasp, a warm gift of flesh to transmit the fever of her discovery. Then she took the next logical step, imagining Hammond, lips pursed, a Sanhedrin unto himself, waiting with skittish impatience for her to be done with any and all perambulations around her vision of earth or soul, to get on with the Routine. The unease, the familiar sensation of having been judged and found wanting, began to creep up her body like a climbing weed. She lopped it off at the base, casting it behind.

Perhaps she should have taken time, then and there, to dig up the whole gnarled, infectious root and destroy it once and for all. The temptation did not entirely escape her. But the human mind does not easily give up its passions and addictions, however destructive. Nor does it easily relinquish its hold on the memory of pains where pleasure was once any component of their creation. So she skimmed the surfaces of her thoughts, leaving their resolution for another day. Besides, Minerva had no time for unprofitable reflection; there was still far too much to see.

And what she saw: arcs of dwellings fanning out from the roseate confluence. White frame buildings, or smartly painted brick, harmoniously topped with further tiers of local slate, led concentrically from the confluence into a dwindling distance beneath where she stood. Crosshatched by short, irregular side-street aisles, the amphitheater panorama of Saint Kathareen's drew Minerva like the lights of vaudeville. She knew inexorably that she would settle in, would set about watching the theatrics of life from a vantage much like the one she occupied at that moment. In time she might well venture a tad closer to the footlights. From one side or the other, she knew her personal Chautauqua when she saw it. Minerva Kathareen Robley Niesenwandering Bolton had, in a manner of speaking, arrived.

At a glowing distance across the Valley, the sun raced toward an irregular, doubly peaked rise. Hardly grand enough to be designated a moderate hill in Massachusetts, the formation stood proudly across the river and above the Valley, bold in its nomenclature, Mount Calvin-and-Levi. Minerva knew it from the map, yet couldn't quite assimilate the intelligence that these nubbins were what she had been invoking in the mind's eye as DESTINATION all along. A moment of gripping terror convulsed her from the inside out. She saw it all—the Saint Kathareen's Valley— with a stark clarity: lovely, miniaturized, enclosed, unreal—and considered the possibilities of living out a life in that impossibly occluded perspective.

Minerva was almost enough ahead of her time to have shouted, "Wait! I didn't leave New England, and Hammond, and hearth and home, to be constricted *again*, like this." And moved on.

But not quite. She stood stock-still, inhaled a heady mixture of apple blossoms and warming soil. For the first time in her life she experienced simple breathing as an erotic act, free, rhythmic, and fulfilling. She tarried a moment longer. Then, at a subtle, ineffable, unambiguous command, she rallied horses and self. Her fatigued but stout team, and her self-directed discipline, the latter of which credited far more of the Robley spirit than she ever would have realized in those days, bore her down the last rutted, hopeful road into Saint Kathareen's.

She drove slowly, partly because of the condition of the seamy gutter which passed for a highway, partly because of her own intense concentration on every landmark about her. On the twin hills opposite she saw modest dwellings clustered around the bottom, a few aspiring toward the loftier altitudes, but not very far. A bit beyond, she noticed a sparser scattering of newer structures. Their bricked uniformity bespoke at once the nearby clay hills, and also their fundamental indebtedness to the traditional houses which lay at their feet and within their venue across the river.

In the geographical center of one of the hills, framed by scaffolding which cast odd shadows in the lengthening day, stood something else again, the sport of the litter, the wildly eccentric monarch whose lack of taste set its own unduplicable standard. It was an enormous turreted building, distinguished by its color as well as its size: a monument of a dwelling, in the process of being painted an unremitting, self-aggrandizing shade of laundry gray.

Upon later, closer examination, inside and out, Minerva would discover gargoyles, putti, blank niches, symbolic pilasters, every manner of visual affectation shamelessly plagiarized from every known period in the history of art. At close range, it would be humanly impossible for the mind to assimilate the details of stratified decor and vulgar overlay. From her comfortable distance, Minerva simply almost went off the road as she guffawed noisily to herself and to the loyal team that had endured a thousand miles of her explosive reactions. "Ye gods! What a monstrosity!" And retrieved herself from near-disaster in a ditch only by the sobering threat of having to abandon her trusty wagon so near to her goal.

Of worldly goods, Minerva had few by the time she reached Saint Kathareen's. Of fortitude she had more than a substantial endowment. Of ideas and originality she had enough to tide herself and an entire settlement of otherwise less impoverished souls over the long hot summer which lay just downstream.

Minerva remembered hearing as a child a story, perhaps apocryphal, from her own father's childhood, during the Gold Rush. A wishful entrepreneur, so the tale went, had set out from New Orleans harbor with a cargo of top hats for the newly rich, socially aspiring residents of the glamorous, mysterious boom town on a West Coast bay. After a lengthy, costly, and agonizing voyage around the Horn, merchant and cargo arrived in San Francisco relatively intact. The only problem was that the slightly mildewed, somewhat soggy cargo was drier and more comfortable by many degrees than San Francisco itself. The new Westerners of the Gold Rush town, affluent though many of them were, lived their days with a greater necessity to stay basically dry and fungus-free than to preen. Their lives were governed far less by cultural yearnings than by the simple challenge to stay afoot on streets where planking set as sidewalk by day disappeared into quagmires of muck and mud before nightfall.

The merchant hatter, supposedly some Robley connection via a remote branch, clearly saw his duty as it lay. He dashed ashore practically before the gangplank was set. Instead of rushing to conquer the large dry-goods emporium, whose manager had for some months been skeptically awaiting

[19]

the supposed windfall, he headed in breathless haste straight for the office of the mayor. Before the sun set on San Francisco that night, the city had become the proud possessor of several thousand gross of mohair top hats—complete with their molded steel-wire substructures and their nearly indestructible gold-patterned packing boxes.

Within twenty-four hours the first sagging wooden sidewalks had been yanked out of the swampy mire and shored up by hat boxes from below. Embarrassed or quizzical workmen cursed, laughed, replaced planks, predicted their imminent and final disappearance into the ooze. Respectful silence gradually fell over the streets as the crews moved on, footholds strengthening as character.

In the end, the hatter presumptive had become a civil engineer. His approach to the civilizing of San Francisco had started from the ground up, so the story goes, rather than from the top down. In the long run, the action meant considerably more to the future of the city and all concerned than anything else he might have envisioned in his wildest fantasy. In a latter day, his dominant qualities might have been labeled: ingenuity, flexibility, imagination.

Minerva Bolton had no handle on the terminology, but she adored the legend. She saw it as a buoyant exercise in the art of the possible, and took considerable private comfort therein. She thought, however, that she'd just as leave tackle Saint Kathareen's the other way around. Starting at the top.

In well over a century of stalwart existence, Saint Kathareen's had solidified itself almost beyond necessity. Brick streets might disappear periodically beneath spring floods, but they always reappeared, inviolate, as the water subsided. Saint Kathareenians, having learned early and independently to survive, had unlearned vanity. Their personal visual lives were as toneless as the endless days of slicing winter rain, except of course for the utter magnificence of their Valley geography, to which most of them were too busy with mundane matters to pay much heed, aesthetically speaking. They worried about molds, rusts, water levels, taproots. Too much water on the soil in April and May stymied the root systems of cash and kitchen crops when the dust and drought of August came. Too little rainfall in the spring, and the plantings grew spindly in proportion to the powerfully thrusting roots heading for the water table. Folks watched the balance as closely as they watched the feedbroker's scales.

The women of Saint Kathareen's stitched poky little sunbonnets to wear against all the elements as they tended the gardens, monitored the irrigation ditches, nudged the rows of shoots into proper conformity. If they remembered to change hats for church on Sunday mornings or Wednesday nights, they donned black or brown stiffly buckramed versions of their workaday gear. Minerva's comprehension of this particular state of affairs

[20]

was based, at the outset, more upon her own imagination and guesswork than any real knowledge. But she happened to be dead-on right.

And she intended to change all that, performing her gentle but relentless surgeries upon the sensibilities of Saint Kathareen's even as she had ruthlessly excised the irrelevancies of her very own name. Her innate style endowed her with a jolly confidence that what was good for Minerva Bolton was good for any right-thinking female person.

She concentrated her attentions upon the newer brick houses on the hills opposite, and, incidentally, upon the gray monstrosity of a mansion a-building with such gaudy impunity. These structures, exuding prosperity, constituted the major external ingredient of Minerva's optimism: her target population, she would say years later, tongue cheerfully implanted in what many observers would admiringly call one hell of a lot of cheek.

As for the church-on-Sunday aspect, Minerva didn't think very much of the idea for her own salvation. She had attended dourly prophetic Congregational services all her life, first as her father's only paragon and angel child, later as Hammond Bolton's dubious ornament. Privately she thought of God as rather remote and impersonal, displaying considerable largess at times, but having also a rather strong and occasionally questionable sense of the practical joke. The representations of the Deity set forth within the austere confines of the New England houses of worship at first bewildered, then bemused her. Finally they began to bore her to tears. Saint Kathareen's churches, somberly if awkwardly modeled after their New England ancestors, would need a bit of brightening up, in Minerva's opinion. And Minerva knew exactly how she intended to go about it.

In the ninety-first year of her age, Miss Minerva is being tape-recorded by an eager succession of history and English majors from Saint Kathareen's College. Hawk Simon is one of them, but there is a specialness to his project. He senses an intensity of communication between the two of them that he is reluctant to impute to anyone else, anywhere. Hawk is awakening to a sense that this project, this triangulation of a Self in eternity, is as important to him as it is to her, even though it is her life with which they are nominally dealing. He does know that Miss Minerva occupies a greater proportion of his daily waking thoughts than does any other living creature.

Hawk has cultivated this sense of importance out of an aimless, dilettantish beginning to its present consuming status in a little less than two full academic quarters. At first the assignment, handed down with barely tolerable arrogance by a junior faculty member in the current graces of the local DAR, offended Hawk mightily. He considered that time spent immortalizing the history and personalities of so trivial an outpost as Saint Kathareen's was an outrageous theft from the puny ration of precious hours of life allotted to Higher Pursuits.

As far as Hawk could tell, the project was illegitimate. The guilty instructor could only have had sly ego games in mind when he designed the Oral History project and designated Miss Minerva as a serviceable fulcrum. Otherwise, Hawk wondered, why bother? The fact that his brown-nosing fellows went about other aspects of the same assignment with patent enthusiasm impressed him not at all. He thought of students and faculty alike as an interlocking protectorate of dupes. Of course, the others had started earlier, listened harder, gone after a different kind of statistic in the first place. From the data they had begun to see that a woman who started as she had, on nerve alone, was bound to amount to more than a quaint period piece. Still, while others plumbed history, Hawk sulked.

After long and elaborate, thoroughly transparent resistance, he finally, and not without serious resentment, had made an appointment for his first interview with Miss Minerva. He managed to accomplish the distasteful telephone call only by convincing himself that as long as he had to serve out an education in dreary little Saint Kath's, he might as well milk it for whatever laughs it might produce.

Something in the amused catch of her telephone voice snared him right away. Lightly she took the reins.

"Yes, indeed, Mr. Simon. I'm a Kathareenian by pure volition. I'd be pleased to discuss it with you, if you like." Teasing, somehow. He couldn't put his finger on it.

"Yeah. Well, maybe we could set up an appointment." Hardly his best company manners, but if he was looking for her to do the rejecting, take the fall for him, he was going to have to find another patsy.

"Tomorrow at two would be just fine," she had retorted, her name Efficiency.

"Yeah. Well." Running out of sullen overtures. "That's . . ."

"Two-thirty, then? Excellent. I'll expect you." Brisk as morning. And clicked off, before Hawk had time to note with any satisfaction that she'd done all the work.

Looking beyond the stand of sassafras to the road from his front door that evening, Hawk had thought for a long while about what it might mean to be a "Kathareenian by volition." He pondered late, indecisively. Finally he went to bed, amused to find himself robed in soft benevolence. He didn't know why he felt so comfortable.

By morning he had modulated back down into benign detachment.

[22]

Nevertheless, the shoulder of anticipation propelled his hours along toward afternoon. By 2:25 an undifferentiated sense of possibility led like a flashlight pointer right up the side of Calvin-and-Levi to the door of Foothill House.

He didn't know what to present to her in the way of a credential. It never occurred to him that she'd demand none. He used Howard Robley, the faculty member he understood to be her relative, somehow—rather like a dog-eared bus pass, still viable, but vaguely embarrassing.

"I'm Owen Simon," he explained.

"Hawk," she affirmed.

"Yes," he acknowledged, as much surprised that he had used that name in talking to her yesterday—or had he?—as that she had retained it.

"I have a good memory," she responded to his ensuing silence, disarming him completely. Whatever thoughts he had had lined up and ready for her undoing went caroming off the walls of his bare skull.

She smiled engagingly. "Come in, please."

He obeyed with a nod, thinking that by keeping his mouth shut he could remain on top, smooth as beancurd. His eyes, however, registering the details of the entry to Foothill House, defrocked his pretensions of disinterest. He could feel Minerva reading him, and felt three and a half years old.

"Won't you sit down, Hawk?"

Aspiring to nonchalance, he crashed into a horsehair sofa, fumbled with his notebooks and recorder, and wished that since, in his embarrassment, he had certainly forgotten how to pray, he could only remember some of the rudiments of how to talk.

Hawk remembers that day with parental indulgence. He cannot yet plot the graph of Minerva's personality, but he has divined with high-resolution clarity the ingredients of her technique. Between wit and candor, she has lured him, entrapped him, wooed him, reeled him in. By the end of that first afternoon he had felt like a brand-new child, never so regretful at having to turn off an episode of *Secret Agent* to go eat dinner as to leave the opening chapter of this vivid, human seriocomedy.

His common sense admonishes his ego, telling him that there are other Oral Historians, other days of Minerva unfolding for other microphones and other consciousnesses. Humble—indeed, paranoid—Hawk decides that she couldn't possibly view him as anything special. He chooses to arrive at her door unannounced from time to time, trying to wrest a meaning—a special pleasure, a disappointment, anything—out of the response she offers when she first sees him through the filters of screen door and surprise. He can find nothing untoward, no matter how often he appears. He appears often.

[23]

Naturally he feeds upon the absence of negative indicators, wills self-esteem tumescent. He hangs on to the feeling that Minerva indeed requites his sense of mission, that she saves the special, haloed moments for him. It is this vision which prevails, affirms his purpose. Keeps him coming back and back and back.

Objectively, straining for academic distance, he does detect a special tone in his tapes. He has listened to all the others. They dissect Minerva as facilely as if she were some kind of inert specimen. Attending fiercely, Hawk might almost believe that her first factory had been nothing but an accumulated tonnage of nuts, bolts, and girders. Felder might have been a gutless robot. Minerva's annual trips to Europe and England might have passed as buying sprees, footnotes. The Chamber of Commerce comes across as a natural development in the evolution of any community. Where is the humanity of it? Hawk wonders.

He can hear in this agglomeration of detail a respectful undertone as each interviewer steers Minerva into the columns of net profit, retail sales, population statistics: one little village and how it grew. He reviews the meager flesh his appointed colleagues have applied to the provocative skeleton of historic Saint Kathareen's, and is scandalized by his peers. Their materialistic self-absorption flatly prevents this entire sample from comprehending Miss Minerva for the vivid natural resource that she is. On the other hand, Hawk is elated to be the exception to the group. Minerva's true confidant, he sees himself, not as one of the Elect, but as The Elect personified.

Everyone else, having come to the end of the project term, has dutifully filed a contribution and gone about other forms of business. This willingness to divest thus of casually garnered portions of Miss Minerva's persona Hawk sees as another aha! in the reliquary of clues to his uniqueness.

Moreover, he feels free to take the liberty of extending his association as far as it will go. He suspects that Miss Minerva understands an ambivalence lurking within his attitudes toward his present academic career, although he hasn't been able to bring himself to talk about it. He assumes by this time that Howard Robley can't wait to spill every moldy bean about everything that goes on in his narrow corridor of experience. What Hawk doesn't understand is that pride prevents Howard from bringing Minerva any tales from a career he considers largely ignominious. Unlike Hawk, Howard Robley possesses no mechanisms of rationalization, no creativity at all.

His own collected tapes, conversations, impressions, have, after all this time, painted for Hawk a pastiche of the building of life and such culture as there was in an earlier Saint Kathareen's. And Minerva, unremittingly alert, has come to epitomize for Hawk the perfect subject for the kind of spoken memoirs which are lately redefining the nation, helping the clumsily assimilated to find a place in it. Minerva's words have real substance. Better yet, she listens. She has become, for Hawk, neither subject alone nor object, but also, especially, friend.

She has told him about the alcove which grew to a workroom, then to a shop, finally to a factory. She has described the instant sensation she created in the dining room of the Inn on the very night of her arrival. She has described the events which launched her socially as well as professionally in Saint Kathareen's. The reluctant progress of the community into modern life seems almost to coincide with Minerva's ambitions for herself.

Hawk has heard her discussed on campus often enough. Students usually approach her expecting a half-hour of mild boredom and spinsterish ramblings. Instead she gives them history as it ought to be taught, from the source. If she really likes them—she leans toward sandy beards and longish but clean hair—she gives them an added bonus. She ends the interview with the offer of a plump, carefully rolled, rainbow-papered joint out of a cloisonné box residing among the selective bric-a-brac on her tea table.

Hawk understands, through a combination of painstaking researches and offhand gossip, that various succulent strains of cannabis have been known to this Valley since before the first transient Frenchmen smoked a surpassingly peaceful pipe with a few extraordinarily peaceful Indians in the 1740s. Legend has it that in the earliest days of the Saint Kathareen's settlement, when rope-weaving was a natural adjunct to shipbuilding, a spontaneous summer conflagration consumed a hemp warehouse several miles downriver from the center of town. Before the fire was extinguished, the valiant folk who braved searing heat to dump buckets of brackish water on the blaze discovered that they were breathing more easily in the environs of the fire than in the normal fog of the congested Valley summers. Slowly the understanding developed. Contrary to all logic, something in that peculiar effluvium was shrinking the agonized membranes of swollen, asthmatic noses and lungs. Something in the infusion was giving more relief than discomfort to those who inhaled it just right. The heady sense of well-being, they accepted as part of the cure.

From that moment to the development of all manner of homespun "asthma powders" and elixirs was no more than a Sunday stroll. If the local version was less medicinal and more placebic than other, similar discoveries already long in use all over the world, no one seemed to mind the culture lag a bit. Thence proceeded the leap from the pharmacopoeia to the purely recreational. Smoking had far outscored the moonshine industry throughout Saint Kathareen's County since long before the revenuers had ever come around to give anybody a chance to think about it. Even today, barely a ridge exists for miles around without its modest stand of "smokin' weed" among the brambleberries.

Minerva, whose perfectly predictable characteristic it was to have been enjoying the weed intermittently with Karraman, who learned it from the local wildcatters, while Bloomer girls were only just coyly flaunting tobacco, still takes pleasure in an occasional puff. Maybelle Three, who still tends the small crop, often joins her. Then goes off to her labors perhaps less speedily but compensatorily less crotchety than usual.

Minerva shrugs off the impression that she can actually focus her failing eyes a bit more accurately than usual lately when she smokes. Nowadays she is reluctant to impute magic to anything. She simply accepts the sensations with satisfaction, and equally enjoys the bewildered gratitude of those she draws into her small ritual. Thus a loose and somewhat bewildered fraternity of Minerva's People forms itself and wanders, practically unaware but tentatively attuned, through the hempy nights of the Valley. Hawk, by virtue of all investments, is the unwitting, unchallenged, and absolutely unacknowledged leader of the bizarre pack.

On one particularly mellow spring afternoon, Minerva is regaling him with the account of her first night at the Saint Kathareen's Inn in her living hat. She has told him parts of this story in the past, but he senses that she is as well aware of that fact as he is. There is no senile dementia here. She has simply chosen, he imagines, to go a bit deeper this time, to say a bit more, to unfold.

Hawk knows, because she has told him so, that she likes his gumption, the way he keeps coming back for more. He never feels that she has descended to the sentimental basement of imagining him the son or grandson she never had. Rather, she offers him great hulking segments of her life in exchange for tidbits of his. Taken literally, the balance is all askew. Taken in terms of length of days, it works out just right, measure for measure. Hawk entertains an eerie notion that if anything of her existence is to remain to posterity, he is somehow to be the vehicle of her memory. The responsibility is awesome. He embraces it as a shipwrecked sailor does his raft.

Minerva goes about recreating that spring night at the Inn—the smoldering gas lights, the genteel murmur of dinner voices, and finally the spreading silence as one table after another caught first the apple-blossom fragrance, then the Juno glimpse of the remarkable female who was entering the dining room alone. Hawk can feel the volleying mixture of bluff confidence and rebellious defiance that must have powered Minerva through a room wherein she still somehow expected to see Hammond

Bolton spring up at any moment, riding crop snapping nervously in hand, ready to play out the villainous guardian in a Return of the Prodigal scene. He can see the mildly critical arch in the eyebrow of the headwaiter who escorted Minerva to a table diagonally opposite the entrance door. He shares her indignation at being forced to describe the most conspicuous passage possible through the room. Virtually hears the collective wrinkling of critical eyes that follow her as if they were on hinge flaps.

How heads had turned! How Minerva had, in the end, loved it, as she finally began to accept the fact that Hammond Bolton was really, permanently back in Massachusetts, stewing in his own bilious nature, not about to come swooping down like a vengeful warlock. A warm and intimate empathetic memory engulfs Hawk with her.

"Hawk, when I first came to this Valley, no one here had ever heard of Freud. I didn't know a taboo from a tattoo. But, do you know, since I've been here, since that very first night, in fact, I've broken every single taboo I've ever heard about."

"Oh, come on, Miss Minerva. You can't mean that."

Her stern glance reprimands. "And why would I be saying it, if I didn't mean it? Yessir, every single one." She pauses. Hawk knows the cadence of her little verbal dramas, holds his peace.

"Even incest," she continues, "if you count distant cousins, of course," an almost apologetic parenthesis.

He almost swallows his tongue. As deep as his affectionate respect for Miss Minerva flows, and as enchanting as Hawk finds her resolute modernity amid the crinolined layers of her exotic history, he is not absolutely sure that she knows what she is talking about just now. He has no wish to offend her by giggling foolishly at the sweeping moral generalization of which she, with not a little smug satisfaction, has just delivered herself. On the other hand, his own discomfiture is pushing nervous laughter over the lip of the cup. He sure as hell doesn't want to get into an explanation of why she's probably wrong. That would entail descriptions and reasonings that he is absolutely positive he doesn't want to hear. Besides, what if she turns out to be right? With her irrepressible curiosity, with her obsessive passion to get at the heart of things, there's no question about whether she'd push him to the outer limits of any conversation he entered. How peculiar it is, he muses, that he spends so much time trying to get anywhere within kilometers of some people's convoluted thinking, while here he is working equally assiduously to stay out of range of Minerva's. He wonders at the paradox, wonders even harder why he comes out feeling so close to his own surface, so vulnerable, in either case.

As for Minerva, she has truly never said a thing she didn't feel she understood in her entire life. When she says she has committed every taboo, she means it. She even goes as far as murder, although probably any tribunal on earth would ride her out on gales of laughter if she tried to explain what she meant. In all her days, Minerva has never lifted an incensed hand against human or animal. She has wrestled lengthily with an abhorrence of others who have done so, understanding fully and ambivalently that her most profound acts of love have held germs as lethal as the fists and warheads others have wielded in the name of defense or justice or power. Nevertheless, she is convinced to a certainty that her tender subterfuges have never directly harmed a fly. Indeed, she estimates that her very existence kept Karraman's marriage intact when nothing else could have done.

No, it is not the little murder implicit in every adultery that brings Minerva's most unremitting judgment down upon her own head. It is nothing more or less than the tormenting wisdom that, had she done the right thing in any one of a number of presenting situations, Karraman would be alive today. If not today, he at least would have been alive considerably longer than the dates on his tombstone record, and his death would have been far less ignoble. She will never really know, but has thought the probabilities through to the point where they are more tangible, more real to her than this morning's English muffin. The muffins she has to import from Pittsburgh. Her fantasies come to her home-bred, fully fashioned, nonconsumable.

Minerva never entertains the thought, although Hawk has openly suggested to her that she might, that Karraman might have died exactly as he chose to: quickly, adventurously, in a state of expiation, however unwitting. She cannot see beyond the bridges that she either burned too thoroughly or failed to burn at all. She does not brood her way through days of contrition or desperation. She believes that what's done is done, and weaves the darker threads through the tapestry of her life with an eloquence that highlights every single shade. But when she says taboo, she means taboo, and means it with the force of a primitive incantation.

Hawk reads the familiar intensity in her eyes, and understands full well that she means it. A breeze blows through the room, tainted with the vague overlay of acrylic smog and held with deadly efficiency over Saint Kathareen's by some kind of climatic inversion. In its fumes Hawk detects the acrid edge of a thousand tribal fires. He shakes off a chill that has emanated from his own body or from somewhere in history itself. It could not possibly have originated in the heat of this day. He isn't sure what exactly he is reacting to in Miss Minerva's panoply of surprises, but reacting he is.

"Jesus Christ, Miss Minerva," he says. Respectfully. "What incredible strokes of fate you've had all along. Every single step."

[28]

Something jolts Minerva into a place where reminiscence obtains, humor ascending. She looks him straight in the eye. "No, Hawk dear," she assures him. "Of that I'm absolutely certain. Neither fate nor Jesus Christ has ever, even for a single moment, entered into it."

II

By the time Minerva Bolton descended into Saint Kathareen's in the spring of 1906, the Inn had already entered its years of great age. If the memory of Fat George governed its simple, graceful exterior, the soul of Queen Victoria pervaded the inside.

Mr. Cyril Cybele, the balding and prissy desk clerk, blanched slightly as the clatter of an alien horse and carriage assaulted the stately tiles of the porte cochère. He fought off the momentary but inevitable association of that unseemly din with carefully vaulted memories of buckboard and manure. No matter what was coming, he already was sure that he didn't like it, nosiree. All he knew was that the dignified clientele which the Inn preferred to cultivate would no more operate or cause to be operated rowdy vehicles than behave rowdily themselves.

Two elderly, liveried bellmen occupied twin armchairs flanking the grand stairway opposite the desk, and at a right angle to the main entry. Neither one moved, nor in any manner acknowledged what was, to Cybele, rapidly becoming an intolerable disturbance. As their custom dictated, they simply sat and waited, languid and impervious, until a servant might enter the Inn to announce the arrival of his gentleman. At length, credentials duly established, suites assigned, Mr. Cybele would ring a mahogany-handled brass bell, simultaneously shouting *"Boy!"* as if in quest of an errant youngster off way yonder across the Ohio to the south. One or the other of the bellmen, or both if rank or entourage demanded, would shuffle with diffident efficiency toward the arriving party. The passengers would be ushered to luncheon, tea, supper, the bar—whatever comfort demanded—as legions of chamberlains and maids labored to unpack, to stow gear, to settle things in. After a leisurely repast, the guests would enter their own suites feeling that they had been residing at the Inn forever.

Thus, hearing what he had heard outside, Mr. Cybele felt violated. Not only had the unearthly ruckus offended his sensibilities; in addition, his sense of rhythm, highly geared to the immediate, efficient appearance of chauffeur or valet, had been thrown off completely. Nervously he waited. Trying not to appear nervous, he squirmed like a baby in church. The whinny and stationary clomping of tired, high-strung horses intruded further upon Mr. Cybele, banished placidity and composure.

Barely a moment had actually passed. Suddenly a bleat not unlike the steam whistle of a displaced river sternwheeler shattered Cybele's precarious poise once and for all. He fumbled for his schoolmaster's bell in order to summon somebody else to rescue him, knocked it to the floor in his trembling anxiety. It fell to the front side of his desk and rolled to a noisy halt universes away, just in front of four highly polished shoes strolling, away from a leisurely tea in the dining room, toward the front door. In his deep disarray, Mr. Cybele had failed to see them coming.

Emmaline Musgrove dipped into her elaborate petit-point handbag to clutch at a lacy handkerchief with which she might stifle a giggle. Her fiancé, Karraman Robley, had no dipping to do. He was not amused. It would occur to him later that he should have cherished every prenuptial burst of laughter Emmaline allowed herself to bray. Happiness as a commodity entered dismally short supply in Emmaline's spectrum of responses in approximate coincidence with her wedding night. He had once feared, in the tentative early days of their courtship, that his seniority might impose unmeasured burdens upon his future wife. For various selfish reasons, he had never broached the subject to her. It would not take long for Karraman to realize, and poignantly regret, that he was not the one who more truly deserved the designation "elderly," years notwithstanding.

Karraman's vague unease at taking a bride fifteen years his junior would melt away to incredulous resentment as he watched her age before his eyes. Her physical body would continue to function with the moon, and bear children over an interminable twenty years. He would watch it ripen each time, and observe with dejection but no real surprise as it gave way to unsuccessfully corseted matronliness. At the same time, her spirit, her countenance, her very soul would catch up to Karraman's years, become

[31]

senescent, and finally leave him ages behind as various undifferentiated bitternesses took up residence in her personality and altered it beyond affection.

But at the moment that he and his skittery fiancée walked through the lobby of the Inn, Karraman Robley's primary concern lay with the temporarily shoddy management of a property which owed a round one hundred percent of its existence and mortgage to Karraman Robley. Thus Mr. Cybele, already quivering in his morning coat, was brought nearly to tears. It was finally the sight of the bell on the carpet that did it.

Karraman dipped his stocky frame to the floor as Emmaline stood giggling and the others remained paralyzed. He retrieved the offending object, grasping its highly waxed handle between his carefully manicured thumb and forefinger. It might have been a snake.

Handing the bell over the desk with patent distaste, Karraman said something pointed and obviously significant to Cybele. Cybele, however, never even heard him. A deafening, not quite identifiable hoot split the air, as if on cue from Karraman's punitively upraised index finger. In perfect synchronization with the opening of his mouth, the offending horses clattered and protested once more. The horn blared again, sounding for anything as if it were right smack in the middle of the sedate old vestibule.

Which, in a manner of speaking, it was.

The bellmen gawked. Cybele's Adam's apple worked spastically about and around his starched collar. Emmaline dropped her petit-point etui. Even Karraman stopped in mid-sentence to stare at the arresting phenomenon which seemed to fill the doorway.

For Minerva Bolton, tired of waiting, dusty and impatient for the civilized attentions of the Inn to come groveling to her, had taken matters into her own hands and entered the lobby. In one of those hands she held an enormous woven willow hamper. In the other she carried a hugely belled parody of a carriage horn. Its tubing was easily eighteen inches in diameter, and more intricate by many turnings than a French horn.

Minerva looked around pointedly. Without so much as a heartbeat's pause in her tempo, she lowered the carpetbag to the floor and raised the horn to her lips. As quickly as she moved, both of the bellmen and Karraman were upon her, galvanized instantly to put a stop to whatever in hell was going to happen next. Cybele stood frozen.

The smaller bellman lunged to retrieve the willow hamper. Instantly he was thrown off balance, geared as he was to anticipate a ponderous piece of luggage filled with matter as intrusive as the lady herself, if "lady" was what he must call her. The bag, of course, weighed almost nothing at all, being filled with sundry ribbons, various small swatches of velvet, and all manner, thousands by count, of feathers.

Minerva smiled dazzlingly.

By that time Mr. Cybele had extricated himself from behind the great desk. He himself relieved Minerva of the giant horn, an action he obviously considered triumphant but which she had intended all along. In truth, her lips couldn't have coaxed a single note out of the monstrous configuration of piped turnings. She had just removed the bladder, which, when squeezed manually, produced the shattering sound that had preceded her entrance. She had pocketed the business end outside the door immediately before she walked in. Had it not been for the slapstick tableau of the handbell, anybody in the lobby might have seen her do it. Instead, the shocked company assumed that the sound had actually been produced, in their midst, by lung power. All that Minerva had wanted to achieve in the lobby had been an effect. She had not failed.

With the softest, most plaintive voice in her cultivated repertoire—after all, there are few diversions in which one can indulge and drive a team of horses across the mountains at the same time, elocution being one of them—Minerva announced herself. "I am Minerva Bolton," she gave. "I believe you have among your files my request for lodgings."

She nearly committed a grave error of protocol, since she addressed her request to the most obviously capable and effective-looking of those present. That figure was Karraman Robley. Minerva also performed, by omission, a second act which cast her onto the shoals of vulnerable independence, but also pacific self-respect. She deliberately omitted, in presenting herself, not only a title but also the entire midsection of her considerable name. She had planned the act, written it, indeed in the very letter that Cybele was at that moment nervously hunting. She had never yet, however, delivered it in spoken word to anyone but the horses. Done is done, she thought gamely, as she left herself dangling in the middle of her chosen wilderness, with neither credential nor cachet. The sensation was not unlike free-fall.

Two happenstances saved her. The first was that Cybele did indeed possess her reservation request, although the date it specified fell three days later than the one on which she had so ostentatiously arrived. Minerva would have accepted gratefully a smattering of applause for efficiency. She had managed to better her most cautious estimates of how long it actually took to turn into a pioneer. She had to settle for healthy self-congratulation, because the audience seemed oblivious of her triumph.

Cybele had taken particular notice of her letter, since he had never before received such a document. Written by a lady on her own behalf, it had betrayed no sign of parent, guardian, secretary, or spouse. Yet the handwriting was cultured, the stationery expensive. He forced himself to squelch the denial that flew to his lips, the protestation that the Saint Kathareen's Inn had no previous knowledge of such a person as Minerva

[33]

Bolton. More distasteful than admitting this somehow irregular creature to his domain was the prospect of seeking other employment in the event that Karraman Robley caught him in the lie or incivility.

"Yes, ma'am," he sputtered, and raced off to figure out where to place her. He was entirely too frayed to remind the bellmen to fetch the lady's belongings. At long last they remembered themselves, abandoned the floor show, and fell to the task.

The other condition that saved Minerva was the awesome fact that Karraman Robley thought he had never seen as fascinating and beautiful a woman in his entire life. Far from feeling insulted at her mistaking him for a nearly menial servant, he interpreted her reasoning precisely as it had evolved. Flattery swelled him like a blowfish.

The spectacle of Karraman's visibly burgeoning ego did not escape Minerva. She watched, amused, as he expanded, plumped his feathers, tried to collect himself with a gulp of stale lobby air. It went down so audibly that Minerva wondered how he would be able to keep from belching it back, heaving forth all the aromas of whiskey, gaslight, furniture polish, and time.

Karraman managed. "Allow me to introduce myself."

Minerva noted the absence of a form of polite address. She waited, fully aware that she had permitted him no hint concerning her status in life, no removal of the glove from the hand which was bare of rings in any case. She wouldn't give him an inch, a fingernail. She had hoped for something a little more imaginative than the stilted phrase with which, she imagined, he prepared to ring up extravagant curtains of significance for her. She inclined her head a trifle in a parody of fluttery indifference. The lusty laugh which was beginning to well at the back of her throat tickled, teased, quickly died by her own hand.

Since he saw that no reply seemed to be forthcoming, Karraman forged ahead. "I am Karraman Robley."

"How do you do." But not a question, simply a mouthed acknowledgment. Then placid, contained silence.

Into which Karraman seemed to grope for an opening so that he could plunge headlong. "Well," and a vaguely discomfited clearing of a throat. "Well."

Minerva shot up a single eyebrow in a gesture that disarmed Karraman, possibly for life.

"Well," he essayed again. "You are, I see, using Saint Kathareen's as a stopover on your journey? A felicitous choice, madam." And a terribly transparent attempt to disguise the curiosity that was obviously driving him to distraction and beyond, into cliché. Karraman had never used language as stilted in his life. Yet something about the stateliness of this exotic stranger, the hint of intimacy in her large, sensuously Vaselined amber eyes, metamorphosed him into any number of things which bore no resemblance whatsoever to his usual self.

Emmaline, at first entertained by all the circumstances attending the encounter, suddenly came to attention. She began to sulk. Some remote, atavistic possessive imperative scattered her docility into fragments as if a twig broom were clearing the cobwebs of premature senility to make way for something insidiously basic. She had not yet learned to recognize passion, let alone lasciviousness. If either had come down and roosted in her pompadour, she would have been hard pressed to give it a name. She did observe that Karraman Robley was looking at this odd Bolton person with an intensity unlike anything she had ever seen cross his features in her entire life.

Karraman's visible admiration, such as it was, of Emmaline's own visage, her style, held all the correct notes of respect and distance, and centered always at an inoffensive locus between eyebrows and chin. For probably the first—and undoubtedly the last—time in conscious memory, Emmaline was viewing lust at first hand, in broad daylight. To an eternal misfortune of which she would never be thoroughly aware, it was all, for her, a spectator sport. She remarked, rather than participated in, a powerful quickening of the atmosphere. Innocent of even the possible ramifications of this meeting between Karraman Robley and Minerva Bolton, Emmaline nonetheless managed to understand to a fine certainty that she was going to do something to nip in the bud whatever was invading her painstakingly cultivated territory.

Far too stodgy (although she would have called it "dignified") to poke Karraman in the ribs, say something gratuitous, pull him by the ear, Emmaline did the next best thing: she again dropped the petit-point etui to the carpeted floor, having accepted its retrieval from Caleb only a moment earlier. This time she pitched it, carefully calculating the gentle clink of its delicate chain-link handle against its metallic frame. Karraman almost jumped, visibly, out of his skin back into reality. Then he dipped and bobbed even less gracefully than he had the first time, when he had knelt to retrieve the bell. He genuflected, eyes up, never leaving Minerva's face, thereby requiring an awkward moment of paw and grope for the delinquent object, which actually had been projected squarely in front of him. His equilibrium suffered disastrously in the attempt to appease Emmaline, restore the status quo, and keep his stare riveted upon Minerva without dropping a conversational stitch. With minimum aplomb, he managed to restore his balance. Handing the small case to Emmaline, whose presence was beginning to reassert itself not entirely pleasantly into the tunnel of his consciousness, he said, "Allow me, madam, to present Miss Emmaline Musgrove."

Emmaline purpled unevenly. Never once in the preceding year had Karraman failed to affix what she considered her honorary title, her dower right, "my fiancée," to his introductions, down to his third-person descriptions of her. Even the scraggy children who bedeviled the craftsmen working on the gray mansion on the hill referred to her thus. From their irreverence, the workmen and journeymen caught the mood like measles. "Place this pediment above the hearth in My Fiancée's sitting room," the foreman would instruct. "Yessir!" would come the reply. "My Fiancée it is!" The entire conversation passed from raucous joke to accepted idiom in a matter of hours. "My Fiancée" substituted for Emmaline's given names so naturally that the word spread through Saint Kathareen's like the creeping waters of a spring flood. During the onslaught, no one even remembered what the landscape had looked like in former times.

Emmaline mustered all the dormant accumulated nerve of her twenty-three years. "I'm his Fiancée." She thrust the statement at Minerva like a dagger or a challenge.

Imperceptibly sarcastic, Minerva flashed an asymmetrically dimpled smile. "How nice for you," she replied.

Minerva's throaty voice, huskiness still heightened by the dust of many roads, belied her age and her experience. She might have been timeless. Emmaline remained innocent, untried, although she technically was the senior of the two by almost exactly two years. She felt childish and uneasy in Minerva's shadow. Younger, without anchor or ballast, and without any of the material securities Emmaline displayed like jewelry, Minerva nonetheless stood calmly centered in her own gravity. Emmaline, who was to feel in her actually insignificant outburst an enormity of pathological shame, looked as if she wanted to leave, or sink into the carpet over the hearth, or die. Unfortunately for her, all decisions concerning her life and its conduct had been structured for her by Karraman Robley or her father, Eusebius, or God for as far back as the undeveloped tendrils of her memory could probe. She had no rational retreat from whatever problems assailed her. So she stood, trying to shrink, trying to loom, watching something terrifying or indescribable happen to the golden links which were supposed to bind her forever to Karraman.

Minerva observed it all in seconds, through the lenses of her own perspicacity. Her next move was governed by instinct.

Better than a guardian angel—it occasionally got her into a scrape, which by her standards was often a more interesting place to be, rather than out of one—she nurtured instinct like orchids. Unpredictability was, to her mind, the bonus, the gravy, the germinating seed of her self-possession. It provided the challenge of Being to her being.

The two women stood eye to eye, princess of light and princess of darkness, neither willing to admit which of those two roles she would willingly adopt for herself. Minerva, for one, ignored the tensions. She addressed her response to Emmaline. Karraman's balding head shimmered obliquely some degrees beneath the tenuous silver cord of their contact.

"It's certainly a pleasure to meet you, Miss Musgrove," came the courtly bow of her voice. Then, with a whisper of a nod to Karraman, "In truth, I've decided to stay in Saint Kathareen's rather longer than you might have imagined. In fact, I've planned to make my home in this Valley."

Emmaline's glance fluttered, searched in vain for a nurturing roost.

Minerva continued, carefully measuring the amount of hard information she chose to release. "I shall stop at the Inn, of course, until a more suitable permanent lodging appears. It's such a charming place!—judging by what I've seen, of course. I've no doubt that I'll be enormously comfortable." She rolled "enormously" around on her tongue like a sensuous, delicate sweetmeat. As she flashed her magnetic smile, Karraman Robley realized that she had just effectively performed the rituals of welcome for herself. There was very little left for him to say, even if he had had the presence of mind to say it. Emmaline, by that time, had thought of a few thousand things of her own that she might have contributed, beginning with the question of where a woman gets away with deciding, *deciding*, with perfect impunity, where's she's going to make her home. Fortunately, she found it impossible to get the first impudent question past her gullet.

Karraman gathered in. "Well, Miss Bolton—"

"It's 'Mrs.,'" she allowed, with demure calculation.

"Mrs., then," and had not the faintest idea what to make of that. "I trust we shall meet again. Do enjoy the Inn. We're rather proud of it, here in Saint Kathareen's." With that, he took rather painful hold of his Fiancée's taffetaed elbow and propelled her toward departure.

Yes, I trust I shall, Minerva thought to herself.

"See that she's taken care of, Mr. Cybele," Karraman Robley ordered. "Spare no courtesy."

Cybele produced a fair imitation of a deferential nod. Karraman turned brusque. Emmaline was grateful to leave the strangely charged lobby behind. She could not have understood that she would have been better off never leaving at all, because Karraman's abrupt departure had become possible only in the moment when he decided what his next move was going to be. Minerva, of course, could not have known with precision, but nothing, absolutely nothing, was going to come as a surprise to her.

"Will you dine with us this evening, Karraman? Mother has had the girls in the kitchen marinating a sauerbraten for days. And cold peach soup, too," she implored. Her accustomed seat in the fragrant leathery interior of the runabout restored a measure of Emmaline's confident territoriality, but not entirely. She did know that she was pressing Karraman. Defiantly she decided that she had every right in the world to do so.

Karraman's response, if unpredicted by Emmaline, was as preordained as floodwater. Even his favorite menu couldn't diminish the intensity of his resolve to get on with the exhilarating possibilities ahead.

"Thank you, my dear, but no. I'm going to deliver you back to Beechwood Street and head out to the fields. I wouldn't be surprised but that the well we've been watching these last weeks comes in tonight."

"We can dine late, if you prefer, Karraman," wheedled Em. "Mummy says she likes to 'get it over,' but she's going to have to learn certain graces sooner or later. After all, she left the farm four full generations ago." Emmaline was grasping at straws.

"Best not to try her these days, I think, my dear. After the wedding, when things settle, we can embark upon the reeducation of your dear mother. For tonight, I think I'd best decline with regret." He paused, looked into her pale, nearly lashless eyes. "Before long, you know, there will be no questions about dinner. Or even," he appended daringly, but with wicked purpose, "about breakfast or midnight suppers."

Emmaline turned blotchy. Karraman leaned across the seat and planted a rough kiss on her forehead. He could accomplish that feat only from a sitting position, due to the disparity in their heights. Emmaline was both aghast and elated at the public nature of the act. Karraman tasted talc, and the cloying fragrance of a wilting sweetness. Not pleasant. Emmaline finally allowed herself to look at him with unalloyed admiration, so he calculated that the assay was worth the investment.

He saw her to the door of her family's noble frame house, a study in restrained elegance. He never would figure out the origins of her own so-called taste. Kissing her hand, he retreated into the automobile and his turbulent thoughts. He sat, idle and pensive, for long seconds before his driver broke the reverie.

"Where to now, Mr. Karraman? The fields?"

"No, Fred. Back to the Inn. Then you're free for the day."

"Yessir."

Karraman wasn't fooled. He knew that Fred knew that he had never entertained a single thought of going to the fields that afternoon or evening. He also knew that Fred hadn't missed a beat eavesdropping on the conversation. Both men were simply engaging in a variation of the Plain-Truth Sidestep. Having paid courteous lip service to the lie, they were free to go about constructing their separate versions of the truth.

Fred, who had watched Karraman Robley from a pup, had also observed the scene in the lobby of the Inn from a vantage just inside the heavy, brass-fitted entry door. He alone had actually caught the business with the horn. He knew exactly what kind of devious plotting was running orbits through

Mr. Karraman's mind. Of course, he had no idea exactly how Karraman intended to go about accomplishing his purposes. If he had, he wouldn't still have been the chauffeur. On the other hand, of course, neither did Karraman Robley. As yet.

Karraman had always resided at the Robley seat, Cricklewood House. The fine old mansion had once commanded a view of the rivers from the head of Crombie Street, well out of the flood plain while still enjoying the perquisites and contiguities of downtown Saint Kathareen's. Yet Karraman Robley cherished his privacy almost as possessively as he cherished Cricklewood. He had no quarrel with Emmaline's uncompromising desire to establish a homestead of her own, apart from the Robley freehold. Hence the endless process of constructing Foothill House, the turreted brick stronghold Minerva had instantly spotted a-building on Mount Calvin-and-Levi, more familiarly known as Settler's Knockers.

All in all, Karraman was not dissatisfied with the decision to leave the center of Saint Kathareen's. He remembered clearly the gradual dismantling of the old downtown family lands, the construction of a full-fledged town upon what was once the kingdom of a few Robleys and the collateral descendants of the other first families of Saint Kathareen's. However well he had loved Cricklewood, he had loved the land at least equally. The mighty Dutch elms, healthy and flourishing in those days, gentled the hot summer air, comforted him by their stolid endurance in winter. But the smaller frame dwellings encroached, the Town Hall rose obstructively between Cricklewood and the rivers whose seasons he had watched with unabashed sentiment. Cricklewood had satisfied him in the old days, but this was the twentieth century. If the relatively untried western bank of the Saint Kathareen's suggested a certain aloofness from the town square and its commerces, Karraman Robley was well past thinking that there was anybody left in the old sense to answer to about it.

On the other hand, Karraman had never entertained a passing thought of abandoning a foothold in the center of town. To that end, he held on to his penthouse, a sumptuous suite on the fourth floor of the Saint Kathareen's Inn. It commanded the loftiest panorama at the riverfront, and in Karraman's mind it epitomized everything he had ever demanded of Power.

The Robley proprietorship of that particular suite of rooms had been an open secret through four generations of male heirs. Just as fathers of a certain station ritually initiate their sons into the byways of illicit sex, the Robley fathers presented their sons with keys to The Apartment. The rest they left to the imagination and the signature on the chit.

Karraman had heard that intricate traffic problems had developed in years past, what with sons, brothers, cousins, and sundry others converging at awkward, unpremeditated times. He himself, the only currently extant Robley male not house-bound by scruple or senility, enjoyed the spacious apartment at will. He did admit that, as grateful as he was for the exclusivity present conditions afforded him, he relished mightily some of the lascivious anecdotes handed down from the days of heavy traffic.

Whenever Mr. Karraman announced that he would entertain or be in residence in the suite, Caleb or Okey would precede his ascent, making certain that the brass-and-polish lift was shining for all it was worth. They knew exactly how to open the balcony doors to the rivers, admitting the fragrances of spring or the teasing bite of autumn, but keeping perfect privacy by adjusting the curtained panels just so.

For once, however, in this pregnant April afternoon, Karraman bustled back to the Inn unannounced. Cybele tried to be suave, unperturbed. His eyes traced a shifty track over to the denizens of the armchairs. Caleb shrugged elaborately. Cybele cringed. He could not believe that Mr. Karraman had come back to the Inn for any purpose other than that of taking him seriously to task for any one of a number of petty or grand irritations, culminating with the incident of the rolling bell.

Nothing could have been further from Karraman Robley's thoughts. The small vicissitudes of Mr. Cyril Cybele he considered as mere farts in the wind. If they discolored the atmosphere, the effect was devastatingly temporary.

Karraman disdained in turn the sycophantic Cybele and then the elevator. He felt energized all out of proportion to his thirty-eight years. For the first flight and a half, he took the stairs two at a time. Gradually the machinery slowed, but the machinery only. Glancing furtively about to ensure that he was alone in the stairwell, he established a more conventional pace, reassuring himself that it was more dignified anyway.

Settled at last in the apartment, he recovered his breath. He prowled from parlor to bedroom, from bedroom to dressing room, dressing room to another bedroom, and back again. He toyed with plumbing, opened windows, closed them again. At last, relatively composed, he tugged at the bell pull that would activate a coiled spring at Cyril Cybele's desk, ring a bell, and continue to vibrate until someone had marked the origin of the summons.

Karraman pulled his ornately carved watch from its fob, and waited. In less than one hundred seconds the knocker sounded at the door. Karraman issued a satisfied harrumph. Proper deference still obtained. He didn't care to know that Mr. Cybele, raised on platitudes and a hickory stick, considered promptness a virtue to be exercised on behalf of all his guests, name and lineage notwithstanding. It went without saying that anyone beneath such elemental courtesy would have been unwelcome in the Inn at the outset. For the privileged, if both bellmen happened to be occupied when the summons came, one of the waiters or pages would be dispatched. Karraman Robley, insisting upon occupying the top floor, actually waited, most of the time, slightly longer than anybody else.

"Well, Caleb, old man, how has the day gone for you?"

Caleb considered. A less seasoned hand, having witnessed the near-fiasco of the bell and carriage horn, might have walked away with the notion that Mr. Karraman was coming derailed. Caleb, who had grown up on Robley lands and watched Robley vagaries of all kinds through the passing years, had learned how to take things as they fell.

"Not too bad, Mr. Karraman. Beans've started a-shootin' out home. Looks like a right good balance for spring. Favorable for summer too, I'd judge."

Caleb was nobody's fool. When Mr. Karraman asked about "things," he meant all manner of things. If there had been a problem at the hotel, that intelligence would have come first. If a stranger, a wildcatter, had turned up in the saloon, his tales of the oil fields would not long elude Karraman's attention. If Caleb talked about the beans, the encoded message read that the status quo prevailed, and that the Robley farmland interests were intact as well.

"Not too much winterkill?"

"Nothin', far as the eye can tell. I'd watch the peaches, though. They're showin' an early bud, I'd say, with the warm nights and all. You know how the Valley can turn back to frost in May as soon as say how-de-do."

"That's true," Karraman agreed, remotely pensive. Small talk and reportage accomplished at one blow, he was wandering back to his immediate purpose.

"Caleb . . ."

"Yessir." Caleb assumed a posture at the ready. His reflex, a parody of deferential response, had been triggered automatically by Karraman's abrupt shift in mood. Caleb had caught Karraman with his pants down in more ways than one through the years, but he still knew a good thing when he had it. The good thing was his job.

"I'll dine downstairs this evening."

"Yessir."

Karraman calculated quickly. "I'll prefer a banquette against the north wall." Facing the main entry. "At seven."

Caleb remained impassive, which flustered Karraman. Karraman had the notion that every aspect of his motive was patently transparent to Caleb, and somehow shameful. The former assumption, of course, was cross-hair accurate. The latter was neither here nor there.

Caleb, who had helped to transport Mrs. Minerva Bolton's outlandish

[41]

baggage to her room on the third floor, already knew that the lady had reserved her own table for 7:30. Karraman Robley rarely entered the dining room before nine when he dined at the hotel. He preferred a robust stint in the saloon with several of his regular cronies beforehand. Caleb could calculate as well as anybody that the lady, after a tiring journey all on her own, would want to dine respectably early, then retire. He knew precisely what Karraman had in mind. He might even have told Karraman what he knew about that evening's reservation book, and saved the sly old fox a half-hour's anxiety, but he chose not to. Such private tabulations kept the balance.

Caleb simply nodded and withdrew. Karraman, turning to an extravagant array of bottles on the chiffonier, began to dab himself with bay rum. The clock on the new courthouse tower began to strike while he was still at his ritual. Like a doleful adolescent on the way to an ice-cream sociable, he looked around furtively, then began to chuckle aloud at his own folly. Here he was, all dressed and ready and smelling like a flower, and it was only six o'clock.

One floor below, Minerva Bolton was trying to get organized. Every material asset she could claim as her own resided with her in Room 314, the Saint Kathareen's Inn. It was a scanty inventory, but efficient. With the carpetbag and the willow hamper, two wicker chests and a few miscellaneous parcels accounted for all she needed to undertake a life.

Finally, in charge of her inventory and her person, Minerva began to pull together the final touches in preparation to go down to dinner. The prospect of eating alone in the public dining room, which should have been anathema to Hammond Bolton's virgin bride, never rippled the composure of one Minerva Bolton, newly of Saint Kathareen's. Her months on the road had settled all matters of self-confidence and false pride. One did what needed to be done. To the depth and breadth that she accepted that kind of intelligence, Minerva was as calm as a mountain lake. Preparing for her mission to the public rooms below, she thought of Karraman Robley, but only fleetingly. She had other business on her mind.

Opening the darker, rougher of the two wicker chests, she began to rummage through its sundry contents. Deftly she extracted a few things she thought she would need. Then she drew a bead on an etched-glass-and-pewter epergne which adorned the top of a lofty highboy in the sitting-room section of her chamber. Minerva didn't even need to stand on tiptoe to relieve the arrangement of the opulent blossoms she intended to put to a better use.

She worked through the late afternoon. At a few minutes before seven she tugged at the tapestried bell pull Caleb had shown her as she was settling in. The tension of the yanking transmitted itself through the network of tensed wires inside the walls. Finally, above the front desk where Mr. Cybele was about to relinquish his post to his evening counterpart, the bell jangled on its coiled spring just as it was supposed to do. As usual, Cybele nearly jumped out of his skin. Composing himself, he managed to turn and catch sight of the spring while it still quivered. He noted that this time the summons had come from Mrs. Bolton. Once again, as usual, he cursed Karraman Robley for being so damnably selective in his excursions into modernity. For the sake of example, the single telephone in the entire handsomely electrically wired hotel, an outside line connected directly to Saint Kathareen's Central, sat in state in Karraman Robley's own suite. Never mind that the help had to be dispatched, on foot, within seconds of every summons from an archaic bell system. Never mind that Cybele's already frayed nerves nearly shattered in the process each time. Never mind that he could hear the jangling in his ears even in the depths of the precious little sleep he got anyway. Oh, no. The Master has his wishes. He insisted upon the "gentle touch of personal service," and he insisted upon the niceties for himself and for every single guest as well.

Thus, Cybele's last duty at the front desk that day was to liberate a busboy from the tiresome chore of shining and restocking many gross of bar-sized crystal glasses in a massive hutch. Dispatching the lad to Mrs. Bolton's room to ascertain her needs, Cybele turned over the keys, messages, and the general running of his grand machine, the Inn, to the night man, Josephus Todd. Cybele gradually wound himself down and left the premises, thereby missing one of the most dramatic confrontations ever to take place at the Saint Kathareen's Inn in all her once and future life. The event was so low-keyed that there remains a possibility Cybele wouldn't have noticed it even if he had been waiting tables himself. Nevertheless, it was a moment that changed lives.

Mrs. Minerva Bolton had indeed, as the book noted, requested a table for dinner at 7:30. Even that hour struck the citified part of her person as barbarously early for dining out, but fatigue, she knew, lingered not at all far behind her temporary elation at having reached the end of her long, long trail. The bellboy whom she had summoned, after a startled look at what seemed to be some kind of dismantled aviary occupying every bed, table, and settee in the room, finally agreed that the dining room was indeed probably ready to receive her this far in advance of her reservation. He

[43]

croaked that, yes, he would see to matters, and would expect her downstairs anon. Bounding out, he left her to the finishing touches.

Karraman Robley's gamble paid off. Feeling flutters of anticipation himself, he had been sitting in the dining room, pensively nursing a single Scotch and soda, since 6:30. Eschewing his regular visit to the lounge, he had had Thomas the bartender place his crystal siphon bottle and the elegantly decanted fifth of whiskey at his table, but he had not touched either container since the first ceremonial pouring. The contents of his glass had warmed from rich, icy amber into an unappetizing solution whose presence he contemplated without commitment. He had never affected the particular eccentricity of the decanter at the table before, but no one on the staff paid any particular attention.

Promptly at 6:45, Minerva Bolton wafted into the kerosene-smogged dining room in an aura of fragrant springtime. The hat accounted for part of it. Minerva's French perfume and female musk accounted for the rest.

Carefully coiffed, she was neither more nor less striking than she had been when she entered the lobby that afternoon at her ramshackle worst. No elemental frenzy could have diminished the clarity of feature, the robust statuesqueness of form. In a flurry of practicality, she had bobbed her hair en route from Massachusetts. Because it grew with such lushness into waves and layers, she was able to maintain the illusion of an upswept height amid a convenience that preceded its time. Hers would be the first such "do" that Saint Kathareen's would see. Tongues would wag even as the scoffers contemplated imitation.

She wore a handsome outfit that looked to Karraman Robley exactly like the tender skin of a baby doe. At her neck, a substantial ancestral-looking garnet-and-pearl brooch rested comfortably in an ecru silk jabot. And the hat.

The hat, on a lesser woman, would have been all gimcrackery and artifice. It crowned Minerva. It said, in measured parlor tones to every male or female occupant of the room, "Do you mean to say that you haven't kept up, poor dears? *This* is a hat, as God meant hats to be."

Thinking himself suave beyond measure, Karraman dispatched his waiter with a message.

Minerva's self-containment had seen her through storm and avalanche, had fended off Indian and highway robber. She could handle horses and baggage and annoyances like Cyril Cybele. She was, in her serious and proven way, a woman of the world. But at heart she retained a certain measure of tender innocence. She had no idea how hoary a cliché Karraman Robley's message contained, nor how very predictable was her reply.

Full of fellow feeling, curiosity, enthusiasm, and, whether she recognized it as such or not, a burning need to make human contact, she said, "Please tell Mr. Robley that I should be delighted to accept his offer of champagne, if he will consent to join me for the toast." Hammond Bolton would have succumbed to apoplexy if he could have seen, but only after laying mighty and eternal hexes on Karraman and Minerva both.

Karraman, although he had embarked upon the offer with confident bluster, actually couldn't believe his good fortune. Not that he was a stranger to women or the oblique byways of courtship. Nor were the final techniques of stalking and capture unknown to him. The simple truth was that, aside from Emmaline, to whom he would pledge himself in—how many weeks now?—he was accustomed to paying for the honor. The champagne would come if and only if a seemly rate were established.

The stabbing possibility drew him up short. Perhaps this provocative Mrs. Bolton . . . But, no. Karraman sidetracked the thought as soon as it came barreling down the main line. He had a tingly little instinct about his own brash, cigar-smoking ability to meet this Bolton woman on his own terms, terms which would turn out to be mutually acceptable. His spirits rose all out of proportion to the two or three sips of Scotch he had absently consumed. Every inch the tycoon, ruddy, just a bit of thickening about his well-tailored middle, he strode the length of the room to Mrs. Bolton's table. Full of his own swagger, he wasn't even disconcerted when he stepped awkwardly on his left foot, his inherently weak ankle buckled, and he had to fumble for a hold on the nearest stable surface. Grabbing a white tablecloth, he checked his fall. Crystal and cutlery tinkled as he bore precipitously down on the edge. Karraman righted himself just in time. He gestured self-importantly to the nearest busboy, who immediately began to straighten things out. Such was his overall poise that Minerva would have to work at the memory all her life to recall that her first two meetings with Karraman were both prefaced by slapstick near-disasters. She would think of him always as a man of breathtaking physical finesse.

He turned slightly away from her, toward the busboy. She noted that an incursion of silver at the temples vied with encroaching baldness for possession of his strongly sculpted skull. She wondered idly which feature would claim the final victory. And wanted suddenly, inexplicably, to stay in a position where she would be able to find out.

Meanwhile, Karraman was busy inking in the final strokes on the portrait of himself as Masterful. He snapped at the bellboy, "Not that, young fool. These things have been disarrayed. Replace them, don't disguise them."

The boy, reasonable to a fault, began to argue.

"You heard me," Karraman intoned, leaving nothing to doubt.

"Yessir," the boy obeyed.

Minerva watched the entire transaction intently. Karraman Robley had some interesting ways of trying to prove that he was in charge. He intrigued her, as she was confident she did him. She had definitely decided to keep the possibilities open. The wisdom of her decision pleased her, and added to the sum of her stunning self-assurance the vestige of a satisfied smile. The net effect was to make Karraman almost wild with the compulsion to have her friendship, know her better, anything—save losing the possibilities of her to the mysteries from which she had come and to which she might return.

"Good evening, Mrs. Bolton." At last. "How good of you to share a small libation with me." He spoke as an attentive sommelier poured champagne for two from an impressively moldy bottle. Minerva thought he sounded as if he'd memorized some of the dreariest lines from the most absurd melodramas she'd ever endured. She couldn't fault him, because she had no idea, as yet, of what passed for manners out here in this wilderness.

"It's my pleasure, Mr. Robley," she returned in kind. "The road from Massachusetts has been long and solitary. It's a pleasure to share a moment with, if I don't presume too boldly, a new friend."

Karraman bowed his head deeply to accept her gesture. Minerva noticed that, seated, he wasn't so small a man after all. Perhaps he only seemed so in contrast to that bulwark of a woman who had been with him earlier in the day. His shoulders spanned broadly beneath a powerful neck. His hands, Minerva noticed, although manicured to perfection, bore betraying calluses. Exactly what they betrayed, Minerva hadn't quite figured out yet. But she was interested.

"In a manner of speaking, I came from Massachusetts, too, Mrs. Bolton," he was saying, "although I must admit that it was my stalwart ancestors who actually made the journey, over a century ago."

Minerva smiled and waited. Karraman Robley had neatly paid a subtle tribute to her courage, and had managed to establish a dual aristocracy of origins for himself at the same time. He continued as if under the schoolmaster's goad. "The first Karraman Robley to lay eyes on Saint Kathareen's was my great-grandfather." Minerva calculated a quick chronology, and nodded. The rest of the story she knew well.

The name that they shared, Robley ancestors had chiseled proudly into the first permanent cornerstones in the Valley, affixed to streets and parks, and stained into glass windows wherever they had the chance. Robleys had been among the first pioneers to stagger into the budding Saint Kathareen's plain after the bruising winter of 1792 claimed most of their animals and half of their party. They threw their own used-up bodies onto the warming silt, the accumulation of aeons of flooding where the Saint Kathareen's River flowed into the Ohio.

[46]

The Shawnee had another name for the gentle stream which, in the late spring of that year, flowed all innocent and bountiful. They called it the Little-River-Which-Rages-Up-Like-a-Giant-When-Times-of-Anger-Come. The earliest Valley Robleys had little personal investment in placating either the Indians or the forces of nature. They promptly rechristened land and water, stamping the Valley forever with their peculiar, shortsighted pragmatism.

Harrumphing their way through the rituals of establishment, they allowed very little to sentiment. The one major concession of emotive value by Calvin and Levi Robley would leave its imprint forever upon their progeny and on the institution of higher learning around which the town would continue to flourish even when the shipbuilding industry and the textile mills went the way of the silt in the flood. They named the town after their mother. Or at least they solemnly believed that they did.

Throughout their young adult lives, Calvin and Levi Robley had seen their salty and irreverent father soften and humanize only on the scattered occasions when, steeped in good Irish, his mind wandered back to the days when he had lived in Massachusetts with his good wife, Kathareen.

"M'love," he would intone into his brew, "how did the winds of fortune ever allow a rolling stone such as me to come to rest in the arms of a saint like you?" (Minerva swore that as Karraman told the tale, she heard the veritable pitch and lilt of the first Karraman echoing through the decades.) Then a pathetic tear or two would roll down the grizzled cheek, usually shortly before the first Karraman passed into a boozy repose. When he sobered up, he refused to allow that any female had even mothered his sons, let alone played any role of importance in his personal life. In response to direct prodding, he threw off weary semblances of replies:

"What was she like? What can a woman be like? Frail, 'tis all. Never could have tolerated the pioneerin'. Best gone." No more. But Calvin and Levi, feeding on sentiment, wishful thinking, and at least the residual fumes of powerful aged whiskey, duly canonized their late mother. Reverently, and with little resistance from the apostate Anglican frontiersmen who were ripe and ready to buy into hearty secular symbolism, they called their town Saint Kathareen's after the mother they'd never known.

Truth to tell, time and whiskey had effectively addled the first Karraman's brain. "Saint" Kathareen Robley in her earthly incarnation had been a petulant virago who drove her husband successively into the bottle and out of the comfortable frame house they had established at the fringes of Greenwood, Massachusetts, toward the wilderness. By the time she died, Karraman had fabricated his memories and his guilts into reverence for the woman who once had saved everybody's life on a midwinter night by scaring off a pack of drunken, marauding trappers. She had wielded only her savage screams, like weapons.

Calvin and Levi, as Karraman told it, thought that they were calling their town after a fragile and demure paragon of Love and Sacrifice. No one was left to say them nay. The last traces of Truth succumbed to Historical Romance. What a strange new destiny for Kathareen Robley, to be invoked as a shared intimacy, a prelude to lust. The old Kathareenians never would have believed it. They were serene in their common heritage, and in the striking physical resemblances that so many of them bore to one another. No matter that from time to time there cropped up a baby with six toes.

"For a closely guarded secret, you certainly know a great deal about it," she remarked as his narrative began to wind down. "And you do tell it wonderfully," she flattered, stoking up his already blistering heat of pleasure.

"Well," he demurred, "I imagine there are quite a few folks about town who actually know more about it than I do. Almost an occupation around here, digging out the lost facts." He smiled confidentially. "We just keep up the impression of a mystery for the outlanders. Makes a better tale to tell."

"A fascinating one from any prospect," Minerva agreed.

"History's a fascinating occupation," Karraman affirmed. "Never know what's going to come up a clue that unearths an entire new chapter, if not a volume. You know, the first settlers in the Valley didn't leave much in the way of writings. Their own past was back East. They only started writing things down when their children forced the issue. Why, we might never have known which Robley was which, or where to look for what, if old Karraman had had anything other than those two sons."

"How so?"

"Easy. Gave him something to name our twin 'mountains' across yon river—if calling those little buttons mountains doesn't offend your ear."

Her eyes sparkled with the wry intimacy of a shared private joke. Massachusetts stock could never soberly dignify such minimal pro-tuberances with so mighty an appellation. Karraman knew it, and he knew that she knew it, and he wanted her to know that he knew that she knew it. The point was made. She continued to sit in magnetic, effervescent silence. Intending only to draw her out, to get at the heart of her mysteries, Karraman couldn't stand the wait. He grew more voluble.

"Of course, the local boys have their own name for old Calvin-and-Levi, but not one that would have pleased my grandfathers, I'm afraid. Nor glorified the ears of a lady, I might add."

He had sent up a trial balloon if ever one existed. As Minerva saw it, he might have had several possible effects in mind. A certain kind of "lady" would have cajoled the nickname out of him with counterfeit innocence, artificial indignation waiting just offstage for the expected off-color epithet. Another type—an Emmaline, perhaps—would have blundered her trans-parent way into a complete change of subject. Minerva did neither. She

[48]

simply sat still, her left eyebrow raised just a trifle. Her deep, oval eyes for a moment looked golden.

Karraman raced on, wondering just what it was she was doing that was making him feel unglued. "I've built a house there," he added. Pride and something akin to embarrassment vied for possession of his voice. "Quite an extraordinary house, I think." He had quite forgotten that the inspiration for and indeed the designer of a large part of the unwieldy structure had dined across town this night, petulantly sharing a groaning Germanic board with two elderly, partially deaf parents, in the secure comfort that Karraman was out somewhere courting a recalcitrant oil well. He had also lost temporary sight of the fact that his usual approach to the house was defensively to disown any role in its creation, and attribute every one of its gauche excesses to their true perpetrator, his Fiancée.

"It would give me great pleasure to show it to you," he told her, courtly as Debrett's, panicky lest otherwise their time together somehow come to an end.

Minerva had divined immediately that Karraman was referring to the monstrous affair with all the scaffolding around its bulk. It would give her great pleasure, she decided, to be the recipient of such a tour, if only for the enjoyment of a loud and heartfelt guffaw. Still, she inclined her head a further modest bit, and allowed Karraman to ramrod the conversation dead ahead.

"There is a balcony facing west on the top floor of this hotel. It affords a splendid view of Calvin-and-Levi and, if I may say so, of my house. Or house-to-be, if you will." He thought with a sudden pang of Cricklewood, and found himself off-guard. He drove the vagrant sentiment underground, all unaware that such lapses constituted some of his most profound attractiveness to Minerva, who could read the hesitant tenderness flickering at his eyes. "Perhaps after we dine, you would accompany me on the first step of the sightseeing tour. The gaslights will be dim at night, but rather nice, I think, no matter how hard old Saint Kath's tries to resist them!"

Minerva marveled at his ability to shift his dialect from primitive to romantic and back again as he described old Saint Kathareen's, then continued to lure her into the life of the present. She supposed that part of that seductive ease came from growing up in a place so small that all classes of the society lived and operated side by side. It was almost like being multilingual, she thought, with growing admiration. Surely especially useful for a local lad who exceeds his neighbors in material advantages, and consorts with educated equals in the outside world, but has to come back and make friends and peace at home. What a talent, she thought, little realizing that she would become a devout apostle of the very same practice herself when her own need demanded, and stick to the principle all her life.

"What about it, Mrs. Bolton?" he was gently urging. "Come with me and see a little of what the real Saint Kathareen's is like."

She had wondered just how he was going to get around to it. Waiters hovered with menu cards, and Karraman surely knew that she would be hungry after her day. After her journey. After her life. He had amply provided her with all the data of his impending marriage, short of the engraved day and date. He couldn't simply invite her to enjoy a further glass of champagne and enjoy the view, the prerogatives of unencumbered men and women. Yet he was doing just that, without apology.

She certainly knew that his intentions were, if not dishonorable, at least not quite open. Still, she felt that, all things considered, she had absolutely nothing to lose by allowing herself to be dealt into the waiting hand. She replied accordingly.

"I think I'd enjoy that very much, Mr. Robley. After dinner, of course."

When she lowered her voice that way, the resultant chord was throaty and not a little seductive, a fact of the physiology of her larynx. It snared Karraman Robley like flypaper.

"Please call me Karraman," he breathed.

She smiled assent as he regained sufficient composure to order dinner. In the gentle euphoria of gaslight and champagne, she became more determined than ever to make a go of Saint Kathareen's, and to do it on her own terms. Allowing a man to order her dinner was one of the amenities to which she could gracefully submit without compromising her purpose. More serious lines of battle were to be drawn in the future. Antagonism at the outset, she decided as Karraman made the final selection of rare German wine, wasn't a luxury she yearned for, let alone one she could afford.

Karraman ordered river trout and spring lamb. Minerva ate with dignified lust. Karraman dwelt purposefully upon the immediate. As the waiter placed delicate nappies of *pêche* Melba before them, he asked Minerva with what he thought was eminently artful casualness how long she planned to stop at the Inn.

"Until I find something a bit more suitable, I suppose," a squelch that couldn't have caught Karraman more squarely between the eyes if she'd been aiming.

"Mrs. Bolton, you'll travel this Valley far and wide before you'll find an accommodation that can even begin to look this one in the eye." Bristling like a warthog.

Delighted at the defensiveness of the man who worked so diligently at keeping a heavy, if inconsistent, camouflage over his consuming involvement in the establishment, Minerva laughed a sparkling shower. "Oh, do call me Minerva. And of course no offense intended, my dear sir. I simply meant that as a permanent resident of Saint Kathareen's, I shall require, shall we say, a more, what?—*adaptable* lodging."

Karraman, who had no idea what she meant, nodded sagely. However, his nod came fully equipped with a heavier baggage than simply the feigned understanding that he was trying to project. It also held his devout and grateful acceptance of the fact that Mrs. Minerva Bolton, late of Massachusetts, had placed herself in a position to provide more than a fleeting, flash-in-the-pan adventure in his life. The rest of the implications he could not yet bring himself to examine. He decided to pursue the jocular note, to try to keep the advantage somehow—if ever he had really had it.

"And how will ye do it, my pretty maid?"

She twinkled in response to his sally, but replied with deadly seriousness. "Hats."

"Hats?"

"Yes, hats."

"You'll sell hats." Not quite credulous. He hadn't pictured her as anybody's shopgirl.

"Not quite. From the looks of things, the heads of Saint Kathareen's have yet to make even a nodding acquaintance with the twentieth century. I think, Karraman, that I am quite well equipped to lead the way."

He still didn't get it.

"Lead the way."

"Yes, Karraman, lead the way." She lifted a glass to her lips and took a sip of champagne while her host scuffled and scurried around his brain case to come up with the least naive question. If it had been Hammond, she would have been ready to throttle him by now.

"You'll sell hats," he repeated.

"First I'll make them." The game ended. "And quite exclusively, I daresay. In the end, I imagine that I shall employ others to sell them for me."

"You'll make hats."

"Yes, my friend, I will make hats." Traces of the old pique were beginning to temper her amusement at the man's peculiar bewilderment. Minerva was becoming impatient to hear some words other than her own flung back at her.

"But . . . how will you begin, dear lady?" Aha! She was pleased to be progressing.

"Begin? Mr. Robley, sir, I have long since begun. Nothing remains now but for me to find a way of becoming acquainted with a few select members of the public. I need to bring my wares to market, as it were."

She gestured toward the blossomed creation on her own head. Karraman realized with a start how it really had been the hat that had attracted his

[51]

attention and ensnared him when she first entered the dining room; then how it had become so proportionate a part of its wearer that he had ceased to sense it as a separate, appended creation. He saw it as a sublime extension of Minerva herself.

"Yes, Minerva, I believe I do see after all. Hats." And as he uttered the word for the half-dozenth or so time in succession, he invested it with a reverence that obliterated whatever prosaic implications he was trafficking with moments earlier. He raised his glass to hers.

"To the heads of Saint Kathareen's, Miss Minerva. And to you."

Minerva accepted the toast gracefully. But despite the feminine delicacy, a stolid determination lurked, inviolate, beneath every inch of her surface. She would not be gentled out of her intent.

III

When Miss Minerva tells him about her self-constructed notoriety, Hawk regards her with no small wonderment. He thinks she is, simply, the most beautiful woman he has ever seen, even into the tenth decade of her life. Wonders: if Cara never marries, if she outlives any old man she hooks up with along the way, ends up alone like Minerva, will anyone ever guess in the old woman at the glorious gymnast, the loving explorer, residing in her youth? He understands vaguely that what he is really asking is a question about Minerva, but can't face up to it.

Hawk, smooth Hawk, wades through the silence, as Miss Minerva sighs deeply. He is buying time. Doesn't want to let her narrative evaporate. Wants to hang on to the present thoughts because there's something . . . a furtive sprout of a thought. . . . Doesn't know quite where to go from here. . . .

Relaxes, calm in the assurance that he can pick it up tomorrow. Whenever. God bless plodding old Saint Kath's. Never need a bookmark, no one ever seems to turn a page. . . .

That was how Hawk had come to know Minerva, really, as the farmer comes to know the spring: slowly, patiently, through mutual diligence. No crop accelerators in Saint Kathareen's. None of that for the native black earth of this Valley. Nature stocks up a richness of her own medium. Hawk laughs at his own simile, because in his cultivations of Minerva he has, inadvertently, come up with something of a medium himself: Professor Howard Robley, whose passionless and meandering writing seminars Hawk Simon, Author, somehow seems powerless to avoid, ends up taking term after term after term.

At first Hawk had relished activating a special set of adolescent passive-vocabulary words on behalf of Howard. Sanctimonious, unctuous, pompous, uppity. Then, at an indeterminate point, Hawk began to realize that everything tied in. As Minerva's seduction of his brain continued, Hawk began to assimilate the fact that it had actually been Howard's offhand interest in his project that inspired some of his first, best interviews, Howard's imagination that had ignited his own. Hawk soon found it possible, even easy, to forgive Howard his graceless xenophobia, his awkward hauteur.

Howard Robley was the first person Hawk had ever known who had a sense of place. Everything about Howard was gloriously Mid-American. Hawk couldn't get enough of the whole scene. He ended up wanting to burrow into the corners of the Robley life every way he knew how, even if it had to be through Howard.

As Hawk progresses in his research, he feels enormously pleased with himself. He extends his benevolence like a spreading flush even to Professor Robley.

Howard himself is more ambivalent about his own worth, which helps explain why he seeks to bolster his standing in the human race through association with Minerva. His own life would not, of course, necessarily be painfully lackluster, except that his own expectations have made it so.

He managed to emerge from his motherless childhood quirky but relatively intact. Every time Emmaline Musgrove Robley had a baby, she swore it would be the last. Nine times she cursed God, her husband, and her infrequent but uncompromising impulses to have unspeakable things done to her by Karraman in the muggy dark of the marriage chamber. Eight times she went back for more. Shortly after the ninth, which had worn her about to a nubbin, she said, she rolled back her small eyes and expired.

That grandiose and selfish exit left Karraman Robley a widower with eight children between the ages of two and twenty, each indelibly conditioned to his own state of original sin and all the guilts and angers thereunto appertaining. The ninth child, Baby Howard, deprived of a mother's love to superintend him through the narrows of self-awareness into the sea of self-contempt, had to figure it all out for himself.

Thus Howard Robley grew. He knew of his brothers and sisters from afar. The older ones gradually sequestered themselves into living paradigms of

Victorian self-torture. One by one they entered convent, asylum, prison, university, or even marriage, the latter of which for the Robleys combined the more austere and satisfying characteristics of each of the others. After a Christmas or two of remembering Baby Howard with inappropriate, or therapeutically crafted, or guiltily extravagant gifts, the elder siblings in turn faded out of contact.

The three youngest before Howard, too tender even by Emmaline's Dickensian standards to be placed anywhere parochial, Karraman finally farmed out to what he prayed would be the logical province, the Grandparents. The Musgroves, their only issue dead and gone, took the arrival of the children as a sign that God wanted them to abandon their wicked city ways and move back to the old family summer compound near Mentor-on-the-Lake. Never mind that Saint Kathareen's was hardly a city, and that no Musgrove had ever tried to brazen out a Lake Erie winter all alone up there. Off they went, and getting access to the children proved more complicated for Karraman than securing a visitor's pass to a leprosarium. Howard, his mother's effective murderer in the Musgrove eyes, was of course never invited on holiday. His brothers and sisters never got to know him at all.

Except for Peter Robley, firstborn son of Karraman and Emmaline, self-appointed keeper of the faltering flame. There also remained several women of Foothill House, who probably did more than anyone to retain for Howard whatever modest grounding in reality he had. Life ensued in its rambling way. An anchor of sorts was in place.

For many years Baby Howard had no clear idea where Peter Robley stood in relation to him. Somewhere, probably out of the combined gossip and fairy tale whispered to Howard by the first Maybelle Kennebec backstairs, he was beginning to understand what parents were. Thinking them a good thing, hell-bent on finding some for himself, he readily settled for Peter.

Karraman was never there anyhow. He spent his days in the oil fields, his evenings God knew where. It didn't matter to Howard, because he had Peter. Peter didn't care how or where his father idled away the widowed hours, as long as he spent them far away from the dour and top-heavy mansion Emmaline had created in her own image.

Peter's qualifications for the proprietorship of Baby Howard's soul consisted mainly in his seniority. Also his presence. Having left Dartmouth College in the autumn of his sophomore year, he was the sole Robley sibling free of a confining institution. Resplendent in his own guilts, he channeled his energies of repression toward the mighty labor of rearing Emmaline's last child.

When Karraman actually did die in 1936, Howard, age five, scarcely took notice. Peter barely had to modify his behaviors. The quarter from which

Peter expected interference was Minerva's. None was forthcoming. Peter was too wrapped up in his own concerns to notice that her solemn taciturnity limned mute grief. She withdrew. Peter's ineptitude as he played substitute father to Howard appalled her. Yet what could she do? To have interfered and been rejected would have broken what was left of her heart.

Howard always knew that Father was an Oil Man. He was confused when Peter showed surprise that Karraman's body was found in the fields. The whole story confused him. He had to assume that the grown-ups were keeping a lot of it from him.

It was said that when they found Karraman, he was dandified down to the last finger ring and spat, and plugged full of shot from his own twelve-gauge shotgun. Not much blood sullied the pristine expanse of snowy scrub beneath him, due to subzero weather conditions. Peter Robley, receptive to cautious suggestion, thought that probably a drunken poacher had mistaken his father for a creature of richer flesh, sweeter meat. He couldn't help feeling a little sorry for the poor disappointed bastard.

The sheriff had a strong suspicion that his no-'count brother-in-law, one of whose undocumented absences spanned the period of Karraman's death, had something to do with it. The coroner therefore determined that exposure after being wounded had killed Karraman, not the gunshots themselves. He ruled death by misadventure, effectively shutting off the due process of law, if not the titillating conjecture abroad in speakeasy and drawing room throughout the Valley. Peter knew that Minerva suspected a different version of the truth, because she told him in one heated moment that a facile exoneration was, in her opinion, every bit as ill-got as a facile blame. She would neither expand nor explain her reasoning, which infuriated Peter further. He incubated a long loathing of her powerful silence. If anybody was ever the mistress of the perfectly guarded confidence, it was Minerva Bolton.

Howard Robley, feeling himself randomly misshapen by a childhood of indiscriminate editings, glories in the conviction that his handicaps are invisible to his students. He vows to protect his charges from the crueler aspects of his own fate.

Howard carries the weary, ironic satisfaction of a tired matchmaker as he observes the growing sympathies between Hawk Simon and Minerva Bolton. Hawk is maturing as a student and as a person. His written prose is tighter. That much Howard can verify objectively. Imputing to him strengths that Hawk is only just on the way to seeking, Howard will both overestimate and overwhelm Hawk before many clouds roll over Saint Kathareen's.

In one evaluation Howard is absolutely correct: Hawk has done splendidly to come upon Minerva Bolton as he has, through a figurative back door that has given time and warmth for the cultivation to proceed. He feels a safety in Minerva's presence that he has never imagined in all his prior life. He feels chosen, eternal. He often wonders if some of the turbulence of the rest of his life would have been obviated, whittled down to a gentler edge, if his introductions to Cara could have been so well stage-managed, or even stage-managed at all.

Cara he met entirely by accident. Technically the accident was his fault, since he plowed his former Corvette into the back of her former Corvair on Old 60 just northeast of the farm. In actual fact the blame belonged to Caravelle because she had decelerated to ten mph and turned off her lights just the other side of a crest of a hill at dusk. She was trying to get the feel of covered wagons, she later explained, and she felt that ten miles an hour was still a little swift for getting the right idea. Hawk assumed that she was merely trying to kill herself, but she hooked him like a dopey river bluegill with her opening comment.

Which was, "What is this, some kind of bloody incest?"

For a minute Hawk stared hard, trying to figure out if he knew her from some historic reunion on his late father's side of the family. Something . . . but not the Simon blood, that was for sure. He gaped dazedly at the pre-Raphaelite person challenging him from beneath a ragtag accumulation of clothing, effusive strawberry hair, honeyed brown eyes, and more symbolic miscellany than he thought he could assimilate in one viewing. At a length which didn't distress the girl because she seemed to expect no better, Hawk looked from distressed Corvette to distressed Corvair and back again. Figured out belatedly exactly to which family relationship she had been referring.

"Shit," he acknowledged.

"Come on, baby. You can do better than that. I'll get the flares while you think." Implying some kind of grudging complicity.

All of a sudden he was wanting her to know him by the pearls that would drop from his lips, but none seemed to be immediately forthcoming. All that seemed to issue forth was raw material. Very raw material.

"Fucking woman driver."

"Uh, do you want to handle that statement grammatically or existentially?"

Hawk gaped. Multileveled linguistics smack dab in the middle of an asphalt cowpath. He didn't know where she had come from, where she was going, or what it was about her that was speaking to his senses. But he knew for sure under the last seepage of light from the great western drain in the sky that she was rapidly metamorphosing into something beautiful.

The strain of a hamstring, the pull of succulent dorsals against the frivolous patchwork smock as she reached and pulled and unearthed several light-stick flares, heightened Hawk's lunatic notion that he wanted to take her right home. Watch her move. Paint her, although he was not a painter. Play great symphonies for her, and watch her listen to them.

Settling, he would make do with talking, listening, sharing a warmed-over pizza. Looking at her: on a country road light-years from New Jersey, a shaggy, freckled vagabond in a wrecked Corvair full of Army surplus light sticks and God knows what else, and whose body language showed nothing but contempt for the rapist of reveries who had shattered her prairie schooner and could now not improve upon the splutters and curses, aborted nacre, that told her nothing about him at all.

"Well?" with elaborate patience. Then another pause while Hawk circled, swooped, and tried again to figure out where he might land without driving off the prey for good and all.

As he maneuvered, a pickup roared by, loopy inhabitants waving and shouting gleefully. Totally engrossed in the immediacy of their cars and each other, both had missed its approach. Neither had thought to flag it down.

"So much for help." Cara shrugged. "Okay, hero. Since you're going to play strong and silent, what do you say we leave the philosophy to the Greeks, and try to get these two miracles of modern technology separated."

"It's not a question of provenance," he threw back, as much for his own satisfaction as to see what kind of an infielder the girl was. "It's a matter of priorities."

"My turn: Oh, shit. I really hoped you might have a better word than 'priorities' all stored up somewhere and waiting to try out. If I wanted 'priorities,' I never would have left New Jersey."

Hawk's sandy eyebrows wizarded all the way up. Her inflection no more bespoke New Jersey than his did. Besides, the plates on her car, what he could make out under the scrunch, read "Cradle of Liberty," not "Garden State."

"Jersey where?"

"What's the difference? 'Trenton uses what the world refuses.' Same goes for the rest of the state."

Hawk floundered. "You sure come a fur piece," he informed her.

"Beg your pardon?"

"It means you've had a hell of a long haul." Hawk laughed. "In this Valley, ya gotta know the language before ya know the territory."

"Oh. Well." Hawk had the impression that she was stammering, somehow flinching away from an interrogation that he hadn't even been aware he was conducting. "I have a job interview," she said deliberately, as if that explained everything.

Hawk wanted to keep it light. "All the way out here? I'm the only person I know in this whole Valley who hasn't lived here forever. In fact,"—abruptly he became a burlesque Dr. Frankenstein, leering merrily—"I did not sink zat anyvun even communicated mit de outzide vurlt." Ghoulishly he wrung his hands, heavily implying that she had wandered into Transylvania, and there was no road out.

"Well, if you're trying to scare me off, it won't work," she retorted finally, fielding his banter. "My late mother's connections . . ." She let it trail off mysteriously.

It did give Hawk pause. It was a strangely couched comment, a half-teasing implication that the "connections" she mentioned came from a macabre netherworld where she now resided. On the other hand, Hawk didn't think that the quiver in the girl's voice was necessarily part of the playacting. He couldn't put a name to what was going back and forth, but he already knew that he was interested in buying into some more of it. So he named himself.

"I'm Hawk Simon." He proffered a welcoming hand. "I live over there." Gesturing beyond a rise on the opposite side of the road. "Late of Short Hills." He grinned.

"No kidding." Surprise and acceptance at once, and a friendliness conspicuously absent in the opening passages of their lopsided duet.

"I'm Caravelle Dragonlover."

Hawk's turn: "No kidding?"

Uncool, said her eyes. "Why would I kid about a true matter like my own name?"

A nonrhetorical question to which, if there is any available answer, Hawk failed to find it. "Wow. Heavy." For an English major, an author, and the putative star in the coronet of Howard Robley, Ph.D., Hawk was churning spume enough for a whole school of porpoises. He was staying above water as best he could, but certainly not with optimum grace.

"For a guy named after a bird, you don't have a lot of call to throw stones, I think." The words bit, but the tone reeked of Helping Professions: calm, serene, detached.

Hawk rallied, although not with abundant confidence.

"Hey—those weren't stones. It's just that in all my benighted life I've never had the pleasure of the company of the famous Dragonlovers of New Jersey."

Caravelle giggled, descended from her Seat of Judgment. "It's an ancient family name, actually, if you know what I mean," she amended confidentially. Then paused. Sidelong twinkle. "I made it up about two years ago when I decided that a Funk was something you might fall into if you couldn't possibly avoid it, but never, under any circumstances, something

[59]

that a person ought to be named, no matter what. God—the years of harassment I suffered with that name."

As Hawk's eyes articulated commiseration, she reeled on. "And, do you know, I never even set knowing eyes on the bastard who laid it on me. He split very early on. At least my late mother said he did. But sometimes I have a sneaky feeling that she set the whole thing up by herself. Me, I mean. I wouldn't put it past her. Kate always said that she liked to do things absolutely alone." Then, meekly, "I guess I do too. Usually."

By that time, Hawk had relaxed. His uncertainties were dribbling down the road the way of the Corvette's radiator juices. Every second that she stood there in the middle of a nearly uncharted highway, beside a wrecked and useless car, spilling it all to Hawk Simon, previous stranger, the possibilities broadened. There she was, watching as star after star punctuated infinity on the nightly round, talking like a compulsive about a father she had never met, said she rarely thought about, claimed she hated when she did. Hawk blossomed in the confidence of his own drawing power.

"Does everybody call you Caravelle? Or are you trying to shake loose of that one too?"

"I didn't choose it, but I'll live with it. It's a family name." She left Hawk innocent of the family associations it had for her. Hawk let it slide, being less drawn to historical disciplines at the moment than biological.

"Caravelle Dragonlover," he said, with Orion at forty-five or fifty degrees in the western sky. "How about discussing it over a cup of something up at the farm?"

"Or a bowl of something?" she asked hopefully.

Whether she meant soup or Granola or hash or something more original yet, he didn't know, but he was pleased to try to oblige at anything. "At your service, my dear Miss Dragonlover." He gave it every courtly affectation he owned. He really had to hand it to himself, he thought, for pulling together such a graceful finale, after making such a botch of the overture.

Caravelle responded in the same vein, curtsying with a sweep of her motley in the macadam. For an instant she looked regal, a monarch out of time and place, worthy of dynasties. Then she parted her lips and said softly, "Right on, Hawk. If only we can get those two fucking automobiles to haul ass out of here."

Hawk can barely recall the days in the clapboard farmhouse before Cara. Lucy the Hound had to abandon his assignment as bed warmer and metamorphose into hearth rug, a demotion which he accepted impassively, as such things go. Paul the Parrot thrived on the new order of ministrations from the start, as witnessed by his rapidly expanding literary consciousness. Radiant, drifting, probably never would have stayed on if Cara hadn't come to round things out, soften the edges. He says she makes him feel nurtured and safe, although neither she nor Hawk fully understands why.

Hawk thinks of the pre-Cara house as a place without aromas of its own. Sensate, Proustian, he loves fragrance. When he goes to Miss Minerva's, he swaddles himself in a private formulation of olfactory comfort: a little must, a little residual cannabis, a touch, sometimes more than a touch, of lavender and apple emanating more or less aggressively from one of Minerva's omnipresent lace handkerchiefs.

One time only he has been permitted to enter the sanctum of Gossamer Fitzmorris Waldron, who is not exactly bedridden in what is not exactly the music room. From behind the oaken door to that forbidden territory, great, ponderous tonalities constantly emanate. Their source, obviously electronic, somehow violates what Hawk is sure was the original, acculturated sensibility of the place.

He expects to find sickroom odors within—alcohol, ether, the masked reminders of an embarrassed excretory system. When the door actually opens to Hawk, he is vaguely surprised at what greets him: a little must, a touch of lavender and apple, and a faint, unmistakable overlay of wet dog.

The music, depressingly overbassed, assaults him like a force field. It erupts like pure energy as soon as he opens the door. It thrums so demandingly within that the knickknacks tremble. Hawk wonders whether the incessant sonic bombardment might not have served to cancel Gossamer's remaining senses.

"I'll talk to you about it later," Cara assures him. "I'm with you, kid, but I have to put on my bearskin and go rustle up some flint so that I can start dinner."

He chuckles, appreciating her appreciation. Goes back to work. A long night of reading about City Fathers, City Mothers, Days of Yore. No beleaguered high-school history teacher would have believed it was the same Owen Simon.

One morning, with the brilliant Valley sunshine barely beginning to warm the dank corners of Hallowell Hall, Hawk made the decision to drop out of Saint Kathareen's College once and for all. Professor Howard Robley, Ph.D., in his alternate role as docent through the dangerous rapids of

Advanced Creative Writing, was telling Hawk that not even a self-respecting high-school dropout would use Kris Kristofferson's eyes as a suitable image for the galvanic shade of blue that Hawk wanted to summon. Hawk was staring idly at Robley, musing after the fate of their vagrant historical intimacies, wondering for the first time in his life what the hell gives a teacher the right.

"Jeez, Mr. Robley, I thought I'd come up with a pretty vivid usage." Not much of a defense, but Hawk was remembering how Robley had described Clark Gable's voice to epitomize irony in a story widely anthologized not too long after the third or fourth rerelease of *Gone With the Wind*. Robley always referred reverently to the publication as if it had hit the streets the day before yesterday. Since Robley had gotten clean away with what Hawk considered a perfectly fallacious metaphor, Hawk bestowed upon himself cheerful permission to appropriate the device. Robley now seemed to be withdrawing both the permission and the device from Hawk's access, irrationally and arbitrarily.

"Simon," Robley pronounced, "Kristofferson does not in any sense serve your purpose as a universal metaphor. In fact, your generation has not yet had the balls to produce anything that could pass as a universal metaphor." He accented "produce" as though it were an epithet.

Hawk was dumbfounded. He had always thought that Kristofferson, graying and sentimental, belonged more to Robley's generation than to his own. But with Robley's response, he felt that he had been turned upon. He kept staring at Robley to make sure that he hadn't put on the wrong bifocals and gotten Hawk hopelessly confused with somebody else.

The tone sounded, signaling the end of the hour. Hawk rose. He stood staring at his Professor, that self-appointed Guardian of the Crossroads, suddenly become card-carrying turncoat. Languid, Levied students filed out between them. As the room emptied, Hawk felt its physical characteristics imprint themselves in his brain with final, indelible gravity. Windows, open to the sweet, lightly fertilized redolence of morning, allowed a breeze to stir. Meekly it churned the accumulated foggy breath of academic years. Hawk wondered not entirely irrelevantly whether anyone had ever dared challenge Marcel Proust, student, about the efficacy of his metaphors in such an aesthetic abomination of a classroom. Talk about adding insult to injury.

Howard Robley looked quizzical. "Well, Hawk?"

He had never called him Hawk before, in almost four years, despite the strengthening line of kinship drawn through Minerva, despite everything. An intimacy of conflict was developing. The same impulse, Hawk thought cruelly, that leads a military surgical team exhaustingly to save the life of a hostile prisoner of war from the wounds inflicted during the brutal capture, beefing him up for the ultimate indignity of incarceration and torture. Hawk had yearned for the closeness of his nickname, would have traded living flesh for it, during all the hours when Howard was breathing life into the Robleys for Hawk's benefit. To offer it now . . . Hawk didn't know what to do, almost thought, anguished, that he was actually going to let Howard Robley get away with it. But he couldn't. Absolutely couldn't. Robley was offering an insult, not a bid.

"Why'd you do it, Robley?" demanded Hawk into the vacated classroom.

"Do what?" Robley too was confused. He had been merely exercising his métier, he thought. In fact, he judged that he had done rather well, concluding an especially pithy hour with a wittily mordant critique of Hawk's piece. He was not at all displeased with his own performance. Or hadn't been.

Actually, the story hadn't been bad. Not bad at all. Robley had watched Hawk toughen and clean up his prose by encouraging increments ever since the very first assignment in Freshman Comp. For himself, Robley's eye had wandered off the main chance long ago. His literary ambitions had dwindled, settling at last on a sprouting image of himself as Pygmalion to the Galatea/Fitzgerald/O'Hara of some as yet unwitting undergraduate. Of all the young innocents who had crossed his threshold of possibility over the years, Hawk Simon had seemed the closest to shaping into something.

"Do what?" Robley insisted into Hawk's seething caesura.

"Do what you did, Robley. Don't be cute."

Howard Robley's confusion immediately took on the taint of righteous indignation. In his entire academic career, no student, nor anyone else in the world, had ever told him not to be "cute." Even as an overprotected, crazily underprivileged infant, "cute" had never been something Howard Robley stood in danger of becoming.

He raged. "You don't know what 'cute' means, do you, Simon? As a slang term, it refers to a cowboy or a specimen of livestock," he spat, "and it means 'bowlegged.' Even in that trumped-up rural mythology you call home, I wouldn't have expected you to know that."

Hawk didn't really have any idea how much Robley knew about his living arrangements. They had always confined their sessions together to more neutral ground, like the seminar rooms in the library or the comforts of the audiovisual labs. Surely Minerva wouldn't have discussed him . . .

Robley drew himself up to his full 5'8", bristled into his beard, and defined pomposity down to the angle of his accusing finger. His straight-on glance would have caught Hawk somewhere about mid-chest.

"I may be aging," he informed. "I may be aging rather more clumsily than I had anticipated in the tunneled vision of youth," pointedly, "but I am not now, never have been, nor do I intend ever to become bowlegged." He waited.

[63]

For a moment Hawk failed to respond. He wondered what the hell he was doing here, or anywhere. The world didn't seem big enough to contain the outrage that was gathering inside his head.

"Well, Hawk? Nothing to say?"

"Why'd you do it, Robley?" Deadly monotone, barely a question. More like a sentence passed on one or the other of them.

Robley's expression told Hawk that he found himself blameless, innocent of implication or nuance. Then abruptly he changed course. "You know, Simon, I never saw a blue-eyed Jew before. What are you, some kind of sport?"

Hawk, who had been a volatile body already, restraining himself for old times' sake, quivered on the launch pad and took off.

"What are *you*, Robley, some kind of faggot? We were talking about creative writing. My baby blue eyes are my business."

"Well, maybe you should have used yours instead of Kristofferson's. It would have been just as effective, you know. In fact," enlightened, "maybe you actually were using yourself, and just calling it Kristofferson as a matter of delicacy," said the world's foremost expert in psychological misattribution. Anger rose, flared, stood stagnant in the middle of a tortured, sweaty limbo.

Something had gone very wrong. What had started as a stimulating literary tête-à-tête was turning into an ugly, uncontrolled series of *argumenta ad hominem*. Robley's momentum was building. He seemed to Hawk not to be able to let it go.

"On the other hand, Simon, you must bear in mind the fact that you're hardly the universal metaphor yourself. For anything."

"Robley, you're a shit." Hawk's vocal control never broke. It was Robley who began to sweat, smelling remotely pasty. His voice, which he attempted to modulate around the high bluffs of good theater, betrayed hysteria, impending defeat.

"See here, Simon—"

"*You* see here, Robley." Hawk, enunciating carefully. "I wanted criticism, and you came down with a virtuoso performance like some kind of feline prima donna. It didn't have one damn thing to do with my work, and if you're any kind of teacher, you know it." Robley opened his mouth, but Hawk streamlined on. "I wanted simple honesty, and you gave me glib bullshit. I wanted a teacher"—to Hawk's amazement, it came out with a reverence that suddenly embarrassed him in the presence of this apostate— "and you gave me an egotistical old fart stinking up the classroom with mindless generalizations about my entire generation, for Christ's sweet sake. *You're* the one with all that . . . that *family*, Robley. That's supposed to give you some perspective, goddammit, some compassion. What the hell makes you think it gives you the Right to do this to people, Robley? Your interminable little tenure with the College of Saint Kathareen's? Let me tell you something, old man: associating with the bunch of troglodytes in residence around here wouldn't qualify you to make moral judgments about a mink farm. Let alone literary judgments."

His voice paused, but his eyes never let up. Hawk gave Robley some credit for his silence. Obviously the attack was losing steam, yet there he hung, poised, communicating that somehow he knew he had yet to feel its full brunt. Hawk didn't keep him waiting long for the final onslaught.

"Well, Robley. Well." Almost wearily, but with a clarity of conviction. "I'm through, old man. If my generation hasn't produced any eternal metaphors, as you seem to be so hell-bent on thinking, maybe it's because we've spent so much valuable time just sitting around in reeking institutions."

He yanked his manuscript folder out of Robley's hand, where it was pilling slightly under the nervous abrasion of Robley's left thumb. Robley looked defensive, half-expecting a bravado gesture, a shredding of paper, a return toss to his face. Something physical.

Hawk surprised him, but only because Robley was expecting Errol Flynn rather than a flowerchild-come-lately. Carefully Hawk placed the folder between the two books he had swooped up from the writing arm of his chair. Count Robley/Masoch registered inordinate disappointment.

"Well, old buddy, consider this particular reeking institution depopulated by one. There's got to be a better way to become a universal metaphor."

Hawk aimed an ambiguous salute in Robley's general direction. It might have been contempt, but then again, there had been that quietly respectful element of having been, at least for a moment, equal enough to have joined in battle as men. Or at least that was what Robley doubtless wanted to believe.

Then Hawk turned and strode from the room. He played it to the third tier, knowing full well that Robley would watch with horrified fascination the elegance of his timing. Neither overly hasty nor self-consciously slow, but amazingly light on his feet, Robley would notice, for a creature so large.

Whatever grandeur Robley might have thought he had mustered for himself at the beginning of the exchange shattered thoroughly, at the end, into confusion and humiliation. Glum, diminished, he could not help but admire Hawk's outward poise, his grit. But then, he had been teaching, one way and another, for a total of twenty-two years, and he had never yet failed to experience a warming, masochistic rush whenever a student bested him on the field of academic honor. It was the only indulgence he had allowed himself in ages.

He sighed feelingly, emitting a potent admixture of envy and dry breath.

[65]

He could see Hawk returning, triumphant, to the farmhouse. He could practically envision the dripping pelt of glory flung victoriously over Hawk's shoulder as he appeared, a hero, before his swooning mate.

Cara is using the telephone as Hawk eases the Healey to a halt at the top of the drive. He swings himself out, then winces as the heel of his left sandal catches the edge of an oversized pebble, causing his ankle to buckle painfully. He limps pokily toward the house, his mind swarming with unkindly epithets diffusely aimed toward the gravel, the highway, the farm, the ceramic ruin of a silo, the whole misbegotten concept of Country Living, and last but not least, Howard Robley, Ph.D. He narrows his eyes, glancing back at the car, wishes for one vain moment that he knew a little less about cars, and had a little less respect for splendid machinery. He would have loved the satisfaction of a grinding, crunching halt, a visceral jolt of the brakes, an emasculating scrinch of gear upon gear. But he has no capacity for taking vengeance upon his car simply because he harbors a set of unrelated, untargetable indignities egging him on toward mayhem.

Hawk doesn't understand why everything has to turn into a production around here, with second-guessing and third-guessing and, What does she think that I think about what she thinks that I think? Arguments don't frighten Hawk in the slightest—or didn't. In a simpler time, arguments were what cleared the air and wove the threads of solitude into understanding. When it was over, the people involved knew one another better than before, which usually worked all to the good. Even if it didn't, Hawk had always felt that people who survive arguments with one another, fellow veterans, are bonded in the experience. He likes the sense of having endured, but even more he likes the idea of mutual endurance.

And he is bone-crunchingly angry because he can't seem to fall into that kind of rhythm with Cara. He still feels that he resides in an emotional terrain where he must skirt issues whenever he detects any potential for volatility. How can she be so selfish, he asks no one, as to put her own nonsense before his real agony? When he wants to talk to her, she's in the shower or on the telephone or at work or who knows where else. How can she not see what he needs? Enraged at her blindness, he is goddamned if *he'll* do anything to brush away the scales.

In small tribute to today's mood, Hawk the graceful, Hawk the stealthy, Hawk the respecter of everybody else's space, decides with plenty of malice aforethought to let the screen door slam as hard as it can behind him on his way into the farmhouse. Radiant, however, has chosen this very morning of life to emerge from his uterine arrangement in the kitchen and replace the corroded and superannuated old doorspring with a shiny, breathily hissing automatic pressure closer. He has even salvaged some of his own money out of somewhere to pay for it. Hawk thus clomps over the doorsill anticipating a thunderous punctuation to his entrance, and is left with a further frustration to pile upon all of that which has already collaborated to form an unprecedented malaise.

The screen door follows his trail at glacial pace, then strikes the frame with all the impact of thistledown. Hawk turns toward the sibilance, missing the familiar sequence of sound and vibration, thinking that someone must be behind him, an inauspicious visitor. Possibly Lucy the Hound, ceremoniously rubbing hindquarters against the screen in his accustomed fandance fashion, amusing the household and infuriating them simultaneously as moths and caddis flies accept the open invitation and buzz their greetings as they enter. Hawk even thinks it might be Howard Robley, hotly pursuing what he has belatedly realized is the best writer he has ever seen or ever will hope to see between the bold banks of the Ohio and the soft streams of the Saint Kathareen's, ready to kneel, importune, and tell Hawk to Come Back, All Is Forgiven. Hawk can't think that there is forgiveness in Robley's bailiwick at this turning, but he does give it a what-the-hell shrug. Whatever Robley's pretense, a reconciliation might not be a bad thing. Hawk would certainly let him in the door.

No one enters behind him. At last the dawn breaks over Hawk. He notes the unauthorized and, to his mind, unconscionable home improvement that Radiant has undertaken, and feels his arms and chest constrict with the beginnings of a new stratum of anger. For good measure, he slams his books down onto the low, polished oaken slab which serves as a table in front of the ersatz harem couch, actually a snarled tangle of pillows and paisley strewn suggestively between the head- and footboards of somebody's massive old Grand Rapids youth bed. His thudding books violate the stolid table just sufficiently to knock over a ceramic mug full of yesterday's snapdragons. Nothing breaks, but the water, which has been economically added to the dregs of yesterday's portion, splays out over everything in sight. It stinks of decomposition. Hawk quickly retrieves his own belongings, lets everything else lie there sopping up the repulsive mess. As if that might show Howard Robley.

The telephone still engages Cara so raptly that she hasn't registered Hawk's arrival. Feigning indifference he hopes will equal what seems to be hers, Hawk wants desperately to know who can possibly be magnetizing Cara so thoroughly on the other end of the line. As far as she has revealed her vital statistics to him, she comes from nowhere, has connections nowhere, has nowhere to go. No wife, no horse, no mustache. Only an oblique reference in a yellowed letter postmarked Habaña to substantiate that she really was kidding on the square when she alluded to her late mother's "connections" that night.

It's Cara he can't connect. Occasionally someone calls from the state hospital with a terse schedule change, or a request for overtime hours. These messages Cara dispatches with nursely efficiency. Aside from that, Hawk hadn't thought that anyone else whom she sees at work holds any remote interest for her outside the walls. He wants to know, *wants to know. Who is it that she's talking to?*

She has the local telephone directory, all half-inch of it including Saint Kathareen's and outlying communities as far north as Creighbill's Bottom, open in front of her. Who? What? Which drawling, twanging, sinewy Valley body will replace his and draw in the nectars of Cara at play, at love? What is it that such a primitive, such a gentile, can be telling Cara? What is the attraction?

He is baffled, jealous, and constitutionally incapable of offering the easy smile, the casual question, that might transmogrify this impasse into a loving, or at least a friendly, exchange between two adults who are, however temporarily, sharing the vestiges of a life.

Hawk casts a malevolent eye about him and says, "Here, Lucy, here, friend," feeling for certain that the dog is the only one he has left. He follows the dog back out the door before Cara has a chance to ask him what he's doing home so early. Although it is he who has erected the final impenetrable barrier between them on this day, he blames her, blames Howard, blames Radiant, blames Paul the Parrot, stores up enough smoldering resentment to carry him through a long, cold interval.

Cara watches Hawk and Lucy as they trail off toward the pasture at the northeast side of the house. Out there on the still-winter-strewn hayfield, they look as forlorn as she feels. It wasn't a telephone call at all. It never is: a question without an answer, a hunt without a treasure, a serve without a follow-through. All those old names, those crumpled, fading numbers, temporarily out of service forever.

Then she goes off to find some talcum powder. She smooths it carefully over her legs, not caring about the effect on her cultivated early suntan, since she's only using it to ease her stockings over clammy, nervous sweat. By the time she has gathered herself into the proper posture and mode to go to work, Hawk and Lucy are out of sight, and Radiant is sound asleep. It occurs to her that she hasn't taken time to pay the telephone bill, which she meant to do, no questions asked, as contrition or apology. She decides that that's all right after all, she can do it when she gets back.

And screeches out of the driveway with a ruinous shifting and burning, the brutalizing kind of expression that Hawk was wishing he could have accomplished only a little while earlier. He hears her from just the other side of a strategic knoll in the pasture. It would not console him to note that the rubbery outburst doesn't relieve Cara one little bit.

No one Hawk knew that day, regardless of station, and with the possible exception of Lucy, felt any other way than completely dispossessed.

But he is unable, mortally unable, to sever the binding ties that need to be cut. When he returns to the farmhouse, he has exhausted his physical energy and his repertoire of silent invective, but his massive hoard of ill-will remains unsullied, waiting in ambush for whatever unsuspecting victim trips his wires next. He is starving, and nothing in the surprising amplitude of their icebox or larder tempts him. What he would really like to bite into is somebody's head.

His mother obliges, managing to be at the other end of the telephone that jangles through the stifling air just as he embarks seriously upon his quest to find something in the pantry to devour. The very telephone he had deplored earlier, vowed not to deal with ever again in this life as Cara monopolized it while he waited, he has jumped to answer on the first ring. Wanting desperately to keep her out of everything, to protect and punish her simultaneously by withholding the momentous events of the morning at the College, he naturally lets fly with everything, including his unreasoned, equally unyielding decision to stay on in Saint Kathareen's anyway. Margo can't comprehend that at all. The problem is, he is intransigent on the subject of leaving that comic-opera little Valley of his. He thinks he has some kind of mission there, and Margo is pulling all the stops to try to make him understand just how silly it all is.

Hawk is not surprised by his mother's resistance, but he is nevertheless undone.

"Mother, you can argue from now to the Second Coming. You just don't have that kind of power over me anymore. I'm staying." He half-expects the receiver to crack under his hand in rebellion to the passion of his avowal.

"Owen, I don't care. Every aficionado of every perilous enterprise since the Vikings has been able to cite a whole almanac of necessity to prove that it's right and safe for him. That doesn't make it so."

"Glib, Mother, but unacceptable." Actually, he is very much impressed. She's ad-libbing into a drama which has taken her by complete surprise, and her improvisational skills dazzle Hawk. He wishes that she didn't read so much, or that she would add a little client-centered psychology to her library.

Part of Hawk's discomfort stems from the fact that he is still privately vacillating about remaining in Saint Kathareen's himself. The events of the morning are still too fresh to slice with a dissecting knife and come out clean. Because he hates the mushy folds of ambivalence, he has stated his position even more strongly than he feels it, figuring that in the ensuing argument Margo Simon will give as good as she gets. With the battle fully joined, he polarizes his wavering stance into a firm position. Partly he is indeed able to clarify his thoughts in counterpoint to direct opposition. Also, he is snagged on the ancient habit of taking the stand opposite to his mother's, no matter what his conviction on the issue.

"Owen, you're not going to get away with demoralizing me by calling me glib. That isn't fair. And anyway, it's beside the point."

"The whole argument is beside the point. I don't even know why we're having it," not a precisely honor-bright statement; they are having it because he has manipulated them into it, and he knows it with all the guilts and satisfactions appropriate to acts of filial mind control. "Mother, why don't you stop worrying about me and just go back to your embroidery. We both know that I'm going to stay. You're just listening to yourself talk."

"Hawk, now you've gone far enough." He knows that he probably has, because she only slips into his nickname when she has lost control of what she thinks is proper. "I do not embroider, as you very well know. And even if I did, I resent the implication. I *really* resent it."

Hawk paces the length of the telephone cord as he talks. As it pulls taut at the end of its radius, he battles the impulse to keep walking, to yank the offending electronic umbilicus clean out of the wall, and just keep walking. He wonders why he didn't do it earlier, when he first contemplated performing the action for Cara's benefit. What remains of his reason convinces him that he wouldn't solve anything at all by that expedient, so he retreats, brazens it out. Sighs.

"And please quit heaving pained sighs, Hawk. It won't work."

"Come on, Mother. Cut it out. This is something I have to work out by myself, but it isn't a problem unless you're planning to turn it into one. Give me some room to turn around, Margo, that's all." He hears himself becoming querulous. Obviously Margo does too.

"Oh, Hawk," she leads into it, "why do we have to argue like this?" Which immediately restores Hawk to full strength.

She might have had him, might have walked off with the Getting the Last Word trophy all sewn up. Now, however, there is entirely too much pathetic self-interest there for Hawk to let her get away with it. Breathing fire and other special effects, he tightens his white-knuckled grip on the receiver as if he could actually inflict pain on someone other than himself that way.

"Well, Mother, here's a thought for the day. As far as I'm concerned, we can go on arguing forever, because it's the best way I know of getting at the truth. In this life you have to face facts. No bullshit, period. You don't write my script, and I don't write yours."

"Owen," out of the depths of what sounds like a sudden, real fatigue,

[70]

"why don't we just say good-bye now? I think I've been sat in judgment on long enough."

Hawk, who has been wanting to terminate the conversation since even before the telephone rang, is suddenly panicked at the thought of a severed connection.

"Just what the hell kind of syntax is that?" he parries.

"Oh, Owen, I don't give a righteous damn about syntax. You're acting like a two-year-old. A minute ago you said how straightforward and honest we were going to be, and now you sit there pontificating about grammar like a Level Seventeen bureaucrat."

"Wrong again, Margo. I don't happen to be sitting at all. No sane person could sit still for all this crap."

"Nevertheless. And not funny, Hawk. Not funny at all. I've had it."

"You only think you've had it, Margo." He sighs, feeling wearily that someone, at least, has had it in this conversation, if not his mother. Continues, "The whole trouble is that your horizons end just west of the Hudson River, and not a damned thing beyond those hallowed borders even enters your serious consideration."

"That's glib too, Owen, and absolutely irrelevant. Save your cracks about provincialism for the real provincials—the ones out there where you, um, live—"

"Low, Mother. Really base."

"—and stick to the issues. Since this conversation doesn't seem to have any that you can keep track of, I'm willing to consider it at an end."

"Do you know what you're saying, Mother?" demands Hawk, aghast. "If this conversation is really over, as of right now, Jersey daylight time, do you know what you're saying?" He realizes impotently that his voice is crawling up the registers of terror. He wants her to let go of him, all right, but on his own terms.

With heavy resignation, then: "I always know what I'm saying, Owen."

He doesn't know whether to believe her or not, but she delivers the line with such recovered irony that he can't keep admiration from warming his gut. He reaches into his diminishing quiver of repartee and digs out whatever he can. "No one always knows what he's saying. That's glib too."

"She's saying."

"What?"

"No one always knows what *she's* saying. We don't assume the primacy of the male pronoun anymore, Owen."

"Oh, Christ. Can't we just stick to the three or four thousand issues that are already on the table, without getting into phony politics, too?"

"All right, Owen. All right. Whatever you say. Nevertheless, I am going to declare this conversation ended. I'm tired, and I'm going to lie down for a

[71]

while. That's all. What you choose to infer is your business. And don't worry about your old mother. I'll be all right."

Nuts. Not that old chestnut.

"Get out of the goddamn hole you've dug, Mother, before you pull it in after you."

"Hang up the goddamn phone now, Owen. I'm going to take a nap."

Over. And out.

As soon as he assimilates the intelligence that she has really gone and done it, he slams the receiver home with a ferocity that he hopes will absorb some of the fury, neutralize it, make things better. Instead, the vibration reverberates off the wall fixture and back through his hand into his wrist, which isn't feeling tip-top to begin with. Something to do with an off-center Frisbee toss. Can't seem to hit the target with anything. Crumples up a piece of old paper napkin somebody was shredding under the telephone, wads it up and hurls it at the wastebasket. Misses that, too. Radiant stirs, wriggles unobtrusively as far as he can get away from ground zero.

Hawk forms a perfect 3-D image of his mother, frosted and coiffed, her jewelry masked in Saran Wrap like all the rest of the hollowware in the house, being hoisted higher and higher on a telephone pole, until she reaches the top. The hoist deposits her, withdraws. She is alone. There is a way down, but it will leave her splintered, sullied beyond her ability to cope with the pain or the indignity. Atop her perch she is momentarily unassailable—until the darkness and the cold winds sweep in. She is temporarily oblivious of the dangers, because she is so jubilant at having overcome the old acrophobia. But the night winds are closing in, and closing fast. She shivers.

Or is it himself?

Hawk fights down an almost insuperable urge to ring her back, to call her "Mummy." He manages to quell the impulse because he doesn't believe that any problem with a woman is ever solved in bed. Clearly the kind of reconciliation for which the child in him yearns is nothing more or less than an incestuous facsimile of passion. It seeks comfort, not syllogisms.

He had hoped for an endorsement, and he is walking away with a dial tone. He knows that Margo's simplistic views of right and wrong have equipped him with the gumption to stand on his own two feet, but he never imagined that his knees would wobble so at the showdown.

Hawk, worn down by assault, still has it in him to curse. Curses Margo, curses Cara, curses himself, curses Radiant for the apparent ability to sleep while souls are being wrenched from their sockets in plain view. Curses the telephone above all. Vows that he will never, ever use it again.

When it rings promptly at seven the next morning, he nearly trips over

[72]

Radiant and pulverizes one of the kittens in his hopeful anxiety to answer. He doesn't ask much: only complete absolution and a small piece of cake to have and eat simultaneously.

"I just wanted to tell you that you have my love and my prayers no matter what you decide, Owen."

He wishes she could have offered up something a little more original or specific, but he is grateful that she keeps it clean. Gamely he thanks her without sarcasm, and says that she's always welcome to come out and spend some time, if she wants to. Fair play.

When he replaces the receiver, this time almost tenderly, he tries to assess the emotional climate that has suffused the room this early in the day. He finally recognizes it as a most uncommon state, a return to normalcy. He doesn't examine it too closely, lest it slip away, especially with the issues outstanding between him and Cara still to settle.

Absently he fondles Lucy, who has come seeking the first of his innumerable daily reassurances. In a not unlikely sweep of his mental apparatus, Hawk thinks once again of Margo, then of mothers in general. Wonders what sort of a one it must have taken to produce the likes of a Minerva Bolton, how any human body could possibly have come to accomplish her. For all Hawk knows, she swept to earth perfectly formed on the day that she entered Saint Kathareen's for the first time. At least, that seems to be the way she prefers to tell it.

IV

Minerva liked to think that everything really began on the elevator.

She moved as confidently as if she had ridden elevators all the way through life in preparation for the capstone of this moment's grace. The truth was that her first experience had been earlier that afternoon, and she hadn't recovered yet.

"The balcony?" Karraman asked as the brass gate enclosed them.

Why not? "For a moment, then."

"Four, Thomas."

"Yes, Mr. Robley." The boy grinned.

Minerva realized the full public extent of her compromise a beat too late. Well, nothing was left for her but to bite the bullet and keep on going. If she was to move inculpably through the rest of her unconventional days in Saint Kathareen's, consorting with the best of families while leading a private life that could make a sailor blush, it was because she decided then and there, right in that handsomely burnished elevator, that she would ever and always *act as if* she were absolutely right, and let the devil take the hindmost. The veneer of confidence would have to varnish over a burden of pain, doubt, fear that would buckle many a lesser back. Minerva simply decided that her indecisions were nobody's business but her own. The officer who rose to her surface was undisputed commander in chief.

As the elevator slowly rose, Karraman Robley seemed to expand by several orders of magnitude. If the Inn was his territorial domain, then the fourth floor was his Throne Room, his Star Chamber, his Holy of Holies. He rose and rose and rose to meet the occasion. Standing nose-high to Minerva, he towered above her.

The door slid open to reveal what looked more like a salon than a hotel hallway. Fragile settees staked intervals of dominion. The panels above them floated in ethereal scenes of heaven as conceived in eighteenth-century France.

"Have a pleasant evening, Mr. Robley," the elevator boy called behind them. Karraman grumbled something incomprehensible as he reached for the solid brass key in his waistcoat pocket.

Beyond the door, Minerva saw first a sitting room less elegant than the mirrored and muraled corridor through which they had just passed, but one whose velvety opulence better suited the rest of the hotel. In the interior, Karraman seemed to resume his proper proportions, Minerva noticed wryly. She liked him better that way, she concluded, than when he appeared as the bull in the china shop of his hallway.

Karraman led her at what seemed to be a self-consciously rapid clip past the portals leading into the depths of the suite, toward the heavily draped French doorways in the western wall. Outdoors, the last sunlight silhouetted the twin hills across the river. It softened even the intrusive presence of what Karraman had ostensibly brought her to see, Foothill House.

They moved imperceptibly closer as a breeze rippled by. For an instant they looked at each other. Then, without either of them knowing how or when the curtain of inhibition had dropped the final inches, they were in one another's arms. If she couldn't quite define her species within the classification "lady," she was certainly on the way to showing him that she was all kinds of woman.

Despite her advantage of height over Karraman, several inches, if one counted the lofty heels of her laced boots, their anatomies managed to match. She felt as though someone had ignited every contact point, potential and actual, on her body. Where she had willingly given herself to Hammond Bolton on the rare occasions of his embarrassed desire, and even provoked some occasions of her own, she felt virtually magnetized by Karraman. When she thought about it, Hammond had been more beautiful by light-years than Karraman: silken blond hair to Robley's balding, graying red; shining blue eyes to Karraman's shoebutton, watery blue-gray; slender, hairless torso, scarcely beginning to run to fat, compared to Robley's tufted, growing paunch. Yet Hammond Bolton was effete, fastidious, somehow dishonest. Karraman Robley exuded power.

The heavens could not have ordained a more fortuitous coupling than that of Karraman Robley and Minerva Bolton, except for several small intervening details. One was the academic reminder of Miss Emmaline Musgrove, Karraman's properly affianced lady. Another was Minerva's conviction that, Emmaline notwithstanding, the strictures of wifely existence were no longer for her. There would be no "honest-woman" chitchat, no moral hide-and-seek between them. Alas for Karraman and his good Robley conscience, she would wait tantalizingly long before imparting to him that he would have no worry about her trying to claim any possession of him, public or private. (She excused herself temporarily with the thought that it would have been presumptuous to address the issue.)

Fortunately for all concerned, neither Karraman nor Minerva had ever learned the good Calvinist lesson that thou shalt not have too much of a good thing. Nor did they question the divine permission to have it at all. And so it was that Karraman led Minerva off the balcony, through the parlor, through another oaken room fitted out as a residential office, and into a stunningly appointed bedroom. She unpinned her hat as they walked, and flung it onto a chair. The unpremeditated gesture elated Minerva even as she performed it, although she could not have put a name to what made her feel such an elevation of the spirit.

Karraman pushed the bedroom door closed behind him, but the plushness of the carpet and a springtime warp in the grain of the wood stopped it short of the frame. Minerva leaned over behind him and finished the job.

"There is no misunderstanding, then, Minerva," as much an assertion as a question.

"Nor should there be, Karraman." She said it very softly, and with grave assurance.

Then Minerva, who had never once loved or been loved by light of day or candle during all her tenure as a lawfully wedded wife, began to undress before God and Karraman Robley and any and all ghosts hovering around the gaslit antiquities of the room. When she reached the tiny buttons of her ecru shirtwaist, Karraman said quietly, "Allow me, Minerva." For a moment she wondered at the absence of a term of endearment, and nearly hesitated. Just as quickly, she understood that Karraman had no need or impulse to depersonalize her into a generality. If such a man as Karraman Robley had many women, and undoubtedly he did, any one or all of them might answer to "my dear." As for Minerva, she would hold on to her own designation with a comprehending pride. She even briefly considered telling Karraman about the full burden of her christening. Then she decided that it was too soon, too soon.

Karraman uncovered her layer by layer. Each successive segment he caressed, savored. Minerva, ripe, felt like the first woman alive. Without hesitation she made up her mind to return in kind—or better—every favor Karraman might bestow upon her. Deftly she released his cravat. With all the instincts of a born modiste if not the knowledge of an experienced courtesan, she unbuttoned, caressed, unhooked, gentled, unsnapped, untied, and caressed again. At length she and Karraman stood, naked and exultant, amid piles of garments and undergarments, the cast-off impedimenta of inhibition. When he had led her to the high, wide bed that had obviously been designed and intended for two, she felt it as a coming together with a body and soul she had known all her conscious life. And she couldn't even remember what Hammond Bolton felt like under the covers. Muslin, mostly.

Even today, even under the pleated and powdery reminiscences of needful flesh, Minerva feels stirrings at her heart and at her groin as she remembers Karraman Robley. She bears powerful tactile memory of breasts that seemed to swell and grow beneath his touch. She feels the magic ripple of his square fingers along her spine, her thigh, the inside of her arm. In bed at night her hand sometimes wanders to the warm, dense haven between her legs, but nowadays she usually dozes before the wanting overpowers her. She can remember to the day and hour the last time she lay with a man. Occasionally, dizzily, she sometimes still believes that she will lie with a man again.

Hawk, on the other hand, belongs to the generation which, statistically, cannot believe that its parents made love any more than the requisite number of times to produce the visible number of offspring. Intellectually he realizes that surely he is wrong, but viscerally he still feels that his generation invented recreational sex.

Minerva understands that he feels this way, pities him because she was more "liberated" seven decades and several generations ago than he is right now. Despite his presumably libertine life in the country within a vaguely assorted, not entirely platonic menagerie, he operates under more constraints of behavior than Minerva did when Queen Victoria's spirit was still casting its shadows of remonstrance over several continents.

Although she can't place the clues, Minerva suspects that Hawk's Oral History project has come to a halt, that he keeps returning to her solely for his own reasons. She senses a special dependency, but feels reasonably certain that he is keeping most of its configurations well-sheltered, even from himself.

He comes and goes. His visits are frequent. Minerva does not specifically invite him, but she barely remembers the quality of the days without his added luster. Her heart always lifts when he appears at the door. Something about him soothes her, calms her like a natural healer. The only other man who ever made her feel that way was Karraman Robley. Nobody else. Hammond Bolton never even soothed her when their life was fresh and trust was at its blindest. If she had stayed with him, he probably would have tried to squeeze humor and security from her with the same obsessive perfectionism he used to eke the last dribble of liniment from the bottle.

It is impossible for Minerva not to wonder at times how Hawk might have made her feel in all the other ways of feeling between a man and a woman. Physically he bears no resemblance to Karraman or any of the other Robleys, except for the power. And the weak ankle. Otherwise he better fulfills the paradigm of the sandy, blue-eyed Anglo-Saxon strain than any of the Robleys ever did. She wonders what virtuoso act of selective breeding has pulled a Hawk Simon out of ghetto and death camp and herring-sucking ancestors, but some well-honed instinct, one sadly lacking in the likes of Howard Robley, forbids her to ask.

She also wonders what a circumcised male is like. Realist beneath the wondering flesh, she fears that she will not likely learn the answer to that one, either.

But, quid pro quo, neither will Hawk Simon *explicitly* learn that on that first night with Karraman Robley Minerva had done exactly what she wanted to do, and so had he, and life was for neither of them ever quite the same again. So much for the inhibiting powers of taboo.

If not magic, Minerva had ambition, guts, and drive. She even had visions, far-reaching ones; but of illusions, none. She always tried to keep her thinking cap on.

She knew that if she were ever to marry again, a possibility she entertained only as mere formality, she would go to no man's bed a virgin bride anyway. Although the concept of "two consenting adults" had not entered the vernacular, that was largely the principle by which Minerva operated.

Cool-headed, clear-eyed, wonderfully healthy, she could not have suspected in advance the enormous, consuming power of the bond between two people who have been loving friends and also successful lovers. Nothing in her mother's guarded, embarrassed stutters about "wifely duties" remotely began to prepare her. During her tenure as Mrs. Hammond Bolton she decided that her mother's distaste for the whole procedure was excessive and uncalled for, but she did not actually begin to pity her mother actively until later, until Saint Kathareen's.

On a drizzly morning in 1906, awakening for the first time in Karraman Robley's bed and stretching like a sated cat, Minerva knew that she hadn't exactly invented recreational sex either, but she suspected that the credit might just possibly belong to her balding, pudgy, middle-aged, absolutely glorious lover. She watched his eyes flicker privately under dreaming lids. Then instinctively she reached for her dressing gown at the foot of the bed. Of course it wasn't there. The only visible clothing was the jumble of last night's mutual disarray, quite out of her arm's reach. With a shrug, she thought that having one little idiosyncratic accessory of fashion would hardly solve the larger logistics looming through the morning anyway. She shivered preliminarily, and slid out of bed to go to the bathroom.

Not that Minerva had never seen indoor plumbing before. Hammond Bolton and his fat wallet naturally provided his dainty bride with a great many of the appurtenances of modern living. Along the route to Saint Kathareen's, Minerva had often had to do with considerably less than the copper and porcelain she had come to favor, but she took sprightly pleasure in making the best of things.

In her own room at the Inn, she had welcomed the conveniences after a tiny flash of regret. She would have to try out heroism in other passages, here, since the creature comforts had certainly been taken care of. And Karraman's own facilities, now that she was taking the time to examine them closely, outdid even hers. They ran the vanguard of everything that was progressive in the building. His tile boasted a handsomer, more intricate inlay than hers downstairs. His towels lay awaiting someone's pleasure on a strange, free-standing rack which turned out to be made of hot-water pipes, keeping everything as warm, comforting, and sensuous as possible.

Slowly Minerva began to appreciate the relationship between Karraman's character and the detailing of the building itself. As petticoats dwindled, Karraman had obviously had the breadth of vision to turn copious and by then unnecessary second and third closets into bathrooms all over the hotel. Simultaneously, his mark touchingly pervaded everything. Complimentary bottles of unguents that Minerva had delightedly discovered in her own room, she found duplicated, and obviously used routinely, in Karraman's. He provided no less for others in those respects than he wished for himself, she concluded happily, and was amused at the depth to which she felt pleasure.

Minerva closed the door and performed for once in her life a venerable ritual of well-loved women. She stood before the mirror, very close. Gazing deep into her own eyes, she lightly ran her fingertips down the bones of her face, and tried to see what Karraman saw. She was uncertain that beauty resided there: her own ideals on that subject had been formed far too early and conventionally for her to appreciate the elegance of her own diversity.

But of love she was certain. And she was just sage enough, for all that, to understand how easily love translates into beauty when the conditions are right.

Eventually she reentered the bedroom. Karraman had propped himself up in bed, his arms folded judgmentally across the tufts of his chest.

"I was right, Minerva," peremptorily.

"Right about what, Karraman?"

"About you, you beautiful creature. You are, without a doubt, the most beautiful woman on God's green earth. Flawless, Minerva. Flawless."

Freckled, she doubted his judgment. But several cautions of ancient wisdom overtook her, and she confined her reply to a modest smile.

"Venus with a cropped haircut."

She laughed aloud, and homed in on the arms he stretched out to her.

They were still lying peacefully nestled against one another when two simultaneous bells chimed, jangling Minerva into solid touch with the world. The more distant gong tolled a rumbling ten o'clock. She was surprised to find that she was running considerably later than she had planned as she contemplated her first full day in Saint Kathareen's from the dated perspective of yesterday. On her first exploratory day, she had wanted to be on top of everything. Yet she felt no regret, no rue. What had changed was a vague and tentative schedule. What had changed it was cosmic. Saint Kathareen's could wait. Karraman Robley had become part of her vision of the future. Everything would come along in its place.

The second bell had an immediate, sharper ringing that would have made Minerva jump, had she not been so thoroughly, lethargically relaxed. Karraman bestowed a passing kiss on her eyebrow, then turned and pulled a strange contortion of an object out of the bottom of the nightstand. It was the first desktop telephone that Minerva had ever seen.

For a few seconds, before Karraman jammed the earpiece of the receiver tightly against the side of his head, Minerva realized that the voice squawking across the mysterious wires belonged to a woman. She gave the first thought of the day to the ungainly person whom she had first seen with Karraman the previous afternoon, the mistress of the mansion on the hillside. As he spoke monosyllabically into the instrument, she guilelessly ran her fingers up and down the inside of his thigh. He responded immediately. He juggled the telephone and repositioned it so that his hands were free to retaliate.

He ended the conversation curtly. "Perhaps. I'll let you know later." And that was that.

Aglow, alive, Minerva was ready to believe that this man's commitment to her matched hers to him. Whatever import the voice at the other end of the telephone had once held, she felt comfortably certain that Karraman would lose no time in demoting it to its appropriately minor cubbyhole. The events of the night and the morning spoke in impassioned tones for themselves.

He looked at her with a piercing depth that struck and resonated every chord in her emotional symphony.

"Minerva?"

"Yes, Karraman?"

"I think I know a way for us to be together, to work together, to plan together . . ."

"Yes, Karraman?"

"You won't think that this is too presumptuous, so soon after our meeting? I mean to say . . ."

She chuckled at the thought. How could there remain any formality at all between them, after what had transpired and the words that had been whispered in the night? She loved him for needing to ask, for being too much the consummate gentleman to take anything for granted.

"No, Karraman. How could I think that?"

"Then, Minerva, we will settle the details today. You will design and create the hats and headpieces for the members of my wedding to Emmaline Musgrove."

At the remove of a lifetime, Minerva barely feels the constriction of her chest, the wildly frightened fluttering of her heart at the memory. Yet barely is not the same as not at all. Like many healed, ancient fractures, the shattering of the heart leaves many residual twinges long after the visible handicaps have been put to rest.

Hawk, observantly attuned, watches a flicker of distant agony in Miss Minerva's features. Charitably he decides that she is experiencing some kind of elderly pain, so he leaves the cues to her. He is still learning the topography of this landscape, and he wishes to preserve all the beauties of its balance. He will not offend her by suggesting that she looks suddenly drawn, unwell. He allows her to test the mettle of her own courage, thinking, incidentally, that he wishes that certain people would return the favor on his behalf.

Tired or not, Minerva continues reminiscing in a mode that combines mellow vision, biting acerbity, and a stunning twinkle of the deep, oval eyes. When she occasionally seems to be mildly abstracted, Hawk attributes it, once again, to confusion of the years, accumulated pockets of cholesterol, synaptic short circuits in so well-used a brain. If it isn't in *Gray's Anatomy,* it must not exist.

In reality Minerva is never confused about anything. The device of appearing that way from time to time constitutes her sole remaining defense against anything that crops up as potential assailant. She carries it off sublimely.

Minerva wishes, chooses, never to grow aged and dim. She hopes and trusts that death, when it claims her, will carry her off in one great cataclysmic moment. She thinks in all honesty that she deserves no less.

Minerva learned to employ the discerning combination of candor and not-quite-candor in thirty seconds flat. That interval was also how long it took her to decide that any part of Karraman Robley was better than no part of Karraman Robley. She knew with crystalline clarity that she was going to return to Karraman's bed the minute the world ordained the proper time, and that Emmaline Musgrove would present no more obstacle to her than Hammond Bolton. Until that moment arrived, she saw no earthly reason to refuse to cooperate with Karraman's wishes in any other matter. Why bother? She had always thought of spite as a terrible waste of energy.

Her mind felt secure, but she was afraid of how her voice was going to come out. She lowered it, hoping.

"Of course I'll design the hats, Karraman. Assuming, that is, that the arrangement meets with the approval of Miss Musgrove."

"Not nearly in the way that it satisfies me, Minerva." He chuckled. Giving her a final squeeze, he headed off in the direction of his shaving mug.

Minerva sat still for a moment longer. Staring at the obstinate drizzle outside the window, she decided that the remainder of the day would be better spent indoors with her sketchbook and some feathers, anyway, than out in such teasing weather.

Karraman shaved, and issued intermittent rumblings Minerva supposed were probably meant to represent music. She smiled affectionately as she tried to reconstruct a sense of order among the discarded clothing on the floor. Thinking it more discreet to finish bathing in her own chamber, she dressed quickly. By that time, Karraman had closed the door to the bathroom. Water ran mightily. Since she had no wish to raise her voice to a level where it might attract the attention of anyone at all, Minerva decided to wait for the gushing shower bath to finish before she told Karraman her intent.

Opening the heavy bedroom door, she wandered through the chambers she had seen only briefly the night before. As she approached the large sitting room, the sight of a table in the middle of the floor stopped her cold. It was wheeled, and smartly covered with white damask. Someone had laid it meticulously for two. A carafe of orange juice nestled in a hammered-silver bucket of ice. A shining thermos promised hot coffee—although it turned out to be chocolate, Karraman's indulgence. A great puff of more white damask guarded croissants in a vermeil basket. From a delicate crystal vase, a spray of forsythia overlooked the whole opulent, discreet tableau. Minerva wanted to vomit. Personal freedom was one thing. The collusion of an entire hotel full of accomplices was something entirely different.

"Damn!" It was an imprecation she had never uttered before any witness less intimate than the two Clydesdales who had placidly borne witness to every vicissitude of her journey west. Naturally Karraman Robley entered the room behind her just as the curse escaped. Minerva felt doubly aggrieved, doubly witnessed.

Karraman, no slouch, instantly grasped the reason for her pique. He stumbled fitfully through the attempt to reassure her that, honestly, no one had spied on her, or upon their activities or exchanges. If he was telling the truth, she failed to understand his embarrassment. She never did understand, until they laughed about it a long time afterward, that it would have served no good purpose whatsoever for him to have explained that the kitchen always prepared breakfast for two when he was in residence, just in case. To his everlasting credit, he understood that there just might have been a demeaning note in such an explanation at the time. He calculated, rightly, that Minerva's dignity would be better served by thinking that the entire staff of the Inn really did know of her presence, rather than imagining herself an anonymous link in an endless procession of night visitors. She would presume the discreet fealty of the employees. And she would not err.

Karraman decided to tread lightly, on a neutral carpet.

"Just a touch of a Continental breakfast, Minerva. I seem to work through the morning better on that sort of thing than on the usual lumberjack fare."

"Usual?"

"Oh. Well, it seems to sustain most of the patrons of this establishment, anyway, according to what we read from the demands on the dining room."

He had struck the perfect tone, enabling Minerva to rally with the least discomfiture. Something of a lumberjack herself under normal circumstances, Minerva assembled her vocal apparatus a few notches above her slowly settling gorge.

"How very wise," she lied dryly.

He agreed, gesturing her into a chair. He allowed her the one with the

[83]

better view of the French doors, partly out of proprietary pride, partly out of good manners, partly because he knew that the panorama pleased the ladies without fail. Minerva, composed, followed the pattern. Feeding upon the vista of the rivers, the dockside tumult, and the not irrelevant contemplation of her own person ensconced right smack in the middle of Karraman Robley's executive milieu, she forgot her trencherman's appetite for good and all. She sipped and nibbled her way, *pro forma,* through a small fraction of what Karraman offered her.

And all the while, he talked. Like a man blessedly retrieved from a long and arid isolation, he talked. As Minerva wondered whether he could possibly give so much of himself to all his women, and whether the surface torrent concealed some even stormier depths within, he talked. With Minerva pondering Emmaline Musgrove and her capacity to fulfill even a tithe of this man's gargantuan needs, still he talked.

Finally, with the unfinished chocolate cold in her cup, Minerva told Karraman gently that she thought it was high time for her to return to her own room. The unuttered thought that irrationally scudded across her mind was that she had to get down there and rumple her bed before a scandalized chambermaid found that it hadn't been slept in. Logical or not, there it was: she could barely endure the thought of being less than a hero to her valet. Oddly, her own inconsistency, fully realized, buoyed her up, humanized her.

On the exterior, she was cool as evening. Beneath the surface, she barely knew how to quell the rising swarm of unaskable questions. They stormed her barricades, deluged her brain. Somewhere beneath the onslaught of all this newness lay the solution to the great unresolved dilemma: how to depose Miss Emmaline Musgrove, remain her milliner by appointment, and keep Karraman happy on all counts at the same time. It eluded the grasp, it . . .

". . . in a little less than an hour," he was concluding.

Minerva hid her confusion behind a small cough, a tiny feathering of her throat. "I beg your pardon, Karraman. I didn't hear the last. After 'an all-day drizzle,'" she added, so that at least he would understand that her attention hadn't wandered up and down the entire length of his monologue, that it had been somewhere in attendance.

"That's all right, Minerva," cajoling, pleased with the flashing fantasy that she was reliving the night and the morning, dreaming of mornings and nights to come. Something deliciously erotic like that. "Our Valley, er, 'mists' often catch in the throat at first. In no time at all you'll find that you've adjusted completely. After all, it's hard to feel hostility toward a phenomenon that accounts for the lushness of the greens out there, as well as a great deal of the agricultural prosperity of the region."

Minerva nodded with what she hoped was an expression of grateful interest.

Karraman plowed right on. "I was just saying that since you probably won't be anxious to do a great deal of exploring in the middle of an all-day drizzle, I can attend to a few items of business right away, and then be ready to take you over to the new house. Emmaline will be there changing her mind about wall coverings again, and causing general pandemonium. That way you can become better acquainted with her, and see something of her sense of style all at once."

Minerva perceived immediately the mild mockery in his last statement. She searched deeply for the humor, the affectionate indulgence, the measure of quiet respect toward Emmaline that should have idled, Minerva thought surely, close to the surface of his words. If they existed, they managed quite skillfully to elude Minerva. She wondered where the fault actually lay: in his expressions, or in her perceptions of them. She couldn't tell, but she hoped for his sake, if he really intended to go ahead and marry the shrew, that it was the latter.

She barely realized that she had hesitated, but the gap was long enough for Karraman's expression to soften into something which touched deeply at the moment's need.

"Please, dear Minerva."

She could not have voiced the multiplicity of conflicts that tore through her. She was definitely not ready, in any sense of the word, for Emmaline Musgrove. Why, she didn't even have with her a completed testament to her pretensions as a milliner, in case Emmaline demanded one. It would be only fair, Minerva conceded, if she did. On the road, she had let fashion go the way of road apples. Last night's creation out of blossoms and freshness and daring had wilted almost completely. Already it smelled mordantly sweet, exhausted, like old, ill-used flesh.

Yet Karraman, even at his gentlest, exuded force. Minerva's thoughts may have wavered, but her destination was inexorable. What she finally said was, "Of course, Karraman. I'll be ready."

What she thought was: Well, why the hell not?

Karraman didn't appear exactly to be waiting for her when she entered the lobby, but that's what he, who never waited for anybody, was doing. To cover, he talked quietly to Cybele about some trivial matter of business. Cybele looked trampled. Minerva noticed that the wooden-handled bell of the previous day's debacle had been removed. In its place sat a rotund desk bell, very bottom-heavy, very stable, not at all in keeping with Cybele's taste for the distinctive.

Minerva stood beside one of the burgundy velvet Duncan Phyfe settees, just within range of Cyril Cybele's remarkable peripheral vision. His eyes darted toward her for an instant only. That was enough for Karraman to note the inattention, surmise from the accompanying scent of apple and lavender the reason for it, and terminate the discussion.

"You will see that the matter is taken care of before evening, Mr. Cybele."

"Mr. Robley, if—"

"Thank you, Mr. Cybele," and left Cybele wondering why he didn't simply toss it all up, wander a few scores of miles downstream, and endow some other hostelry with the benefit of his experience and finesse. Probably, he allowed with weary resignation, because nothing along the lengths of the rivers and the breadth of the countryside could equal the Inn at Saint Kathareen's in beauty, gentility, ambience. And if Karraman Robley had the lion's share of tyrannical tendencies in business, he also had a relatively generous purse and a fine, if eccentric, eye for innovation and creature comfort. Cybele returned, as was inevitable after each periodic inner tantrum, to his duties. And Karraman turned to face Minerva.

She was hatless, but gloved. She wore no wrap or shawl, but carried a French parasol that matched the splendid challis of her outfit. To Karraman's eye, what she was wearing was a dress, and as fine a silhouette as he had ever seen. In actuality, it was a shirtwaist and skirt. Since tailored two-piece outfits had come into fashion, much like men's trousers and shirts, Minerva had discovered that she could parlay four simple garments into a minimum of six cleverly coordinated outfits. She had no desire to trade on this fashionable invention as she did upon the creation of hats. In fact, she positively preferred to keep her crafty, attractive economy to herself. She would laugh with untranslatable glee fifty years later when Lord & Taylor reinvented her wheel, and offered it to the public at five hundred dollars in a flimsy, matching drawstring bag as "The Perfect Weekender." Minerva lived on not much more than five hundred dollars for her first year away from Massachusetts, and collateralized her first millinery shop into the bargain.

"You are lovely, Minerva," Karraman greeted her.

Nothing, she thought, if not direct. Not "You *look* lovely," or "What a lovely frock," or any bush-beating flattery. Never leave me, Minerva. Come and meet with the woman who is about to be my wife.

She had known that he would have a motorcar. She hadn't known that it would be white, or that he would be driving it himself. From the driver's seat he sang out the landmarks as they chugged past. Expecting passersby to gape and wonder, she was slightly disappointed to realize that everyone in Saint Kathareen's was cheerfully accustomed to the sight of Karraman, with or without his old retainer Fred, careening by in his mildly gaudy 1904 Humberette. Minerva would learn in time that Saint Kathareen's always forgave, indeed often relished the peculiarities and peccadilloes of her own. And no one was more "own" to Saint Kathareen's than Karraman Robley.

Townsfolk, heads down or averted against the insistent drizzle and the rising winds, had no reason to glance up at what everybody naturally assumed would be the expressionless face of Emmaline Musgrove, aka My Fiancée, tooling past at Karraman's side in the touring car. The few who did happen to glance up absolved Karraman and ignored his vagaries. Kathareenians had forgiven Robleys as long as money, power, and family longevity counted for anything among human beings, which is to say forever.

In the spring drizzle of 1906, Minerva still had the Valley character to fathom even as she and Karraman still had to enter the first phases of mutual knowledge, compared to the scale of human time. They had not yet learned the skills of tender battle and reconciliation. They had touched one another's ancient histories, but not personal pasts. On they rode in the Humberette, each swathed in tentative pride, from a small circuit of the town back down to the levee. Happily.

"Up much?" Karraman was bellowing into the dockside tumult. Minerva's eyes widened at the evil-sounding locution.

"Inches maybe, Mr. R. No fear yet. Won't see twenty-five this time."

"Wal, she has t' hit forty before she starts wettin' up the elevator beds, but y' can't be too careful."

"Said a mouthful, Mr. R. Never will forget 'ninety-six, m'self. First we was out a-wadin' 'mongst the tall grasses, and the next I know'd, we was a-boatin' out m' gramma's attic dormer!"

Karraman laughed sociably. Minerva listened enthralled. In an incredibly short span the language of the river would seep into her vocabulary like the insidious moisture into every basement and root cellar in the center of town. For the moment she listened, absorbing phrase and cadence, not quite believing that such a cheerful litany of disaster belonged to the real world and not to some berserk fiction. She had a great deal to learn about the ways and means with which people manage to accept that which they are powerless to avoid. Rapt with the mise-en-scène before her, she barely noticed the ferry-barge approaching, guided into its berth by a plucky little stern-wheel tug.

[87]

She had never seen anything like it. In Pittsburgh, all up and down the Ohio, tugs pushed or pulled just as Minerva expected any right-thinking tugboat ought to do. Here in occluded little Saint Kathareen's, the tugboat rode fixed to the downstream side of the barge like a curious asymmetrical, inorganic limpet.

"Ready, Minerva?" She had scarcely had long enough to begin to take it in. Already she was craving more time to savor the throwaway details of this emerging universe. Already she was coveting hours, lifetimes, of digging in.

"If I have to be," she replied pleasantly, her bantering tone an imperfect ground cover for the wistful honesty at base. And took up her parasol, waiting for Karraman or one of the deckhands to help her from the car. Instead, Karraman waved broadly to the grinning fellow who had been chatting amiably about the state of the river. Obviously well-attuned to Karraman's patterns, he waved back with a jovial salute and began to crank the vehicle without another word. As it sputtered back to life, Karraman released the brake. Slowly, very slowly, he eased the auto, kit and caboodle, onto the gangplank, onto the barge.

Minerva had always thought that composure was her long suit. She hadn't braved the wilderness for nothing. She had seen sights and experienced adventures alien to most women and all but a few of the most intrepid men of her time. Nothing, nothing at all in her remembered panoply of vivid moments, had prepared her first for the autocar itself, then for the autocar, herself inside, on the deck of a boat, all on the same incredible day.

With Karraman and the vehicle safely stowed as passengers, the captain of the tug waited for no further cargo, human or otherwise. Off they steamed, the little tug bravely breasting the swift springtime current, losing barely an inch of its intended trajectory as it bucked the insistent flow. When they reached the opposite shore, Minerva was as breathless and triumphant as if she had accomplished the entire portage alone, and on foot.

"By God, Karraman Robley, not even Chadds Ford could have been like this!"

Karraman reached over and squeezed her hand. "Minerva, there is considerably more to Saint Kathareen's than meets the eye. I promise you that."

Smiling: "It might just take a lifetime to probe the bottom of that statement."

"I'm still learning it myself, Minerva. Just when I think I know every single nook and cranny and seventh cousin, this Valley offers up another surprise, and then one more for good measure. It's a fine life, I think, as long as you don't mind the challenge of what's strange and unfamiliar every single day."

[88]

"What do you think, Karraman? I've made it this far, haven't I?"

Upon retrospective reflection, she couldn't believe her own naiveté. As if a simple voyage of discovery across a few tame mountains could have prepared her for the quality of her life in this new country.

V

Hawk cannot remember ever in his life having felt so strange. He isn't sure whether to relish the situation for its lunatic eccentricities or to heave its ingredients into some literal and figurative compost heap for good and all. What he is doing is trying to choke down a midday repast of groundhog sautéed with onions in Hudepohl. Caravelle has acquired the animal from one of the transient Kentucky cowboys who has just spent two or three days on the place. He has reciprocated the hospitality in whatever way he knows. The other element of the stranger's gratitude consists of the offer of his fine bronzed body to both Caravelle and Radiant, in that order. Although he has behaved as graciously as he knows how, both of them, for reasons of their own, have seen fit to decline.

At least that's what Caravelle has said. Hawk, assuming the authenticity of her physical satisfactions, believes the sexual component of the story. He is even secretly pleased that she has attracted so flagrantly physical a specimen as the cowboy. He becomes indignant only when he learns that Radiant was included in an invitation that pointedly left him out. Not that he would dream of participating. He merely wonders about his drawing power.

What Hawk doubts seriously is Cara's explanation of where the groundhog really came from. She has, to Hawk's amazement and distaste, proven herself a serious adept at this entire small-game business, thereby casting some disagreeable question upon all her declarations of broad-spectrum innocence.

She has expertly skinned and gutted the malodorous creature, and hung its pelt. She has even read its entrails, or if she hasn't, it certainly isn't Hawk who will be able to say her nay. They have informed her, she claims, that an older rival will enter her life. Hawk thinks that she is fabricating the whole thing, that she couldn't possibly have the vaguest idea how to read anybody's entrails, let alone a groundhog's, that she is obliquely ragging him for the increasing number of hours he spends in the company of the old lady in the house across the river. Probably jealousy takes forms as multifarious and bizarre as there are relationships, Hawk allows charitably, but he still thinks that this nauseating display is overdoing it.

Obviously Cara does know how to handle a dead animal. She publicly attributes her peculiar skill to all the years of laboratory cuttlefish and fetal pigs, to months of pathology and O.R. duty before she settled on psychiatric nursing as her real affinity. With the groundhog monopolizing his thoughts, Hawk meanly wonders whether she would favor universal lobotomy, brainectomy, for her current charges. Shifts his eyes, deeply ashamed, because he knows how unfair it is for him even to think that way.

Hawk takes Cara with a grain of skepticism under the best of circumstances. He wants her attention; adamantly, he *requires* it. Between her job, her assorted crafts, her incessant telephoning, her "mysteries," she calls them, he feels that there is nothing left of her for him. Attention is simply not being paid. If she thinks she's going to find her "identity" in Saint Kathareen's, Hawk can't believe she's going to do it by hiding behind such posturings. She doesn't seem to be getting closer to herself at all. His problem is, neither is he.

As for the matter of the groundhog, Hawk straightforwardly believes that she has gone beyond simple misunderstanding into outright lying betrayal. No one has ever dressed and cured a fetal pig or skin of *rana pipiens,* as far as he knows. Caravelle has demonstrated with the groundhog that she is no stranger to the last nicety of slit and timing. He believes that, for reasons of her own, she prefers to keep her image squarely in the category Healer, even though the facts do not necessarily support her pretensions.

Just then Radiant bursts through the low-slung open window in the front room, disdaining the newly modernized expedient of the door. He would have had the devil's own time wrestling it open by himself, because of the three grocery bags of very gritty freshly picked lettuce which he is trying not to crush in his parody of an embrace. There is enough lettuce in one bag alone to feed the Vienna Boys' Choir for several weeks. Hawk sullenly hopes that Caravelle will be happy, but knows that she is pissed because she is going to have to be the one to clean it, or let it go dirty. Hawk will take off

[91]

with his tape recorder and his notebooks, and Radiant will retreat into his security sleeping baggie for his next version of the duration. Before she can settle on which variation of the riot act she is going to read them, Radiant blows her cover.

Sniffing: "Finally cooked that little bastard you caught, eh, Cara?" He has acquired "eh" as a permanent locution from the period when he was contemplating defection to Canada to escape the draft. His number never came up, but he enjoys sounding international.

"Radiant, could you just kindly shut up, please?"

"I don't see why, Cara." Ingenuousness personified. "What's done is done. If that's how you get off, we're all going to have to be up-front enough to deal with that." Radiant has never strung so many words together while sober in all their association.

Meanwhile, Cara, whose usual temperate style dovetails perfectly with both Radiant's laid-back lassitude and Hawk's uprisings, is turning redder and redder. Her freckles seem to be acquiring a third dimension. Hawk can virtually see a band of hot rage encircle her at the depths of her belly and climb the ladder of her ribs to her full consciousness. Projecting mightily, he imagines that she is furious at Radiant for not being her brother or her son, not intimate enough to attack and retain at the same time. He understands: this is the frustration that Hawk experiences every single time he wants to tangle with Cara, yet can't because he fears the repercussions. What is so wrong with all of us, he wonders, that we give up so much just to feel a little bit safe?

Unguessed at by Hawk, who is still sufficiently miffed to disallow Cara any humane motives whatsoever, she is feeling very much the same way he is about the various irresolutions that are abroad in the air of the farmhouse. She is sick of playing games, sick of watching Hawk hoard thoughts like contraband, leaving one or two out for her to trip over and wonder about, only to have him snatch them back before she can see them in daylight, acting as if it's her fault for getting in the way.

At first Saint Kathareen's had seemed so right, Hawk and his household so welcoming, that she couldn't believe her good luck. Now things seem to be falling to pieces. Whoever heard of a full-blown, World War III conflagration over *groundhog*? With Hawk acting half the time like a double agent, and the other half like a premenstrual fishwife, Cara scarcely knows which way to turn.

"You want to know why, Radiant?" She begins to grope her way out of the latest booby trap. "I kept you out of it because I respect you. Ordinary people don't usually want a tour of the slaughterhouse while they're eating. There's a basic conflict there, you know? I only had your sensibilities in mind," she patronizes, sarcasm dripping like blood from the carcass. Radiant shrugs.

Hawk considers the mess on the plate, which doesn't represent too radical a departure from the veal Marengos and lamb ragouts of his youth and his dearest preference. He knows that the groundhog is unequivocally fresh, having recently watched it in the throes of its demise, fresher than anything routinely offered up by the purveyors of the nominally sanitary. Only his olfactory equipment signals his visual organs to hunt down maggots, dry rot, decomposition, God knows what else. So pungent, so gamy a liquor, so insistent a wildness can't be right.

Finally Hawk can't stand it anymore. He pushes back his chair, eschewing a particularly enticing salad featuring dandelion, alfalfa, and other more and less cultivated sprouts. He hopes that Cara will think he isn't hungry anymore, even though he would really like to polish off the salad in a trice, obliterating with blessed chlorophyl and vitamin K all traces of repugnant memory. Silently he berates himself for whatever kind of capitulation he is committing, but shrugs it off when he fails to find any suitable alternative.

"I think I'll go into town for a while, Cara."

"What a surprise," flatly, gazing at the salad greens. Hawk is unaccustomed to hearing sarcasm employed by anyone in the house other than himself, and doesn't know what to make of this turn. Cara has retreated into an old and unsatisfactory form of verbal ordnance because she is otherwise at a loss. She can't think of a way to phrase and fashion what she needs into something that can be purchased, parceled, and brought home in a string bag. She is convinced that they will break up housekeeping very soon, if that's the proper phrase to apply to what they will be doing to what it is they have already done. The thought of laying in one more supply which will then have to be rushed through, donated away, or somehow subdivided terrifies her.

For long seconds, neither Cara nor Hawk speaks again. She looks distracted. He can't define it. Sorrow casts a momentary pall over him. To think that he has shared bed, board, stash, and intestinal flu with this woman—for how many months now?—and he can't even read her properly to distinguish with assurance a legitimate case of *angst*.

Cara, although she has spoken last, feels that the burden of breaking the silence belongs to her. When she frames a statement, it comes out of times long gone, in a voice driven up an atavistic octave to the misty childhood when everybody kept leaving. Fathers, everybody. Even her mother, who promised that she would keep in touch, who said once that she would love Cara always. Who went off and died in a fluky accident involving sugarcane in Cuba, a scythe, and a systemic toxicity which she refused to acknowledge

[93]

or accept until it had driven every last hale red blood cell out of her body. Finally the marrow had gone too, and that was that. Cara hadn't even learned about it for weeks. It was for that final negligence that Cara never forgave her.

Cara, adult, deals with departures by stage-managing them to suit herself. Professionally she ministers to crazy people who neither die nor get well, the chronics. She travels light. Even animals, which she had once loved, fondled, held as confidants, she now relates to as Diana, huntress, objective viewer of the food chain and the cycles of nature—birth, death, decay, destruction, necessity, inevitability. Caravelle is deeply into natural determinism. Lucy the Hound she leaves to Hawk.

She opens her mouth to say something that will put a dressing on it, but Hawk is halfway out the open window.

"So long, Cara. Don't wait up," and strides across the sill. She starts to call after him, then figures: Let him stew in groundhog juice. Almost automatically she turns toward the telephone.

Hawk pauses at the door of the Healey, still hungry and freshly contrite. More than he wants the salad, he wants to know that matters will be in hand when he returns. He is about to rise to the level of his maturity, going back to the house, even entering by the conventional passage, when he stops short. His salad is still on the table, but not because Cara has tuned in with magic, parterly communication upon his intentions. Nothing as normal as that, Hawk rages to himself. Caravelle Dragonlover, New Jersey's own Benedict Arnold, is on the goddamn telephone again. Hawk is seeing fiery, destructive, misdirected, self-immolating red.

If he were to snatch the receiver from her, roar imprecations, give himself over to all the jealousies whose existence he refuses to admit to the theater of his emotions even though they've taken all the seats in the front row—if he were to listen for the retort, try to catch the special music that has resonated to Cara's frequencies, he would be amazed and probably abashed. He would hear no whisper or murmur of seduction or tryst, but only the crackling static of an interminable open-ended long-distance circuit waiting for no one who will materialize today.

Hawk's fantasies are everything but right, not surprising since Cara's quest is everything but ordinary. She wants a past, a pedigree. She wants casual hints in ancient letters to materialize into living folk who will be at home to her calls and alert to her needs. Hawk, in truth, perceives those needs quite clearly. She threads them through their quiet moments so consistently that he'd have to be insensate to miss them. He refuses, on the other hand, to accept the fact that they represent real problems. Hell, she has a job, a future, a direction, a whole set of marketable skills. What does she want, egg in her kefir? Now, as far as he's concerned, he's the one with a *real* problem. Stated baldly: Where does he go from here?

He feels gummy with the heat of the day and with the inner tension of having his life undermined in every way he can currently imagine. Probably another long, guiltless shower in the sulfuric water of their own artesian well would help, but Hawk is temporarily feeding on masochism. He needs a high colonic of the soul, he decides, and is convinced that Cara's training cannot include such a refinement.

Kicking pebbles does nothing for him. He wanders up around the barn, peers listlessly into the ruined silo. The crops, at least, seem to be thriving. Sullen, he moves back toward the house. Reenters, this time using the conventional aperture. He wants it to be a statement, but of what, he cannot be absolutely certain.

If his reappearance surprises Cara, she doesn't let him in on it. "Hi, Hawk."

"Nothing high about it, Cara." He twirls the verbal cat by the tail until it's ready to shriek. "No high spirits, no high expectations, no high grades. In fact, no grades at all." Having baited her, he waits. When she rises to it, he turns on her as if she were a renegade.

"I'm sorry, Hawk," she softens. "Want to talk about it?"

"I thought I did," he snaps, "but I can only hold up in competition with a telephone for so long. Then I'm on my own. That's the human condition, isn't it?" Then thunders back out of the room before she can even agree with him. He has gone up, this time, not out, however. It's a subtle signal, but it means that he's allowing pursuit.

"Oh, Hawk," she mouths despairingly, but she mouths it to herself. If he has private settlements to diagram, so has she.

When he slinks ambivalently back in, it is easy for him to see why she hasn't followed him. Still, he pretends that he couldn't care less. She is casually scraping groundhog into a Tupperware bowl.

"Don't think you have to apologize," he tells her. His tone communicates the contrary.

"I don't have anything that I need to apologize for, Hawk."

"You don't mean that. How can you mean that, Cara?"

"How I can mean it is that I mean it. I don't even understand what in the hell you think I've done."

"It isn't one thing, it's thousands of things."

"Hawk," she says reasonably, "I haven't even known you long enough to have done thousands of things. I just wish you'd tell me what's plucking your beard. Maybe if we were both in the same ball park, we could put an end to the game."

[95]

"It's no game, Cara."

"Oh, Hawk, you know what I mean. I feel like you've got this elaborate
. . . *thing* going on, and here I am locked outside the gate. Minerva Bolton
gets your time and your energy, and I get your . . . your hassles. I don't
think that's exactly equitable, do you?"

"Oh, shit. Look who's talking about *things* going on. The original Queen
of *Things*, glossing right over every key issue in sight."

"I don't know what you're talking about, Hawk, and I'm pretty sure that
you don't either."

"Is that right, Cara? I don't know what I'm talking about? Every time I
walk in the goddamn house you're off on some magical mystery tour with
the telephone, you won't say a thing about it, I don't even know who he is,
but I sure as hell know he's *there*, you can't even wait until I'm down the
driveway, for Christ's sake. Why don't you just invite him to move on in,
Cara? The two of you can live happily ever after on groundhog."

Cara laughs in spite of both of them.

"You think it's so funny, Cara? Well, I don't. I think it's downright
crude. And I haven't seen you offering to pay any phone bills, either, by the
way. Mr. Whoever-he-is is getting some kind of nifty free ride, I'd judge."

"Are you talking about my telephone calls, Hawk? Is that all it is?"

"All? I'd say that was more than enough."

"That's ridiculous, Hawk."

"I don't know how you can say that, Caravelle." Hawk plasters
Wounded, Indignant, and Hurt across his features. "I came home because I
thought for a minute that my own four walls might just be a safe place to be.
And what happens? You're on the goddamn telephone again, and if I don't
see the back of your head, I hear the back of your voice. Nothing in it for
me, huh? All I'm good for is a roll in the sack and an occasional
conversation." He is running out of energy.

"Look, Cara," he informs her, "I'm going into town. Do you want
anything?"

A tremulous child inside, Cara offers nothing.

"I'm going to Foothill House," he continues, having no choice but the
truth.

"I know."

"You think it's a monstrosity, don't you." Not a question.

"It is a monstrosity. That's given. But once you get past all those phallic
turrets, I'm sure—"

"Listen, Cara, I never—"

"Hawk, just go. Please." He hears: *See if I care. Keep her to yourself, and see if
it bothers me.* He'd love to deny her accuracy, take her along, show her that it
doesn't amount to a hill of sugar-snap peas, but he cannot bring himself to

invite her into a world he cherishes as exclusively his. He feels cornered. Not sufficiently shackled, however, to stay home.

He enters the Healey, leaving the remnants of the stew to Radiant and the bluebottles. And to Lucy, if he doesn't take umbrage at the relegation. One must always be attuned to the sensibilities of others, Hawk thinks, wondering how in God's name he is going to balance all the sets of data he is accumulating willy-nilly, and still keep the sensibilities at bay. He is not absolutely certain that he can do it. Worse yet, he is not absolutely certain that he even wants to.

Miss Minerva has been sitting on the screened sleeping porch at the rear of the house, facing the northwest vista from an upholstered wicker armchair. Once the porch had been a summer kitchen. Emmaline, Minerva remembers, had tittered mightily at the prospect of a mudroom filled with the residue of children—slung-aside mackintoshes, grubby little mittens, rows of galoshes in homey disarray. With more accuracy than cynicism, Minerva knows these days that what must have tickled Emmaline pink was anticipating the mysterious procedure of getting all those children, because from the time the first one of them was old enough to track a single genteel rainprint, Emmaline was already shrieking and railing blue murder at so much as a dancing shirttail. Muddy footmarks, if they had been able to hear her outrage, would have retreated and fled on their own. Consequently the much-vaunted mudroom portion of the summer kitchen would have passed for a disinfectant airlock. It never held so much as a stray overshoe in Emmaline's time. Of course, she hadn't lived to oversee the sanitation of Howard's upbringing, but he would have preferred torture to soil anyway. He confined the various garbage and detritus of life to the interior of his skull case.

Then she hears the front doorbell intone the first four notes of Beethoven's Fifth. Howard Robley had had the thing installed in what he probably considered his finest hour. Minerva ignores the cliché, as she has been doing for all these years. She rises, and crosses toward the end of the porch nearest the music room and its peculiar annex. The French doors open from the porch into a fringed, hideously overstuffed chamber, another century.

The room would undoubtedly have been able to accommodate the lacquered black Steinway, the harpsichord, the ancient harp, even the medium-sized cathedral organ. It would also have managed to contain the furnishings, the menacing roseate flowers upholstered into fields of black, the mauve velvets, the opaque and faded lampshades. Not even the gargantuan Gothic fireplace, installed with slight, disconcerting asymmetry under Emmaline's tainted eye, would have been too much for the heroic room, given the massive proportions of the space, and the very history of it.

But for Gossamer. Gossamer, pyramiding down from pendulous jowls to the rest of her enormous self, as motionless as a growth on her vast mahogany bed. She reminds Minerva of a weirdly distorted stingray, something that should have been extinct millennia ago. Her bed fits its alcove so snugly that she has ordered the four mammoth speakers for her sound system to be wall-hung above the four pillars which mark the corners like totem poles. The control panel for the sound system, looking like the interior of a cockpit, is mounted also, onto a sturdy shelf slightly above the foot of the bed, surrounded by shoe box upon shoe box filled with eight-track tapes. They constitute Gossamer's filing system of choice.

Minerva stands just outside the door, riveted to the spectacle of Gossamer making her way down the bed to replace *The Best of E. Power Biggs* with *E. Power Biggs Visits the Great Cathedral Organs*. It is not unlike observing a formless monster arise fully grown from the primordial bog, wallow its path toward an unwitting prey, and wallow back again, shuddering with a mindless caricature of pleasure before disappearing back into the bog. Minerva still catches herself fantasizing from time to time that it would really end up that way, Gossamer simply oozing out of sight, a sea slug in the sun, but of course nothing can be done. So Minerva braves it again, even though the combination of the room, the inhabitant, and the omnipresent roar of the most depressing music on earth invariably makes her feel like she's descending into an overheated coal mine, or purgatory. She feels stifled even in the hastiest passage.

Of course no passage ever turns out to be quite as hasty as she would wish. Pairs of tables flank tables. Pairs of bibelots flank bibelots. A Rose Medallion punch bowl, far too graceful for its ambience, strangles with dying roses. Minerva remembers when Karraman bought that bowl for Emmaline, remembers piercingly, but refuses to feel guilty. Refuses. The water stagnates. The nectars of springtime stand the danger of losing out to attar of rancid.

A further obstacle to Minerva's progress through the room is Gossamer's expression. When it is passive, Minerva always wonders for a panicky moment whether she has slackened once and for all into the Eternal Slack. When it shows signs of animation, as it does right now, Minerva's compassion or conscience slows her down to a pause. She knows that Gossamer has something to say, but the circuit from brain to tongue has been obstructed by some miscarriage of the electrons. Minerva throws in a "tut, tut" or a "there, there" and promises both of them that she'll surely give it the time it demands in a little while. Usually she does, although the torpor of the environment daily encroaches further upon her sense of liberty, like kudzu unchecked. Nor would she dream of changing anything. She lives with what she has to.

Some time after Minerva had admitted Hawk into the sanctum to meet Gossamer, he mustered the nerve to ask about the origins of the whole overpowering setting. Minerva's twinkle outrode incipient mischief and settled into leering malice quite unlike anything Hawk had ever read on her features before.

"Actually it's Emmaline's room, dear Hawk, although Gossamer has appropriated it." She spoke as if the present Army of Occupation had just taken up residence yesterday and would leave, all of its own accord, any minute now. Gossamer, in temporary and inconvenient residence for the last thirty years or so, Minerva wished to view as just another piece of obsolete overstuffed furniture, part of Emmaline's legacy. "I want to remember her just as she was," came Minerva's heavily sugared malediction.

Minerva unremittingly continues to whet Hawk's already insatiable appetite for history, *her* history, to be precise. To hell with the voluminous statistics the others have amassed. He wants to divine the real roots of this place. She has addicted him to the delicate or brutal complexities of everything in her. He thinks that if only he is discriminating enough in his questions, he will find the key to the universe in this microcosm of hers.

Sometimes in the velvety bunting of deep night, he wonders if some latent perversion governs his attraction to Minerva Bolton. Sometimes, awakening suddenly, throbbing and hard out of some phantom pursuit without a locus, he lies beside Cara and finds Minerva grazing the borders of his consciousness.

On such nights he turns to Cara, loses himself in her. Lucy the Hound, mysteriously attuned to such activity, howls a baleful descant to whatever sounds and sighs reach his floppy sensors. Zeroed in on the ultimate shared selfishness, neither Cara nor Hawk ever hears Lucy until much later. Only Radiant, thirsting after diffuse satisfactions, thrashes in his narrow bag.

Sometimes, while Hawk broods through the hours, dank, menacing auras swarm around Cara. She sleeps fiercely, privately. Hawk often lies wanting, but not wanting her. Wandering fantasies waft toward Minerva in fits and starts. But not the Minerva who is. Something else . . .

Sometimes he catches a wild glimpse of Cara time-capsuled into Minerva. In a panic, he shakes the image from himself. In so threatening a mode he never reaches for Cara. He has convinced himself that it is she who exudes the palpable message of exclusion. In truth, it is he who is doing the excluding.

He gets up and prowls through the house on those nights, cursing the dormant Radiant for obstructing the path to the larder. Hungry for anything that might nurture the boundless lacunae of his soul, Hawk devours books and magazines with his eyes, smokes joints, inhales the night, wanders into the garden, harvesting anything in season. At length, bloated and gassy with scallions or new peas, pods and all, he makes his way back upstairs and throws himself onto the bed, feeling exaggeratedly like an upended walrus. Cara, deeply at rest, rarely stirs. When she does, Hawk pretends vast torpor, which pretense usually spawns its own reality.

He awakens from such fuddled comas confused, angry, and even before he is fully alert, devising reasons to get to Minerva's pronto. Thus, whatever his excuses, Hawk's appearance at Minerva's door in an afternoon heavy with the familiar chemistries of Valley air does not surprise her.

What she wonders about this time is the conflict that she reads so patently on his face.

The first time Hawk had heard the doorbell intone the Fifth, his eyebrows had leaped to his hairline. He scarcely notices it at all anymore, the way he hardly notices what Radiant is wearing or whether Howard Robley has shaved his mustache this week.

Minerva reaches the door and flings it open, after a fashion. She catches Hawk in a frozen frame. Marks his discomfiture. She can neither qualify nor quantify the tensions coursing through him, but unerringly senses their depth. Under other circumstances she would tactfully allow him to come in, sulk, settle down, bide his time. She would powder her nose, make lemonade, plant the lemon seeds, and wait for them to mature. Allow him whatever he needed.

Today she feels an avalanche of emotion transform itself into something heavy, and localize in a faintly alarming nexus beneath her ecru silk jabot. Thinking herself beyond sentimentality, she assumes that the sensation has something forthright to do with the mortal coil. She will not start, therefore, to squander time.

She plunges in abruptly. "I'm delighted to see you today, Hawk." She glances pointedly, for some reason, at the vicinity of his low-slung belt buckle. "It seems that we need more and more time for the completion of our mutual project, doesn't it? I was just thinking of you, too." She implies heavily that she knows for a fact just how much of his mind she occupies. Hawk is pleased somehow, before he realizes with astonishment that he wouldn't tolerate that kind of possessiveness from anybody else on earth.

Businesslike, she conducts Hawk through the foyer, wondering why it is that today she has the feeling he needs to be shepherded. Trying to put herself in his place, she asks herself whether he ever feels the claustrophobic crush that overwhelmed her when she first entered this capacious structure anticipating vastness, and found herself in the middle of an oversized Chinese box.

Which thought leads her instantly to comprehend the source of the nostalgia, the unprecedented deluge of bittersweet that surrounded her moments ago as she answered the door. Not for Karraman, nor any man. Indeed, it is none other than Minerva Kathareen Robley Niesenwandering Bolton for whom she yearns, the only Minerva, the very Minerva, who lived and loved and verified herself as she was reflected in loving eyes.

At the core of every grown woman, she believes, there lies a passionate girl. Beneath and between the rayon snuggies and the flaccid flesh there lies a moist and supple nest waiting to give, to take, to clasp, to sing. The observed person exists only in the moment, but the private person exists in all the eternities of her span, all at once. And, she realizes, it is young Hawk who has brought her to this acute concordance of insights for the first time.

Minerva, intoxicated by what she knows, leads Hawk to the formal parlor. She gestures him toward the horsehair ottoman, where once, ages and ages ago, he tripped headlong into his own future. This time he seats himself with somewhat rigid grace, but grace nonetheless. Minerva follows closely behind, nudging him toward the opposite end of the couch. Then seats herself, edging Hawk a little farther yet in order to reach for the cloisonné box. Hawk is beginning to feel cornered, yet safe. Ensconced. Relaxation sweeps over him.

"Excuse me, Hawk."

Minerva opens the box with the usual ceremony, and proffers it to him. He receives the crystal-based table lighter from Minerva, and helps her light up. The sweet aroma of her first toke produces in him an anticipatory contact high. He is good and ready to leave outside the door all the ponderous emotional baggage with which he entered. He drags deeply, privately, on the joint.

A beat passes. Another. Through the softening light of her own vision, Minerva waits. Not long. The tension leaches out of Hawk's face like lime out of unsized plaster. He doesn't even feel like talking anymore. None of them belongs in this house—none of the assorted travails of Margo or Howard or Caravelle. What was Hawk's anguish has become his peaceful apotheosis. All he wants now is more and more and more of Minerva's life, if that's not asking too much.

Minerva grumbles something just beneath Hawk's threshold of hearing. He has never before experienced her as a person who mumbles incomprehensible asides, and he is concerned. He has never met a person as straightforward as she usually is, and all of a sudden he can't make sense of her. An iron fist grips at his entrails. Things happen to people at Minerva's age. What if something is happening to her right now? He can't bear the thought of losing some crucial part of her to a stroke, or a brainstorm. He wants to ask Caravelle Dragonlover, R.N., what can be happening, but he doesn't want to hear that, either.

Suddenly Hawk jerks to his feet as Minerva gropes for words. He wants to put a stop to guesswork once and for all. "Miss Minerva, maybe you're not feeling—"

"Sit down, Hawk," she snaps, fully herself. "I'm always feeling. Did you come here to talk to me or not?"

Nonplussed, compliant, he sinks back down. He is frightened, elated, Alice on the verge of Wonderland, fantasies of Future coming down fast as History.

As Minerva weighs words, Hawk tries to shudder his head into clarity, like a great waking beast. Distantly the strains of Bach's "Toccata and Fugue in D minor" thunder from a pipe organ. Hawk is dimly cognizant that Gossamer has jammed E. Power into the tape deck again, full volume, business as usual at Foothill House. He thinks that E must stand for Electric. Hawk is nearly cataleptic under the weight of his surroundings. He can envision an endless dungeon, dank, cobwebby, sour, a hunchback curled over stops and keys. He follows the motions . . .

Minerva reaches for a lace handkerchief in her sleeve and shifts her body slightly. Something contorts her face, reintroducing Hawk to the trepidation that he has felt intermittently since he entered the house. He is mistaken, however. It is not pain, it is labor. Minerva is about to deliver herself of the message and meaning she has been privately gestating for most of her life. At the last minute she nearly falters, fearing that she has spawned a monstrosity.

But traffic in the birth canal flows one way.

Dilating.

Hawk inducing.

"Tell me what you were going to say, Miss Minerva," he urges evenly. Suddenly it is he who is back on the line, cajoling, edging forward with eye and tenor.

"There's so much to tell, Hawk. It involves such a long, long expanse of time." She repositions herself yet again, to shift into the long narrative.

And just as the downbeat signals the entrance of Miss Minerva, the soloist and prima donna, the front door opens, crashing noisily against its springed backstop. Minerva and Hawk, whose collective universe had a moment ago dwindled to their mutual consciousness plus the scratchy dimensions of the horsehair ottoman, jolt uneasily back from somewhere distant. Expecting a phantom.

Instead seeing Howard Robley, Ph.D., humid, panting, smiling in awkward anticipation of an effusive welcome. Which is not forthcoming.

"Oh, shit." Hawk, who is then mildly surprised that the expostulation elicits not a stir. Probably no one realizes that it is he who has vocalized it, the sentiment being so palpable in the surrounding air. Or perhaps he hasn't.

Robley advances. He smiles a trial balloon at Hawk. "Well, Simon." False hearty. "Welcome to Foothill House." As if he, having been born and raised there, can lay any greater claim to its mysteries than Hawk can. As if he doesn't know that if opening exercises were to have been conducted, the time has long since passed. Hawk won't buy Robley's pompous possessiveness for a minute. He, Hawk, assumes a proprietorship of Minerva based upon hours of shared confidences, empathies, even love. He refuses to attribute such capabilities to Robley under any circumstances. Once he would have, but no longer. Besides, it is Herr Professor who has burst into an already fulminating situation, and it is his proper role to be still and to wait to be welcomed or not welcomed.

Hawk lowers into intentional silence, which is just a step away from the aphasic state he has occupied since he arrived. Robley sniffs the air, forms a trenchant comment about the waft of grass about him. Sadly he aborts, somehow unable, Hawk divines, to follow through with an obvious impulse to be hip among the hip. Instead, he thrusts ahead into the charged silence.

"I've often admired the little Healey, Hawk." He pauses long enough for any and all volunteers to enter the colloquy. None does, so on he pushes. "Since you haven't pulled up stakes in Saint Kathareen's, I may have my chance to ride in it yet."

Fat chance, Hawk's reflexes signal. He notices that in double-knit slacks, Robley's pelvic bones seem to be wider than his shoulders.

"I imagine she corners like a dream." Another memorable metaphor from the creative folks who brought you Clark Gable, Hawk sneers to himself, and offers no help whatsoever.

In truth, some native compassion prods Hawk to help this sorry little man out of his humiliation. But in the emotional bloodletting into which they have all plunged, sacrifices will be made. It is Minerva who will perform direct euthanasia.

"Howard," she pronounces, "you don't have enough of a sense of timing to perform a proper 'Chopsticks.' Why don't you go off and regale Gossamer with your witticisms. I'll receive you later."

Mortally snubbed, Howard begins to grumble his way out. He gropes for a blistering retort, clumsily fails. Minerva feels a momentary stab of guilt at having cast a bona fide Robley out of the parlor of Foothill House. Yet, with Hawk sitting, expectant, across the decades of sofa, she feels inexorably that nothing else matters except going on with what she has begun.

Howard throws a to-hell-with-Gossamer scowl toward the music room, and retreats. With him he takes the shards of whatever minimal confidence enabled him to open the front door in the first place, what with Hawk's car already parked big as life outside.

Minerva, considerably subdued, turns back to Hawk. "Well, Hawk. Once again now."

But as she begins, Minerva startles Hawk all the way over toward what he had thought was the far boundary of his capacity to be surprised. Minerva isn't talking about herself at all, Hawk is perceiving. To his utter consternation, Minerva Bolton seems to be launching into what he has awaited so long by giving him a detailed description of somebody *else's* wedding.

Old people! There are times when Hawk cannot fathom what is at other times his tireless infatuation with them. What a plentiful waste!

Well, settling back, he had come to be instructed. . . .

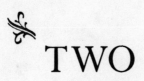 TWO

TWO

VI

At the wedding rehearsal, Karraman Robley had received solemn, explicit instruction concerning Emmaline's passage down the aisle and thence into Robleyhood. He was to face the rear of the church when Lohengrin's herald sounded, with eyes for Emmaline only. Rapt, he would receive her, lift the veil, welcome her, lead her to face the reverend clergy as he would thenceforth lead her through life, face lift, fortune, whatever came down Old 60, over the river, and up the hill.

If events had proceeded as outlined, if Emmaline had wafted in on a cloud of fragrant silk, their lawfully wedded life might have taken a far different turn at the start. As it happened, Emmaline caught her heel in a newly installed heating grate at the head of the aisle. She didn't trip. Nothing so definitive. Her father's stolidity and amazingly agile reflexes prevented the obvious disaster. She simply clattered. To Karraman's eternal disgust. He saw her advancing bosom. It threatened to crush him. In an endless measure or two of Wagner, she lost him completely and irrevocably.

His eyes darted around the church. Beneath its stone battlements, the overall picture he found was surpassingly beautiful.

It was not a person, not a face, not an individual countenance that caused the awareness of beauty to burst upon Karraman. In fact, the single, freckled presence he actually sought was absent from the scene. Instead, he saw a meadow alight with blossoms. He saw a universe full of grace. He saw tulle and crepe and pliant straw; streamers playing in the breeze that wandered in through the angled windows; a whole herbiary of colors and enticements.

The hats. It was the hats.

Karraman had seen to it that the ladies of Saint Kathareen's met Minerva. They had first trickled, then scurried, then stomped in droves to the room that had become Minerva's first residence and workshop in Saint Kathareen's. Karraman, for his part, could hardly believe his good fortune at having the most exclusive milliner between New York and Chicago headquartered at his hostelry. The fact that he had engineered the entire situation, including Minerva's popular exclusivity, never inspired a rational thought in his head. He was as grateful to her as she was to him. The Inn's coffers jangled with the coin of the ladies who lunched before or after the rituals of millinery—or even during, when it became the height of stylishness to enjoy a repast right in Minerva's studio, courtesy. of the breathless room servants.

Karraman had neither the time nor the breadth of vision to imagine such a future on his wedding day. He saw the church filled to the last pew like the glorious multicolored finale of a showboat musical drama. Schooled on the panoramic visions of the likes of Asher Durand, Karraman fell in natural love with the pink-and-golden vista before him.

Under every eloquent hat he sought the flash of Minerva's eyes, but to no avail. As a consequence of his passionate researches, he very nearly missed the moment when Eusebius Musgrove arrived, clammy and panting, at the altar with his equally heat-struck daughter. The fact that she towered over both men and the minister as well did not add to the traditional expectations of the tableau.

Emmaline looked daggers. Karraman nearly missed them, as well, engaged as he still was in a scan of the church that combined welling pride at Minerva's aesthetic accomplishment with despair at her apparent absence. By the time Emmaline was able to impale him on the rapier of her glare, Karraman had already established a pattern of formal acquiescence that would last a lifetime: he behaved himself, he played the role, his body acted it out to the teeth and toenails. And like the slave Epictetus, he was in his soul a man forever free, a man whom Emmaline could never touch with any punishing expression. Moreover, it took the merest shaving of a moment for him to decide to exercise the exquisite freedom of his body as well, and at the earliest possible opportunity. This he decided precisely in the second before, at the cue of the absence of the monotonous liturgical drone, he pronounced to Emmaline a definitive "I do."

Yearning for Minerva all the while.

*   *   *

It would be difficult to pinpoint just which of Emmaline's ineptitudes had clicked the blockade forever into place. The final trip down the aisle, the catastrophic whinny of an "I will," the jagged hangnail that marred the perfect passage home of the diamond-encrusted wedding band, the sheer top-heaviness of her cosseted and corseted bosom—possibly none alone or together would have quite sounded the order to the garrisons of Karraman's brain, if it hadn't been for the hat. Her hat.

It was lovely, a flower in the rubble. It was daring: no tiara or cloche, nor even a coronet to suit the expectations of all the congregation for Saint Kathareen's monarch presumptive—for wasn't the event as much a coronation as a wedding, welding together forever two founding strains of power and money and guts? For the occasion Minerva Bolton had created for Emmaline a simple touring hat, laced it with white *peau de soie*, and swathed it in the softest, sheerest tulle. When Emmaline's matron of honor, a nameless soul with the face of an aging Doberman pinscher, unhooked the tiny frog which secured the veil over Emmaline's left ear, yards of mist, practically and artfully concealed, released themselves into a billowing fall at her back. The effect drew a gasp of approval from the pews. Even Karraman uttered a sigh, which might well have been taken for connubial emotion by anybody who didn't know the truth.

What a waste, he thought, and surreptitiously scanned the church once again as he pecked Emmaline's dry lips.

And still couldn't find her.

Along with wanting Minerva, he felt an unfamiliar welling of pain, a tug at the heart, a longing to which his analytic brain could scarcely assign a name. Practical as he was, Karraman understood that he was surrounded in that church at that moment by Beauty. He was absolutely, impotently, incapable of separating that perception from his concept of the woman whose elegiac mind and deft fingers had created it. He strained again for a glimpse of her. Failing once more, he impatiently beat the retreat up the aisle encumbered by far more than a new wife.

For on his wedding day, Karraman Robley had positively and completely fallen in love. Amid a demeaning shower of rice, at which Emmaline brayed to show her demure approbation (forcing him to wonder if it shouldn't have been oats), Karraman vowed another, a totally private vow. He was going to make it up to Minerva Bolton, "it" being he wasn't quite sure what, "make up" he wasn't quite sure how. Divorce was naturally out of the question. But Karraman Robley, nothing if not a man of his word, was going to get it worked out, come hell or high water.

And high water was what made it all possible. At least that was how it began.

Karraman and Emmaline were to have spent their wedding night in

Karraman's suite at the Inn. Much as he disliked the idea, it seemed the only practical thing to do. The train that would bear them away to the luxury of a wedding trip in New York chugged sootily through town only on Sunday mornings. Although Karraman bore a complicated remorse about bringing his new and peremptory wife into the domain of his small and large peccadilloes, he could hardly spend the night at Foothill House amid the noisy and communal aftermath of the most elaborate wedding reception Saint Kathareen's had ever seen. He took care of it in the best stiff-upper-lip tradition, buttoning the anguish of his need for Minerva into a tight compartment, standing guard over its integrity, building poignancy into what might have descended into farce. He carried it off well enough that Emmaline might never have suspected a thing.

The weather held for the garden reception. Aromatic breezes from the southwest reminisced rain. Here and there an elm or a maple began to invert its leaves, but not a soul, caught up as they all were in a sea of hats, an ocean of champagne, noticed. Somewhere in the nearby country a tortoise crossed the road, but such signals bid feebly for attention on such a day.

By evening, the puffs of decorative cumulus had begun to thicken and roil. Emmaline was changing into her traveling costume and roiling a bit herself, anticipating the initiations yet to come. Although the journey that night would carry her only across the river and up the few steps from the levee to the broadly porched Inn, the symbolism was monumental. Therefore she dressed the part.

Karraman was less concerned about his own appearance than he was about a great many other practical matters. He wrestled for some moments with the decision to order the shutters at both the house and the Inn to be closed. Then he moved decisively toward the negative. He reasoned that if the weather turned bad enough to justify the precautionary act, performing it would be too dangerous anyway. Besides, the natural perimeters of the Valley always provided their own protection from the worst ferocity of the tempests. As long as the rivers contained themselves . . . And no reason why they wouldn't. Matters seemed to be well in hand. Karraman turned his attention to Emmaline's luggage, which was considerable, and which he judged to be largely a waste of adornment.

Amid a building squall and some embryonic river whitecaps, the robust little tugboat ceremoniously ferried them across the river. Space would have permitted a plenitude of wedding guests to have gone along for the trip back to the center of town, because Karraman and Emmaline were traveling without the Humberette. The ladies and gentlemen of Saint Kathareen's, however, chose to a person to stand on ceremony and allow the newlyweds the solitude of the river. They would enjoy the enforced fellowship of the wait at the dock for the ferry's return trip. No matter that their paths would undoubtedly cross later, over a late supper at the Inn. Proper was as proper did.

Karraman looked up at the sky, down at the water. Emmaline had Romance written all over her posture. She sidled up to her husband. Actually she was engineering herself so that she could look up, rather than down, at Karraman. Alas, all she succeeded in producing was an unfortunate contortion. In the face she earnestly presented, miming passion, Karraman saw living rictus, and felt heartsick. Fortunately for both parties, his sudden assessment of their potentially perilous condition on the water kept him from dwelling lengthily upon his newly acquired millstone.

Moving unexpectedly up the river, boiling and tumbling at a fearful rate, the storm actually entered Karraman's field of vision as a contained, rampaging body. The valley which bounded the mighty river also held the storm, perfectly. Sheets of rain tore and bulged upstream into Karraman's full view like a maddened flag corps. The storm was bending and tearing at trees on the banks all along its fearsome path. He knew that the captain was now racing the elements to the levee. When the brunt of the storm hit the confluence, at which precise point the tugboat was fighting for its passage, the disciplined enclosure of hill and valley would break ranks, causing what kind of surge and destruction Karraman could only dread.

Suddenly the ferry seemed to halt, to drift. The captain was shouting something up to Karraman from the tug. Under the building pressure and din, Karraman could only make conjecture about what he was saying, but the experienced guess was totally accurate. Emmaline, not often a soul to take careful note of what was going on in the world around her, couldn't help but be riveted. The tug was pulling out from the port side, the downstream side of the ferry. She screamed, and dug her stumpy fingers into Karraman's upper arm with such frenzy that a clinically trained torturer couldn't have homed in between tendon and nerve with greater accuracy.

"What in God's name is he doing? He'll leave us here to die," she howled. Karraman might seriously have considered the suggestion welcome for a moment, had not the fever of the challenge already begun to inflame his blood. Intent upon appearing imperturbable, he responded in measured tones. The inevitable result was that Emmaline couldn't hear a word he said.

"What?" she roared.

"Shut up, Emmaline," he roared back. By that time everything was roaring. The heavens, the waters, the valiant little sternwheel tug, Emmaline. Even, to his immediate dismay, the bridegroom himself.

"I said, shut up, Emmaline. He's pulling to starboard in order to take on the upstream thrust. He's saving our lives, is what he's doing"—although God knows why bother, he wanted to add.

Tears mingled freely with the rain that was now beginning to slash at the confluence. "You have no right to talk to me that way, Karraman. I deserve better than that." Her nasality pierced the storm. Even at the height of peril, she was worrying about just deserts. Karraman would gladly have jumped the rail and swum to some distant point in order to eradicate the lifetime arrangement he had so smugly architected for himself. But somehow he managed to pull old Epictetus out of a soggy hat. He wasn't a Robley of Saint Kathareen's for nothing. Ignorant as a pup about the true history and character of Saint Kathareen Virago, his ancestor, he nevertheless had inherited undiminished the Robley sense of pragmatic accommodation. The welding of dynasties had been accomplished, would be consummated, would endure. No Robley had ever walked out on anything before (after the small matter of New England). None would again so long as Karraman retained the upper hand. In his own stoic way, he would also manage wife, family, hearth, home. And accommodation.

"Forgive me, Em," he bellowed. Passing by all manner of rationalizations, any number of which would have been acceptable to Emmaline, he formulated a certain shaggy phrase for the second time in a single day, this time out loud: "I'll make it up to you. I promise."

That second occasion bore no resemblance whatsoever to the first. It had become a martyr's oath for Karraman, bereft of joy, tasting of gall. Moreover, he knew that it came not as a gift freely given, but as an exacted tribute: throughout his life with Emmaline, an Enforcer would be standing by, making sure he never forgot a word or overlooked a gesture. Already it was in place.

Emmaline smiled a tremulous little smile, which caused her jowls to quiver. Appeased, and with a mild, ceremonial pout, she extended her lips for her husband's tribute. Already conditioned, he delivered the obligatory kiss, wondering how in hell she could still manage to have dry lips in the middle of the wildest typhoon the Valley had seen in his lifetime.

They hardly noticed that they had docked. The usual jolting and lurching of the procedure, normally the most turbulent aspect of the trip, passed as mere incident, compared to the drama of the crossing. Mr. Cybele stood nervous and drenched at dockside, barely managing to control two open, thoroughly irrelevant umbrellas. Just as Karraman escorted Emmaline clumsily off the gangplank, a gust of wind caught at one umbrella and tore it inside out. In his frantic, ill-coordinated effort to restore its questionable utility, Cybele let go his grip on the other one. Like a rigid parachute, it sailed upstream. The Sturm und Drang devoured it before Cybele could get sufficient voice out of his throat to send a bellman in pursuit. Karraman thought Cybele was going to weep. Or had already started. In the downpour, he couldn't be absolutely sure.

"Don't stand there gaping, man. Get on in and check the elevator beds."

"Yessir. I did. I mean, I'll do it again." He took off with a lurch, then turned around. "They're dry, sir. They'll stay dry, I'd bet my paych . . . I'll just check again, sir. Yessir!" And fled.

The bellmen busied themselves with Emmaline's luggage as unhurriedly as if it had been raining rose petals. Karraman and Emmaline negotiated gingerly the twenty feet of mossy brick between the levee steps and the portico of the Inn. Just as they were about to gain the entry, they were jolted nearly breathless by a gust of wind stronger than anything that had preceded. Emmaline flailed toward a lamppost and held fast. Karraman finally pried her away, noting with distaste that the pristine dove-gray of her costume had become impressed with a vertically striped, sooty dampness, the positive imprint of the fluting on the post to which she had anchored herself. Registering his reaction, Emmaline looked down at herself, and assumed an expression she usually reserved for social inferiors or references to intimate bodily functions.

With an absolutely uncharacteristic surge of earnest amelioration, Emmaline pronounced upon the only positive note she could conjure as they entered the Inn. "Well, thank heavens for my hat. It's kept its shape, and kept my hair reasonably dry, and I don't suppose I'll catch my death after all."

Karraman grunted, pleased at the credit issued, anxious nevertheless to remove from Emmaline's purview a subject he cherished as his personal domain.

Emmaline, oblivious and also unconsciously buoyant at entering the Inn as consort and presumed equal for the first time, plowed ahead. "I must admit, Karraman," chattery, "that my first impression of that Minerva Bolton was not at all a salutary one. After all, one didn't know a thing about her . . . origins, did one?" Emmaline at her most supercilious often took on a tincture of the Sceptered Isle. "And that complexion! Really! One does wonder about freckles"—she pronounced it like "pox"—"on a lady. How *does* one pass one's time?"

Bellmen, baggages, footmen, chambermaids, most of them hovering damply, waited for a word.

Emmaline, reigning, sailed on. "Of course, one couldn't help but feel a touch of pity. Such a gawky thing"—Emmaline's own height—"and barely a hint of bosom under all those dull shirtwaists."

And *vive la différence,* screamed Karraman's brain, before he finally shut her off. *"Emmaline!"*

[113]

"Why, what is it, dear?" Astonished. All over innocence, followed by a simpering little retreat which might, just might, have become a girl two-thirds her age and half her size.

"Oh . . ." Broadly, "*Bosom*," she cackled. "Well, after all, Karraman. It's time to acknowledge these things, don't you think." Not inquiring of him at all, actually, she sought charmed approval throughout the gathering entourage. She found sodden impatience in its place. Promptly she regrouped. "Well. Obviously some subjects remain better relegated to the privacy of our suite. Shall we?"

The plural possessive rankled Karraman, but he had other fish to fry, and he hoped that they weren't gathering anywhere too close to his elevator beds.

"Mr. Cybele. See Miss Emmaline to my quarters. I'll need to check the storm precautions at the lower levels."

"I think you'll find everything shipshape, sir," ventured Cybele. Robley glared him down before he remotely intuited that his nautical metaphor was unfortunate at best.

"You will nevertheless see Miss Emmaline to my quarters while I check matters elsewhere, Mr. Cybele. Excuse me, Emmaline," he said, turning his back on any further possibility of a reply.

Emmaline, miffed, misdirected her pique at Cybele. "You may call me *Mrs.* Robley." Unmistakably a ukase. Imitating her husband's militant about-face, she headed toward the elevator and pressed the summons bell. When the doors regally parted, the gilt-framed baroque mirror, carefully selected by Karraman to flatter his companions of the evening in its dusky glass, abruptly reminded Emmaline of the striped ignominy visited upon her person by the storm outside.

Well, *Mrs.* Robley was not going to permit herself to be troubled with such a detail at this moment. Miss Emmaline might quiver with uncertainty, but *Mrs.* Robley would ignore the facts until such time as she could easily discard the reminders.

She drew herself up to her full height as the elegant cell groaned its way to the top floor.

Emmaline was far too self-concerned to have felt any of the negative reverberations thrumming through the lift and the occupants thereof. Her mind, having dwelt sufficiently for one day upon the problems of status, turned with wicked glee toward the next scheduled activity, the loss of her own girdled virginity. Her breath whistled heavily through large teeth. She lacked even the simple Victorian modesty to blush.

On a floor below, Minerva Bolton was not blushing either. It was something else, but she could not satisfactorily explain to herself the hot, prickly feeling under her skin.

She had been in the church. Hatless, her cropped curls hidden under a modest chapel veil, she had ensconced herself behind the largest woman she could find. As a bonus, an enormous, load-bearing column, a row ahead of her and to the right, had masked her completely from Karraman's scouring sweep of the church. For good measure, she had placed herself on the groom's side of the aisle, since she correctly surmised that Karraman would expect her to join the Musgrove entourage, for purposes of discretion. She regretted neither her decision to attend the ceremony nor her virtual invisibility there.

Nor did she regret having avoided entirely the reception at Foothill House, with the inevitable hypocrisy of every congratulation and greeting. Consequently, she regarded with an overlay of wonder the frequency with which she sauntered to the window, squinted between the louvers, and reassured herself that considering the impending storm, she was better off in her room with her tea and her sketchpad than abroad in a garden of rain and clichés.

Steering clear of the reception had not been a gesture to spite her face. She thought of it as more a sensible effort to avoid redundancy.

Emmaline had suffered Minerva to spend a number of hours at the house before the wedding, showing swatches, draping fabrics, revising designs. Minerva planned it from the dressing room to the honeymoon wardrobe. My Fiancée didn't have to sacrifice a moment of the attention she devoted to the workmen who were laboring against all odds to quit the premises in time. Karraman had plumped out with exhilaration as Minerva's faultless taste insinuated itself down to the last detail. Imagine rice thrown from the folds of individually crafted fabric blossoms! How like Minerva!

Em's gradual recognition of Minerva's aptitudes remained draped in the mantle of reluctance. With Karraman it was another story. Nights, he couldn't wait to return to the Inn. Most nights they repaired to her room or his, where caress invaded conversation, and a word or a touch signaled untold chapters of infinity. Between times Karraman had watched the wedding plans as they unfolded into a work of art. The intricacies of Minerva's mind, he told her, reminded him of the whorls of her fingerprints: visible yet unfathomable, constructed of the same stuff as everybody else's, yet uniquely hers.

By the time his wedding day arrived, Karraman would have qualified as the quintessential bridegroom, sporting Cupid's arrow like a talisman, madly in love. The only problem was that single detail of misplaced identities: he was marrying the wrong woman.

The right woman, Minerva, held to the straits of reality. She had mentally rehearsed every detail of the afternoon, the part she'd witnessed, and the part she'd eschewed. Safe in the hotel room, nothing could hurt her.

When the storm approached, it jolted her doubly, in both its physical magnitude and in its perfect effrontery. Minerva Bolton, for all her exquisite control, had not planned a tempest.

From her aerie she watched the mounting splendor of the storm as it tore willfully upstream. A thrill of terror electrified her as she realized that the wanton wind and water were approaching Saint Kathareen's at point-blank range. Almost accidentally she caught sight of the little tugboat laboring its way across the menacing channel. In spite of the fearsome gale, which was by then hurtling rain in sheets against her window and field of vision, she had known instantly why the brave journey was just then in progress.

Nearly hypnotized, she watched the starboard maneuver of the tug, followed by the safe docking, Cybele's opera buffa interlude with the umbrella, everything. When Emmaline collided frontally with the lamppost and came away branded, Minerva began to laugh. She laughed until she shook. She shook until the tears flowed freely. She cried for a long time.

Reaching desperately for any avenue of comfort, she even tried to mull over Hammond Bolton, to give tentative audience to the theory that perhaps she should have stayed by his side after all. Then again, all she could think of to support Hammond's advantage was his not unpleasant profile. Karraman's, while less classic, had more character in any one of its inches than Hammond did in his whole six feet.

Some people, Minerva concluded, are not meant for consorts. Some people require power—power to nurture, power upon which to feed. Surely Hammond understood that. He was narrow, bigoted, stultified, but not stupid. Minerva never could have selected a stupid partner for even a schottische at a tea dance. But, whatever Hammond might have concluded about his wife's requirements, he hadn't the faintest idea of how to go about living with them. Minerva didn't think he could ever flex his brain cells long enough to learn something new, and act decisively on his newfound wisdom.

She had left Hammond with impunity when she finally understood that the way things were was the way things were going to be, but a tiny corner of herself would always lie in reserve for thinking about him. That corner she would seal over with paraffin, indulging herself with access to it less and less often, more or less objectively, as the years passed. Hammond, on the other hand, never really had loved anybody at all, Minerva included, as she defined it. What he had mistaken for love, she sadly realized, was simply an aggravated case of compulsive possessiveness. While Minerva, caring but determined, was able to put him out of her conscious thoughts most of the time, Hammond, wooden and benumbed, thought about Minerva every single day. He couldn't help it.

He never dreamed. At least he had always claimed vehemently that he never dreamed, whenever Minerva succeeded in humanizing him sufficiently to engage him in so personal a discussion. He would never have countenanced the irresponsible, alienist notion that surely he dreamed every night of his life, just like the rest of the human race. He would no more have believed that he was repressing something, had he known the word, than he believed that anything about his part in their marriage owned any of the responsibility for Minerva's departure. Hammond's world came neatly packaged. He survived as long as nobody, not even himself, violated the wrappings.

He never dreamed, he maintained, but he awoke thinking of her most mornings, and often during the middle of his thrashing nights. That was when he wrote the fragments of letters, never finished, never mailed, carefully squared off in neat parcels, squirreled away in a cedar chest, along with his notebooks. (When they finally reached Minerva after his death, they smelled like questionable relics, annoying tickles from the beyond. He told her more than she wanted to know.)

The sound of music, any music, reminded him of her. Consequently he listened to music as little as possible, never owned a Victrola. He grudgingly bought a radio only at the time of the Great Depression, when he decided that a man of his station ought to have quicker access to the news than that which the newspapers usually afforded. Some days he thought that he couldn't stand another moment of the torments of his soul, but of course he never seemed to do anything about it. He simply took more and more constricted refuge in the familiar.

Thirty years later, in Minerva's estimate, a complete index of his personality would have shown that he had neither matured nor managed to align in reasonable order the factors that might have turned him into a creative member of society. He chose to remain a reclusive zombie of a millionaire. All he did was run to fat.

Even on Karraman Robley's wedding night, even trying to ride out a personal storm which contained as much potential for havoc as all the gale winds that were churning the world into a caldron of destruction, even in the midst of all that, imperceptibly Minerva's inner climate had modulated from torrid to temperate, temperate to cool. She looked up with moderate surprise to find that no Hammond Bolton stood cowering before her tirade. Only the storm bore witness to her tumultuous emotions, and she was relieved. She was also smart enough to know that she needed the passage of time as well as miles to bring her thoughts together into a manageable mass. She was content, that night, to smooth out the wrinkles of her own sheets.

Gingerly Minerva slipped her fingers under the quilted tea cozy covering the pot on the tray beside her. The china had gone cool to the touch. Resolutely she ignored the symbol. Such warmth as teakettles hold she hardly viewed as balm to the innards. The true feelings have to start somewhere else.

With which thought she immediately felt a quiver between her legs. Yet, in some respects true to her Victorian ambience, she rose quickly, mentally changing the subject with the act of altering her position.

More tired than she thought, she was relieved by the comprehension that she was all right, still herself, not losing her mind, not losing her grip. She was neither disoriented nor disarmed, just bone-tired. Who wouldn't have been, after designing a visual triumph like the Musgrove-Robley wedding? Strong backs have broken under less strain than Minerva had placed upon her own clever head.

Walking toward the dressing room, she began to unfasten the bodice of her shirtwaist. Once her mama had done that for her, then a nursemaid named Erna. And Karraman Robley. But not Hammond Bolton. He performed all his intimacies in a stuffy, camphorated darkness. Minerva's preparations he left entirely to her. His underworked organ was an ostrich, wasted in the fertile loams of her body.

Long months had passed since Minerva had felt the need to devote ponderous moments to Hammond and his shortcomings. Now, as she eased her way through her ablutions before sleep, she realized that it wasn't actually the person Hammond who had triggered her thoughts. It was the idea of marriage, for one thing. And it was Karraman Robley, for the other.

Slowly, as she settled into the restless night, Minerva reviewed the factors she would have to reckon with to sustain her through the days ahead. While it could hardly have been called the end of her perfect day, and while her fulfillments were severely limited to the territory above the neckline, she at least fell asleep with a sense of honest self-appraisal. Her sketchbook teemed with her visions of the coming autumn in Saint Kathareen's. Fulfilling them would nicely occupy her days and nights. She could afford to bide her time, to relax, to force nothing. In her position, time was an ally.

While Karraman, upstairs with his sense of personal command immobilized in a leg-hold trap, battered lovelessly away at Emmaline's intractable hymen. At every thrust she whinnied. At every whinny he winced.

Believing that his responses had something to do with spasms of pleasure, Emmaline whinnied louder. Karraman praised the thunder and lauded the lightning. Without their might, he feared, Emmaline's vocalizations would have rivaled the string quartet in the dining room for the attention of everyone in the Inn. In the Valley. In the world, the universe.

Until a few scant months before, Karraman had actually found himself titillated, if perversely, by the prospect of his wedding night with Emmaline. Although he was certainly able to cast off most of the inhibitions with which he had been duly catechized as a pup, certain mythologies continued to hold fast his imagination. Perhaps his favorite fairy tale was the legend of the *virgo intacta*. He probably never would have brought himself to contemplate marriage to Emmaline, dynastic considerations notwithstanding, if he had not entertained elaborate suppositions about maidens chaste, pure, and not exactly beautiful, who somehow blossomed into something exquisite, body and soul, at the touch of a certain Magic Wand. With vain, hopeful romanticism he had managed to cast the unlikely Emmaline in the role of Sleeping Beauty. Her awkwardness, her overwhelming homeliness, even her unfortunate laugh would fall away like the pod of the milkweed when the right moment came, revealing light and airy wishes-come-true. The new Emmaline would float up to him on feathers of love and soft whispers, capturing his heart forevermore. All in all, it was an incredibly unrealistic set of expectations for a pragmatist such as Karraman to harbor. But there it was.

Then, with the spring creeping into a middle-aged heart which was craving even a mere crocus or a snowdrop, there came the spectral garden of earthly delights. Minerva. No matter how ferocious the struggle of Karraman's business, no matter how wearing the complexity of his dealings, life was reduced to perfect simplicity at the end of the day, when he could nuzzle her fragrant neck, run his fingers along her freckled cheekbones, kiss the proud crowns of her splendidly sculptured breasts.

He deluded himself eloquently. He reassured himself that his control of the situation was well in hand. By consummating his marriage to Emmaline, he would successfully merge the Musgrove and Robley lines after all. Moreover, he kept reiterating to himself, he would establish a lineage of impeccable blood. Mathematically speaking, and Karraman Robley loved to speak mathematically, he could become progenitor to whole generations of dynasts and tycoons who would sit behind massive Regency desks and proclaim him as a most uncommon ancestor.

All those visions had seen Karraman through the cold winter of his betrothal to Emmaline. His grandiose prognostications warmed him as he crunched through hoarfrost, and still hung on as he slogged in waders through the fields from rig to rig. He saw the future he needed to see in the clock-smooth mechanism of his dining room at the Inn, and in the wake of the little ferryboat which would shortly become part of his empire. He saw it every time he watched the frame of a KR Lumber company house go up on a piece of land being developed by Musgrove Enterprises, Incorporated.

Out of harm's way, in Foothill House, he envisioned a wife who would preside authoritatively at tea and table. If winds of war swept over the land, as some whispered they were bound to do after that abortive peasant uprising had been put down over across in Russia, perhaps it would be so much the better. Emmaline could always roll bandages. Karraman, although far from seeking out profiteering as an avocation, God forbid, would certainly not look askance at utilizing the opportunity to consolidate an interest or two.

Until Minerva. And the warm dusks. And the fluid laughter that had never needed to metamorphose into anything more or less than it had been at the start in order to define perfect bliss.

The dusk that settled on Karraman's wedding night felt very different indeed from the ones he had come to anticipate with such glowing security. This night was damp, dulling, dripping with rain, sweat, and fatigue. Young Lochinvar, feeling suddenly as elderly as sin, drew back to regard his prize. There she lay, hair frazzled, teeth and eyes equally clenched. She had abandoned her extravagant negligee to the humidity. Her sweating breasts lay splayed, drooping over the sides of her torso like a pair of contrary porpoises. Having nowhere else to go, Karraman, in dismay, plunged farther in.

At last Emmaline's sound effect matured into a full shriek. Karraman, despairing of any personal surcease, withdrew himself from her and imagined that if he looked down he would find his poor, ill-used member savaged and bleeding. Whatever it was that had eked out of him during the process was a poor substitute for pleasure, blood from a shriveling, reluctant turnip. No relation at all to the rocketry, the loving pyrotechnics he and Minerva were already perfecting à deux, so easily, in the lengthening spring evenings.

Karraman lunged toward the bathroom door after endowing Emmaline's shoulder with an absentminded pat. He hoped it conveyed something connubial, because it was the best he could do.

Letting the water run hot, he began to bathe, almost caress his beleaguered genitals as if in consolation. When the snowy linens came away tinged with pink, his worst expectations flared like phosphorus. It took him long pulsebeats to bring himself back to containment, to realize that the blood was Emmaline's. Well, at least he had been right about the *intacta* part.

He fell asleep wondering what on earth there could possibly be left to look forward to.

VII

Some twenty-two miles upstream, at Creighbill's Bottom, another sort of barrier was under assault. The Bottom, as the local river rats preferred to think of it, lies just far enough north and west of Saint Kathareen's to be vulnerable to the far heavier onslaughts of wicked weather that periodically cross the county's midsection in a band. Increasing automobile travel, with its godless speeds approaching twenty miles per hour, was making the public generally aware of the odd meteorological properties of the Mid-Ohio Valley. Sage farmers and rivermen have always known that strange air currents mingle and dally in a strip stretching for endless miles west to east, but scarcely more than the reach of a good south forty going from north to south. A traveler, chugging down Route 60 at any reasonable rate, might to this day find himself running into a fathom's width of hail, or an ocean of pollen, a blanketing blizzard, or any selected seven out of ten plagues, and pull right out again before he even knows what's hit him.

In later years, a lighter-than-air craft, buffeted hopelessly in those very crosscurrents, would crash spectacularly and bring a greater measure of public credulity to the old wives' weather bulletins that had circulated around the area since time immemorial. In the fateful spring of 1906, however, neither scientific prediction nor the testimony of organized experience would avail Creighbill's Bottom.

[121]

A punishing rain had been falling in a neatly contained west-to-east corridor for over seventy hours at a place just above the bend in the river. The God-granted bottomland was beginning to let growing rivulets back into the already swollen Saint Kathareen's. The water table was so thoroughly saturated that springtime taproots would rot at topsoil level or, at best, bottom out far above the strata which normally provide relief against the parching summer ahead. No capacity remained to absorb another drop. Earthworms knew it, and drowned in surface puddles in spite of lethargic scrambles to avoid the subterranean flood. Ferrets, gophers, and shore rats knew it, scurrying for cave and hollow tree, most of which they would find already occupied by other refugees of their ilk. Folks in the lowest-lying areas knew it, and were busily moving what provender they could to higher ground.

In Saint Kathareen's, no one paid much attention. The storm as they were experiencing it had moved into the area from a due-southerly direction, from downstream, not from anywhere near the Bottom at all. The central force had veered off toward the east at the confluence. By midnight the assault had dissipated into a steady pulse of moderate rainfall, without any of the menacing tenacity of the usual flood-storm. There was no apparent reason to look to the north for a further onslaught. No nautical Paul Revere had yet carried the alarums from Creighbill's Bottom, primarily because all the likely candidates were too busy battening down. Moreover, there was already enough flash flooding in the dips along 60 to have turned a great deal of its gravelly length into a particularly hazardous form of abrasive muck, making passage treacherous at best.

Downstream, the broad confluence was quickly reaching its capable boundary. The Saint Kathareen's, accustomed to a felicitous welding with the larger stream, found literally no place to flow. And yet the runoff came. What the earth rejected, the streams had somehow to accept, as long as they could.

One additional factor lent a sense of security, however spurious, to the drowsing little hamlet of Saint Kathareen's. For anyone who was thinking about it—and in that secure midnight after the worst of the rains, not many were—the knowledge of the new earthwork dam a dozen safe miles upstream, between the Bend and the Bottom, gave comfort. Surely so revolutionary a construction would prevent a disaster such as the Flood of '96. The locals didn't understand a great deal about flood control, but they believed, Lord how they believed, every word that the Board of Agriculture people told them. It didn't matter how it worked. What mattered was that a number of old county families had a fine new recreational lake on some otherwise nearly useless scrubland, and the population in the end of the county below the dam went to bed at night with the expectation that every house would be staying right dry from now on.

[122]

The County Square regulars spun nostalgia bordering on regret after the floods gone by. They were almost sorry, one might have inferred, that the old hardships were gone. They were right about one thing. The impending devastation would not duplicate the Flood of '96, or any other. It would be unimaginably worse.

When the flood had struck a decade earlier, it had come in the usual way. Slowly, with ample warning, it had rolled its way down the Ohio from Pittsburgh on one side, with a little help from the vicinity of the Bottom on the other. Its waters, still reasonably untainted with industrial poison, converged at Saint Kathareen's, leaving her with the lion's share of the damage. They carried off a measure of good topsoil, but left a rich, loamy replacement as compensation in their wake. As usual, the incursion carried off a number of riverfront shanties, but most Kathareenians deemed those quite ripe for some unauthorized urban renewal anyway. Every charitable soul in the Valley had the chance to visit all manner of good works upon the impoverished victims, most of whom ended up better fed, clothed, and housed than they had been to begin with. If anybody chose to cry crocodile tears and revert to his antediluvian ways, it was very little skin off the bluenoses who had already garnered a satisfying surplus of credits toward grace.

Impromptu soup kitchens had hummed with activity and goodwill. Merchants, for the most part, enjoyed sufficient warning to move goods to high ground, subtly ignoring the safety of merchandise which might later be sold as "damaged" for a price, rather than remaindered at the end of the season. Sage old-timers checked the inch-wide knotholes in pine floors to ensure that the water would come up and through in predictable fashion. Confined behind an impenetrable, solid slab, it would finally force the floor into a floating raft. Given the simplest escape valve, the fundamental structure would hold. In the true spirit of the community of discomfort, old flood hands coached the younger tradesmen in the manly arts of drilling holes, sealing up, lashing down.

When it was all over, most agreed that the sky above shared a freshly washed aura with the earth below. Old Kath had held fast once again. Most residents were, in a peculiarly Protestant way, quite as pleased with the idea of facing the drudgery ahead as with having endured the arduous days just passed. A few of the more fastidious arrivistes did begin to select new homesites which cobwebbed higher and higher up the sides of Calvin-and-Levi. Far it remained from anyone, however, to attribute such a choice to any motive less salubrious than the fine view, the unspoiled terrain, the upwind relation to the slaughterhouse.

No, no mere breakdown in the persistence of memory proved the nemesis of Saint Kathareen's in 'aughty-six. No one forgot. It was simply that they trusted. They put faith, confidence, and a sense of the supernatural amulet

in a virtually untested variable: the holding capacity of a quivering, functionally underdesigned, critically overstressed earthwork dam.

Shortly after two in the morning, the river bass, bluegills, and giant cats began to flail. A few water moccasins, throwbacks to a more primitive and peaceful age, hissed their malevolent way inland out of the swamps, looking for shelter to share or to preempt. Livestock edged nervously uphill as tingling premonitions of a shift in the natural order worked against their hides.

Downstream, south of the weather belt, the rain had completely stopped. Its residue dripped from the leafy corridors of Saint Kathareen's like water clocks. Aggressive slivers of moonlight skimmed the slowly parting clouds. Karraman Robley, after a patch of restless sleep on the night, stood on his balcony contemplating the placid scene below in contrast to the restless unease chewing him from within. He attributed this chafing insomnia to his recently established bondage; to a burgeoning need to share his thoughts, his very life, with the spectacular creature sleeping in solitude in her own rooms below; to the dreadful triage which he did not doubt Emmaline would try to perform if she ever suspected that he harbored any of these thoughts, let alone acted upon them. Only many weeks later, after he had had time to reflect on the day as a whole, did he attribute a grain of his restless irritability to any innate instinct about what was going on upstream. He always assumed that it was a coincidence, although generations of river people operated then, and still do, on a philosophy that says otherwise.

Whatever the reason, Karraman's highly attuned senses became suddenly aware of a distant clatter. He recognized the sound immediately, even before it resolved into elements distinct from the rustle of night and the vestigial droplets of rain from trees and gutters. The sound was as old as he was, as old as Saint Kathareen's, older. Ancient wooden wheels cobbling across brick streets. A single lame horse. A raspy driver urgently prodding an ailing animal on some transcendentally desperate errand.

In advance of thought, Karraman lurched through the French doors back into the living room. Completely oblivious of the snoring mountain inhabiting his bed, he snatched his trousers from an upholstered rosewood valet, knocking the piece of furniture over with a crash in the process.

Emmaline jumped alive. "My God, who's there?" she croaked, wild-eyed.

Damned fool of a woman. "Hush, my dear," Karraman managed to force. "It's your husband."

"Oh," she exhaled, bovine in her appeasement. She reached a stumpy paw in his general direction. With a sympathetic resignation born of the understanding that he was about to get the hell out, if temporarily, of a former haven that had become a trap, Karraman grasped her hand gently in both of his. It was as unwelcoming as her lips.

"Seems to be a bit of a something going on downstairs, my dear," although the distant hooves hadn't even clattered as far south as the range of Emmaline's hearing yet. "I'll just be a moment or two."

"Karraman." Focused, abrupt, she drew herself upright. "If I had known. That this sort of thing. Would come between us. Night after night." The enormity of her illogic alone rendered it unassailable. "And at a time like this. I never. Would have consented. To . . ."

"Nor," pronounced Karraman, "would I," patience exhausted, "have asked you." Waistcoat in hand, he exited well in advance of her spluttering reply.

Cyril Cybele had stayed the night in the first-floor room reserved for such upper-echelon-staff use. He had foreseen that the social frenzy of Mr. Karraman's wedding day and night might place outrageous demands upon the staff, even though none of the nuptial festivities had taken place on the premises. He frankly allowed as how he couldn't have predicted the nature or the scope of those exigencies, but he wasn't one to allow himself to be caught short on Mr. Robley's time. Despite the unquestionable air of martyrdom which he managed to affect, he welcomed an occasional night's respite from his bleak and humorless home life. His existence outside the Inn he shared in a dismal and drafty farmhouse with his invalid mother and half-wit brother. Perpetually torn between loathing over the burden and guilt over the loathing, he had painstakingly fashioned for himself at the Inn a universe where his origins were irrelevant.

Relaxing thus, feeling as close to confident about his situation as he could manage, Cybele watched the curling smoke of his cheroot layer the air. He lounged semicomfortably on an imitation Empire fainting chair, a foppish dressing gown covering his full front-desk regalia. Outside sounds barely touched his reverie. Still, when the unsteady rhythm of the wooden-wheeled dray approached the Inn, Cybele got himself to the front door even before Karraman Robley, in spite of the fact that Karraman's cognition had preceded his own by a considerable gap. Cybele needed only to shed the robe in transit. Furthermore, he had no human obstacle intent upon

Epithalamian dialogues to counter and appease in the process. Most important, he had a pressing, vested interest in getting out to that ruckus and rerouting it before anyone else discovered its source. He had known unequivocally what it was from the instant that the off-gaited horse and its ill-inflected driver had entered the sphere of his hearing. He had grown up in the same house with the latter, and by extension, he often thought contemptuously, with the former as well.

He darted across the lobby. The drowsing night staff straightened up a mite, but they needn't have bothered. Cybele didn't give so much as a recriminating glance in any direction but dead ahead. He gained the front door a split second ahead of Karraman Robley, just in time to hiss, "What in the name of God are you doing here with that rig at this hour of the night?" at his scruffy, malodorous only brother.

Even Karraman, who prided himself on knowing just about everybody in the Valley, nearly remonstrated with Cybele on the spot for representing the hotel so rudely, regardless of the apparent circumstances. Then he remembered that the bewildered creature facing them with an expression of hopeful idiocy plastered all over his asymmetric features actually was the lunatic brother. With no alternative in mind, he had to suppose that at least Cybele knew something rudimentary about handling him. Failing that, he granted Cybele the right to treat his own blood the way he pleased, as long as he did it with dispatch.

Karraman was about to beat a reluctant retreat back to his own quarters, assuming that some private domestic crisis had triggered the unprecedented visitation. Obviously Cybele thought as much himself, and was far more anxious than Karraman to have the premises quit of the visitor. Then something not quite definable caught at the hem of Karraman's resolve. The brother sat still, up on the high seat of the buckboard, maloccluded jaw and protuberant Neanderthal brow thrust into twin parodies of hostility. Between the guarding ridges of bone and flesh, startlingly clear blue eyes caught the lights of the Inn and focused some kind of mute plea from Karraman to Cybele and back again.

Cybele was beside himself. He wanted the creature off the grounds, blood kin or no blood kin, before he brought disgrace upon his brother by the revelation of something even more hideous than the relationship itself. Cybele couldn't think what that might be, but he was taking no chances. "Whatever it is can wait till morning," he snapped, his voice closed tightly. "Go home and see that the wolves don't attack your mother."

"Your mother" echoed in Karraman's ears. A total disclaimer of both relationships at the same sweet time, he thought. Jesus Christ, which one is the idiot?

Other matters pressed. "Shut up, man." Cybele looked aghast, but Karraman's time of life for telling people to shut up had just come hard upon him. "Can't you see the man's come here with something to say?" Then, to the brother, with a gentleness he had despaired of bringing to use this night, "Come on, friend. We won't whip ya. What is it?"

The brother cocked his head to one shoulder, foolishly dropped his jaw and simultaneously contorted it into a pointless grin. "Damn thing's a-fixin' ta bust." He beamed.

They both knew instantly what he was talking about, but Cybele led off in response, due to a lifelong habit of biting off his brother's infrequent comments a half-step before they had been completed.

"Nonsense, you jackass. It isn't even raining." The habit of denial flourished like a fungus, regardless of the facts.

"Up t' home it's a-rainin', all right. Has been since . . ." and he began to labor off the days on his fingers.

"Now, see here, you—"

Diverse clouds of uneasiness began to swim into focus for Karraman. He was listening first to the brother, then to the silence. Instinct and reason flowed all together, and all of a sudden he knew what he knew.

"Now, *you* see here a minute, Cybele." He listened acutely to the gathering rush of the waters around him. No mistake. "This man may just have done this Valley one of the biggest favors in history. We aren't going to stand here arguing about it. We have to move." He took on urgency. "What about your house? Your mother?"

"But, Mr. Robley, he's just an—"

"I said shut up, man. Whatever else he may happen to be, I think we have plenty of reason to believe that he's also absolutely right. Listen." He paused. "The air is wrong. The water's wrong. If there are mistakes to be made, they're going to be made on the side of keeping people safe and dry. It's getting on to three. We can't have more than a couple of hours. Now, let's move."

"But, Mr. Robley, he's—"

"That is, if you're still planning to come back to work at the Inn?"

Cybele's eyes widened. Then he rallied. "Yes. Well. Mother's all right. The house sits on a knoll. She understands that she's safe. But if he really is right, he'll never make it back."

"Then we'll put him to work down here." Turning to the brother, he put a deliberate brake on his accelerating speech. "Can you do that, man? Do you understand me? Can you help us move some tables and chairs so they don't get wet?"

The brother waggled his head eagerly. Karraman only hoped that his ability would match his will. By that time his lungs and his ears were registering the subtle shifts in air pressure that inevitably heralded nature's wrath. They had very little time before the water would begin its rise.

Minerva drifted in and out of a demiworld between rest and not-rest. Her mind had been wandering from one reality to another. She felt neither alarm nor surprise when Karraman's insistent knock came to her door sometime after the Town Hall chimes tolled 2:30.

What startled her was his disarray. His private person she had experienced in every manner of loving deshabille. Publicly, even for a midnight passage through a deserted hallway, he presented an impeccable front, armored, never a thinning hair out of place. The Karraman Robley who appeared at her threshold in shirtsleeves tore at her heart. Man and boy he stood, vulnerable dimensions of humanity revealed in the simple anomaly of an absent cravat.

Nothing rushed his kiss or changed its character. Nor did the taste of Emmaline linger. No remaindered sweetness threatened to draw Minerva to the banquet as guest or prey. In spite of everything, Minerva had an honorable sense of propriety. She absorbed in a flicker that it was not passion that brought Karraman to her door.

"Minerva."

"Yes, Karraman." The tender, intimate goodness of their communion.

But injected now with a quiet, extrapersonal urgency.

"Minerva, the dam has burst at Creighbill's Bottom. The water will rise."

The pause of a soft breath. "How bad will it be, Karraman?"

"We don't know, Min, m'love." She noted the grave endearment, but marked that he designated her with her name, still there, still in place. "But I want you to gather your important belongings and meet me in the lobby in a few minutes. I'm going to send you to Foothill House while there's still time to get across."

Minerva, suddenly strangely charged, stared at him as if he were Noah run rampant. "My God, Karraman, this is the third floor. Surely—"

He interrupted her. "It isn't a question of the water rising this far, Min. It's a question of isolation, of damages that might undermine the foundations, of how long it might take the water to recede. There's no way to judge these things." Not to mention what feeble resources might be left to husband on this side of the river when it finally receded. Who would have thought that Saint Kathareen's would have gone complacent so soon after '96?

"I won't be five minutes, Karraman." Minerva brushed his lips and sailed off in a wave of determination. Karraman, still tentatively poised to counter arguments in spite of himself, spent precious seconds watching in ecstatic disbelief her serene and competent movements toward evacuating the hotel. He understood that this was no subservient female pandering without thought to his arbitrary and masterful orders. Rather, she had an intelligence to match his, unencumbered of false vanities. She had absorbed his message, accepted it on the merit of his experience, and prepared herself to act.

Minerva hadn't given a lot of thought in those whirlwind moments to where Karraman had said they would be going. The words "Foothill House" grazed her sensibility, then wandered on as the urgent situation began to impress itself. In the lobby, ready with her abbreviated baggage, she began to think concretely about what lay ahead. Her thoughts led back toward the direction from which she had first entered Saint Kathareen's, an epoch ago. A path that bisected the angle of the confluence would lead neatly and efficiently to the hills of her first splendid vantage. She could head straight out, on high ground all the way, hightail it back to Massachusetts, where right-thinking oceans never had the effrontery to flood, and never be heard from again. She considered the possibility for the length of one full heartbeat, then tapped it straight back into her well of reserve. If Foothill House was to be the next port of call, then so be it. What shelter they would find or make there, she hardly knew, but she was primed to make the best of finding out. Her trust in Karraman never wavered.

Minerva waited in the frenetic lobby. Seething activities, methodical by some internal standard, but not to the naked eye, flurried around her. Out of nowhere, a backstairs staff had materialized and begun to haul all movable furnishings to higher floors. Specially measured chains were hooked to drapery rods by prearrangement. The draperies themselves were then threaded horizontally through the chains, and the whole business hoisted so that it was parallel to, and on a level with, the ceiling. The water would have had to inundate the entire twenty-foot height of the lobby floor before a single thread of fabric got wet.

Four young men diligently rolled the giant Shiraz rugs into tight cylinders. Simultaneously, Cybele and an oddly clad fellow whom Cybele had called away from hauling furniture climbed a pair of ladders. They eased free and lowered on a powerful set of chains what Minerva had at first assumed to be merely an unusually broad ceiling beam. It swung some two feet below its accustomed location. Then Cybele released from its concealed locale what seemed to be a simple winch and pulley. Slowly, with an eventual grin of triumph, the assistant followed suit on his side. Easing the apparatus to the floor, they watched as the boys with the rugs received the gear. Cybele looked grimly satisfied as the workers loaded the rugs into the hoist. On the other ladder, the helper seemed to have fallen into bewilderment again. Cybele gestured the motions of drawing the hoist up hand over hand, and finally the helper grasped the purpose. Minerva released an intake of breath that she hadn't even realized she was holding. She almost laughed when the helper, anxious to succeed and please, applied himself with such ardent strength that his half soared up most of the distance to the ceiling in a sprint. Cybele nearly lost both balance and temper. Only the urgency of the task held him in place and in check.

At last they had stowed the rug and replaced the beam. Cybele skittered down his ladder like a gun-shy rodent. With sweating palms he withdrew a checklist from the depths of his waistcoat. He shrilled a question here, an order there, in a falsetto which, to Minerva, lacked even the simplest elements of authority. Apparently nothing he said made a whit of difference anyway. All operations, according to the drill with which every staff member was intimately familiar, were either completed, or in progress, or well on the way to getting started. As a result of Karraman's frequent and thoroughgoing practice sessions, no one tarried about his task or questioned its necessity. Of all those in various stages of energetic preparation around the building, only Karraman's mulish bride balked, indicting the activity about her as premature, somehow embarrassing. Even Cybele's brother, who had never done a day's work in the company of other men, joined every team that needed an extra hand or back. Cybele, seeking him out again before he got into any mortifying mischief, turned and found him lifting ponderously framed oil portraits from the walls and stacking them vertically in a cart. For his pains, he received an incredulous stare from his brother and, from a few of the others, the first nods of gratitude anyone had ever telegraphed his way. Someone even asked his name.

"Roscoe," he offered, grinning. Somewhere in the depths of his awareness, he knew that the confession of his name would displease Cyril mightily. He wasn't really sure what it was anyhow, since his mother called him Junior when she could remember, and Pa when she couldn't. Cyril always called him You Idiot or Imbecile, and he knew that wasn't right. He chose Roscoe for the old sheep dog out on the place. He knew it must be a good name, since no one ever made a mistake and called Roscoe anything else. Often they said it softly, like a song. And if the dog got lost in the flood, or anything, there would always be a way to remember him, now.

"Well, we're obliged for the hand, Roscoe."

He grinned, and kept up the patterns of labor.

Minerva watched, fascinated. Despite her inclinations to join the effort, she knew better than to offer. Karraman's plan was a tight one. The interference of a woman, even one who had braved the Alleghenies alone, would only disconcert the working harmonies of men whose expectations were of a different sort. Minerva understood the mechanics of point-making far too well to sacrifice anyone's safety on behalf of someone's principle. So she waited, confident that her major role in the drama of the night had yet to be played out.

Emmaline, on the other hand, had decided that the starring role belonged to herself alone, as she was convinced befitted the new Mrs. Karraman Robley. Suddenly there she was, descending the staircase *fortissimo*, snarling cautionary instructions to bellmen and servants, who needed none, and who, moreover, had better things to do than give precious minutes over to obsequious groveling. Between other comments, she was reading an intermittent riot act to one pinched, livid Karraman Robley. He maintained a most ungentlemanly clip several steps ahead of Emmaline, and looked as if he'd prefer to open a trapdoor to oblivion for her just after he'd passed safely beyond it himself.

Why were they taking off so unceremoniously on this night of nights, she wanted to know, when any self-respecting Kathareenian knew that there couldn't possibly be a flood these days. And if there were, what could be safer than the fourth floor, mind you, the topmost floor of the tallest building in the whole Valley? And if they did have to leave, why on earth drag her flight after flight down these dreadful stairs? A little water in the elevator bed wasn't going to turn it into a chambered nautilus, was it? And how long was it going to be (this latter while gesticulating, free-handed, at nine pieces of luggage) before she could fetch her real clothes, instead of just these few toss-ins? It certainly seemed to her that some sounder management, of the standard, say, to which Papa Musgrove subscribes, might . . .

"Ah, Minerva, I'm grateful that you're ready."

"What's she doing here?" Emmaline demanded, as if she had caught sight of a dead rat floating belly-up.

"Of course, Karraman." She spoke softly, but managed to make herself heard above everything. "I'll help in any way I can." Turning slightly: "Emmaline, my dear, perhaps I can carry something for you. Oh! You're not carrying anything at all. Dear me! I must try to learn efficiency from you."

"Well, Minerva. Well. If that's a compliment, this hardly seems the moment for social niceties."

"I didn't mean to offend you, Emmaline. Truly I didn't." A soft, bemused curl played around the corner of her mouth.

"No. Well. This is certainly. Not the time for flattery. In any case."

Minerva simply planted that in a flourishing garden of non sequiturs provided by Emmaline.

"I suppose My Husband. Had one of the servants. Rouse you. This hysterical false alarm."

[131]

"Yes," replied Minerva, omitting the part about how Her Husband could take care of all the "rousing" he needed to do without any help from anybody, thank you.

"Well, where has he suggested that you go, dear? This prophet of mine."

"Actually, I . . ."

"Minerva is going with you, Emmaline," Karraman rescued, having returned from several rapid tasks to see with disgust that Emmaline still had the backbiting department open and running. "While you chattered, your luggage went to the ferry. Foothill House will see you through. Doremus has the keys to the Humberette over there, and one of the boys can ride horseback as far south as Gantry for provisions, if it turns out to be necessary. I doubt that it will."

"Karraman. I'll hear of no. Such. Thing. The rugs haven't arrived for the master bedroom, and the telephone is completely unreliable, and the electricity goes . . ." Emmaline continued to argue halfheartedly, even as she allowed herself to be propelled toward the door.

"Karraman," breathed Minerva, who had lingered a step behind, "what about you?"

He removed one hand from Emmaline's arm long enough to stroke Minerva's cheek. "Don't worry, Min. Saint Kath and I have weathered a flood or two before this one. We know the ropes. You'll have far more of a challenge at Foothill House, I daresay," pointedly. "But you'll manage. I'm not worried about you for a moment."

At that instant, getting on toward the hour of four in the morning, the angle of the levee permitted the strange trio to catch a glimpse of the little tug and the ferry. Minerva could have sworn that they were already riding many feet higher in the water than she had ever seen. Emmaline, at first sight of them, remembered the trip across earlier in the day, and tried to bolt. Even Karraman, although he would have been loath to admit it, felt an anxious turn at the sight of the little vessels bouncing high and alighting with groan and clatter on an angry, watery roadbed.

What had happened at the confluence was a simple conflict of currents. As a general rule, the Ohio flows more swiftly than the Saint Kathareen's, so that the downstream current at the crossing is directionally reliable, if often mildly choppy. With the approaching engorgement of a broken dam upstream on the Saint Kath's, the current of the small river was taking on the might and personality of a battering ram. Unable to overcome the vigor of the mighty Ohio despite all her efforts, she nevertheless sustained the fight. In a few short minutes the Ohio would win, forcing the Saint Kathareen's up through storm sewers, back into creeks and runs, and finally over the banks.

For a moment the two streams, each mindlessly absorbed in its own kinesis, met and collided just north of the confluence like two hostile hands clapping. They thundered together, spumed white, rolled back in angry retreat, leaving less and less distance to carry the bravado of each onslaught. Moored perilously close to their point of juncture, the tug and ferry jounced and shuddered with every infuriated collision. Captain Perley Stevens had come close to moving them into his midwinter inlet, a few hundred yards upstream, when someone bellowed Karraman Robley's orders down to him.

The captain measured the situation decisively. With a keenness born of a lifetime on the river, he reckoned that Robley's intent was indeed the more sensible course—if the battered craft didn't shatter into flotsam before he had a chance to make his foray out into the free waters. As he saw it, considering the westward bend of the Ohio just outside of town, and the corresponding bowing of the Saint Kathareen's, the Calvin-and-Levi side of the river invariably ran a smoother, more consistent current than the downtown side. In fact, mooring the tandem vessels in open water across the river could even be safer than trying to let her ride it out in the accustomed inlet. One or two significantly large pieces of debris, floating tree stumps, whatever the rivers decided to give up, might well prove the destruction of a vulnerable sternwheel in a semienclosed space. The inlet was easy enough for river garbage to float into, but much harder to get out. Why, once Perley had watched the entire Tabernacle Church of Ephraim, Ahia, float downriver in a flood. The whole town of Saint Kathareen's held its breath as the roof and steeple approached the railroad bridge. They knew it would never clear, and it didn't. Off went the rest of the hallowed building on its way downstream, but that gol-danged steeple floated into the inlet just like it know'd where it was a-goin', as they said. No boats in there to get knocked about that time, but the steeple bell ran its mouth day and night for a week afore anybody could get down to it and set it back on dry land and hush it up for a moment's peace.

Karraman gamely tried to hurry his party along. They'd sent luggage enough for forty days and forty nights, but old Perley would have to find room. He'd done it before, and his daddy and granddaddy before him. Karraman knew he'd do it again. Minerva hadn't been around long enough to comprehend his confidence, but bravely she bought into it.

When Karraman Robley finally reached the gangplank, flanked, as Stevens saw it, by the one he'd married and the one he should have married, it was all Perley could do to keep a civil tongue in his head. Valor strove, but passion won.

"F' God's sake, man, can't ya get the rest a your party ta make some tracks about now? There's no tellin' how long it'll be afore these waters quit actin' jist as hospitable as they are right now."

Karraman, who hadn't seen them as hospitable to begin with, suppressed a smile at Perley's obverse optimism.

[133]

"This here's the party," Karraman shouted above the increasing din of the waters. "Get you going, now."

Perley balanced at the edge of disbelief. "Karraman Robley," he bellowed, "you've got no guarantee from me that I can bring this vessel back across this river one more time tonight. I'm tellin' ya this," he huffed, "because I'll not have the torment of a hotel full of drownded people on my conscience." He drew a breath.

Emmaline made a move in an indeterminate direction. Karraman held on. "Rest easy," he returned to Stevens, the directive falling in morbid contrast to the urgent tone in which it was delivered. "Everything's seen to. The Livery's busier'n bejesus, movin' folks upland every which dry way. They're haulin' as far as Marietta, takin' the inland route. It's . . . ah, hell, Perley, that's none a your problem. Just move this cargo safely to port. I'll never forget." He gestured to the two women. Then he kissed Emmaline's fold of cheek. He never touched Minerva, but he never took his eyes off her, either, as he said, ostensibly to Perley Stevens, "It's worth its weight in diamonds."

Pivoting abruptly, Karraman fled back to the business of salvaging his hotel, leaving the conjunct fate of the two women up to the river gods and Perley.

"Karraman! Wait!" Emmaline, wailing.

"No time now. I'll be over soon. Keep calm."

Minerva, trying to guide Emmaline's heaving shoulders up the rest of the gangplank, automatically began to croon small comforts to her hysterical companion. Finally, amid considerable cajoling plus some rather pointed pokes and thrusts, Minerva managed to get Emmaline onto the creaking deck.

Emmaline turned her watery, fireshot eyes to Minerva and said, "I'm sorry. I should be grateful to you for coming with me. I'd never survive it alone." She ended with an ill-suppressed belch.

"Nonsense, dear," a vulnerable little catch at her throat, "we are all here to help each other." But, she thought, as Emmaline sobbed and hiccuped all the more, if you throw up on my good suit, I'm going to toss you overboard, I swear I will.

Minerva had no need to make good her mental threat. Every time Emmaline vomited, it was over the rail. Little bits of spittle clung to the corner of her mouth so tenaciously, washing away only to be replaced anew, that Minerva stopped worrying about Emmaline's vomitus and began to have some trepidations concerning her own. Her toughness prevailed for the length of the crossing, probably by willpower alone.

All in all, it could have been much worse; had been much worse, in fact, hours earlier when Perley had bravely borne across Karraman and his virgin bride. At least the winds had calmed somewhat. Thus, they arrived at Levi's Landing shaken but safe, with Perley taking an adamant stand by that time in favor of returning to the levee. Usually he was a man who stuck by his earliest decision. In this case, in the calming air, he was willing to make an exception. More to the point was the human payload packed solidly onto the lantern-lit jetty, jockeying for position in line to board the ferry, as the moon tore westward among the stormy clouds, racing morning home.

"Look, Minerva! It's the house staff, and half of the mountain, it seems, waiting to welcome us home."

Not with all that luggage, thought Minerva. There are enough carpetbags here to cover your bedroom three times over.

Not to mention cardboard cases, string-tied parcels, even a bird cage. The faithful retainers of Mount Calvin-and-Levi, most of them, were making a time-honored beeline home to their low-lying families on the other side of the river as the flood encroached. Regardless of the dangers, they were electing, singly and severally, to catch up with the homefolk and flee inland rather than to watch loftily from above as their houses, earthly goods, and newly planted seedlings washed away. For a moment, seeing the throng, Minerva doubted the wisdom of Karraman's planning. She couldn't imagine what all these people knew that she didn't know, to cause them to flee the mountain like this.

Quickly getting a grip on herself and the situation, she took Emmaline by the arm and propelled her off the boat, weaving a path through the crowd.

"I want to go back to where Karraman is." Petulant, stamping a verbal foot.

"Nonsense, dear. Karraman has made the right decision. We'll be safe as houses here."

"But Karraman. What about Karraman?"

"He'll do much better at rescuing himself, and a slew of others, I imagine, if we can simply do our part by doing as he asks."

"But, Minerva . . ." More imploring, less imperious.

"Hush, dear. We don't want to create a spectacle in front of everyone," who were so busy trying to crowd and jostle onto the ferry that Emmaline could have paraded the length of the jetty in her birthday suit, and no one would have noticed.

But it got to her anyway, just as Minerva had calculated. The only spectacles Emmaline considered respectable were those in which she manipulated others into pitiful carnage, not those in which she might come out second best. Randomly her eyes scanned the crowd. A few seconds earlier it had appeared as a wretched jumble, her first ego-ridden idea of its purpose having been promptly disabused. Emmaline in need became transmogrified into Emmaline in command of the name, rank, and genealogy of every pleading soul on the bank. She would have felt no compunction about commandeering any number of them to her purposes, if Minerva had not taken matters firmly into hand.

The Humberette was parked at dockside. At the sight of it, solitary, proud, and driverless, Minerva registered the final reality of their situation. She had thought that at worst she might have to scale the hill, reach the house, and find someone to fetch her and Emmaline and the luggage. At best, the telephones might even have been working, and someone would have had both the time and the foresight to get through. The abandoned car told her in a flash that creative hoping would do no good. The lady who managed to conduct two horses for eight-hundred-odd miles was now going to have to do something about driving a miracle of modern technology for a few thousand yards.

"Well, now what? I want to know."

Minerva inhaled carefully, as if each molecule of air might contain an alarm that she would trigger if she didn't remain in a state of perfect, calm equanimity.

"First we'll each take something that we can carry in each hand to the car. Then, while you rest, I'll get everything else. After that, we'll go to the house. That seems the sensible approach, doesn't it?" She wanted to include Emmaline in the action so that she wouldn't feel completely railroaded, and stop cooperating altogether.

"You must be mad, Minerva. I thought you were mad from the first day I saw you, but now I know you're mad." She was talking softly, with staccato rapidity. Her eyes darted from side to side. "Women don't drive cars."

"This one does. Here, Emmaline. You take this little case. I'll take those two."

Emmaline acted mesmerized, but she complied. For the rest of the ordeal home, including more than one futile attempt to crank the automobile, then get it properly into gear, she sat blankly clutching the small case Minerva had handed her. Minerva, having watched Karraman start the car dozens of times, had a rough idea how to go about it, but not a whipstitch of practical experience. With the zombie seated on her right, and the fast-encroaching water just outside the car, she almost wished that Emmaline would start to rail again. That at least would be a sign of human contact.

But, nothing. Not a single word until they had chugged and bucked all the way up to the driveway of Foothill House, at which point Minerva finally mastered the tempo of the gearshift. They rolled smoothly over the final yards to the entrance, and landed with the headlights pointing doorward, in what Minerva decided was a pure inspiration. That way, she reasoned, their trail would be better illuminated in the murk of predawn, and the glow would see them as far as the first interior light.

She wanted to weep with relief at having gotten that far. Automatically she looked to Emmaline for a word of gratitude. She should have known better. The glaze lifted long enough for the mistress of Foothill House to say, "Well, I must say I'm shocked that a perfectionist like Karraman would want to saddle me with such poor quality helpers. 'Companion,' indeed! Doesn't even know how to drive a proper car." As if Emmaline did. "I'll see to this in the morning. Meanwhile, bring in my things. I . . ." with a sudden hand to her serpent-tongued mouth, "don't think I'm feeling very well."

VIII

At least Foothill House was dry, even if the bedroom rugs hadn't arrived yet. The larder had been providentially stocked to the rafters by Emmaline's mother, who apparently considered food an essential part of the dowry. Holding no truck with iceboxes or other newfangled tools of the devil, she regarded as legitimate provender only that which could be canned, bottled, smoked, dried, packed in brine, kept in a root cellar, sprouted in a jar, cultivated in a winter garden, or maintained on the hoof. Of the above, nothing was wanting. It was almost as if Mrs. Musgrove had never believed they'd go on a honeymoon at all.

Nor did she have confidence in electricity or piped-in gas. Fragrant hickory by the cord filled the woodshed. Tallow candles stood at the ready in every decorative candelabrum and sconce. Boxes more filled the giant side panels of the hulking dining-room buffet. Minerva, who had watched the assembling of this veritable supply depot during the prenuptial preparations, nevertheless felt as if she were walking into a house that had been occupied for generations. Despite the aromas of new wood, paint, and plaster, the overstuffed aura clearly belonged to some quirky denizens of a former century. If the bedroom rugs were missing, everything—every single thing—else was in place. Every expanse of furniture bore the weight of ormolu, porcelain, art glass, silver, crystal. Potted palms strangled corners.

Ball fringes hung from everything. Instinctively Minerva loosened her collar.

"Well, Emmaline dear, the baggage isn't going to come in by itself," to a vacant hallway. Brisk, calm, no grass growing.

Minerva was surprised to hear, from a darkened room behind a partially closed French door, "Yes, well, you begin. I'll be along." Some of the imperiousness had drained out, but Minerva could still see with dead certainty who was going to end up carrying the bags.

She moved toward the front door to begin unloading. As she turned, her peripheral vision caught Emmaline in an uncultivated lunge toward the stairway. Right then, she made the conscious decision to let the hellcat wear herself out with tantrums, if that was what she wanted to do. She'd get no sympathy from Minerva's quarter. If any humanity lurked beneath Emmaline's uncooperative exterior, she'd come around. Besides, Minerva assumed that Em was bound to get hungry sometime. Let her see to her own scullery.

But for once, Minerva's keen reasoning fell wide of the truth. Emmaline had not been headed for the warming rocks of self-pity after all, but for the sparkling tile of the bathroom, a convenience whose utility both women would have increasing reason to laud as the days wore on. Neither had Emmaline meant to play to the grandstand for the purposes of enlisting Minerva to pursue and console. She wanted nothing more than to be alone with her misery, at least at first. Hunger was, and would be for many days, the furthest thing from her mind and her body. It would be Minerva who would ply Emmaline with sweet teas, salt crackers, clear broths, anything to keep up her strength. Minerva, in the dark solitude of early mornings, would find herself praying for Emmaline's recovery, reminiscing compassionately toward the mewl of her laugh, the slash of her tongue, any sign of her life. Partly she was to feel terror in the face of her own unaccustomed impotence as the rains went on and the water held. And partly she dreaded to present Karraman, when he finally slogged up the hill to reclaim this branch of his empire, with damaged merchandise. Or, far worse to contemplate, with no merchandise at all.

For Emmaline had gone upstairs to vomit. And she kept on vomiting through the rest of the night, the morning, and all the rest of the following day. For better or worse, Minerva didn't discover what was going on until she had lugged every last trunk and grip into the foyer, thereby dissipating a small but righteous fury in a rugged, sweaty self-satisfaction. Then she felt she could face Emmaline with fair perspective.

The bathroom stood opposite the head of the long stairway, across the cavernous main portion of the upstairs hall. Karraman had had a florid La Farge window designed and placed in the bathroom to trap daylight like a diadem. At night, the single luminescence in the house shone forth out of a tulip sconce above the mirrored medicine chest. When she had first seen it, Minerva had wondered seriously about devoting such profligate expense to a domestic lavatory. It seemed to represent a shameless monument to human excrement and other unmentionable details of private form and function. Cautiously scaling the staircase in belated, exasperated search for Emmaline, she resurrected the memory of the proud bathroom beacon, hoping at least to orient herself according to its light. Unfortunately, a testy perfectionism on the part of carpenter and journeyman had prevailed. Not so much as a crack of light presented itself beneath or around the oaken door. Everything had been cut to fit tighter than a hold. The pestilential dampness of the air itself had completed the seal.

A barely human noise from somewhere straight ahead of her caught Minerva up short. Before the time it took to think it through, she understood what was happening, and shouted for Emmaline. Her fingers methodically prowled the wall where she thought the light switches ought to be.

Emmaline retched again, dryly, then gave herself over to deep, rasping bids for breath, for air.

"Emmaline! Open the door!"

Minerva had no idea whether to expect resistance or not. Emmaline had changed the rules so many times in the last hours that Minerva was no longer sure what game they were playing, although she was wryly aware that she did not possess the advantage of the home arena. Moments ago she would have brooked no rebellion. Having just located a light switch, turned it both ways, and received not so much as an anemic flicker of a response, she felt her confidence wane. She was almost ready to beg, to implore Emmaline to reveal herself, retching or not, and she wanted enormously not to turn herself into supplicant in the situation. To her immense relief, she heard a rustle of movement followed by a small crash, a muted exclamation, and finally the turning of the knob.

The bathroom door opened into a dimly flickering arc. The candles. Of course. When she realized that the power had failed, Emmaline had been more than ready. Her mother's child to the last jot and tittle, she had never held much with electricity either. She had had no intention of entering that prison of a bath cubicle after dark without having every single backup system in full working order.

Even in semisilhouette, Emmaline looked ravaged. She held on to the doorknob with her right hand, and reached out to Minerva with her left. Quickly Minerva rearranged her balance to support Emmaline. She seemed to want to be guided to bed. Minerva glanced briefly over their shoulders at the mess of a bathroom, the floor littered with towels, bottles on the vanity upset altogether or balancing in a precarious heap. In the sink lay the shattered fragments of a particularly handsome shaving mug. Minerva recognized it as a duplicate of one Karraman kept at the Inn.

"Min, I'm sick," whimpered Emmaline.

"It's all right, Em. I know. The crossing was awful. On top of all the excitement, you're just taking a while to resettle."

"No, Min. I'm sick. Really sick."

Surprisingly, Emmaline's voice was for once free of pretense or drama. Its openness sent an alert through the layers of Minerva's fatigue. She reached a hand to Emmaline's forehead, which felt alarmingly hot. A sour effluvium surrounded her over and above the combination of unguents and fragrances which she had apparently spilled all over herself when she savaged the bottles on the dressing table.

"Hush, dear." To Minerva's surprise, affectionate condolence was beginning to come almost easily. "We'll get you to bed, and I'll make a nice tisane for both of us. Tomorrow you'll be right as rain." Propelling Emmaline by the dim light toward the master bedroom, Minerva caught them both up short. "Well, maybe not rain," and chortled throatily. Even Emmaline managed a weary smile. Then, in easy intimacy, Minerva conducted Karraman's wife to her bed, sponged her as far as modesty would allow, and tucked her in. Exhausted, Minerva lit another candle from the guttering remains of the last one, and set off in search of tea herbs and honey. She wouldn't have sworn an affidavit at that point as to which one of them needed it more.

Not long after first light, Minerva awoke with a cramped start. Accustomed to functioning from the first wakening, her intelligence needed no reminders of where she was or what she was doing there. Her body, on the other hand, screamed rebellion at the unaccustomed lugging, hauling, straining, and good old-fashioned overuse to which she had subjected it only hours before. Slowly she uncurled herself from the overstuffed boudoir chair and moved quietly over to the bed in which Emmaline still angrily tossed.

By daylight the bed seemed less imposing, smaller. Minerva fought a surge of pain rising like a tide. Karraman, between nearer boundaries, seemed closer to Emmaline, farther from reach.

Emmaline opened her eyes opaquely, closed them, turned painfully on her side with a profound snore. Minerva tiptoed to the front windows. She drew a crack in the fringed and gussied edges of the drapery. Her eyes widened. Beneath a low overhang of billowy gray sky, the river had metamorphosed overnight into a glassy lake. Minerva couldn't begin to guess at its breadth. It had already risen to encompass the entire base of Calvin-and-Levi beneath her, and the very heart of Saint Kathareen's on the opposite shore. The point where the confluence should have been had dissolved into a muddy pool. At a closer examination, Minerva could make out the activity of boat traffic, rafts, all manner of makeshift floating craft, amid the channels that had been complacent little streets less than a full day ago.

Somewhere in the house a clock marked the half-hour. Seconds later, a steeple somewhere in the Valley followed suit. Minerva wondered what had happened to the courthouse sentinel. Its absence marked for her another step in understanding the enormity of a flood's aftermath. Yet, to think of "aftermath" was, she understood, premature in itself. When those clouds outside decided to open again, they weren't going to rain butterflies.

Minerva started through the house. She needed to begin to inventory the means of comfort and nurture for herself and Emmaline. Before it all ended, she realized, it was going to take every gram of patience and ingenuity she could muster.

Doctors in a later day would have called it influenza. They would have administered sulfa and prayed for the best. Emmaline survived it due to a combination of Minerva's considerable knowledge of folk medicine, pure orneriness, and her own reserves of girth and blubber.

Minerva brewed her camomile and comfrey. She laced it generously with honey, and fed it to Emmaline by the spoonful. When Emmaline showed signs of a beginning cough, Minerva made her poultices of pungent pastes. Day melted into tedious day, and Minerva began to augment the tea with a ration of whiskey. (Emmaline swore that her mother couldn't possibly have laid in any wicked spirits, but someone had, thank God.) When the skies cleared temporarily, Minerva ransacked the raspberry brambles for leaves above the growth line, and brewed a concoction of that and rose hips, just for the change. She exploited every clear minute, and carried in bundles of greens, flowers, berries. She used every resource she could think of. She felt that she could only retain her grip so long as she continued to vary, in any way she could, the interior patterns of boredom and ennui.

The clear skies, though counterfeit, kept Minerva going. She would awaken facing the window, cautiously crack the draperies, and start joyfully at the overlay of cottony billows on spectral blue. This was a world she knew, could manage. Then she would follow her eye downward—and back came the sinkerweight.

Minerva, feeling as weathered as an ancient tar, was nonetheless innocent as flood-hands went. She had yet to learn that the flood depth at the confluence, paradoxically, had nothing to do with the temper of the immediate skies. Conditions as distant as the headwaters of a mountain feedstream could, and did, influence the times and tides of seemingly unrelated terrain.

It had been raining intermittently but with some force in Saint Kathareen's for over three weeks, since the wedding. On that basis alone, clear skies augured nothing especially hopeful. To complicate matters, a late thaw after a vicious winter high in the Alleghenies brought new volumes of water downstream daily. Land that Minerva and her team had crossed as permafrost was now washing, unknown to her, right past the very levee from which she had crossed to the hill. She did know that there was too much water. She hated it.

She thought at times that she was going mad. All that wind, all that sunshine, and still the waters stayed. New freshets deluged old benchmarks. At a loss, she brewed more tea. Thus did she keep hold.

Then one night, at the beginning of the fourth week, after a stretch of unrelenting days when Minerva thought she would collapse if she had to haul one more pail of vomitus to the septic system, Emmaline's fever broke for the first time.

Minerva had been sleeping on a chaise that she had moved in to substitute for the boudoir chair across from Emmaline's bed. She lay hovering between torpor and consciousness, a condition which she had come to regard as her natural place in life. Weakly, in the back horizon of her mind, she heard a meek voice pipe her name, drift out, pipe again. Was she dreaming? Hearing things? Hallucinating, in this mad companionship that was more solitary than isolation? She opened her eyes, and saw the first light above the still receding lake. Yearning in every sinew to turn her back, curl up and let nature take care of its own, she sat up to check the summons that she could have sworn she had heard. Unmistakably it came again, from the tangle of hair and linens and relief into which Emmaline had woven herself.

"Min?"

"Yes, dear. I'm here."

"I'm sorry, Minerva," pitifully, resembling no person Karraman Robley had ever had the pleasure of meeting or taking to wife. "But my bed covers seem to be drenched. I've had some horrible kind of accident, and I don't even know what happened." A pitiful desperation saturated her tone. Minerva sniffed the air, came up with nothing untoward. She had thought that they had weathered all possible crises of the human body to date, but she fairly leaped from the chaise across to the bed. She dreaded the rupture of some unknown, some sac or organ or small element of humanity with which she had no manner of coping.

Emmaline was indeed drenched, from head to toe. Dank curls clung to her forehead in dispirited circlets. Minerva thought, dared hope, that the fever had broken.

"It's all right, Em. It can only be a good sign. Let me find some more clean linens, and in a few minutes you'll be . . ."

"Right as rain" again fluttered across the reliquary of clichés that she was accumulating exclusively for Emmaline's benefit. Deciding once and for all that as a form of comfort, it would never do, she tried to fashion the dry ingredients of a smile into gentle solace. Without words she clasped a capable hand on Emmaline's sodden shoulder. Emmaline's eyes, which would have been lovely if they hadn't been so close together—and actually were rather expressive, if you took them one at a time—broadcast relief. Minerva scurried off to find something suitable in which to dress the bed and its occupant.

Well, this wasn't exactly what she'd had in mind when she'd said that she'd do anything she could, but she was morally certain that acting as a nursing sister at Foothill House had some kind of advantage over digging out of a flood.

Still a month would pass before Karraman Robley set weary foot back in his mansion on the hill. The threat of typhus would quarantine the Valley. Karraman would, for once, allow common sense and an incipient populist fellow-feeling to deter him from crashing the barriers, flaunting his sense of personal invulnerability, and lending his own authoritarian advice and consent and presence to the conduct of Foothill House and the mixed bag of inhabitants therein. Since he had unquenchable optimism (seriously misplaced) about the loyalty of the retainers he assumed to be running the property, and since he had complete confidence in the resilience of both of his women (misplaced too, if only by half), he plunged his waders back into the slime of Saint Kathareen's and kept right on going with the job of restoration.

By sunset each night, Karraman barely cared whether the telephone line to the house was going to be restored or not. (It was, but only when they finished getting the river ooze out of the jacks in the Central switchboard.) He wanted simply to share a few minutes of camaraderie and rotgut with his fellows, to put down a bowl of the steaming mess they were cheerfully dispensing at the soup kitchen in the grammar school, and crawl into his cot at the Armory. He ached to the geographic center of his bones.

After interminable days, the rains stopped, not only in Saint Kathareen's, but upstream on both rivers as well. Some of the upper benchmarks began to come into view. With each new subsidence there came a small, weary, solidly unified infusion of glee to the Kathareenians who were toiling filthily to get things back in place again. Karraman was unkempt. Excruciating blisters, earned at the handle of a shovel here, a guy rope there, had barely begun to harden into callus before new spots rubbed raw. He labored to keep in view the brighter days, which were surely not very far downstream.

None of the damage at the Inn would prove irreparable. Even the rugs had held dry. When he thought about it, Karraman harbored benign fantasies even about Emmaline. Partly he had constructed a wishful vision of the domestication going on at Foothill House; partly there was growing in him an increasing inability to separate Minerva out of the image when he tried to picture "wife." His present vision for eternity, soon to be mercilessly revised, consisted of a delicate blending of Emmaline and Minerva, the real and the ideal, the ridiculous and the sublime. When late-night fatigue let loose its claws long enough for him to yearn across the water to the hill, he thought "Emmaline!" but saw, felt, remembered the face, the voice, the touch of Minerva. Had he thought it out clearly, or discussed the situation with anyone, it would have been quite clear that he had gone slightly mad— a convoluted form of civilian battle fatigue. The malady, fortunately, was to be a temporary one, although throughout his life there would be moments when he would have given his eyeteeth to have been able to retain the illusion.

The march of the floodtide through the Valley had imbued Karraman's life with an undeniable sense of purpose. Selflessly he addressed the task of providing basic needs for the suddenly displaced. As soon as it was possible to enter the Inn by rowboat, he opened as many of the hastily vacated guest rooms as were accessible to the dispirited stragglers or laborers who had nowhere else to go. Tugging pathetic belongings behind bowed backs, they tracked mud and silt and a greasy, underprivileged stench into rooms that had been hitherto unsullied by the indiscreet invasion of the waters.

Cybele stuttered. "This will mean, I mean, Mr. Robley . . . do you mean, what do you mean?"

"It's you who seem to be acting disgustingly mean, Cybele," said Robley. "If the rooms get dirty, clean 'em. Period." He left little doubt, by the thunder of his inflection, that he damn well meant Cybele could clean them himself, hand, knee, and scrub brush, if he couldn't work anything else out. What the hell did that dandy think that every other able-bodied man in the Valley was doing all day and all night, anyway? Hardly sitting around and checking reservations.

Cybele cowered a little, then progressed into his customary resentful submission. Karraman walked away humming a brusque, barely vocal little air. He looked like a man satisfied with his life and the advancing direction of events. He was never to know how differently things were going on the hill from what he could have imagined at his most creative.

While Emmaline's fever had continued to rise and fall, Minerva had continued to cope with it as best she could. That final sweat-drenched morning, when Minerva tentatively deemed the crisis over, had been a false armistice in the cosmic sense. Emmaline's temperature did hold at normal.

Some virulence or other had indeed seeped out of her and the house. In pathetic gratitude, Em had wolfed down Minerva's offering of tea and cinnamon toast. Moments later, before she even had the chance to wipe the last tidbit of crumb from the corner of her mouth, she had chucked it all back up again. All over the linen and the muslin, and this time even the counterpane.

"Oh, Em." A wail of disgust or despair.

Choking and gagging: "I . . . can't . . . help . . . it."

"I know, I know. Just aim for the pail."

More heaving. Then, breathless, contrite. "I shouldn't. Have eaten so. Soon."

"I shouldn't have given it to you so soon."

"Not. Your fault."

"Well, it certainly isn't yours, Em. Here. Just roll over. I'll change the bed like this, and I won't forget to thank Providence that your mother laid in enough washing soda for the whole Confederate Army."

"SheneverharboredaConfederateinherlife!"

"That was just a figure of speech, Em," with a demichuckle. "You rest now. You'll feel better soon."

"I feel as if I never got off that damned boat."

Raising an eyebrow, Minerva twinkled down at the again-restored Emmaline. What she said was, "I know, Em," softly. What she meant was: Well, well! I didn't know you had a spark of blasphemy in you, old girl. Maybe there's a ray of hope left yet!

Gradually it became obvious that the fever was going to stay down. The torments of the nights receded in direct proportion as the rivers. The mornings were something else again.

While there were still the linens to wash, and still no sign of servant or helpmeet to aid her, Minerva silently thanked all the fates for the strength and energy to go on washing. She scrubbed her hands raw, then turned her milliner's gifts to the arranging of rhododendron blossoms, slips of dogwood—anything she could find that would bring the memory of beauty to the tedious atmosphere.

One day, when the sunniest of the peony shrubs had finally been coaxed into bloom by its resident ant colony, Minerva plucked the fairest of its plump pink blossoms. She had admired, on the heavily encrusted oaken sideboard in the dining room, a massive but strangely delicate hand-painted two-piece porcelain punch bowl. It sat high on a separate self-base, which would in turn invert into a large compote, if one chose to make use of it that way. The bowl itself, subtly sculptured at the edges, bore smooth dusty-rose billows of flowers nesting in hazy, soft green bowers. Minerva carried the outfit upstairs piece by piece, in two trips, to make sure that nothing dropped or scratched. Then she filled the bowl with water drawn from the bathtub, and floated the peony in the center. It looked as if it had been born there. She set the whole arrangement on a vanity just opposite the foot of the bed. A perfect setting, she decided. Low enough for Emmaline to admire from the bed, elegantly reflected in the triptych mirror of the vanity. Minerva hadn't needed to displace a thing to find its home. Emmaline's battalions of unguents and masks still rested within reach on her bed stand. What she hadn't needed were still packed since her trip from the Inn.

Minerva's creative sense had been chafing. She thought she had repressed it in the mixed rewards of her labors, but she took inordinate satisfaction in the sight of the fresh, uncluttered, artfully placed peony. It reminded her of a hat—and didn't; proved to her that she could still translate her gifts to any unlikely locus, create a small island of form and freshness wherever she chose, justify her existence as an artist or artisan, even while she structured her time as a body slave.

And, as no small part of her pleasure, bring joy to Emmaline, whom she could not bring herself to despise.

Emmaline opened her eyes to an unspoken cue, having slept or feigned sleep through the unsubtly muted bustle of arrangements. Minerva watched her focus into awareness, comprehending without embarrassment that what she wanted from Emmaline at that moment was a word of praise, an appreciation, a word that expressed a feeling of sisterhood, that acknowledged Minerva's own humanity.

The pathetic wraith in the bed had vanished. The touching frailty, the hook which had snared Minerva's sympathy, had fled with the night. Not that the wasted frame had suddenly rematerialized as the burly specimen who had married Karraman Robley. No, the figure nestled in the slightly rumpled but for once largely immaculate trousseau bedding looked as if it would take two of her to fill the real Emmaline's wedding dress. It wasn't that. Rather, it was the voice. Tone, inflection, tempo—all of it took Minerva back in a whirlwind to the very first of their encounters in the lobby of the Inn. It was as ugly as sin, as demanding as Satan. Minerva thought she could see Emmaline's entire visage transform back into something awful at the single vocal cue.

"And who, may I ask. Placed that object. On my vanity?" She might have been referring to excrement, or worse. Minerva, in the interests of maintaining the household that had held together so far, chose not to reply, but set about efficiently removing the arrangement.

"Who, I said." Bellowed, not asked.

"Really, Emmaline, with just two of us in the house, the possibilities are somewhat limited, don't you think?" Her answer was spurred by rising ire, but tempered by a sudden debilitating fatigue.

"I deserve at least. The courtesy. Of a reply." She might as well have been talking to a stranger with some repulsive deformity that rendered real confrontation out of the question.

"Emmaline," through teeth clenched like a fist, "I can't begin to tell you what you deserve." And wheeled out of the room, defiantly carrying the arrangement with her. Only to dart right back in, sloshing water all the way down the front of her dress and practically losing the peony, when Emmaline gasped, "Min . . . the basin . . ." and promptly threw up into the punch bowl, which Minerva had automatically proffered as the receptacle nearest at hand. All over the peony. When she had caught her breath again, contrition crept into her first imploring word. "Minerva—"

"Em, just shut up. Don't say anything. Don't talk about the punch bowl. Don't apologize. Most of all, don't apologize. I could no more bear the thought of having to grant forgiveness to you just now than I could swim the white-water rapids upstream, and I don't do well in a farm pond. Now, I'll be back to change you in a few minutes. You just sit still."

"But, Minerva—" As close to supplication as she would ever get in her life.

"Later, Emmaline. *Not now.* For the time being, just you leave me alone, and I'll leave you alone, and we'll both feel much better about everything."

She wanted to thunder down the stairs, to crash and barrel through the house, but her noxious burden prevented her. As it was, she set it down so percussively when she finally arrived, trembling, at the kitchen sink, that the base chipped. That alone would have been bad enough, but its reverberations trembled through the bowl itself, and started a hairline crack which looked exactly like part of the tracery of the design, except that Minerva knew it wasn't. She expected the whole thing to vibrate out in a huge web and shatter into her hands. She expected an explosion, brimstone, lava bubbles among the regurgitated gobbets of whatever Emmaline had eaten last. Holding it like a steaming caldron in her bare hands, Minerva thrust her way out the kitchen door, through the mudroom, into the yard. With all her reserves of strength, she tossed the bowl, pedestal, contents, praying that the earth would swallow them.

Instead, porcelain collided with shale and crashed with epic volume on a stepping-stone right underneath Emmaline's open side window. Rapidly the liquid contents merged with the muck and slimy residue of all the rain, and slid anonymously on down the slope. On the relatively flat slab of rock where they had landed, hand-painted shards lay, disgraced, looking all the more incongruous for the bruised peony leaves scattered randomly among them.

Minerva, not exactly contrite, but nevertheless aware that she was not at liberty to play havoc with Emmaline's personal property, either, bent to see what she could salvage. The answer was clear and immediate: nothing. As she straightened her aching back, she glanced upward and caught the unmistakable image of Emmaline's stealthy form at the curtains.

If indecision consumed Minerva for more than the flicker of a hummingbird's wing, she never showed it. With lips set, she turned defiantly back to the house to remount the horse that had thrown her. She didn't bother to rehearse the fusillade of words she would aim at Emmaline. Unconsciously she knew better than to dribble such fury through the strainer of her reason. Her intention echoed through her footfalls. She threw open the door to Emmaline's bedroom with a regal flair.

And faced, not two feet away, a pallid and bedraggled Emmaline, eyes streaming, struggling to bundle the rancid bed linens into a parcel for the laundry chute.

"Oh, Em, for God's sake, let me do that."

Emmaline crumpled quite noiselessly to the floor, and buried her head in upturned palms. "I've ruined everything." Snuffling.

Minerva could imagine the snot mucking up Emmaline's hands, her face, her clothing, the floor on which there was not yet, thank goodness, a priceless rug. Something held her to the spot, however, and kept her from running to fetch one of the hoard of Emmaline's lacy handkerchiefs.

Emmaline's volume increased. "I'll never be well again. I tried to change the bed, and it stinks so. And *I* stink. If Karraman ever comes home, he'll think he's wandered into a slaughterhouse by mistake." Snuffle. "Or a morgue."

"Now, Em," softening, "nothing is as bad as all that. We're taking care of things as we go along, aren't we, and it's not going so badly. Besides, by the time Karraman can get back across the Sargasso Sea out there, you'll be well, and the house will be in fine order, and everything's going to smell just like summer."

"Horse manure."

"Emmaline!"

"That's what Saint Kathareen's always smells like in summer: horse manure."

Laughing. "Well, springtime, then. Whatever you like. When he gets home, the lord of the manor will never even believe that the battlements have been under siege. Trust me."

Emmaline, having wiped her eyes, nose, mouth, on her sleeve, looked with naive gratitude up at Minerva. "Min, oh, Min . . . I never would have survived any of this without you. You've kept it all from going to pieces."

In view of what had just befallen the punch bowl, Minerva found Emmaline's choice of words a bit peculiar. However, no malice lurked in her eyes or her voice. No one, not even the elder Mrs. Musgrove, ever mentioned the punch bowl again, at least not in Minerva's presence. Minerva, guilty, pussyfooted around the subject for some time, waiting.

Finally she decided that Emmaline must have realized every friendship has its price, and that for Minerva's companionship and thoroughly reliable support, this was indeed a negligible tariff.

Some months later, after a business trip to Savannah, Karraman brought home a beautiful Rose Medallion bowl that had been imported all the way from China. It would have bought and paid for the porcelain many times over. Emmaline kept it on the vanity opposite the bed in the master bedroom, and fresh flowers were placed in it daily.

One day Maybelle Kennebec came back. She bore the grand epithet Laundress, but actually she considered herself, among other things, the official keeper of Emmaline's life, possessions, and sacred honor. She had midwifed Emmaline's own birth, and considered herself entitled to access to Emmaline's soul and her household. All this was true in spite of the fact that she possessed neither the organizational ability nor the proper degree of sanctimonious noblesse oblige to have been designated Housekeeper in all her years of indenture to the Musgroves. That, to her, was mere formality. In Maybelle Kennebec's dance of life, she alone called the tune.

No one could figure out why she had fled Foothill House when the flood came. She and her namesake daughter, Maybelle Two, had been assigned by seniority to the most capacious and attractive of the servants' suites. Her own shanty, still occupied by an undifferentiated assortment of her grown stepchildren and their incestuous progeny, stood less than half a mile down from the Robley property on the hill. Maybelle had been overjoyed to move herself and Maybelle Junior out of the squalid and leaky frame house over into respectability. In equal measure, she was pleased that the live-in employment with the Robleys, a step up from all those years of day work with the Musgroves, would keep her closer to home on the hill, blood and water being what they are. Problem was, of course, that Maybelle had a time distinguishing the one from the other, especially when she was drunk. Those periods were only intermittent, but they struck with gale force.

Maybelle's own house, despite the leaks and sags, faced no greater danger from the incursion of the floodwaters themselves than any other structure more than halfway up Calvin-and-Levi. Despite optical illusion to the contrary, it lay acres out of the flood plain. Her family, safe in its very numbers, hardly needed the brambles of Maybelle's personality as an additional obstacle on their journey through the testy days. Nor did they particularly need the two extra mouths to help them deplete the paltry pantry stores. The raspberries, their only cash crop as sold in individual pint boxes to whichever of the specialty grocers down street were buying on steamy June mornings, had washed downhill in rivulets of mud. The moldy specimens left were hardly fit for piecing. Still, with things as tight as they were, for whatever reasons she never explained to a soul, Maybelle chose to sit out the worst amid the friction and the clatter of her own four creaking walls. She stayed drunk, somewhere between coherent and brainless, for the entire time.

At last she, or her poor abused digestive tract, decided one day that enough was enough. She pushed the jug aside, and slept the sleep of the dead for four whole hours. At five o'clock one breezy morning, she nudged Maybelle Junior awake and told her in no uncertain terms that they were going to be late to Miss Emmaline's if they didn't get themselves and their clothes cleaned up right smart right now. She gave no indication that she hadn't appeared for work yesterday, or the day before, or the day before that, or for countless days and weeks stretching back into a former season. She could not then or later give any adequate explanation of her tacit acceptance that Miss Emmaline was indeed "on the place," but she asserted forever after that, planned honeymoon notwithstanding, "Maybelle knowed," she knowed. Nor did it ever occur to her that anyone in either of her two households would question or upbraid her for any part of her behavior, either the absence or the triumphant comeback.

The two Maybelles slogged over spongy lawns and avoided the pond-sized puddles where they could. When they arrived at the circular driveway leading to Foothill House, they found the cobblestones grown mossy from weeks of disuse, and the moss grown slimy from the incessant moisture in the air. Intrepid, they negotiated the treacherous footing, and burst into the formal foyer just in time to hear Emmaline scream with unalloyed horror.

Maybelle Fille started like a nervous squirrel. She looked as if she would gladly have swum back to the crowded, rickety shack, where at least no banshees were in residence. Maybelle Mère, equipped with a less perturbable nature and also a backlog of experience, more and less sordid, with Miss Emmaline Musgrove, grabbed her skittish child by the nearest blond pigtail. Instinctive reflex, old as the hill, told her roughly from what segment of Emmaline's humanity that screech had emanated.

Minerva, who thought Emmaline had surely exhausted her repertoire of unearthly noises in the weeks preceding, had come flying out of the parlor clutching a copper watering can with a serviceably long spout. At the sight of the two disheveled creatures in the vicinity of the staircase, she almost thought that she had apprehended the perpetrators of whatever ghastly deed had driven Em to these new heights of vocal virtuosity. Then she realized that they were heading up the stairs, precisely the opposite direction from a path of flight.

"Stop!"

She wielded the watering can like the barrier at a railroad crossing. "What's going on here?"

Maybelle Kennebec, her pale Appalachian visage frozen into the granite of intent, barely bothered to appraise Minerva, who was, in her opinion, the only obvious intruder in the ointment. "Honey, y'all dassn't get in Maybelle's way when Miss Emmaline's a-callin'. Y'hear?"

If Minerva had been one to nonplus easily, that undoubtedly would have done the trick. Her character being what it was, she simply fell into step with what was obviously a more knowledgeable procession to the upper regions of the house than she could have conducted herself.

Rounding the landing neck and neck, Minerva and Maybelle aimed instinctively for the crack of light framing the slightly open bathroom door.

On the chilly white tile they found Emmaline. She lay curled into a ball, her knees clasped to her chest. The small of her back she had braced against the fluted base of the sink. Minerva winced as she thought of the ridges it would dig in the brittle flesh. Emmaline's nightgown was stained. In the unflushed toilet floated a mess of blood and tissue and nothing else Minerva could recognize.

Minerva and Maybelle shot queries at each other's eyes. Whoever was the asker and whoever the respondent, they both understood what was happening.

Hefty Maybelle the Younger, who had been squeezed out of the race at the turn, clomped in, breathless and excited. "Ma?"

"Git down them stairsteps and start the water t'boilin'."

"Is she dead, Ma?" eyes aglow.

"You heard me. Move."

"But, Ma—"

"I said do it, Miss Uppity. I didn't say wait till the new moon."

Her offspring clomped out reluctantly. Minerva began to croon small consolations to Emmaline, who was by that time emitting large, pitiful sobs interspersed with nauseating snuffs and coughs and hackings. Reaching for a washcloth with one hand, Minerva continued to smooth back Emmaline's hair with the other. Maybelle tolerated that for the better part of seven seconds. Then she clasped Emmaline's available shoulder with an iron grip. Minerva watched with fascination.

"Now, listen up, Emmaline Musgrove."

Emmaline practically snapped to attention. "Maybelle! Thank God you're here!" Renewed sobbing.

"Now, Miss Emmaline, how do you expect me ever to see you through childbed and all, with you settin' up such a caterwaulin' about losin' one so early on? Why, it ain't even a babe worth swaddlin' yet."

A wide-eyed pause, followed by a blanching shock of comprehension. "Do you mean to tell me that *that's* what happened to me? Oh, my God." She threw her head back to the tile with such fury that it would have cracked if Minerva's knee hadn't been at just the right spot to cushion the blow. Also, it absorbed the impact from both sides at once. And knocked Minerva off balance. And pulled Maybelle down for good measure, since she had failed to compensate her shoulder grip for the corrected angle of Minerva's fall.

Thus, when Maybelle Junior appeared at the door to announce sullenly that she couldn't find no matches nowhere nohow, in a house well enough equipped with matches and candles to serve as an overendowed tinderbox, Minerva didn't know whether to laugh or cry at the whole absurd situation. Gathering herself in, she thought for a moment of the child that had been lost. Karraman's child. And decided that the best thing to do was to get busy, clean up Emmaline again, and restore some kind of order to Foothill House.

Emmaline didn't have the strength to push her away, but Maybelle finished the job. At least in spirit.

"Who's she, Miss Emmaline?" gesturing over her shoulder toward Minerva.

"Oh, that's Minerva. Nobody." Then, as she rose into a private universe containing only herself and Maybelle, on their plodding way back to the bedroom, "Oh, Maybelle, I can't begin to tell you how hard the last weeks have been on me . . ." as she rested herself on the crutch of Maybelle's questionable support.

"Poor baby. You more'n likely had to do chores and drudgery you never was in your life drug up to do."

Sigh. Assent, but so martyred, so brave. "Maybelle, no one will ever know. . . ."

From the day Maybelle arrived until the day Karraman appeared a full two weeks later, Emmaline barely offered a sidelong glance to Minerva. Maybelle did, because she knew she had seen Minerva somewhere, and couldn't find her way back through the alcoholic haze to place it. Instead, she remained stricken with the notion that Minerva was some new breed of servant, hired expressly to usurp her own rightful place at Emmaline's side. Minerva couldn't have been more relieved to have another body in the house to take over the duties of the laundry, if nothing else. Naturally Emmaline did nothing to dispel Maybelle's misapprehension, so Maybelle barricaded the way to the washtubs. Minerva, after a single game attempt to shoulder her part, let it go without a regret.

Her next move was off the chaise longue and into a smaller, more blessedly private bedroom. Whatever conversations took place between Emmaline and Maybelle regarding her selection of sleeping quarters or anything else, Minerva neither heard nor chose to hear. She caught Maybelle-the-child regarding her quizzically whenever their paths happened to cross, but Minerva managed to stifle whatever conversational urges she had with very little difficulty. She was content to wander in the gardens, potter reservedly in the kitchen, commit to her sketchbook the effulgence of ideas she had conceived and stored mentally during the long days and nights of her indenture to Emmaline.

Daily Minerva made it a point to check Emmaline, to exchange a pleasantry or two, if "exchange" was the proper description. Daily she was tersely assured that her services were not required, so she returned to her solitary occupations in relative peace. She enjoyed the release, she enjoyed the reflection; she relished the freedom from bondage to another human being.

Since the rivers had finally begun rapidly, noticeably to recede, a restoration of the status quo in Saint Kathareen's seemed within reach. On that basis, Minerva went about her business, planned, sketched. She worked out several drafts, each one increasingly intricate, of a system whereby her hats could be fashioned on an assembly line of sorts, up to the point where she or a trained assistant would apply the individualizing and striking ·handwork details. It strained her own credulity to think that the fruits of her brain, so carefully worked through and yet so inchoate, somehow, would ever come to that. Then again, when she reflected upon the present state of her life, she could hardly believe any of that either.

Finally, on an innocent and memoryless summer day, the little ferry started to run again. A rivalrous excitement, a quiet little contentiousness, suffused Foothill House. Emmaline dressed herself importantly in a dusty-rose faille suit which was not only inappropriate for the season but also miles too big for her since she had lost so much weight. She positioned herself among the fringes of the formal parlor, looking like a relic, but not as useful. Maybelle had materialized a black uniform out of somewhere. It came complete with starched white apron and frilled cap. Somehow she managed to keep her frowsy air intact despite the primness of the getup. Still, there was no mistaking the festive anticipation over all. Maybelle Junior appeared with two unmatched bows haphazardly adorning her pigtails. Minerva recognized one of the ribbons from the small hoard of materials she had hastily assembled and brought over on the night the dam broke. She kept her counsel with Maybelle Two on the grounds that reprimand would be lost on anyone amoral enough to display the booty with such impunity in front of the victim of the looting. Why waste precious energy on anger in all this heat? Besides, there was no reason to overturn so delicate a domestic balance as the one currently obtaining, over a simple piece of pilfered ribbon.

Minerva looked fresh, slender, artless. She stood much in the background when Karraman mounted the front steps. He put his arm around Emmaline, who simpered audibly. "Beautiful girl," he told his wife, "it seems like a lifetime since we were together." But Minerva knew infallibly and forever that he was looking directly at her.

Minerva could smell Karraman's essence, he was that close. He could barely, nor did he try to, hide the proprietary satisfaction in his smile.

"Well. Well, well. Foothill House seems to have done well in my absence."

Simultaneously: "Certainly, Karraman"—Minerva.

"Well enough, I suppose"—petulant counterpoint, directed straight toward a forthcoming litany of complaint.

Which Karraman nipped in the bud. Ostensibly he was addressing his wife. Actually he was responding to Minerva.

"Excellent, excellent." An engine, he rolled right on. "Then you'll be delighted to know, my dear, that Minerva will be staying on with us for a while."

"What?" croaked Emmaline.

Even Minerva's eyes went several phases wider.

"Oh, Karraman, your hospitality is too generous. But the time has really come. I mean, I must get back to my own place and start getting to work on the—"

Emmaline's interjection of enthusiastic accord was unprecedented in Minerva's experience. "Oh yes, it's high time."

Karraman quashed both of them in a stroke. "Minerva," impaling her on the gentle sword of his voice, "politeness has its place, but I'm afraid that this is absolutely not it."

"Karraman!" Emmaline sounded as if she were gargling.

Caution, excitement, trepidation crept into Minerva's newly chinked armor. "What do you mean? I'm afraid I don't understand, Karraman." She gestured toward the northeast. "The ferry's running. I can see the streets again. So what if they're a little muddy? Do you think I've never seen mud before, for heaven's sake? What d'you think they've built the mountains out of, Valley bricks?" Her grin reflected her proud perspective on her trip out. "Besides, Karraman"—she paused solemnly—"you're here now."

"Ah, Min, if only this were as simple as you make it out to be."

"Oh! You don't mean . . . Is it something about the quarantine?"

"Quarantine? What quarantine?" The ruddy rose of Emmaline's furious face had begun to outdust the hue of her outfit. It was the most color Minerva had seen in her cheeks since the wedding.

If Karraman was surprised either that one of the women in the house was aware of the situation or that the other wasn't, he didn't betray himself. Minerva thought that was a shame: the explanation would have tickled him.

When word of the quarantine had come flashing across the river in Morse code, Minerva had painstakingly separated out the dots and the dashes. She had closed her eyes and thanked her stars for a childhood in which she had never been denied access to such modern innovations as the telegraph office on Ralston Street. The overweight young man who operated the key had pretended to be annoyed with her, but actually had worked with diligent, secret pride on teaching her the Morse alphabet at every gap in his round of getting and sending. Minerva had learned her lessons well enough.

Reading the scattered and ominous messages broadcast for the general welfare from across the river, Minerva had reflected that Mr. Morse's convenient little system was at least as responsible for her being in Saint Kathareen's as any other single factor. She had been so thoroughly imbued with a sense of easily spanned distances, at such an early age, that leaving New England when she left Hammond Bolton gave her no more real pause than the interval between dah and dit. Everything was reachable. And thus did she muse, sitting in a darkened monster of a house, staring at the flooded earth below, reading in code the message that her only link to civilization in this forsaken valley was shadowed by the threat of a plague. She had shivered with excitement. The whole drama was as distant as Mars, as near as her wits. She was living by them now as surely as she had in her westward wagon.

For a time she had declined to share the information from the other shore with Emmaline because she thought that Em was too ill to accept the news without potentially drastic shock to her entire system. When Emmaline had improved, the danger seemed to have abated to the populace as well as to Em. Minerva decided it would be cruel and superfluous to burden her with something that might still cause consternation on account of her own family and Karraman. Finally, with Emmaline on the road to recovery, and firmly in league with Maybelle against Minerva and all reason, Minerva stubbornly avoided the occasion of having to give up a whisper of her private self if it wasn't required. That included the intelligence that terse messages had indeed been flashing irregularly across the darkness.

"The quarantine's lifted, Emmaline." Offhand, but impatient. "How

[156]

would I be standing here and trying to talk civilly, if it weren't?" Emmaline just stood there looking gawky. Karraman's tone shifted subtly. "No, Min. It isn't the quarantine. It's the hotel."

A sharp intake of breath from Minerva. "What do you mean? Has something happened?"

"No, nothing's happened," a coded explanation to an understanding ear that despite tempest and inundation, reasonable organization still prevailed, and normal conditions were at least foreseeable, if not already established. "We've had to reassign the rooms, that's all."

Emmaline decided to recover. "Reassign? What do you mean, reassign?" Not knowing remotely what to imagine, she knew that she didn't like the sound of it. "Karraman, I asked you what exactly that is supposed to mean, reassign?" She didn't need to add that it was her right to know. All hands present already understood that she felt that way.

Karraman decided not to inform her that he had heard her asking what he meant, reassign. He simply declined to reply.

"The Valley is teeming with refugees, Min. We opened the Inn as soon as we could run a raft to the front door. Everyone has helped in one way or another." He stared at Emmaline, his voice as much a dare as a warning. "No one ever knows how much good labor there is in an honest soul until the hard times come."

"A-men," keened Maybelle from somewhere. Nobody paid any attention.

Minerva thought with a strange remoteness that the word "labor" would probably bring Emmaline up short. Any minute, she feared, Em would remember to match Karraman's recounting of his ordeal with her own, horror for horror. Then, of course, she would stand, frail but starchy, waiting to accept her award for the Most Valiant Survivor of Anything, Ever. Minerva felt tentative, disengaged. What if Karraman's lost, unformed child had the power to draw tight the bindings of guilt, pity, ownership—any of the components of family—around him and Emmaline for good and all? Minerva wondered, from a distance outside herself, how she might assess her strength to bear that possibility, when all the blood had suddenly left her hands, her feet, her brain, and flowed into one hard, pulsating bolus located just at the base of her throat. She couldn't swallow. . . .

But Emmaline bypassed her own advantage like the dauntless leader of a suicide mission. "Refugees? What do you mean, refugees?"

"I mean, Emmaline, what one normally means when he says 'refugees.' I mean homeless victims of a devastation. I mean, I might add," looking at the clotted paraphernalia of opulence around him, "people far less fortunate than we are."

"I daresay. Well." New direction. Minerva watched keenly. "Karraman, our hotel has maintained standards of quality and discretion for generations now." She was jabbering far too quickly to have caught the elevation of Karraman's eyebrows as she casually appropriated ownership of the Inn all to herself. Fascinated, Minerva watched while the gesture drew attention to a vein at Karraman's temple which she had never noticed in all their times together. Its rhythms amplified the thudding Minerva still felt at her gorge. She wondered if that were visible, too.

Emmaline, oblivious, ran right on. "Don't you think, Karraman, that you might have been just a little more selective about opening the doors to just anyone? After all, your father could hardly enjoy seeing the splendid reputation of several generations resolving into a dew overnight, thanks to your charitable little impulses, could he?"

Karraman's expression had modified from displeasure to disbelief to contempt, beneath which Emmaline obviously fell at that moment.

Oblivious. "How disgustingly"—she poked around the rancid oils of her brain pan for a word—"sullied." Mean, triumphant.

"Perhaps, then, my *dear* Emmaline, you'd better not sully yourself with the likes of me. After all, don't forget that I'm the one responsible for the sullying."

Karraman angrily hurtled himself in the direction of the car that had brought him up from the wharf. Minerva stood momentarily paralyzed with the perverted sense of having won a competitive battle and at the same time, in a not quite delineated way, having lost the war. She had no time to clarify her thoughts, although they boiled down to a very simply essence: under present circumstances, her cachet with Karraman depended very heavily upon a symbiosis of needs among herself, him, and Emmaline. Until normal conditions returned to the Valley, she was stuck. If Karraman walked out on Emmaline, he was walking out on both of them.

Except that Karraman wasn't walking out on anyone. Before Minerva even puzzled up to her first labyrinthine turn of mind, Karraman was back up the walk, lugging baggage that included bits and pieces of her own and Emmaline's, as well as his.

"Here, Karraman, let me help." Her offer was a prayer of thanks.

"Don't bother, Min," chugging gamely. "This is all there is. I'm not even sure what I brought. Don't worry—everything is safely stowed back at the Inn. But, you know, material geegaws start not to mean much when we're bending backs to the breaking point just trying to keep a town from going under. And I mean going under."

Minerva rushed to take one of the straw cases from Karraman. She brushed his hand, at least partly by accident.

His index finger shot out like an adder's tongue, trapping her fingers for the whisper of a moment. "Are you all right?"

"I'm all right."

"You and Em have," pointedly, "managed."

Her eyes smiled, but she replied solemnly. "Did you ever think that we wouldn't?"

"No. Never."

"Good."

Emmaline took in what she saw, from her remove, as a tender pantomime. She missed the dialogue, and wouldn't have understood its import if it had been illuminated for her in Gothic script. She did know that she felt insulted, but she couldn't come up with the words to meet the occasion. She tried to pivot smartly, but she almost tripped as she caught her heel in the ridiculous swish of faille and crinoline. Recovering equilibrium, she cast a poisonous look at Minerva, and went off to seek whatever consolation she could among the geegaws.

IX

Hawk, replete with anecdote, stops the Healey at the gas station at the downtown end of the bridge. He fills the tank, and goes to pay the cashier inside the cubicle of a building. As he returns to the car, Cara pulls up beside him.

"I thought you were working afternoons," he greets her.

"I am. Later."

"Then what are you doing way the hell down here?" The state hospital is out Old 60, the other direction from the farm.

"I was going to meet you up on the hill. Then I saw your car. Anyway, it works out fine. I want to leave mine to have the oil changed."

"You know, it's really hard to keep up with you. If you had wanted to come with me in the first place, all you had to do was say so. She'd have been perfectly happy to have had you come," flatly.

"How about you, Hawk? How happy would *you* have been if I had up and gone along?"

"Look, Cara, I'm not up to playing games. Just tell me what in the hell it is that you want to do, and we'll take it from there." Hawk is frustrated because Cara has clearly made up her mind to trespass on his territory with Miss Minerva, and now he wants to revoke the halfhearted invitation altogether. Everything is so disjunctive. He needs to regain his ground, but cannot see well enough through the layered fog to tell exactly what is forfeit. He needs time.

"I want to meet her. It's time. Nobody knows more about this Valley than she does. Everybody else is dead. Maybe she can talk to me about some of the things I need to know. Obviously no one else will," she appends sarcastically.

Hawk is burning because what she calls a need strikes him as a whim or fancy. He understands that Cara's intrusion, for that is how he sees it, will alter the parameters of his relationship with Minerva permanently. He is as angry with himself as he is with everyone else, in or out of sight.

"Look, Cara, do you have to put your life together on my nickel?" Getting into the car, furious, but obviously waiting for Cara to come along and hold up her end of things.

"Jesus, Hawk," as he skids out into the street, narrowly missing a collision with a station wagon.

"What do you mean, Jesus Hawk? I always thought it was Jesus Christ, simpleton Hawk." Now he is shouting for sure. "She's *my* old lady."

Cara's eyes narrow. Hawk realizes the absurd layers of innuendo he has brought down. Yet the false notion that he sleeps, or does something even more kinky, with a woman into her tenth decade of life does not bother him nearly as much as what he really meant, which is that he resents anybody poaching on the territory he has painstakingly staked out with Minerva Bolton.

And it isn't even Cara's fault. One warm night on a lonely highway she suggested a riddle, and Hawk wove it into a schematic drawing. He has, by his own offices, tantalized Cara into wishing distance of this relationship, and now he resents the intrusion.

Hawk, not Cara, has been the one fixated upon Minerva all along. That gracious old woman has brought windows to his tunnel, invited him to step through the leaded looking glass into worlds he never dreamed or sang. He had not realized that the windows were there to be breached. He's not ready to lose, share, dilute this relationship. Minerva is his tour guide, his wizard, his unlikely guru.

"Hawk?" Back to normal decibels, gentling.

"What?" Still sharp-edged.

"Who is she, really? She does know everything about everybody in this town, doesn't she? I just have an image of her carrying around a huge brass key ring in her mind, and it can unlock anything. Please, Hawk." Sweating anguish.

"No," carefully. "I don't think you have the right picture, Cara," tiptoeing on eggshells of truth. "I think she's just a polite little old lady who caught the genealogy bug. What does that have to do with you? Nothing, that's what."

Many beats pass. Cara wants more than that, Hawk knows it, doesn't have the thrust, the tenacity, to birth it.

"Hawk," determinedly, abandoning the minuet, "what if she knows something about my family?"

"Come off it, Cara."

"No, Hawk. It's not impossible."

No response. Cara swallows, raises her head a notch, staring straight ahead.

"I mean, really, Cara. So you landed in Saint Kathareen's because the name looked like something you found in an old letter. Big deal. Look, I know what it's like to be out here in never-never land, wanting like hell to be a part of something or other. To be family." He is rattling because he's swirling so fast on the carousel of his own guilts that he doesn't know how to get off. "Good Christ," he tacks on, not quite irrelevantly, "we're so far west of the Hudson out here that folks think the Hudson is the jalopy Cousin Denzil has jacked up on Coke boxes out back. But there are fantasies and fantasies. You can't let it take you up like that. Expectations only get you into trouble."

Silence.

"Besides," into the breach, "you don't know anything about her."

"Oh, Hawk, honestly. That tears it. I know everything about her. You never talk about anything else."

Hawk comprehends her hyperbole, glides right over it as he corners onto the last several miles of Old 60 to the farm.

"Cara," he argues, as if his non sequitur were in itself sufficient data to conclude the argument, "she started making hats on the very first night she got into Saint Kathareen's."

Cara's eyes are about to ignite. "Hawk, so what? That doesn't mean she never took time to do anything else, like live her life."

Hawk, knowing he sounds absurd, flails on. "Cara, I'm only trying to make you understand. She worked day and night, hardly had a private life of her own," a statement absolutely true and absolutely false in such blatant proportions that it's a wonder he can fit it all into one sentence. "She always kept a suite on the third floor of the Inn so that she could be living right where she was working."

"So what?"

"So what? So she was the Valley's first bona fide tastemaker, is what. The old girls loved her. They monopolized her day and night, is what. Her life was their life." He's distorting more and more wildly, getting deeper and deeper. "They'd have tea served by a liveried butler, all the exclusive works a New World aristocrat could have asked for. And the young matrons— well, for them, going to Minerva's was practically a *rite de passage. That's* what."

"*What?*"

"Rite of passage. You know. Like in New Guinea. Margaret Mead—"

"I know about Margaret Mead, Hawk."

"Well, you didn't know about *rite de passage.*"

"Of course I did. I just couldn't understand your accent, that's all."

"Cara, is my accent the point of this conversation? Because if it is—"

"It isn't, but I'm not sure you understand what is."

"*Me* not understand? Look, Cara, if you think that Minerva Bolton has any more to do with your life than . . . Margaret Mead . . . Goddammit, Cara, why don't you just quit pushing?"

Then Hawk stops short. Cara isn't pushing at all. It is he, Hawk, who is giving her the very reinforcement she seeks for the idea that he wants to obliterate. Right when the argument is neatly shunted onto the siding of the millinery business, Hawk himself has pulled the switch back to the main line.

But Cara doubles back on him. "What makes you think that everything has to be exactly the way you see it? You must have a terribly limited interpretation of human capability, especially when it comes to women. The old biddies had to go home sometime, and when they did, I'll bet Minerva had the energy of two normal people. What did you tell me she had? Three hundred employees? Executive dining room, of all things?"

"It was an employees' dining room," he mutters. "And *four* hundred."

"Well, whatever. It still sounds to me like she was resourceful enough to keep her private life separated from anything she wanted to be away from. And I'll bet that the more mysteries she left dangling, the more Saint Kathareen's ate it up. Why, she could have had twenty bastard children and this bloodthirsty little paradise would have lapped it up like cream."

"Are you crazy? That makes absolutely no sense at all. What are you trying to do, Cara? You can't rebuild her life to suit your identity problems."

Hawk's attack jolts Cara, who had actually been building up an unanticipated steam of affection for the old girl. "Hey, that was a bull's-eye, Hawk. Right on the cheap-shot target. Which happens to be about five hundred miles away from the main point."

Hawk mellows back a couple of notches. "Okay. I didn't mean that. I guess." As much of an apology as he can muster. He's getting ready to get back into the center ring.

"If you didn't mean it, then why did you say it?"

"You won't let it go, will you?" He is preparing to ignite. "I said it because I wanted to, dammit. Oh, shit."

He is driving offensively now, cutting into the inbound side of the two-lane highway because the discussion isn't getting anywhere, and he feels that the least he can do is make some progress on the road. The tractor

[163]

ahead has edged to the berm to allow passage, but Hawk doesn't realize until a horn dopplers him back to sanity that the passage is reserved for an empty milk tanker already barreling its way past both him and the tractor on the way back to cow heaven. He veers back into line, narrowly avoiding a fender-to-fender confrontation with the tractor. He purses a ballooning collection of epithets behind narrowed lips.

Cara has never seen him out of control of the car, either. She inhales, exhales, inhales again. Breath still controlled, lungs partially retentive, not relaxed. "Hawk."

"What." He is trying with just fair success to force the adrenaline levels back down.

"We were talking about what happened to Minerva. So she became successful. That's wonderful. Big deal. Are you actually trying to tell me that you think a woman can't have a success trip and a private life at the same time? You think the success thing is only the prerogative of someone who's willing to sacrifice a normal home life and family? Because if that's what you're telling me, and it sure sounds like it is, your ideology sucks."

Hawk jams on the brakes, not oblivious of the chaos he is creating in the line of traffic behind him, but not precisely caring about it, either.

"My ideology sucks? What about your manipulating, conniving . . . Or is it only open season on me today? What about using a little righteous common sense here, Cara? We're talking about the year nineteen hundred and aught six, not the last enlightened quarter of this glorious century. Don't make me out to be the pig, because that's not where it is, or where I am, and you know it. If you'd ever gone to any real school after you got that nurse's diploma in your hot little hand—"

"Hawk."

In the phlegmatic mode of the Valley, the drivers behind the Healey are gaping at Hawk and Cara as if voyeurism were their dower right. At least they are keeping their opinions to themselves, although the line of traffic is beginning to stretch back to Kentucky.

And Hawk, sickened, knows for an absolute certainty that he has gone too far. He and Cara are alone in a universe, and the universe is expanding between them. The heavy air fills with sour rancor.

"Cara, I didn't mean that. I meant . . ."

His experience of human dialogue decrees a two-measure rest, into which Cara is supposed to rush with tender dispensations, a hand on the thigh, or somewhere. And: It's all right, Hawk. You're all right by me.

But Cara has no intention of helping him out of the hole. Coolly she sits back and lets him idle out the guilt. Although there is virtually nowhere for her to move in her bucket seat without actually getting out of the car, Hawk has the distinct impression that Cara has receded into some remotely visible

[164]

but thoroughly unattainable distance. He feels a sober panic, is suddenly bereft, laden with cosmic emptiness in the space between him and Cara. She has wrapped her total communicative self inside the antique paisley piano shawl which formerly adorned only her shoulders and her drawn-up knees. Without moving an inch, she has totally fled.

Hawk throws the car back into gear. One driver, attempting to pass him just as he decides to accelerate back into highway comformity, shoots Hawk a dirty look. With poise and fury, Hawk returns the favor with the official finger. He has never performed that public gesture in his life, thinking it far beneath his dignity and certainly unequal to honest rage. Furious at his own lack of self-control, he blames Cara. Who doesn't even emerge from her swaddle to catch the silent fit he's pitching.

They reach the turnoff to the farm. Hawk peels into third gear, raising choking dust around the flying gravel. At the top of the hill he exhales so fully that it seems he has been holding his breath ever since downtown Saint Kathareen's, fourteen glacial miles ago. He pulls into his parking place beside the disused chicken coops. Cara opens her door before Hawk has finished his power-off ritual. Usually companionable, she customarily stays for the closing festivities, then walks with him to the house, admiring the terrain as it changes with the light and the seasons. This time Cara gets out with neither a bang nor a whimper.

"Cara! Wait!"

She turns back, her face a passive study.

"Cara—"

"Don't tell me you're sorry, okay, Hawk? Just don't tell me you're sorry."

"Jesus, Cara, I have a right."

"A right. Just what kind of right did you have in mind, Hawk?"

"A right to apologize, at least," he improvises. "Not to expect you to forgive me, just to have an apology stated and heard. Is that asking so much?" Then he wants to bite his tongue, because as confused as he is, the notion of apologizing hadn't even introduced itself until Cara brought it up herself. He feels manipulated all out of bounds. In fact, he doesn't have the vaguest idea what he wants to say beyond, perhaps, "Cara! Wait!" Perhaps he wants simply to sit in the cocoon of the car for a few minutes, waiting for the monstrous space between them to contract into something manageable. It's just that he can't stand by and watch her let herself in for a thudding fall by constructing a real live grandmother from a set of coincidences and a batch of fading freckles. But, my God! What is he saying? Caravelle has never even seen the woman. It is his head, no other, from which this shattering thought has arisen. He wants to regress, efface, simplify.

But it's too late. Cara is outside the car, and by now so is Hawk. Radiant is approaching from the direction of his usual window exit, walking faster

[165]

and looking more distracted than either of them has ever seen him before. Both Hawk and Cara pick it up, but only Cara is capable of response.

"Radiant. What happened, baby?"

Radiant's composure, such as it is, implodes. He is crying and his nose is running copiously. He is barely comprehensible. "Lucy's dead."

"Say it again, Radiant. I must have misunderstood."

"No," he sobs, "you didn't misunderstand. Lucy's dead."

Hawk is catatonic. Cara does better through the course of the crisis. Hawk tends to think sometimes that her nurse's training has leached the compassion right out of her, but he is wrong. By nature plus a judicious dollop of her mother's perverse conditioning, Cara has learned to react with restraint in the heart of the crisis; to burst open into jagged fragments, privately, later.

"What happened, baby?" she repeats. Hawk's mute rage grows, not only because of his own impotence, but also because he believes that Cara doesn't give a red-hot damn whether anything has happened to Lucy or not. He can almost see the clipboard on which Cara will write the dispassionate details, to be transcribed later in a cavernous department of medical records in the bowels of a vast and futuristic hospital. His imagination is in full sail, even if his reason is disengaged.

"I decided to jog to the mailbox"—at the foot of the gravel hill, a run of three-quarters of a mile or so. He is sobbing and sniffing. Hawk reads it as a bid for sympathy rather than honest, open, guilty grief. Is furious. "Lucy wanted to come. He played, and wanted me to cuff him all the way down. He was running in circles around me. The way he always does?" He searches futilely for a handkerchief in pockets that have held nothing remotely civilized since he left home, indeterminate years ago. Cara hands him a tissue. Hawk witnesses it as a consummate intimacy, and wants to scream.

"So what happened then?"

"His circles got wider, you know? And he was running off into the tall grass at the bottom of the hill. All of a sudden he screamed."

"Screamed? Dogs don't scream."

"No. I mean screamed. Really screamed."

Even Cara winces.

"I ran after him, but by that time he was on the way back out to where I was coming from." Unconsciously, Hawk takes Radiant back up a notch for trying to follow the old dog into menacing and unknown perils. And Cara for wincing.

"I thought prob'ly it was a trap, but that was crazy, because who'd want to poach that close to the highway?"

Hawk finds a growl somewhere and tells Radiant to quit the theorizing and get on with what the hell happened.

[166]

"Well, I don't know for sure."

"How can you not know for sure? You were right there." Within minutes, Hawk has seen his most cherished perspectives on Minerva upended, then his status quo with Cara, previously tentative but at least holding, blasted away in one verbal sweep. Now Lucy. . . . He is having wagonloads of trouble dealing with what are stacking up to be three perceived losses in one day, even though this latest one is the only one that's actual so far. He doesn't stop to think that under the circumstances he probably wouldn't know for sure either. What's more, he realizes with a hard jolt of shame, he might not even have had the exquisite gut to follow the animal into the high grass, either.

". . . but I think it was a copperhead."

Cara isn't supposed to shudder, according to Hawk's increasingly myopic vision of her emotional repertoire. When she does, he hates her for an irrational instant.

"LUCY'S MY DOG."

"Why do you think it was a copperhead, Radiant?" Caravelle, Psychiatric Nurse speaking. Just how long have you had the feeling that·you're Napoleon, your Majesty?

"Because there were no bullets or anything like that, and no noise, and no flesh wounds. He wasn't even limping, or favoring a leg. There wasn't a single sound, except the scream. Then after he screamed, I think I saw the grass maybe sort of waving in a diagonal line toward the stand of sassafras. Like something was slithering away."

"You think. YOU THINK. Radiant, I don't think you ever think at all." Hawk is shocked by the raucousness of his own voice. Radiant does think. He is probably beginning to understand right now what the guilt of the survivor means. Hawk has no monopoly.

Cara oozes sudden sweet mockery. "And just how would you have done it differently, Hawk?" Remembering all the times he and Lucy romped through the tall grasses, raced to the mailbox, rolled over and over one another on the sweet, innocent earth. Innocent, Hawk sees, because it had not yet chosen to reveal its destructive capabilities, not because they weren't there.

Hawk refocuses. "Okay, Radiant. I'm sorry." But he is addressing Cara, Minerva, poor dead Lucy, even Howard Robley, from whom he might have parted in any one of a number of less wounding attitudes. His mother, his neighborhood, everyone on earth to whom his farewells have been irrevocable or not irrevocable, or guiltless or tainted simply because he made it so. "Okay? Okay. Then what happened?"

Radiant glances at Cara to ask if he has just imagined something, or has he been granted safe passage after all? Subliminally she encourages.

"It's okay, Hawk," looking at his feet. "What happened was that first he started whimpering like a sick puppy, and then all of a sudden he was breathing funny. Finally he was walking like all four of his legs were paining, but at first there hadn't been anything wrong with his legs at all."

"Systemic," Cara affirms.

"You said he wasn't limping," says Hawk, more inquisitive than quarrelsome, but not yet up to Cara's comprehension.

"That's right. Not limping. Just walking sort of stiff-legged, or something. I tried to pick him up, but he snapped at me."

"Did he bite you at all, even a little nip?" Cara, accepting the fact that a snakebite was actually what had occurred, knows that the stricken animal might have transferred the venom unwittingly to a loving friend.

"No. Wouldn't let me near him, is why. Except that he kept sidling up to my legs, but whenever he accidentally brushed me or anything, he'd whimper some more, and go away again. Meanwhile, his breathing was starting to sound like he had emphysema, or maybe worse. By the time we got to the front steps, he just couldn't make it. He just put his head down and curled his body up and shivered. He seemed to have, like, shrunk. I thought maybe I could rig him onto the bike and get him into the vet somehow, but by the time . . ."

"It's okay, Radiant. I don't need to hear the rest."

"Let him finish, Hawk." Cara knows what she's doing, for everyone's sake.

"I said, I don't need—"

"Hawk, I know what you said, but I'm not sure that you know what you need right now." She is taking a colossal risk, but the greater risk of legislated silence is the capitulation of self. Hawk knows it as well as she does.

"And you do?" The words are designed to bite, but they are extruded tamed.

"For now—yes, I do. For later—one step at a time." She turns back to Radiant, who looks like he wants to suck his thumb and twiddle his stringy blond hair. "What happened then, Radiant? What did you do?"

"Nothing happened. I mean, nothing . . . happened. By the time I ran in for the backpack and the webbing—I mean, by the time I got back outside, he wasn't breathing. It couldn't have taken forty-five seconds from out to in and back."

Hawk looks at Radiant through his regular eyes for the first time since the beginning of this monstrous conversation. Radiant is too fogged up to catch the improvement, so he flinches when Hawk extends his arm. All Hawk wants to do is clasp Radiant's shoulder in friendship, gratitude, solidarity, pain, everything. To ground them both. To regularize something. To thank him for doing the best he could. The best anyone could. Cara, watching

[168]

intensely, gives Radiant a mother's nudge in Hawk's direction. All of a sudden the three of them are knotted into a sobbing cluster. When they gradually withdraw, something close to normal has been restored. But Hawk still knows that the sudden release had little, if anything, to do with Lucy the Hound; and also, that the collected events of this day have somehow changed the structure of his life. He wishes he knew how.

Radiant has placed Lucy in state on the kitchen table, which he has cleared of honey, tamari, peanut butter, unshelled nuts and their various impedimenta for the first time in recent memory. The dog hasn't yet begun to smell, but he looks very stiff, quite dead. Paul the Parrot keeps broadcasting the officious reminder that "Something Happened, Something Happened." As if anybody needed to be told.

Radiant, as though by entitlement, steps forward first. Cara grabs Hawk's hand, which each accepts as a gesture for the benefit of the other. Then with a preliminary squeeze Cara releases her grasp and steps professionally toward the table. With a careful squint she begins combing through Lucy's fur. She scrutinizes the neck, throat, stomach. Finally she announces, calmly, that Radiant is quite right about the snakebite, which they all knew all along anyway. For all Hawk knows, Cara is not only sure of the variety of snake, but could also supply its name, rank, and serial number, if pressed. It is that sort of instinct that makes him believe, at his well-guarded core, that she is probably quite right in whatever she's hypothesizing about Minerva too, somehow. It scares him silly. He chooses not to challenge anything else right now, preferring to rest with whatever securities he can salvage. It is a highly marital syndrome.

They observe moments of silence, of grave intimacy. At last Hawk breaks the reverie. A glance at Cara tells him that she's been waiting. "We'll have to bury him."

Radiant, having expended a month's worth of conversation, sighs deeply and looks away. Since he feels responsible, he'll go along with anything.

Cara manages to straighten out the perspective. "Hawk, dear, it probably isn't legal unless he's in some kind of coffin, and very, very deep."

Hawk, who flies in the face of legality with baggies in his pocket every day of the week, suddenly turns holy crusader when an image of desecrating his beloved animal flickers across his field of reckoning.

"Then what do you suggest we do?" Resentment showing.

"We take him to the vet, and he takes care of it for us."

"How?" Suspicious. Old Hawk-of-the-Suburbs, for all that he's adopted the Valley and the turning of the seasons as his own, still lives with some gaps of experience that boggle even his own mind. Lucy was his first dog ever. His first pet.

[169]

"Very professionally, Hawk," says Cara, and Hawk wonders what it is she's afraid to say. Then she says it. "By cremation."

Hawk struggles visibly. He believes unflinchingly in dust-to-dust, but he believes that the process should be left to take care of itself as naturally as possible. He grapples for a decision. Is suddenly sure.

"I'm going to bury him, Cara." Radiant and Cara both start to protest, but their collective gentleness gives Hawk the space he needs to ward off the objections. He raises a forestalling hand. "I want to do it myself. You don't even need to be implicated. Really. No one will ever find him. And if anyone does, you won't know anything about it." Hawk's determination makes it very clear that he means what he says.

Silently Cara goes to find a big green plastic trash bag. Hawk realizes what it's for, and that becomes the hardest moment for all of them. Radiant finds a spade propped up on the cellar door. Hawk carries it awkwardly, because he insists on cradling the plastic bag like a babe in arms. He goes out the front way, but circles around back. He doesn't want Lucy buried anywhere near the tall grasses or the stand of sassafras.

The next day, Hawk's hands are painfully raw. His arms and shoulders and back are so agonizingly stiff that he must focus all his energy upon keeping tears from welling as he and Cara drive into town and across the bridge on the way to Foothill House. Consequently they do not discuss the tiers of significance that surround this visit. Yet in a way that he would be hard-pressed to explain, Hawk feels more at home, at peace, with all of it than he did yesterday. He does not wonder whether his unaccustomed new feeling has anything to do with the fact that he has now consecrated someone he has loved unto this land.

Hawk and two buddies thumbed their way to California late in the summer after their freshman year. They arrived in San Diego before dawn after an all-night hitch with a golf-supply salesman out of Phoenix. They camped in Ocean Beach. As the sun rose, Hawk was more disappointed than surprised to see that grubby orange smog could blanket the legendary Pier at the End of America just as effectively as it could obscure the Statue of Liberty closer to home.

Later that morning the Santa Ana winds had begun to blow in emphatic gusts from the desert. Looking eastward, Hawk experienced actual physical elevation as the hot breezes raked the sky clean. When he turned oceanward, he noted with perplexity that the foul pollutants were still poised, suspended, a few hundred feet—or miles—offshore. Before redirecting his attention inland, to the day ahead, he wondered briefly whether the tainted clouds would scatter at sea, or press toward Asia, or glide naturally back to muffle the coastline when the winds abated.

It didn't matter. He and his friends caught a lucky ride straight to the San Diego Zoo, where the driver parked and deposited them directly under a standard marked by a giraffe.

Hawk feels similarly about everything on the day after Lucy's funeral. No resolute conversations have taken place. The noxious clouds still hover in the distance. But he has finally agreed that he must do what he must do. If Cara feels so strongly about meeting with Minerva, who is he to think he can stop her? If Minerva has questions, about seeing him back so soon, about anything, she does not allow as much. She is as serene as she was yesterday, as gracious as nobility about receiving the unexpected patchwork princess he is presenting to her now.

"Come in, Hawk, Caravelle. You're just in time. Maybelle Three has just made lemon squares for Gossamer."

Maybelle Senior Kennebec and her daughter have both been dead and gone for more years than Hawk has been alive, but the current Maybelle still insists upon her distinctive enumeration. Minerva, as well aware as anybody of the myriad identity problems accruing to this household, understands perfectly. Appalachian hill women to this day often transfer their names from generation to generation of daughters, unsullied by marriage or evolution. Liberation has nothing to do with it. Babies simply come, somehow unexplained, with the regularity of the dogwood blossoming. Mothers, having so little else to endow, pass on their Names.

Minerva is surging on. "Gossamer, of course, should eat absolutely nothing. She could metabolize for three years on her body fat alone. We will simply do her a favor and relieve her of the burden of one-half of this batch. Please excuse me for a minute."

Caravelle is ready to be enchanted, Hawk realistic.

"Where was she yesterday when I had the munchies so badly I almost ate the arm of the sofa?" he growls to Cara under his breath as Minerva recedes kitchenward.

"My gracious, Hawk," replies Minerva from two rooms away, over the omnipresent backdrop of E. Power Biggs on every pipe organ in Europe and the New World. "All you had to do was mention it. Foothill House is no place to be shy."

X

With Karraman in residence after the flood, Emmaline infuriated, and herself effectively stranded, Minerva didn't know whether to be shy or not. As far as actually moving away from Foothill House, absolutely no argument availed. The most she could do was to remove herself from the bedroom she had occupied in Karraman's absence, during the period when she wasn't doing a fakir's penance on Emmaline's useless and fashionable chaise. Given a dizzying array of choices in the tentacled mansion, she elected the quarters which were to be hers, in one way or another, until she died.

It was one room, tower-shaped, never intended to be any more than that. Its unique character attracted Minerva from the outset, and would have been quite enough to suit her. However, the room came equipped with a sterling bonus: a suspension-sprung ladder leading to a beamed garret room above. It was the garret which appealed instantly to Minerva, despite Karraman's spinsterish worries about the difficulty of keeping the hexagon, an architect's fancy, warm in winter and tolerable in summer. The architect and Emmaline, partners in folly, had obviously planned the room as they had planned most of the rest of the house, that is, with only the outer façade in mind. The narrow access to the garret precluded any serious storage, and the unfinished floors precluded any other practicable use.

Except to Minerva's imagination. She hauled the smallest of her wicker chests up the ladder, along with three or four of the overstuffed harem pillows with which Emmaline had smothered every available surface and ottoman, mistaking excess for fashion. Minerva was appropriately confident that Emmaline would never even notice their absence. For some reason the tower bedroom itself, although as overwhelmingly electrified and candled as the rest of the house, also boasted a handsome oil-burning student lamp to bolster its *de rigueur* inventory of miscellaneous lighting aids. That accessory Minerva appropriated for her loft as well. She rearranged the abundant knickknackery so that it would no more be missed than the pillows, even if Emmaline were to venture across her *non grata* threshold.

She also took a sketchbook and a box of pens and inks up the creaking ladder. For reasons she chose not to analyze, she left another, similar set of artists' materials casually arranged on the writing desk in one of the bays in the bedroom. Not that the tower loft was a secret, or that the work she planned to do there was classified. She simply felt the need to indulge a small but real impulse to maintain a certain integrity of her person within the sprawling complexities of the household. The geography of the loft left her satisfied that she could do so.

Minerva also learned quickly that the geography of her hideaway offered her wonderful advantages otherwise. She could see without being seen, hear without being heard. Bless the central heating: through its bewildering system of ductwork and grilles, odd currents of sound circumnavigated the house in bizarre, sometimes hilarious patterns. Especially in summer, when sound waves didn't have to share the conduits with air or water or any other manufactured energy.

One day after Maybelle seemed to have the routines of the place well in hand, Minerva had stolen upstairs, sketchbook in hand, to enjoy an hour of organized solitude. Gradually the sound of approaching voices pitched to conflict snagged her attention. When she realized that the subject of conversation was herself, she pattered mischievously down the ladder just in time to hear Maybelle Kennebec announcing, "But I ain't startin' in doin' up her room every day, like she was some Queen of Sheba or somethin'."

Minerva, already expecting Emmaline's hearty, selfish second to that motion, didn't think a thing of it. She welcomed the privacy, as a matter of fact, and at the same time felt grateful to be able to perform any quid pro quo she could in what she saw as her immeasurable debt to the household. Even if the reception accorded her was less than wholehearted in certain quarters, she was guest nonetheless, and recipient of bed, board, shelter from the storm, and other perquisites. Minerva saw her debt as boundless. Characteristically, she refused to see that her tireless presence during the weeks of Karraman's absence might possibly have placed the shoe on the other foot.

Regardless of who owed what to whom, Emmaline remained true to form and gave Maybelle the only answer that was perfectly unpredictable. She swallowed all resentment toward Minerva in one stunning gulp when confronted with the suggestion that someone other than herself might be the ultimate arbiter of any phase of housekeeping.

"You're the one taking on all the queenly airs, Miss Maybelle Kennebec. You'll do up Miss Minerva's room the same as you do up the rest of the house. With the rest of the staff back, and that slattern of a daughter of yours occupying space and eating up pastry all day long, I'd think you'd be hunting up and down river and stream looking for work to do, not trying to find ways to get out of it. Besides," afterthought, transparent as window glass, "Miss Minerva is a guest in this house." She stood waiting defiantly, as though she were supposed to be the one on the defensive.

Maybelle just shrugged. Silence.

"Well?"

"Whaddya mean, well?"

"Have you nothing to say?"

"No, I ain't got nothin' to say," and wouldn't allow if she had, either.

"Yes you do."

"You tellin' me I do?"

"You do. What you have to say, Maybelle Kennebec, is, 'Yes, ma'am, Miss Emmaline,' and what you have to do is follow my orders and keep a civil tongue in your head." Although she sounded more like the nasty little child Maybelle had helped to rear in the Musgrove house than the lady of the manor she would pretend to be, she rapidly communicated to Maybelle the picture she was trying to paint. A menacing pause hung over both of them as Maybelle decided whether this was going to be the time to call her bluff.

Minerva had backed slowly out of visual range, but she still thought she could hear every one of Maybelle's inner wheels clanking. This was going to be better than the theater in Boston, because she herself was part of the denouement.

"Well, Maybelle? What's it going to be?"

Maybelle finally remembered, in the nick of time, where it was she had seen Minerva before. It was before the wedding. With all them hats. And sassier hats Maybelle Kennebec had never seen or craved. Her final answer to Emmaline came with the clarity of a military strategist.

"Well," snorted Maybelle with copious borrowings from one of the idioms popular in the house where Emmaline had been reared, "seeing as how *she's* hardly a lady given to idleness," pause, allowance for all the deep

[174]

innuendo to glide in and light, "I guess I can see my way to helpin' out. After all," Maybelle dredged a fathom or two further into the Musgrove ethic, "she's a more contributin' member of society than certain others I could name."

"That will be enough, Maybelle. Just do the room."

Minerva, suppressing laughter by the gale, almost stumbled over her own feet as she heard the angry whirl of skirts and the movement of triphammer heels in her direction. The figure that clattered through the doorway a moment too soon for her retreat, however, turned out to be Maybelle, not Emmaline. Instinctively expecting a friendly gesture of complicity, Minerva winked. She wilted like steamed lettuce under Maybelle's opaque scowl. Minerva, wryly subdued, returned to her room with the clear and distinct understanding that neither she nor Emmaline had come out on top of that particular fracas. Upon reflection she decided that, considering all the peculiar circumstances surrounding the arrangement of the household, it was probably just as well.

It couldn't have been his need to have proximity to Minerva, to work the knots out of his mental laces in the comfort of her presence. It couldn't have been the wanting to touch her, to make love to her, to feel her making love with him. All that had to be left for the Inn. The house was a constraint on truth, a lie to the mythology of the paper marriage that existed therein. The walls knew. The solitary pillows knew. Probably Maybelle One knew too, since she seemed to know everything else, but no one was saying.

It couldn't have been an attempt to flog Emmaline with her own inadequacy. Karraman was not that cruel, nor Emmaline that perspicacious. It couldn't have been thoughtlessness, because Karraman left very little in his life to chance. It couldn't have been insecurity, because Minerva never hesitated to let Karraman know exactly where he stood: beside her every step of the way.

Whatever the reason, Karraman insisted, and Minerva stayed. It wasn't that she had nowhere else to go, either. Karraman assigned her the large suite on the second floor of the Inn as soon as the space became available. It tripled the size of her first room on the third floor. She was ecstatic over the endowment of air, light, space, and windows. She found a number of inventive ways to lick her gratitude into Karraman's ear, massage it into his temples, knead it into the base of his spine, let him know how truly pleased she was with the accommodations. All of them.

Neither her gratitude nor her expression of it diminished. Her space, on the other hand, kept shrinking. Within days Karraman realized what was going on, and freed an additional room to add to the suite. That one Minerva reserved for the "public touches," the final crimps and adornments which personalized her creations so attractively, and for sales. She reasoned that, even though the real labor went on behind the scenes, customers loved to see gracefully competent fingers finishing up their precious hats. It gave them a lovingly bespoke quality. Minerva's insight scored again.

Page by page, her record books filled. Minerva had started by documenting in her own hand the execution of the Robley wedding from the first presentation of sketches to the final rendering of accounts. By the following autumn, despite the commercial hiatus occasioned by the Flood, she had fallen hopelessly behind in the thorough archives she had hoped to preserve. Orders were simply pouring in too fast. What she had, she realized, was no longer a lyrical little fantasy of a workshop to diarize prettily at her convenience. Her fledgling had rapidly outstripped not only its nest, but its entire corner of the garden.

When Karraman announced that he and Em were going to take a prolonged trip abroad to compensate for the honeymoon which had been outwitted by the storm, Minerva was phlegmatic about it. As much as she would miss Karraman, she could certainly take advantage of the found time to reorganize her systems. At the rate women were flocking to her with orders, she certainly needed to do something.

A full contingent of Musgrove relatives from Kentucky had sent a portfolio of orders in with the new Wells Fargo man. They had been so impressed at the wedding that they had decided, en masse, to knock the Confederacy on its ear with touring hats in the latest fall colors. They'd be much obliged if Miss Minerva would please inform them as to what the new fall colors would be.

A friend of a friend of Emmaline's from Pittsburgh had heard about the wedding in such vivid detail that she felt as if she'd been there herself. She was enclosing a swatch of the imported fabric from which her new winter coat would be made, and would Minerva kindly design something appropriate for herself, and for her little girl to match? Her head size, she thought, was quite normal, but her darling daughter's was positively lavish with golden tresses.

One of the forbidding dowagers of Saint Kathareen's sent a lady's maid with the following message: Madam's French lilac bushes have finally arrived by steamer and will be in full bloom by next spring, God willing. Would Minerva kindly design a hat for Madam to wear at a garden party concurrent with their flowering and include the colors of the lilacs, their greenery, and other spring flora *and* fauna as well? Madam simply knew that Minerva could capture her vision in something lovely. Minerva rather doubted that, since not even Madam herself had seen in bloom the colors she wished Minerva to duplicate. Minerva was game, however. Ideas formed, and methods would follow.

Every day brought orders. Sometimes they came by post, sometimes by messenger. Minerva jotted down everything and filed it carefully. She knew that her reservoirs were outgrowing the casual assumption that she could recall everything just by the act of wanting to. It was imperative that she segment her carefully narrated record book into divisions of various kinds. She perceived clearly that the records of the little workshop would one day need to be both kept and deciphered by more people than herself. Soon she had a filing cabinet with drawers for Ideas, Orders, Requisitions, Billings, Disbursements. And still it grew.

Meanwhile, Minerva tried to be rational about Karraman's absence. One day toward Christmas, calendar in hand, she calculated that he had been gone for more than the total of days they had actually spent together, deducting for the flood. How could she miss him so totally? How could he have entered so intrinsically into her very patterns of thought that she couldn't remember what it was like to plan without listening for his responses, without listening inwardly to imagine what he might have said?

She refused to become mired in it. Instead, she set about to change the patterns. And she felt she had the need, the desire, and, not least, the wherewithal. Minerva was moving toward her factory.

Her current receipts, orders, and billings probably would have been collateral enough for any bank to start her off, but Minerva felt that it was important to show a dollar credit column at the outset. Her financial security resided at that time in the Saint Kathareen's Livery, rested, curried, sleek and strong, ready to be offered up to the highest bidder. Junior Plenderlieth, Prop., knew as well as he knew horseshoes that this new automobile madness would never last. The great horse breeders in the Valley, who disagreed with him, were gradually converting to studfarming thoroughbred racers. He obviously felt differently, and apparently wasn't about to take the risk that he might be outsmarted when the word came over that Miss Minerva, that stubborn cuss of a gal, was finally going to get herself quit of those two fine Clydesdales. He thereby submitted to her a whispered bid that totaled roughly three times what Minerva had calculated would be his final offer. She accepted on the spot—and fled with the cash. She was only mildly curious as she watched Junior retreat with a rodeo whoop in the opposite direction.

Minerva worked fast. Karraman and Emmaline arrived home on the day of Christmas Eve. By the time Karraman had maneuvered through the exigencies of homecoming, Minerva was fairly bursting to tell him everything. She waited, working in her suite, knowing full well that Emmaline would do everything in her power to keep him from leaving, with dusk descending on Christmas Eve, but dead certain that Karraman would do what he wanted to do, no matter what.

He arrived at the door just when she thought that she could wait no longer.

"Karraman!" she cried, joyous as an angel, "I'm going to have a factory!"

Karraman hadn't seen such rubble since the Flood. He had always felt more at home in her suite than anywhere. He thought he knew her sense of organization inside out. After all, he had been at her side as she planned every step of it. Now when he asked her what the hell everything was, Minerva inquired whether he wanted it in narrative, chronological, or structural order.

It was her factory—her destiny. She loved every niche and box room.

"Minerva, what in the name of God is this?" He jabbed at a blueprint.

"What? Oh, that's the dining room."

"Minerva, we *have* a hotel. I thought you were building a factory."

"I am, Karramar," relishing it.

"Well, what in the hell is a dining room doing in a hat factory?"

"Now, Karraman," she cajoled, "you probably thought Mr. Astor was mad when he first set up a dining room where men and women could be together, and in a first-class hotel, too—"

"Did not." Garumph.

"—but where would the Inn be now if you'd refused to see the wave of the future when he introduced it? In the Dark Ages, that's where."

"There's no comparison, Minerva."

"There's every comparison, Karraman. If people can work together, they can relax together too. They can be comfortable, and eat together, or eat separately, if they want to. But it's going to be their choice, not mine. *Or* yours. And it's going to work. You'll see."

"One of us will," he agreed. He couldn't contain his skepticism because she was building a factory around an absolutely unheard-of standard: the comfort and safety of the people who operated it. What an idea!

Gradually, by the time she had worked through the master diagrams from raw material to finished product, with lines of access drawn down to the smallest dressmaker pin, he began to reflect appreciation. Then a great deal of appreciation. Then unalloyed respect. Minerva watched it flow from the light in his eyes all the way to the bulge in his trousers. She would have loved to share the creative moment with him in the communion of the bed, if she had been able to find it under the blueprints. She had to settle for a modest little clearing on the floor.

So still she went back to the hill. She stayed on as a favor because Karraman urged that someone other than the servants be on hand while Emmaline recovered from the trip abroad. Then she stayed because the suite at the Inn had to undergo further remodeling and renovation if the standards of her "showroom" were to duplicate the tasteful modernism of the rising factory. She could have taken another room at the Inn if she had pressed the matter, but she didn't want to monopolize too much of Karraman's commercial space at one time.

Next, in an entirely new round of developments, Minerva found that she was staying because she and Emmaline had reached an armed truce. It was dawning on Em that Minerva's social grace and artistic flair made up for her own lack of same. Their partnership, which began with the homecoming party Emmaline gave in her own honor, set the standard. Before long, the "little evenings" on the hill became the envied highlights of every social calendar in the Valley. Minerva stage-managed the events beyond anybody's wildest imagination. Karraman's hostly pride blossomed. Emmaline was too busy taking credit to show resentment. Minerva just worked on the guest lists and kept her judgments to herself.

After a while all the socializing began to pale, and Minerva found that she was still on the hill. At length she realized that it wasn't a bad idea all around. Maiden ladies of remote connection were often fixtures of many large and creaky mansions in that era. That particular cachet seemed to satisfy Emmaline as well as Minerva, each in a way that Minerva felt would probably fail to stand under further scrutiny. She consequently declined to give it any, and devoted herself to utilizing in full the combined facilities of the factory, the Inn, and the tower room. They comprised a solid universe.

Minerva never intended to capitalize on the genealogical fact of her Robley connection. When she first arrived, she had decided to bide her time, not to presume to trade upon a coincidence of blood. Later, when she might have wanted to clarify matters, she felt not unlike a person who has missed the name in an introduction, but has allowed animated conversation to proceed to the point where it has grown too late to ask. For her, it had simply grown too late in the day to tell. Minerva had always harbored a cautious ambivalence about making too much fuss over bloodlines anyway. She tended to think that when people paid too much attention to that sort of thing, they were inclined to breed the brains right out of themselves, like collies. Her visions worked out, after all, because she was very practical about fulfilling them. And since Karraman's household needed her in a variety of ways, she was equally practical about staying on. There, for many decades, matters flourished and stood, notwithstanding wagging tongues up and down the Valley.

"I didn't come here to invade her privacy," Cara insists *sotto voce* to Hawk as Minerva calmly arbitrates an escalating altercation between railing Maybelle and thundering Gossamer above the relatively dulcet tones of the pipe organ.

"I didn't think you had, Caravelle."

"Quit patronizing me, Hawk. I'm not getting into that kind of thing with you."

"I'm not patronizing you," he denies, realizing that he'd better cut it out right now. "Seriously, Cara, I didn't think you came here to invade her privacy, because I didn't think you came here thinking of her at all. No, wait . . ." kindlier, as she flares, "seriously, baby. C'mon. I mean, *you're* not here to do any oral history."

She doesn't need to affirm with her voice, because her eyes articulate clearly.

"Good. Now." He slows, paces himself. "You're looking for something besides a job in this glorious Valley climate, right?"

"I . . ."

"Come on, Cara. You told me that much. About how your mother died, and how that old friend of hers didn't know anything at all except maybe, *maybe* this weird connection. And the letters with the name spelled wrong. So now you—"

Cara is trying to keep it down, but obviously straining at it. "Hawk, *so what?* What am I hurting? Not you, not her—"

"Cara, that's the point. How do you know it isn't hurting her? If she had anything to tell about your family, believe me, I'd know it." Cara shoots him a Well-who-the-hell-are-*you* look, but he's too busy dissembling to catch on. "I mean, you have so much going for you—your looks, your brains, your sense of humor, you have a really operative profession—"

She is outraged. "Well, thanks a thousand. You're finally getting around to crediting that, are you?"

"Ah, Cara, I apologized for that a long time ago."

"Oh, rilly? I guess I must have missed something."

"Well, I meant to, anyhow. Look, could we forget that for a minute, and go on?"

"Why, naturally, Hawk. Forget old Cara's self-respect any old time, for the sake of literary exposition."

"Aw, Cara, don't. All I meant is, well, we're getting close to something really important. I don't want to snag it over something that I said in a careless, blind fury and never meant in the first place."

"I accept." She smiles sadly, having just received more of an apology than he ever intended to bestow. "You were saying?"

"Yeah. Well, you're . . . secure. If you end up not finding any clues about who your family was, or if Saint Kathareen's turns out to have been the wrong place to land, you don't have to worry about salvaging a shattered reputation, or lost pride, or a lifetime structure that all of a sudden gets blown up in your face. You just pack up and move on—or not, as you see it. No sweat, right?"

She isn't sure, her face tells him. She doesn't encourage him, but neither does she call a halt. She has bobbed somewhat out of reach, but is keeping her head above water.

"What I'm trying to say, Cara, is that she has a hell of a lot more to lose than you do. If you keep this up, she could be very badly hurt."

"I don't believe you said that."

Hawk is astounded. "Don't believe I said what?"

"That *she'll* be badly hurt."

"Well, she will. You can't deny that."

"I can't deny it or not deny it. I don't live inside her skin, I only live inside mine. I can't vouch for her feelings, but she's had a hell of a lot longer to get in touch with them than I have with mine."

"So . . . ?"

"So what about somebody, you, for the sake of a vivid example, caring about whether or not *I* get hurt."

"Christ, Cara, of course I care." He hasn't really meant to say that either, but having said it, he suddenly realizes that it happens to be true.

"Then why all this speculative business about hurting her, hurting *her,* by talking about something in her past when she's practically set herself up with a license from the FCC to do just that, and I'm sitting here hurting in every pore and follicle because maybe she can tell me what I need to know, and you're censoring me like a goddamn subcommittee?"

"That was quite a mouthful, Cara."

"No kidding. But if you didn't agree with me, you'd have a lot better comeback to hit me down again with."

"Now, just who is going to hit whom, Cara, dear? I thought your generation rather disdained fisticuffs." It is Minerva returning from the music room with the weary triumph of a victorious chess player.

Hawk is tongue-tied. All he can do is sit. Cara holds the cards. He feels that something momentous is about to happen. The professional in him wants to turn on the tape recorder in order not to miss a drop, but he fears that the click and whine of machinery might destroy the balance in the room and spin the three of them out into infinite distances where they'll never touch anything real again, let alone each other.

He and Cara exchange glances. She keeps silent. Hawk, having planned to head her off with an ambush of words at the pass, finds that the troops have deserted.

"All right." Minerva smiles resignedly. "If you've nothing to tell me . . ."

"Miss Minerva, I didn't . . . We didn't . . ."

"Nonsense, Hawk, of course you did. Both of you. If the fact of your being here, in my company, weren't germane to your argument, why would you have chosen the parlor of Foothill House for the occasion?"

"How can one, uh . . . person know so much about so many things, Miss Minerva?" Hawk asks with gut-felt emotion.

"You were going to say 'old woman,' weren't you, Hawk? No—don't answer. It really is all right, you know. You don't understand it yet, but when I dream my dreams, I'm never a single day older than you are. Don't ever forget that."

Just as Hawk is about to reply, take the bull by the horns, Cara makes an identical decision. "You're right, Miss Minerva," she tells her. "At least you're right about our discussion belonging to this house. What we're really arguing about is whether it ought to be discussed at all. Hawk and I disagree."

"That's enough, Cara," Hawk warns.

"It may be enough for you, Hawk, but it certainly isn't enough for me. Go on, Cara," Minerva commands. "I don't think I'm excessively inquisitive, to want to know what's going on under my own roof."

"Cara—"

"Hawk, it's my problem. My decision. Keep out of it. *Just keep out of it, now.*"

Hawk hears something momentous in her insistence, and doesn't want to hear it. Doesn't want to be right. Does not want to pursue this conversation to its conclusions. Hawk doesn't want his mind ransacked, his secrets stolen. And he has brought it all on himself. What a fool, what a goddamn mindless fool, to have fallen for her pitiable-orphan routine, and brought her over here, just because the dog died. Goddamn dog. Why couldn't he have let well enough alone?

He looks down at Cara's slender hands, oval fingernails, and feels assaulted. There seem to be two pairs of identical hands in this room.

Something is going to be settled here, he feels it surely. But what? What?

Cara's eyes tell Hawk nothing except that the matter is no longer his to decide. He defers, and she takes her place.

"Miss Minerva," cautiously, "I believe that I might have had some family of my own in Saint Kathareen's. You've been here a long time—"

"Longer than God." She chuckles.

"—and I thought perhaps you'd know somebody. Be able to help me. I don't know."

"Well, what is there that you do know, Cara? Perhaps we can go from there."

"Yes. But I really don't know anything at all. I don't even know where my mother was born."

At that instant, as if visited by a galactic laser, Minerva's features transform. Cara is busy staring down at those hands of hers, trying to cool the fire flaming in her cheeks, but Hawk is convinced that Minerva in that second has seen a revelation. Minerva *knows,* and Hawk knows that she knows, and no philosopher in the world can parse the grammar of the psyche that has led to these various epistemologies. Hawk only knows that he is right.

"Your mother wasn't born here," snaps Minerva so sharply that Hawk and Caravelle both start.

"But how do you know?" Caravelle is stricken, but not too dumbly for the most critical question of her life.

"Because," Minerva announces firmly, "I do believe I knew her. And her mother as well." Minerva inclines her head then, and closes her eyes.

"This isn't easy for her," Hawk hisses at Cara.

"Did anybody say it was going to be?" counters Minerva, like a shot. She struggles for a moment then. Hawk, who sees that she is ready to go over the brink, wants to help, but not by abetting this exercise. He wants multilateral disarmament, withdrawal behind safe borders.

At last, with a laden sigh, Minerva clears an avenue down which she might proceed. Her neck pulsates with the effort. "Are you ready, Caravelle, truly ready? Because there's no retreat once this has begun. You'll have no Erase button for a refuge."

But Caravelle's answer doesn't really matter, because Minerva has made up her mind. She has had this agenda in storage for more years than the combined lifetimes of her guests.

"For one thing, to know all is to understand all, and to understand is often to forgive. Karraman always said that. I always indulged him when he pontificated, but very often it turned out that he was right. In any case, whether or not forgiveness is the order of the day right now, you owe it to yourself to open that avenue of possibility. It can't help but make you feel

better about yourself, as well as the rest of this unlikely cast of characters."
She gesticulates into the corners of imagination and memory, as if the
entire family sat or lolled in lawn dresses and white ducks all about the
room.

"There's something else, too, Caravelle. Perhaps I overleap myself in
telling you this, but I have nothing to lose." Hawk is getting smothered in
. . . *language,* and he wants to know what in the hell it is all about. This isn't
like Minerva, to defend, apologize, build breastworks of prolixity. Slowly he
begins to realize that she needs to temporize. Her measured flow of
conversation is buying the interval in which she must absorb, process, and
come to terms with the most remarkable confrontation of her entire life.
Meeting Karraman was one kind of turning; Minerva was chief engineer all
along in that lifetime route. Caravelle is something else entirely. He feels for
her, aches in her pain.

But this is Hawk's moment, too. If Cara and Minerva have found one
another, what will be the use of him? What can he possibly contribute to the
terrible richness vested between those two? Threatened all out of mind, he is
nonetheless compelled to force the rest of the tale out of Minerva. He is
ready to force her, to set upon the defenses she's erecting before they petrify,
when quite straightforwardly she dips right into his mind and reads it for
him.

"All right, my dears. No more pussyfooting." She pauses, but only to
breathe deeply, to inhale willpower. "If you have specific questions, ask
them. If I can answer them, I will. If not, I'll try to help you find somebody
who can. But no more games. You have to decide for yourself whether or not
it really is answers that you're looking for. You'll never really be liberated
until you can stop chasing all the vague setups and oblique hints that your
mother planted between here and, I don't know, Cuba, or whatever madcap
place. Before that's settled, you'll never really know whether the pursuit is a
safer refuge than the real quarry. No—don't interrupt me now, Cara. It's
too late."

She would have. She has been working up to a classic rejection, a
storming out, a denial that will wilt Minerva on her vine, that will take them
back to a safe time when Hawk frolicked with Lucy in the night and Cara
had never set foot in Foothill House. She was going to say something vulgar
with irony, but now she can't even begin to think of pulling it off. It doesn't
matter. Her unexpected rescuer is in place.

The Hawk who reenters the conversation at this point is the Hawk that
both Cara and Minerva have known at his best: cool Hawk, composed
Hawk, Hawk who has begun to see what is unfolding now with a greater
clarity than either of the two women, since he is still, barely, at a distance
from it. He is engorged with joy and pain, and with a sense of anticipation
almost beyond endurance. He has never stared this particular kind of truth

in the eye either. God knows he resisted long enough, for everybody's sake. Now, at the breach, all he wants to do is move along, see who it is who's been right.

"It's going to be okay, Cara. Really."

"Hawk . . ."

Hawk's memory suddenly streaks back to an evening last fall when he and Cara and Radiant were in the kitchen at the farm making tomato juice. They had all pitched in to chop onions and bell peppers, celery and carrots, because what they really liked was a vegetable juice with a zing to it. They had salvaged all of their own bruised tomatoes, and augmented the supply by buying two bushels of somebody else's for a grand total of two dollars. Hawk was stirring the contents of the huge kettle as everything cooked down and blended. Radiant and Cara were taking turns pressing the first batch through a funnel strainer with a wooden pestle, and filling the jars to be sealed in the canner.

Hawk kept his head right smack in the middle of the sweet, spicy steam that rose in a cloud from the batch he was stirring. "If my mother had seasoned the vaporizer like this when I was a kid, I would have been content to stay sick forever."

Cara laughs. "That's pretty strange, you know."

"Strange? What wholesome American kid would rather smell Vicks Vapo-Rub than home-cooked tomato juice still in the kettle? I ask you."

"Uh, I always kinda got off on the Vapo-Rub," Radiant contributed, deadpan. All of a sudden Hawk felt such a surge of love for the people sharing his labors that he wanted to take all the emotion and put it up in a Mason jar too, so that it would keep forever.

He shifted gears quickly, wanting to avoid the occasion of maudlin. "How many quarts you figure we'll have when we're done, Cara? Fifty?"

"Closer to a hundred, I imagine. Next year we probably ought to double it, though. We'll more than likely run through this before Christmas, if we're not careful."

"Even if we are careful. Radiant here can drink two quarts in a day without half trying."

"Hey! What's that? Do I hear someone calling me a glutton or something? Me? Radiant? What a wound. Trashing me, the best tomato-juice pestler in the county? Shoot, man. Where's your sense of decency? Do I get paid for this?"

Hawk remembers the high pleasure of hearing Radiant tease. He remembers the tug of happiness at Cara's remark about how they ought to handle the project next season. He isn't sure to this moment how far he's willing to commit himself in advance to anything, but it is a mightily fine and potent feeling to think that Cara isn't going to be the one to pull the plug.

[185]

Amid the rumble of Gossamer's stereo, Hawk remembers the country silence of their kitchen on the farm, how the crickets can sound like tree frogs in autumn. How that night they had sat around, no records, no music, little conversation, listening to the lids snap into seals as the sterile jars cooled, one by one, then all at once in a tender little percussive flurry. The hominess of that moment stays with Hawk like a compliment. He pulls it out and polishes it from time to time just to feel the glow.

He knows why it has surfaced all by itself, in Foothill House, just now, and there's nothing to do for it. He wonders what it will take to restore that kind of peaceful order to their living arrangements, and there is no answer he can embrace. Nothing.

"Honest, Miss Minerva," he attempts, rising, "we have to go now. I've been unexpected company for you two days in a row now. I don't want to take advantage."

"Sit down, Hawk. You set this in motion the very first time you asked me to talk into your machine. I'm sorry if you think it's gotten away from you, but it's too late to reverse it now."

Minerva talks. Hawk wants to interrupt, to go over some of this—all of it—again, get ready for the Final. Then he realizes that this is the Final. He wants to close his eyes, to glide through time back to where Minerva's nearly perfect recall has taken them. Then he fears that he'll lose his place, that he'll come up spluttering if he comes up at all, that he'll misplace his sanity and his bookmark at one and the same time.

"Miss Minerva!"

"Yes, Hawk dear," her voice firm. In Hawk's estimation it ought to be seriously diminished, after all the use she has given it, outstretched like fingered bubblegum, until no resilience is left.

He has her attention now, and he doesn't know what to do with it. "You're saying that you always came back to Foothill House. Even if you didn't think it was right."

"On the contrary. I always thought it was right. It just wasn't always easy."

"You never had doubts?"

"Now, that's not what I said, Hawk. I've always regarded doubts as nature's checks and balances. I use them. I don't let them run me. Remember, I homed in on Saint Kathareen's in the first place because of the Robley nestled at the middle of my name. The final extension of that act was to end up in the house as well. Don't you see, Hawk, Emmaline always considered the mansion a demonstrable asset. No emotion connected to it at all. No . . . heart. For me, even when I was arguing most vehemently for the right to sleep elsewhere, Foothill House has been my only true home."

"But—"

"Quiet, Hawk," Cara interjects tensely. "You've designed this production, now don't disrupt the audience."

Hawk draws himself into check, but his emotions have entered a state of all-out war.

XI

The armistice, for such there was in Foothill House, lasted for nearly five years. It took but a fraction of that time for the exits and entrances of the various denizens to become accepted facts of life.

Minerva went to the office every weekday, most Saturdays, and often on Sunday as well. If her working on the Sabbath raised any eyebrows in town, Minerva considered that part of the necessary price for her professional fulfillment. As long as nobody let a little religious indignation interfere with a woman's natural appetite for a new hat at regular, seasonal intervals, the business would survive.

More than survive, it prospered into a rapidly expanding, continuous undertaking. She exceeded her own sets of expectations nearly as fast as she was able to formulate them. She had thought that borrowing Maybelle-the-Daughter from Foothill House might be a useful way of keeping the salon picked up and pumping some independent finances into the garbled Kennebec economy at the same time, but she quickly realized that the frenzied pulse of a thriving atelier required far more intensive maintenance than even a competent domestic could have provided. Quickly Minerva observed that her assistant, Molly Godwin, was trying to enlist Maybelle as a general factotum. Maybelle probably couldn't have handled so demanding an assignment even if she had been full-witted. As it was, the pressure of mounting orders, interfering with Maybelle's basic lint-picking functions and general domesticity, ended up paralyzing her effectiveness for good and all. When Minerva sent her back to Foothill House with a gentle word of thanks for "tiding me over," Maybelle fled with relief.

"I told you so, Minerva," Em chided smugly.

"You're right, dear," Minerva replied.

"A woman has to see to her own business," Em amplified, having no idea what it would be like to do so even if she were capable of having any.

"You're right, dear," Minerva replied.

"Things will straighten out now that Little Maybelle is back where she belongs."

"You're right, dear." That kind of acquiescence cost Minerva nothing. She did, then, go on to see to her own business, and she did it by appointing Molly supervisor, hiring three assistants for Molly's custom workroom and a helper to help the helpers. Minerva herself presided over the salon, where her fine eye was always in demand. She did the sketches, she mixed dyes, plucked feathers, and even ransacked the countryside periodically to learn whatever lessons nature had to teach, season by season. But when one of her ladies rushed in clutching a dress box, newly arrived from New York or Paris, and said, "Oh, Minerva, tell me what we must do to crown my outfit," Minerva managed always to appear calm, leisurely, at the gracious service of one and all. No Fabergé could have handled his jewels more lovingly than Minerva treated those "crowns" of hers, and the heads that bore them. She was a genius, they agreed.

So did Karraman, who couldn't do enough for her. The traffic that she was generating through the Inn at lunch- and tea-time was more than worth whatever investment the Inn placed in her operations. Minerva, who had thus far resisted monopolizing even one more square inch of commercial space there, began to overcome her diffidence when she realized that she was able to pay top dollar for whatever else she needed. She and Karraman concluded independently, but simultaneously, that she was going to have to take still an additional room, a bed-sitter, if she was to have any peace at all.

"I'm beginning to realize that I can't have a private life in here, Karraman," she told him one night as they lingered after a late supper in the studio. "Every time I open my eyes in the middle of the night, I see the moon outlining something that I want to adjust or redo or try out. I no sooner start, it seems, than it's morning and I haven't slept another wink." She tempered the complaint with a wry smile, but the truth showed itself in the hollows of her cheeks and the smudges under her eyes.

"I've thought about it, Min. Always *seems* to be a crowd in here, whether there is or not." He smiled. "Not that I'm complaining—"

"—but it does seem a bit disconcerting," she agreed.

"Yes. Well, I've been thinking about the bed-sitter down at the far end,

[189]

here. Old Mrs. Knight has been there for four months now, but her daughter will be back from the Tour anytime."

"Yes. I had a letter the other week. She said that her hats were sensational in Paris." She smiled modest pleasure.

"I don't doubt that. Well, she must be about to restock her supply, because they're docking within the week. The old lady's going back with them, and that frees one of the best views in the house."

"Oh, Karraman, you know that she'll be wanting it back for the next time. For her, the Inn without that room would be like the Mass without the Eucharist."

He laughed appreciatively. "Aren't you sacrilegious tonight, Minnie?"

"That may be," she retorted, "but that woman strikes me as canon law incarnate. Why, every time she looks at me, I feel as if my underwear is showing. I'm surprised that she even nods greetings to me in the lobby. I keep expecting that she'll cut me dead, and that that'll be the end of my social standing in Saint Kathareen's."

"Now, Min, you've never worried about anybody else's opinion before. Who the hell is Mrs. Knight, anyway?" He was cajoling.

"Nobody, actually," Minerva agreed. She could hardly explain it to herself. Perhaps it was her own future, her own censorious old age she was facing, disguised as a stranger. She presented it to Karraman, however, as a casual conversational sally. "What on earth could an old lady of sixty years of age think about *my* life?"

"Minerva, my innocent, I don't think dreams develop wrinkles. I don't suppose her priest would approve of you—"

She arched that evocative left eyebrow at him.

"—all right, of us," he amended cheerfully, "but I think her imagination sings hosannas every night."

"Silly. You can't know that."

"Well, maybe not, but the fact remains that her room is going to be vacant, and I think you ought to have it."

"And when she wants it back?"

"She can have the identical accommodation on the floor below. It'll be two dollars cheaper by the week, and that will pacify the Scot in her."

"Oh, Karraman, I think it will work out just fine." Then she glanced back sidelong. "What about *my* Scot? How much *is* that gorgeous view going for this week?"

"Don't you worry about a thing, Min. We'll work it all out, one way or another," his finger tracing along her cheekbone a memory that traveled the length of both their bodies and settled in, warmly, at the core. As they entered each other's arms, Minerva decided that she wasn't going to argue the point now, but she would settle it with Cybele in the morning. That evening her satisfactions were many, varied, and deep.

She didn't know until years later that Karraman had outthought her before she even started. Already he planned to endorse each of her rent checks for deposit to an account earmarked for her when the time came. Probably she won the last round when she finally learned the truth, because she invested what was by then a small fortune in enclosing and furnishing the splendid bamboo-and-wicker sleeping porch at Foothill House. The balance she used for upkeep and maintenance. At worst it was a split decision, which might not be all that desirable for a pugilist, but seems an eminently satisfactory way to run a life.

Finally, then, she had her comfort and privacy when she needed to rest, away from but in secure proximity to the constant quiet frenzy of Hats of La Vallée.

The name had come about in the way much of Minerva's life took form: through the improbable combination of pragmatism and romanticism which suited Minerva as winter suits Eskimos. She knew that French settlers had first arrived on the banks of the Saint Kathareen's long before the first Robleys had landed and taken root. Also she knew that they had been driven off by the combined hostilities of the land and the aborigines. The mystique of the French culture had appealed to the later pioneers sufficiently to have lent its accents to street names, creeks and rivulets, and other small landmarks wherever Saint K. had disdained to squirm in and take over.

The notion of combining French glamour and Valley earthiness had darted about her thoughts for months, but every time she sat down to think it through, to ink out a trademark that would convey the qualities she fostered, Molly Godwin or Garnet or Bertie Lou would stream in from the workroom twanging questions and comments about what they were "a-fixin' t' do" next, and Minerva felt hopeless about ever getting a glamorous name to flow gracefully from Valley tongues.

One day, the entire process turned to her advantage, and it came in the person of a little errand boy who had, she'd have sworn, the most indecipherable regional dialect she'd ever heard; and she'd thought that with the Maybelles she'd heard it all. The lad had come with a crate of packing twine Minerva had ordered from a supplier called Valley Distributors, commonly called the Valley by those who worked and dealt there.

"Uhm frm thu Vallay?" he announced.

"Pardon me?" she responded, momentarily out of phase, as with a foreign tongue.

"Thu Vallay?" he insisted, giving the second word an almost glottal underline.

She had it. She had his message, and she had hers: the name that said everything she needed to say, but could not possibly be vandalized by word of mouth. Hats of La Vallée was born.

She signed the invoice for the twine with a flourish, and tipped the boy what amounted to nearly a day's pay for his efforts. She reckoned that he probably thought she was more crazy than generous, but he would never know what he had done for her. Recounting the story years later, she would observe wryly that she couldn't have ridden on the subway from Grand Central to an ad agency for what her trademark had cost her, and no professional could have done a better job.

"Girls!" she summoned, before the happy messenger was fully out the door. "Drop what you're doing and come here for a minute. We're going to do some signs, and some labels, and give ourselves a good old-fashioned christening party. You are now employees of La Vallée, and we're going to do it up brown!" Enthusiasm crackled through the air, and business went full steam ahead.

It took no time at all for La Vallée to become synonymous in the world market with the careful elegance which had always been the hallmark of her work. Before long Minerva even grew accustomed to being greeted as Miss La Vallée on the street by those who weren't among the initiated, but wished they were. It didn't bother her in the least. In fact, it remained possible for her to continue living at Foothill House for exactly that reason: she not only had a carefully guarded identity of her own; she had two of them.

By the time the bells of the Town Hall were ready to toll in the new year 1911, La Vallée occupied the two-story factory-warehouse building on Market Street, with the river at its front door and the railroad at its back. The salon thrummed its way along as well. For the growth and success of the business, Minerva was grateful, never smug. She attributed the stupendous success of the undertaking to a lot of luck, a generous measure of Karraman's sound business advice, and the cooperation of a group of employees whose loyalty and competence were peerless.

The largest measure of Minerva's pride she vouchsafed in the factory. All about her, child-labor filled the newspapers and scandalized humanists and reformers everywhere. Minerva refused from the beginning to hire a worker under the age of sixteen. When she was decried for depriving the market of labor and the family of income, she offered to provide support for any child who would complete her education and then come to work. When twelve- and fourteen-hour days threatened to turn even sixteen-year-olds into pallid, middle-aged drones who rarely felt the kiss of a sunbeam, Minerva declared that a workday on her premises would last for precisely eight hours, with extra pay for limited overtime. When other owners placed the vanities of the customers above the failing vision and tortured fingers of the hand workers, Minerva installed sewing machines. Additional electric lighting, combined with other structural improvements in the facilities, ameliorated conditions for those who put the deft finishing touches that made the difference between just any hat and a La Vallée.

Minerva, preparing to be accepted on her own merits, prepared equally to be accepting of everybody else. Since Ohio was so close to West Virginia, formerly a Confederate domain, many residents of Saint Kathareen's shared the Confederate sympathies and regarded the Negro as a species apart. Minerva deplored the attitude, and embraced humanity for the qualities that made them human. She hadn't met a Jew since she had left Massachusetts, but she was positive that for all their mystical and Oriental ways, she would accept them quite as freely.

When she heard from Felder, she knew it was going to be the chance of a lifetime. He had received her name from the architect in Cincinnati who assisted her in the design of the factory. He was in touch with such things, and knew that Felder would want to be in touch too.

Felder worked for the National Labor Recovery Board. Its title sounded official, governmental; reeked of mandate. Actually the organization operated under no imprimatur whatsoever except that of a few wealthy, long-settled Jews whose compassion was strained to the breaking point by the plight of their recently arrived fellows. To the founders of the Board, a human being who was wasting away was wasting away, period. One tuberculosis bacillus had no better credential than another; watery lentil soup was watery lentil soup, whether the water was carried from the village pump or the fire hydrant on the block. Human gifts could stifle as easily in Hester as in Krochmalna Street, if no one had the resources to cultivate them.

The National Labor Recovery Board was, in the eyes of its founders, a reasonable solution to the Jewish problem. It looked to the frontiers of the American continent in more than one dimension at a time. The western movement was part of it; the growth of industry was another; the possibility of scatter-seeding the continent with one of the most fertile motherlodes of European culture, an element that would otherwise be trading off its sensibilities for bread and chicken fat, was a third.

The Board offered two commodities: management and labor. On each level, the sales point was experience. Recovery people, as they were known, could furnish a concern with workers from the bottom up, or they could augment the work force that was already on the premises. It didn't matter. These folks were so desperate for reestablishment in benevolent environments that they would use their abilities to the last full measure.

C. J. Felder set the principles out in a series of eloquent letters to Miss Minerva Bolton. Since the first inquiry had elicited an immediate, gracious request for more information, the letters and prospectuses had surged across the mountains. Minerva was enthralled.

She had always loved it when the business of ordering Things occupied her. The selling process she found so seductive that often she allowed the salesman to continue long beyond the point where she had already made up her mind to buy.

With the Recovery, the idea of transacting business had attained its highest level, she thought. What was at stake were lives, nothing less. She could influence countless others, by her direct action, by her example, by her conviction. She could, incidentally, serve La Vallée superbly at the same time.

The Valley, in fact, had never suffered underemployment. Every time she shortened a shift and added another one, or augmented her labor force by even a small percentage, she did place a drain on the human resources of the region. When irate employers turned upon her, a woman who should have served as their example and ally rather than their adversary, they did indeed have an honest rivalry for a body of folks to do the jobs that were demanding to be done. Minerva was not unaware of that.

She bargained with Felder, by mail and wire, for twenty-five families to resettle in Saint Kathareen's. Letters of ornate prose forewarned her not only about the crop of workers who would be arriving, but, she fancied, also about the fussy and self-conscious character of their shepherd himself:

From these numbers, my dear Madame, your operation will yield a total of not less than thirty workers, highly qualified, fully vaccinated, and, if I may presume upon Madame's charity, and mention such delicate but, I fear, essential matters, fully guaranteed to be disease-free in the social sense, do you understand my meaning, and if so, kindly accept my humble apologies for the reference, as it is a matter of utmost embarrassment, yet one on which I do believe that a Lady such as yourself ought to have complete reassurances.

Minerva always felt that she had to take a few deep breaths at the end of one of Felder's sentences. She hated the typing machine which framed them, obviously the proud property of the Recovery. She wanted to see Felder's handwriting for herself. She could just imagine the flourishes and curlicues with which he tried to embellish his basic, crude illiteracy. That is, she reflected, if he actually had handwriting at all.

At least he seemed to have a serious eye for the organization of his little band of aliens. As Felder envisioned, when they finally arrived, they would enter without a ripple. At least from the Kathareenian point of view. Whatever else might have been rent asunder in the process, Felder's people kept to themselves. On the surface, the arrangement couldn't have been better. Two families, that of the rabbi and the *schochet*, would provide nothing directly to Minerva except the spiritual security of her new employees and the sanctity of their respective homes and tables. For that development Minerva felt all the more virtuous herself.

The housing would be simple. The Robley-Musgrove building concerns would provide new frame dwellings for cash down payments at five years, interest-free, or ten years at the lowest possible mortgage rates. Karraman would quietly donate a two-story frame house up on Sycamore near Fourth to be used as the synagogue. The rabbi and his family would live on the second floor. Minerva understood from Felder that they would be wanting to do some construction in the basement of the house, but that was perfectly all right with Karraman. The house was to be deeded to the Hebrew community in perpetuity. If they wanted to build altars of Ba'al on the premises, it wouldn't bother him a bit, as long as it didn't interfere with the flow of business in Saint Kathareen's. Minerva reminded him that she didn't think Ba'al had anything to do with the Hebrews, but Karraman said expansively that it *still* didn't matter. That was the end of that.

So Minerva got ready for Felder and company. He was to assume supervisory duties on the night shift at the factory, and the rest of the Hebrews were to be scheduled for the convenience and betterment of the business. Minerva thought she recalled that the Jews had their Sabbath on Saturday, and wondered about that. Felder informed her delicately that there were, indeed, a few traditionalists among his group who would prefer not to work during the span from Friday dusk until Saturday at nightfall. The others, however, would surely not be electing to move to Saint Kathareen's if they had had any exotic medieval rituals accruing. She kept wondering who had done the English for him.

Felder sounded as if he thought that his people would blend easily into the landscape at Saint Kathareen's, and he would in fact prove to be right. They would pass through the larger community like summer shadows, always in place at the right time, often felicitous, occasionally annoying, but never obtrusive.

Minerva had no such neutered ambitions for her benign social experiment. She looked forward to the dark mystery of Levantine noses and gypsy eyes, wild gesticulation and loud, keening prayer. She would hover inconspicuously around Fourth and Sycamore for their Holy Days and their

Sabbaths, wanting to imbibe a little of the color and the culture come from afar. Her success as arbiter of fashion hadn't exactly gone to her head. It simply gave her the confidence that now she could arbitrate a whole village's humanity as well as its sense of taste.

The man who disembarked from the train first had over his arm the identifying topcoat that Felder had promised, and his immaculate broadcloth shirt also fit the description. But where was the rest, not the part that Felder had written about, but that Minerva had assumed would be there? Where were the side curls? The skullcap? Where were the cigar, the eggbread crumbs in the unruly beard? Most of all, where was the nose? What happened to the goiterish eyes, the full lips? Where was the Jew, in short, with his portable redolence of rendered chicken fat and onions?

The man who disembarked from the train carried the gear of Felder, but Minerva was looking for something more like the mark of Job. Instead she saw a beardless, hatless Anglo-Saxon of a man, looking down across his graceful nose from his considerable height.

"Miss Bolton?"

"I am Miss Bolton," she agreed, confused, confident only in the title and the name. She had wrung the usefulness out of "Mrs." ages ago. "Miss" served her professional purposes admirably. Beyond her first declarative sentence, however, Minerva was suddenly speechless. She had rehearsed her lines thoroughly, but this slick impostor was delivering all the wrong cues.

"I am C. J. Felder," he announced in rounded tones. His smile revealed splendid teeth, with not a speck of unleavened bread or anything else in the crevices between them. "How do you do?"

She mistrusted him on sight, was insulted by his cultivated voice and his worldly, erudite manner. She had been prepared to accept him as a queen accepts the humblest of her subjects, to forgive him his origins and his idiosyncrasies, to embrace him in spite of the way he might happen to smell. Instead, as she stared at him incredulously and tried to retrieve her mental footing, he stood and gazed patiently around him, and looked as if he were quite ready, willing, and able to forgive her hers.

Finally it was he who took the reins. "I can't tell you what a pleasure it is to meet you at last, Miss Bolton."

She nodded dumbly, failing to add that it was mutual. At the time, it wasn't.

"Your efforts here in Saint Kathareen's have attracted the attention of organizers and workers throughout the East."

"Is that so?"

"More than you know." He lowered his voice just a fraction, but the implied confidentiality rang straight through. "As a rule, a labor organizer travels with me. Conditions where my people enter the factories are often as bad as where they came from. We go on in with the guarantee that if things aren't cleaned up within ninety days, we pull them out for resettlement under the kind of tolerable circumstances to which every man and woman in this entire country has a God-given right."

Minerva was thinking that in all that avalanche of written words he had never before turned political on her. He had dwelt impractically long on practical matters ranging from hygiene to skirt lengths, but never on ideologies. What kind of duplicity was this?

"Mr. Felder," Minerva interrupted what was shaping into a harangue. "Just a minute, please."

He seemed startled. "Yes?"

"Our communications didn't concern organizing. My people—"

"But don't you see, Miss Bolton?" The interruption, absolutely alien to the amenities of Valley conversation, jolted her. Perhaps *there* was the evidence of the aggressive Semitism she vainly tracked. "That's exactly the point! La Vallée presents no problem at all! When the organizers arrive, it will be strictly to study *you* and your extraordinary success. The harmony . . . Don't you see?" he repeated.

"No, Mr. Felder, I'm afraid I don't see," cold as stone. "Organizers were never part of our communications in any way. Never. If my operation is such a paragon of employee justice, why make an issue of it?"

"We—"

"*I.* I want to leave well enough alone. My people are not experimental animals. We are not a classroom."

"Miss Bolton, I meant no—"

"Never mind, Mr. Felder. You'll want to settle in for the night. I know your journey has been difficult." She looked at the first-class railroad car from which he had alit, thought of a flatbed wagon, and wondered if her sneer had been audible. "A car is waiting to take you to the Inn. I'll see you in my office at the factory in the morning."

"At nine?" She could have sworn that the opaque courtesy masked something else, but she was prepared to best whatever it was.

"Seven-thirty," and wheeled off into the crowd. It was a good thing that Felder had come a week before his party, as an effective scout. Perhaps she could still head the rest off at Pittsburgh.

In the morning Minerva arrived promptly at seven-fifteen. Felder, already deeply engrossed in the materials on his desk, looked busy, scholarly, clean. "'Morning, Miss Minerva." He grinned.

"Good morning," primly. "I see you've begun your day."

"Begun my career, is more like it. I have nothing but admiration for what I see so far. You astonish me."

I astonish myself, she thought, flushing, if I'm going to be taken in by flattery. On the other hand, she had not come up with a persuasive reason to eject Felder, either. A contract is a contract.

So she began to teach him the business. It was important to her to be careful, lest she be accused of instigating his failure by omitting critical information. On the other hand, she watched him carefully to catch mistakes, carelessness, excess. He never committed any. Still, she could not find a way to trust the man. He had, after all, betrayed her expectations.

He continued that kind of betrayal until, within weeks, he could anticipate Minerva's needs before she expressed them. He had come as a manager, not a milliner, but he learned the language of the hat trade as masterfully as he had obviously learned English.

The garish, ornamental correspondence Minerva had gleefully attributed to his crassness had demonstrated no such thing. His chief amanuensis, a thorough and clever immigrant lad who, perhaps, still lacked a few of the refinements of the written language, had been responsible for it. Minerva, at first aghast, grew slowly appreciative as she learned that one of Felder's rarest gifts was the ability to delegate authority, and then leave the delegate alone to do the job and learn from it. His subordinates thus grew confident in themselves, and in him at the same time.

Minerva could already see small evidences of a new energy abroad in the factory, and there was no doubt in her mind that Felder was generating it. Subtly, wasting no time, he had reorganized a hierarchy of foremen and subforemen and stewards whose growth he then encouraged through their participation in short-term competitions with each other. In some places Felder defined the goal in terms of material output; in others, speed, or the reduction of waste. Occasionally the object was to solve a technical problem before someone on another shift found a better way. The rewards were usually spiritual, but occasionally Felder contributed a round of liquid refreshment after work to the winning foreman and his team.

After grudging reflection upon the growing conviviality between the employees and Felder, Minerva finally called him in and announced that his financial profligacy in frivolous areas would have to stop forthwith. Felder knew exactly what she meant.

"It's not so very much, Miss Bolton," he argued diffidently. "Besides, where else is there to spend a dollar in Saint Kathareen's? A penny or two for the sake of company morale—that doesn't infringe on my monthly budget so much."

As he spoke, Minerva belatedly realized that the petty cash Felder was spending was his own. That made her even angrier.

"Felder, I'm not asking you. I'm telling you. Put a stop to it right now.

Your money isn't my concern, but the encouragement of using alcohol among the employees is bad policy, and I won't have it."

"As you wish, Miss Bolton."

Before he was out the door, she knew that her anger was rooted in embarrassment. Why hadn't she thought of Felder's useful little methods herself? She hated being bested on her own court. Not another word was ever spoken on the subject. But before the day was over, Felder received a handwritten memo to the effect that a small fund labeled "Entertainment" would be budgeted to his disposal. He was to utilize it at his discretion, "to attend to the well-being of those connected with La Vallée."

Minerva set up the official mechanism, but that was the true story of how C. J. Felder invented Minerva's corporate expense account. She slowly was learning to give him that much: he had an apparently infallible sense for what would make people happy.

Fortunately, he was equally perceptive about many of the things that angered them, too. It was less a matter of knowledge than of instinct, but long before the first light snows fell in Felder's first winter with Minerva, he knew where the factory was vulnerable as well as he knew her strengths.

Felder hadn't known about a planned brick-and-bottle assault on La Vallée, but he did know that rival manufacturers up and down the river vied bitterly against Minerva's higher pay and far better conditions for perennially scarce workers. When a violent few stormed the factory one sleety night, Felder might have been prepared for it all along. That was how quickly he rallied himself and his forces.

Minerva was already there, whether coincidentally or not, she never said. Nor did she ever take Felder's appearance anything other than casually. Presumably she knew that it was his habit to return during the swing-shift hours, mingle with the night staff, get ahead of things. What enraged her was that, as he reached the top of the stairs, he stopped on a dime and shot back in the opposite direction. Hmph! she thought. Wouldn't he just be the one to turn tail in a crisis.

She couldn't very well fire him for insubordination, since she hadn't issued any orders that he had disobeyed. Still, there was something ugly about a man who would abandon and forsake an employer in serious distress. She should have known.

Then, suddenly, there he was, returning to the vortex. With him he had brought a good dozen of the burliest men and the toughest women in the evening-shift contingent. Each one was lugging or hauling or hefting a crate of something. Except Felder. With a grappling hook in his right hand he was tugging along not one but three boxes. In his left he pulled two burlap bags, a brace of pliant reinforcements. Barking orders, he emplaced himself beside Minerva, in the most vulnerable location on the floor. Still in jacket and waistcoat, he fought like a man possessed, if fighting was what anyone could have called it, with flowers as shrapnel and language as bomb. At his side stood Minerva hurling her barrage of weapons—clump after cluster of artificial flowers. There she was, a hostile bride, catapulting her angry bouquet into history's face.

Minerva's eyes blazed. She couldn't have estimated accurately how long the entire skirmish took. It went on and on, the air filled with curious missiles and strange exhilaration, until she thought her arm hadn't the strength to lift one more projectile to the window, let alone throw it. The attackers below were slowing down, too. Most of them seemed to think either that their point had been achieved or that it wouldn't be that night.

It was at that juncture, just before the various cavalries retreated, that Felder sustained the only real injury of the encounter. One bottle, which must have been flung by a colossal arm, reached the top of the window from whose bottom half Felder was leaning. The raised, double-hung panes both shattered, shards flying everywhere. Minerva actually saw it happen.

Felder's hand flew to the intersection of his head and neck, where, it seemed to Minerva, the natural angle had suddenly, ominously shifted its entire cant. She saw Felder's face and neck go crimson. She screamed. She thought he was going to be decapitated. Frantically she pulled him away from the window. Blood streamed between the fingers of his clawing hand.

"Felder! My God!"

"It's all right, Miss Bolton," he gasped. He withdrew his fingers from the region of the bloodied collar beneath his jawline, bringing a huge sliver of glass and most of his earlobe with him. His fastidiousness had saved him. The fragment that had lopped off his earlobe had fallen, spent, unable to penetrate the layers of worsted, broadcloth, shirt, waistcoat, and necktie that had bunched up to protect his arteries and jugular.

Somebody had already run for first-aid supplies. Minerva ran toward a visible bolt of muslin, snipped a huge swatch, and folded it into a solid compress even as she ran back toward Felder.

"Thanks, Miss Bolton," playing with a wry smile beneath the agony. "This sure beats a tourniquet around my neck."

"Oh, Felder. I'm so sorry. So truly sorry."

"S'nothing. Could you just hold this in place while I loosen my collar?"

"Of course."

Meanwhile, the police had arrived downstairs. There wasn't much of a tumult left. The aggressors had apparently decided that the pitched battle was over anyway. Saint Kathareen's finest, all three of them, apparently didn't want to alienate either side. Ankle-deep in slush, they simply looked at the artificial flowers, shooed the remaining participants on their way, and left.

"Felder, we'll get you to the hospital."

"Nonsense. The bleeding seems to have stopped. We'll put a bandage and some sticking plaster on this, and start to clean up below."

"That can be done in the morning."

"Nonsense. We'd waste two shifts that way, instead of just one."

"You're a remarkable man, Felder," said Minerva, tearing adhesive tape.

"Not at all. You were in trouble. I did what I had to do."

"Can I ask you something?"

"Why not?"

"What would you have done if I hadn't been here?"

"What's to do? I would have done what needed to be done. Do you think I don't have my own pride in La Vallée? Do you think," he added with a trace of the accents she knew that he was only burlesquing now to cover whatever emotion he really felt, "that you're the only person watching the store? Let me tell you something, Miss Bolton. When you took on Felder, you took on a very responsible person."

"Oh, Felder," she said again monotonously, not knowing whether he had any idea what kind of apology she owed him. "Call me Minerva."

Together they worked through the hours helping, leading the rest of the night shift in cleaning up the mess, temporarily sealing the broken windows with plywood and asbestos. Shortly before dawn they both left. Minerva told Felder, as he left her at the porte cochere of the Inn, not to come back to work until he felt better, a day or two, whatever he needed. He nodded and thanked her, but they both knew he'd be back on the job at the usual time.

Upstairs, as Minerva began the excruciating task of removing the slivers, she understood clearly that a great deal of the blood on her hands was his.

When the dust settled, Minerva was a heroine. Felder had not hesitated to report the events of the siege to the Recovery, who in turn informed its friends on every major newspaper east of the Rockies. In Felder's version, he had barely been present as an observer. It was Minerva Bolton, already known as a champion of the worker, who had mounted the battlements on behalf of her principles and her people. Minerva thought that if Hammond Bolton had followed the story, and he undoubtedly had, she would certainly be receiving the divorce papers any day now.

Well, let him. But let him do it through her attorneys. Minerva decided that she was going to get herself out of the Valley, out of harm's way for a while. It was time.

Not that the siege had left her intimidated. On the contrary, she felt consolidated more than ever, and sublimely supported by Felder, whose asymmetrical ear, at last healed in a clean, geometric line, added a dashing touch. She felt not only the confidence, but the strong justification to go to

Europe, come back with ideas, techniques, enthusiasm. Knock Saint Kathareen's, and her growing national clientele, off its collective pins.

She couldn't have picked a more auspicious time to do it. After five years during which all of the principals had privately wondered whether indeed it could happen, Emmaline Robley had become pregnant again.

For five years Minerva had had no tangible clue that Karraman had ever touched Emmaline after their wedding night. Their marriage, while it had settled into a domestic arrangement that included civilized conversation at table and on most public occasions, hardly radiated blissful communion. At times Minerva had reason to wonder whether it entertained any communion at all. When Minerva stayed over at the Inn, Karraman often joined her. There they inhabited a universe of mutuality, a sharing that kept a safe distance from a world where one's private pain or suffering might be visited upon another soul. In other words, they never talked about Emmaline, except insofar as she was a member of the population they knew in common.

For five years the thought that Emmaline might one day bear Karraman's child had bobbed around on the surface of Minerva's mind, but without persistence. She had no reason to think that Emmaline had become barren with her first miscarriage, nor had she any real reason to believe that Karraman did otherwise than act as a husband to his wife. Moreover, she no longer felt any more threatened by the advent of a child than she did by the presence of a wife. Karraman's commitment to Emmaline had been sealed from the first. Minerva had not truly coveted Emmaline's nominal position at the beginning, and she did even less so as the days wore on. She saw quite clearly that Karraman had great need of the mansion, of the lady of the house, the "little woman" at home with her needlepoint and her menu planning. If Minerva was the great love of his life, Emmaline was the great rock in the middle of his public diadem. Minerva wouldn't have had it any other way. She had tried rockdom once, in Massachusetts. It hadn't worked out at all.

But now there was the thought of a child, suddenly quite real after five dormant years. To her utter consternation, the impact of the news jolted her. She knew that she would recover, that everything would regularize, that she had no right to any negative emotions that she might in any way transmit to Karraman, tainting the air, diminishing her humanity and thereby her importance to him. She needed time, precious time. She needed distance, and diversion, and the healing air in the cobbled streets of Europe. She needed a gestation period of her own, to use in developing the output of her factory—possibly adding something logical, like gloves, or scarves crafted to order from fine imported silk. She had some ideas running through her head about actually painting on fabric. What an opportunity it would be to talk with the people who knew the materials and the techniques she wanted to work with. Europe was the place where she could unite herself for the future.

What was most important, she'd be damned, tarred, and feathered if she was going to endure one single minute of Emmaline's morning sickness a second time around. She picked up the telephone and began to make arrangements. Poor Karraman. He wouldn't take the news of her impending journey lying down. But that position was just where Minerva wanted him to be. She had no logic, no force of reason behind her. Yet she was bound that she would prevail, by whatever powers she could summon.

Without ever having left the shores of the mighty Ohio at Saint Kathareen's, Minerva had acquired a loose but interconnected network of friends who summered, wintered, or just plain lived abroad. A flurry of invitations greeted her when she first arrived at her hotel in Paris. Instead of dwindling to a trickle as she quite expected them to do, they continued day and night in France, and then either trailed or preceded her everywhere she went for the length of her stay.

Social badinage had never exhilarated Minerva. She was far too devoted to reality to take sustained pleasure in surface conventions. The breadth of opportunities, villas, titles, activities, failed to turn her head even a degree. They did expand her perspective so mightily that she felt she ought to declare her gratitude as a treasure before Customs when she returned home.

England was the last stop on Minerva's tour. She had planned to sail out of Southampton, feeling that somehow the transition back to America would come more naturally from there than from anywhere else. She would later revise that opinion, but she would gravitate to England from that time on. No matter what else changed, the one constant aside from Karraman would be her friendship, initiated as her first visit to London was drawing to a close, with a gifted and original young milliner named Claire Nikolai.

Claire ran a shop in an unexpected little cul-de-sac in Bloomsbury. Minerva happened to wander up to it one morning. She had decided to poke around the quaint streets with the booksellers and tearooms that epitomized what she had expected of London all along. Hats, for once, had been the farthest thing from her mind. She wasn't even wearing one.

The gilt letters on the door of the shop etched simply NIKOLAI into ancient, rippling glass. The windows were draped so heavily that Minerva couldn't tell at first whether or not it was a commercial establishment. Something delicately handsome in the drapery fabric caught her interest, and she tried to peer in through the murky atmosphere to see what might be lurking inside. She jumped back with an audible start when a pair of eyes like black almonds suddenly stared through a break in the curtains and right back out at her. She stood transfixed as the door opened and a sweet, spicy incense wafted out. Minerva thought she had blundered into an opium den or white slave headquarters for the entire British Isles.

"I'm Claire Nikolai. Do come in." Her accent was thoroughly British, but the quality Minerva ascribed to her was vaguely Balkan. The drapery, the smoky fragrance, Claire's costume—a cossack-looking embroidered shirt, girdled at the waist above a pair of billowy trousers (trousers!)—everything contributed to the impression. Minerva wasn't sure what she was being invited into, but that gloriously tense uncertainty had guided her through some of the most auspicious turnings of her life. She decided to follow it.

And couldn't believe that a simple coincidence had brought her there. "I'm Minerva Bolton. How do you do," she replied, with her head about to swivel off her neck as she began to absorb the most disorderly, ill-lit millinery workshop she had ever seen. In every corner of the sizable salon there were scattered finished and unfinished hats whose design and component parts would have boggled the most experienced eye. Claire, amused, let her take it all in.

Finally Minerva found voice for a comment. "This is . . . a marvel," appreciatively.

"It would seem that you know something about hats."

"How could you possibly . . . ?"

"Either that, or you're an artist." She smiled genially.

Minerva chuckled. "Either that, or you're a gypsy fortune-teller. Please tell me what you mean."

"Rather simple, really. Customers don't come here. I go to them, and show my wares in comfort. They find my working style a bit . . . off-putting, to put it delicately. But they pay. My dear, how they do pay!" She laughed huskily, pleased at the secret shared. "But you—you're not put off by my . . . workshop. Not in the least. Do tell me, Mrs. Bolton. I am correct, aren't I? Hats—?"

"It's Miss. I mean, actually it's Mrs., but . . . Oh, why don't you call me Minerva?"

"A bit forward for England, don't you think?" and went off into gales of laughter as Minerva registered horror at her gaffe.

"Call me Claire, my dear, and do tell me just what it is you know about hats."

If Minerva had mentioned La Vallée at first, Claire would have recognized the name immediately. She did a better job than Minerva, at that juncture in history, of keeping up with the competition. On the other hand, Claire was admittedly harder to keep track of. Her hats sold, unlabeled and unidentified except by the excellence of their style, to a select group of fashionable women who preferred to retain the exclusivity, rather than the popularity, of their costumers. To divulge Claire's name and address was to express an intimate confidence of a type that women did not often choose to share, sisterhood being what it was and wasn't in the dawning years of the twentieth century. Claire didn't disdain publicity, but she never courted it. She had been for years content to let things proceed as they always had. She belonged to a breed unknown to Minerva. As their friendship progressed and her predilections began to unfold, Minerva would be perennially fascinated and envious of the life that Claire was able to maintain by refusing to squander her privacy. Claire, on the other hand, recognized that Minerva was a genius at the art of balance as well as business. Their relationship settled into comfortable mutuality after about forty seconds. It remained undisturbed despite the intervention of war and distance for almost an equal number of years.

Claire had come by chance upon a method of molding felt with minuscule infusions of steam. The result was a technique that could be applied after decoration had been affixed to a basic hat form. The product, while still custom-designed and individually crafted, could be turned out with far greater efficiency. Minerva had first been impressed by the artistry of what Claire was doing, hidden away in that unlikely oda of a workshop. She ended up nonplussed by the cool professionalism behind everything Claire did. It was impossible not to conclude that the maelstrom wasn't a camouflage designed deliberately to keep out the idlers and the high society crowd.

Claire had not identified herself as Miss or Mrs., and with Minerva's help the conversation had progressed to first names before she had a chance. By the time they sat down to share a glass of sweet tea Russian style, with lemon, at midmorning, Minerva's curiosity had progressed beyond the realm of business. Claire had mentioned a daughter. Minerva wanted to know what kind of man it took to grapple with a creative life as independent as Claire's obviously was. Could Karraman Robley have a European counterpart, a man who took pride in this woman's achievements outside of his kitchen, bedroom, parlor? Then again, Karraman was someone else's husband, not Minerva's. Had Claire had to pay a price, too? How to ask?

Through the obvious channel. "Your daughter, Claire. How old is she?"

"Ah. The child of my old age, my personal revolution," replied Claire, who was not yet forty. "She's nearly five years old. A charming little thing. I already regret having to send her to school next year. It's almost like setting the felt to the mold, I think. It serves a purpose, but something of the lovely purity is lost in the process."

"Who looks after her now?"

"Her grandmother. My mother. A true Russian babushka. She speaks to Tasha in Russian and French of palaces and czars. I'm not sure that Tasha remembers she's a proper English child, by the end of each afternoon." Claire's complaint was more wry, more affectionate, than bitter. Beneath the lacquer-black coolie haircut, Claire's eyes laughed and danced. Her tailored severity, Minerva had begun to realize, was as much a surface mannerism as the shambled condition of the studio. Claire's emotions ran eloquently through her conversation after all. And drew Minerva in.

"What about her father? How does he take to all of this?" There. The plunge taken.

"Father? Ha. Tasha represents as nearly an immaculate conception as anything I've heard on earth. Nikolai doesn't know that she exists. Actually, I'm not even sure that Nikolai exists anymore." She spoke in brash accents, but the eyes had it differently.

"I'm sorry, Claire."

"Whatever for, Minerva? The bastard never could stand competition. I never even had a chance to verify that I was pregnant before he walked out." Her expression hardened. "Of course, calling him the bastard in the case does rather muddy things up, doesn't it? I wish we could do away with that particular epithet. I can't imagine how I should cope, if someone were to tack it on to Tasha."

"Claire . . ." Minerva wanted to tell her that she understood, and that there but for the grace . . . , all those things.

"Don't, Minerva. Tasha was my choice. She's a truly capital child, father or no. And I know what you're asking me, besides. You'd like to know how it is that one runs a family and a studio, creates a hat and a child all at once. You'd like to know how it all fits together. Whether or not one can be responsible for the arts of the household alongside the arts of the marketplace. Yes?"

"You're uncanny, Claire."

"Not uncanny. Just experienced. This so-called independence is an uphill and lonely route, one I've handled for all of my adult life, long before Tasha came along. I wish I were as long on optimism as I am on experience."

"You don't think it can work?"

"Does that disappoint you?"

"No. It confirms my suspicions."

"Suspicions or fears?"

Minerva paused. She felt blissfully unconstrained. "No, 'suspicions,' I think, is the right word. I was married once, before the birth of La Vallée. It didn't take. I have no regrets."

"Did you find that you didn't need a man, then?"

"On the contrary. I found that I have an abiding need for a partner, the kind of man who accepts what I do, and respects the ways in which I go about doing it. Not a man who tries to rebuild me in the form he thinks I ought to occupy."

"Nikolai wasn't even that considerate. He wanted me completely formless. Malleable. Going nowhere. There was room for one artist only in his universe. And even that wouldn't have satisfied him. He actually had room for only one whole person, and that cut me out, didn't it? When the possibility arose that he might have to be responsible for yet a third, he disappeared into some far-off caldron of artistic ferment and never was heard from again." She snuffed out a long mahogany cigarette.

As Claire talked, Minerva's compulsion to tell her part, to explain her own self, began to grow into something she could barely recognize. Suddenly the world had assumed a new dimension. Its possibilities peered out at her from beneath a set of luxuriant black bangs. Minerva, who had begun to look mightily forward to her return voyage to Saint Kathareen's, found herself feeling at home in a way she had never previously imagined. By the end of the afternoon, she and Claire knew as much about one another as perhaps two acquaintances of such duration can ever hope to. By the time they had enjoyed a splendid dinner at Claire's mother's table, Minerva had agreed to cancel her return passage and stay on for an additional month.

Baba, Claire's mother, made it much easier. A small woman, she had the kind of carriage that suggested imposing height and unshakable calm. Minerva loved the way her lush voice ran in trills around the *r*'s and gutturals of her conversation, and she accepted with profound gratitude the effortless hospitality that offered piroshki to eat, plum brandy to drink, and a brass bed to sleep in, as though Minerva had all her life been at home with such exotica. Her hotel would undoubtedly have found a way to accommodate her beyond the prearranged length of her stay, but Minerva chose not to discommode them. On the day appointed for her departure, she saw her belongings deposited in a taxi, settled her bills, and directed the driver to take her to Bloomsbury. In the four weeks that followed, Minerva became part of a warm and emotional and effusive family to whom she rapidly realized she could trust her very life.

For four weeks Claire and Minerva worked all day, sharing ideas and techniques, experimenting with styles, inventing the designs that would delight and flatter discerning women in the coming seasons. At nights, by the murky lights of oil lamp and candle, they sat with Baba and Tasha, each of the four in turn making her dreams and memories come alive for the benefit of the others and herself. Sometimes Tasha fell asleep listening, a glass of sweet tea half-finished on the table next to her. Minerva marveled at Claire's tenderness as she removed the child's shoes and covered her gently, letting her pass the night where she had settled rather than disturbing the placidity of her dreams. Once Minerva awakened on the plush davenport in the middle of the night, and realized that the same tender care had been accorded to her. She pulled the eiderdown higher against the chill of the room after the fire had died to embers. As she snuggled in on the way back to dreamless sleep, she realized that what really blanketed her was the unequivocal openness of love and welcome. She was so completely touched, so grateful to the core of her being, that she thought the feelings would burst out of her if she didn't hold on tightly. She clenched her muscles and gritted her teeth against waking so disruptively a household which had offered her nothing but comfort.

As far as anybody else in London knew, Minerva might as well have left the country. She kept that far away from the hub of her previous social circle, and equidistant from the byways of fashion and commerce. When the time came for her to sail for home, she left with a giddy feeling of stealth. She refused to let Claire, Baba, and Tasha accompany her to Southampton, on the grounds that the parting would be easier if their farewells were abbreviated and natural.

As she steamed out of sight of land, Minerva realized that she had acted selfishly. She knew that they would meet again as friends, and serve as creative spurs to one another whenever the time seemed ripe. But there lingered a vestige of guilt that circled her like a gull as she crossed the Atlantic, because she felt quite certain that Tasha would have adored seeing the ship.

It was more difficult to develop a fellow feeling for Peter Robley, the scrawny and blotched little creature who had been born to Emmaline in Minerva's absence. He was colicky and cranky on his mother's milk. When he abandoned his squalling long enough to look around at the world and find it wanting again, Minerva noticed that his right eye had a tendency to wander toward his nose no matter which way the other one went. Emmaline was about to convert the child to a formula made of corn syrup, against her doctor's judgment. When the weaning was accomplished, the household would be indistinguishable from what it had been before Minerva left, since various servants had been assigned to virtually every aspect of Peter's nurture, except for the twenty or so minutes a day during which Emmaline consented to dandle a rattle far too close to the baby's nose. Minerva was sure that that couldn't be helping that eye a bit, but who was she to say?

She wanted to love the baby. He was, after all, flesh of Karraman's flesh. He was also a newborn infant, innocent of whatever loveless grapplings had gone into his making. She wanted to feel protective surges toward this baby as she had so quickly grown to feel them with Tasha, but there seemed to be so much, too much, in the way. One twist of logic told her that a new little life, unformed and uninfluenced, should have been so much easier to love than a child who had spent one hundred percent of her prior life under a tutelage alien to Minerva's experience. Still, Minerva knew that logic had nothing to do with it. The feelings were too intense.

So was the press of business. Shortly after her return to Saint Kathareen's, she realized that she was spending more nights at the Inn than at Foothill House. She had to admit that in this phase of her life the arrangement suited. If Captain Stevens decided to close up shop earlier than usual, or if the water was too choppy for comfort or safety, Minerva would have no plans that she would be forced to change. No obligations to phone up and tell Emmaline not to wait supper for her. No expectations that would have to be altered.

She supposed that Emmaline would rejoice silently at her announcement that she was going to call the other side of the river her official home.

Emmaline surprised her. "After all this time, Minerva? It seems a bit silly to me. After all, one hardly expects you to be here all the time," making it sound like an indictment somehow, "but at least you have a place to rest your head when it suits you."

Minerva was taken completely aback. "Em, you've been too generous. It really is your home, even though you've always made me feel so much a part of it. I—"

"Well, Min, if that's the way you really feel." (An additional count of ingratitude to be charged against your record, Madam Prisoner.) "But I'll keep the room as it is for a while. Just in case. Oh. Will you still be coming to dinner on Sunday? Mother and Father will be asking." Perhaps that was it. Perhaps she simply couldn't face up to the censure of a community that might accuse her of turning poor, defenseless Minerva out into the cold world where she would have to pick up all her mail and messages at a front desk. Or perhaps Em understood that beneath the hostility and the rivalry, the socially prominent Mrs. Karraman Robley had no other female intimate in the world, no one who, in the absence of any discovered blood tie, had tolerated her over such a long period, with such acceptance and equanimity, and without pay, as Minerva had. Or perhaps the real truth was that Emmaline, in whatever unrealized manner, actually did recognize the real truth. Perhaps she had known all along about Minerva and Karraman. Perhaps the thought that haunted her nights and plagued her days was the real terror that if she lost the one, she would lose them both.

Minerva was never to learn the answer to that riddle. Indeed, it is entirely possible that Emmaline never articulated the final analysis of it for herself. Nevertheless, for whatever reason, Emmaline always kept open the invitation to return. She never revised a detail of the room that Minerva left, although whenever Minerva came back, she saw that it was entered at least often enough to keep it in high polish and perfect repair. She discovered that even when Emmaline finally had the garret equipped with a real floor of varnished teak, she had the harem pillows replaced exactly as they had been scattered in 1911. Minerva flirted briefly with the theory that Em had simply forgotten what the original arrangement had been, but at rock bottom she knew that wasn't right. She felt ineffable gratitude, like an errant sailor for whom the light in the window has never been extinguished.

XII

By the time Minerva became pregnant, Emmaline had two more children, little Peter's eyes had straightened out, and La Vallée was operating four overlapping shifts twenty-four hours a day. Through outlets in seventeen cities, La Vallée boutiques were also selling the gloves, scarves, and imported soft leather accessories that the factory manufactured, warehoused, or finished from imported materials. Minerva had worked almost nonstop for nine years. Thanks to Felder, who had risen to occupy the position of virtual alter ego, she still went to Europe annually. Her trips were never vacations; however, she looked forward to them with the glee of a child anticipating the Glorious Fourth on the village square. Unlike such a child, she never fell asleep before the festivities were over. And she never, never came home disappointed.

When she realized and had confirmed medically what had happened to her, sets of implications raced through her like tumbleweed across an unfenced veranda. It wasn't that she had ever thought of herself as barren. Forever and ever birthing ideas and designs, she thought herself perpetually gravid in all the senses that were important to her. The gloomy concept of barrenness was far from her way of viewing her universe.

Years before, when Emmaline had conceived with such lightning efficiency on her wedding night, Karraman had asked Minerva, with touching awkwardness, if she would prefer him to use some kind of galvanized rubber sheath to protect her from Emmaline's fate. Minerva had little idea of what the thing would look like or how it could work. She kept picturing an automobile tire, and couldn't shed the images of treads and blowouts. Mischievously relishing Karraman's vast embarrassment, Minerva allowed him to answer every petty question, to overexplain, to apologize himself into a crimson sweat. Then she told him kindly that she didn't think such a thing would be necessary at all.

"Seriously, Karraman, consider the facts. Emmaline is one sort of individual, and I'm assuredly another. I'm simply not the mothering kind. People buy my sort of offspring and wear them on their heads! It's . . . well," she lowered her voice, "it's my calling," reverently. And thus did she see "facts."

Karraman traced the line of her cheekbone down his favorite path with his index finger. It circled around her lips. She kissed the toughened whorls of his fingertip as if to seal the veracity of her conviction.

"All right, Minerva," he had assented, grateful to be relieved of the responsibility. To him, the use of a "French letter" secretly signified the demarcation between the fancy ladies of Pike Street and the women of valor who belonged to his sundry houses and lives. If Minerva chose to consider herself "above" Emmaline's assorted fates, Karraman could only accept her decision with relief and chuck out with the jetsam of other problems he regularly consigned to the women's department whatever anxieties he had harbored on her behalf.

What a snaggle of contradictions Minerva had represented in those days! She accepted her monthly "friend" with the equanimity and comfort of a modern athlete. She never in all her life comprehended the woes of benighted souls like Emmaline, who took regularly to her bed, whining and mewling with "the curse." On the other hand, Minerva remained medievally oblivious of, although not precisely ignorant of, the various causes and effects pertaining to that particular sector of her being. Heaven knew that she and Karraman had had ample opportunity over the years to have started any number of babies. The fact that they didn't for so long simply reinforced Minerva's conviction that her will chiefly, if not exclusively, governed the situation. She never squandered a moment's anxiety over her biological calendar in ten years. There was far too much to keep track of among the orders, invoices, and bills of lading.

Not entirely unsophisticated, she did know that it was possible to "lose" a baby at will, if one knew the right people. She was also quite certain that she could find out who the "right" doctor was from Karraman with very little difficulty. He always knew such things, every bit and shred of arcanum in the Valley. She gave that possibility about sixty seconds of careful consideration before she realized that such a course was completely out of the question. Something deeply buried in Minerva suddenly quickened and leaped to the instinctive, permanent defense of her—and Karraman's—unborn child. She couldn't see sufficiently far into the future to figure out what she was going to do with it after it was born, but she did know that she wanted to bring it into the world more than she had ever wanted anything before in her entire life. As a plan started to form in her mind, she went to her personal desk, opened a drawer, and began to write a letter.

"Karraman, I'm going to spend a bit longer in Europe than usual this year. Felder is in complete control, and I'll need the time."

Karraman responded exactly the way any loving mate might answer when faced with the prospect of a war, a separation, and all of the unknown elements designed to strike fear into the hearts of mortals under the poised dagger of ultimate loss. He bound all his tenderness and need and protective instinct up into one fragile package and delivered it to Minerva at the top of his lungs. "What in the hell's the matter with you, Minerva? Have you completely taken leave of your senses?"

Patiently: "Now, Karraman, you don't need to shout at me. I can perfectly well hear you just the way you were. If you want to go about shrieking like that, you might as well wait until I'm gone. I'll still be able to hear you."

"Minerva, you're not being funny. Or even remotely reasonable. There's a war going on over there."

"Not in England, there isn't."

"Not yet, maybe, but England certainly hasn't hesitated to involve herself right up to her royal ears so far. I don't give those damned fools six months before they're sweeping mortar shells off their own front doorsteps."

"Not according to Claire."

"And just who the hell is Claire?"

"You know perfectly well who Claire is."

"Yes, I do, and that's exactly what I mean. Just what the hell kind of an expert is she supposed to be? You can sell her under the table without half trying, and now you're trying to tell me that she's an expert on international diplomacy, too? Don't delude yourself, Minerva. Claire can no more predict the course of this thing than she can fly the ocean on a pair of homegrown wings. She doesn't have half the brain you do."

"I think that was supposed to be a compliment, Karraman, but it won't help. It wasn't even a very good compliment, if you stop to think about it. Twice as good as not much is just about like multiplying zero. No matter how high you go, you still come out with the same thing: not much."

"That wasn't what I meant, and you know it, Minerva. I'm telling you that just because your friend has a lonesome urge to spend a month or so cooking up ideas for the new season with you doesn't necessarily mean she can see the forest for the trees." He paused long enough for inspiration to strike. "Say, Min, if that's all it really is, this might be the perfect time for you to invite Claire over here. After all, she's never seen the operation at La Vallée. She'd have all the time, all the space . . . And I think, with a little luck, she might even find that she could end up as a nonpaying guest at the finest inn the United States of America has to offer. I—"

"No!" Like the report of an unexpected weapon, catching Karraman completely off-guard.

"What?"

"I mean," straining toward graciousness, "no, thank you, Karraman. Thank you with all my heart. And Claire's too, I'm sure. But not just now. I'm going."

"But what on earth for? You're behaving absolutely absurdly, do you know that? This isn't like you, Minerva."

"Claire has . . ." flailing, "she has so much else to think of, Karraman. I can leave La Vallée, and with Felder and the crew, it's as if I'd developed a second body and brain to take over while I'm gone. Claire has nothing of the sort. Just herself. Once in a great while she contracts out some handwork, but that's all. If Claire goes, Chapeaux Nikolai goes right with her. And she can't afford that," omitting the details of the various independent moneys on which Baba seems to draw from somewhere at will, allowing them security if not luxury, comfort if not elegance. Still, what Minerva had said in the main described the situation. It was indeed Claire's income that kept them all from day to day. She guarded that source of livelihood as if it were all she had.

Karraman's equanimity went up like a magnesium flare. "Well, that's as goddamn imprudent a way to conduct a business as I can think of. I don't know what you think you can learn from her, but it sounds like she needs some goddamn basic lessons of her own in practical living."

"She seems to have done all right so far, not that it's any business of yours. Besides, she has Baba and the child to support, and she's done as creditable a job of that as anyone could possibly ask. I only wish you could see Tasha," she added as a lesson, uttering it like a curse.

"And that's another thing. That child is no one's fault but Claire's, no matter how you look at it. Talk about poor management . . ." He did not seem prepared to leave the sentence unfinished, but Minerva saw her choices clearly: terminate the statement, or get the hell out of this room, out of the kind of life that could produce such utterances. Get far, fast. Perhaps forever. She went for the sentence instead of the exit. At least that was an action open to revision if necessary.

Her fire had converted itself to dry ice, searing and deathly cold. "Every child on earth has two parents, Karraman, even if one of them chooses to absent himself from the premises. Fortunately for Tasha, Claire is more than capable of bearing the responsibility of both. If you consider my friend's managerial skills so terribly poor, sight unseen, then no amount of argument on my part is going to change your mind. I'm sure you have more important things to do right now than sit here listening to me waste my breath."

He reached for her hand, which she withdrew gently and without rancor. If she had pulled away in a dramatic gesture, he would have pulled her back, swept her to him, buried the differences between them in the kind of crushing embrace that had, with the years, never gone sour or a tad less exciting than it had been in the beginning. But that was hardly the resolution that Minerva wanted to that problem just then. She saw no point in sweeping the dust over the chasm in a cloud. The gaping hole would be invisible for a while, but as soon as somebody tried to take the first step back into the ordinary, an unprecedented disaster would become unavoidable. Somebody would crash.

"I'm sorry, Karraman. The last thing I wanted was an argument about this."

"Min, if you'd just be reasonable."

"I am being reasonable. There have been restless times before, and there will be restless times forever, if the entire roster of recorded history is any indication. I have a business to think of, and a life to lead." Or vice versa, she thought. "I can't just keep myself in a state of suspended animation because a few Balkan princes insist on getting themselves blown up in Europe."

Karraman chuckled in spite of himself. He didn't know that she had deliberately engineered her phrasing so that he would. "You make it sound like a chess game, Min. It's not nearly that simple. I only wish it were. This is the real thing. I'm telling you. If you go to England now, you're liable to find yourself in the middle of it at any time, and it's no laughing matter, I assure you."

Minerva may or may not have been chastened, but she spoke as if she were. "I know it's not a game, Karraman. I've never been more serious in my life. I promise you that I won't be rash, but I'm going. I must go. Now."

"And that's that?"

"That's that."

"Min, you're such a babe in arms. A modern war—nobody on this earth knows what it's like to live through one . . . or how to survive. Min . . . I don't want you to go."

"I'll be safe, Karraman. I'll be back before you know I've gone."

"Fat chance." That time she went to his arms when he opened them, and wished that nothing in the world could ever make her leave.

She thought that the conversation had ended. She thought that her bullheaded refusal to listen to reason had been the most effective acting job of her career. A grateful prayer went up to the powers that had enabled her to get away with it. All she wanted was to get packed and sail away in peace; peace being, of course, a state of nonharassment by anyone who loved or could otherwise influence her. It had absolutely nothing to do with the condition which was the opposite of war. One woman's peace can obviously be very much another woman's holocaust.

Unfortunately, Minerva's hymns of grateful praise came prematurely. Karraman found her intransigence winsome, her stubbornness seductive, and her gaping (and feigned) ignorance about the progress of the war the most attractive aspects of her whole posture. He loved her more, wanted her more, didn't want to sacrifice ten minutes of her gumption for the sake of anything.

He dragged the conversation all the way back to the beginning, as if it had never come up before.

"Hmmm." Musing. "You know, Min, this seems like a good year for me to visit Europe, too, now that I think of it. Before the whole continent explodes politically, that is, and in every other way I can think of. After a, um, decent interval, you might say, we might perhaps just accidentally run into one another over there." He looked enormously pleased with his solution.

"No!" Sharply.

"What?"

"I meant, I'm not sure that's a good idea, Karraman. If there is going to be trouble, I'd feel considerably safer if you were here at home keeping your eye on everything. I need you to keep La Vallée under control, as well."

"I thought you told me you trusted Felder implicitly."

"Oh, I do. He's the best employee a business could hope for. But that's it: he's an employee. You're . . . well, you know what I mean."

"I'm not all that sure that I do, Minerva," he said, puzzled. "In all these years, I've talked to you about your decisions whenever you've wanted me to. In fact, it may be presumptuous of me, but I've felt like a part of the business from the first—"

"Oh, you are, Karraman, you are—"

"—but you've never actually asked for a thing. Not a word, not a cosignature, nothing. Now, for some absolutely incomprehensible reason, you're hinting to me that you want me to run the whole shebang, or at least see that it keeps running, and you've just gotten through telling me that Felder can do it with his eyes closed. And all you can say about it is that you want to go gallivanting off to Claire Nikolai all the way across the damned ocean, in the geographic center of a damned war. I just don't understand it, Min."

She cast about for some logic somewhere. "Well, for another thing," she essayed, "as soon as Em recovers from this last confinement, she's going to be champing at the bit to get away from Saint Kathareen's for a while herself. How would she feel if you tore off to Europe when I just happened to be there, and then didn't have the time or energy left to take her where she wanted to go when the time came?"

"I suppose there's some truth there," he allowed. "But this entire attitude is so unlike you. I almost feel that you plain don't want me with you. That's a strange sensation, Min. Oh, I know that this arrangement of ours can't be every woman's dream for you, yet here I am nearly begging you to spend a month or so abroad with me, no strings attached, and you seem to be dredging up every excuse in the book to get out of it. It would be the first real freedom you and I have actually had, and here you are running a country mile in the opposite direction. What happened to all those plans of ours? They were so damned realistic that I could practically feel the ship rolling and pitching under our bed." The reminiscence painted a depth into his eyes.

Something heavier than pain stabbed at Minerva, not so much about the separation she was about to enforce, and not so much because she wanted in every fiber to tell Karraman of the real reason for her prolonged journey and knew that she wasn't going to, but because of what she was going to say next. She was going to lie, boldly and barefacedly. To a woman who lives the kind of deception Minerva had to endure perpetually concerning Karraman and his role in her life, truth in every other matter becomes a sacred principle from which she cannot, must not, deviate if she is to keep her self-respect intact. Moreover, she was about to hurt him, when she had never knowingly done so before. She had no idea of how or whether he'd be able to take it. Or whether she would, either.

"Karraman, I just don't think it would be good for us right now. I need a break of some kind, that's all. This is the way I'm going to do it this time. Don't worry, dearest heart. I'll be back." She wanted to implore him to be waiting for her. She wanted to turn her back, to foreclose the possibility of any reply at all, let alone one that she might not be able to answer or absorb. She wanted to be gone right that very minute, before she changed her mind and told him that she wanted nothing more in life than to wander through the world with him, at leisure, to have him there beside her when

[217]

their child was born. Instead, she stared him down, hoping that he would be unable to see the torment in her eyes through the pain in his own.

"If that's the way you want it, Min, I suppose that's the way it's going to be."

She tried to make light of it. "Minerva Bolton Triumphs Again, eh?"

"I wish somebody felt triumphant about it. Maybe you do."

"It isn't that, Karraman," softening. "Just please believe that I know what I'm doing, and that for once my judgment is right."

"For once? Min, that's the problem. Your judgment is more right more often than anybody's I've ever known, my own included. I just hate to think of being the one who's left behind again. And I suppose you'll call me old-fashioned, but I hate the thought of your making that crossing again all by yourself. Especially under the circumstances."

"Of all the things to worry about, Karraman. I'm such an experienced hand by now that I'm practically part of the crew." Besides, for one time in her life she was going to be anything but all alone. Not for a single second.

They let it go at that. She didn't want to leave too soon, because she really wasn't quite sure how long she'd have to wait after the birth of the baby before she came home. On the other hand, she didn't want to wait too long, because she didn't want Karraman to begin to suspect. Besides, who knew when the shipping channels actually might be blockaded once and for all.

Fortunately, she had picked up the habit of wearing flowing chemises and all manner of Oriental smocks and caftans from Claire. Her bohemian exoticism, cattily well-remarked all over Saint Kathareen's, precluded any worry about her wardrobe. As for Karraman, he had always told her that he'd love her just as well with a few more pounds on her lithe body. If she had to play that kind of bluff before she left, so be it.

When she finally got ready to leave, Karraman did decide firmly and irrevocably to accompany her to New York. Minerva never found out whether Emmaline knew exactly where he was going on that trip, because the night before the morning of the scheduled departure, Em had an all-out *bon voyage* party for her at Foothill House. The most likely explanation that Minerva could settle on was a feeling of "good riddance," which Emmaline would hardly have been cultivating if she had understood fully that her own husband was going along for a hearty part of the ride.

Minerva did not anticipate that her *voyage* could possibly be as *bon* as all that, no matter what the motivation behind the wishes. Her only previous experience of pregnancy had been Emmaline's. She would never forget the first time, when the aborted fetus had flooded out of Em as uncontrollably as the waters out of the dam at Creighbill's Bottom. It never entered Minerva's mind that she'd lose her own baby. She had too much faith for that. What she did remember from that time and every other was the incessant vomiting, the changing of linen, the mornings when a drop of tea on Emmaline's tongue was enough to send her into paroxysms of gagging that went on far into the day. Minerva had felt remarkably hale so far, but she couldn't imagine that an ocean voyage in her condition could possibly be anything but complicated. She only hoped that she had the stamina to get through it without becoming a burden to anybody.

She took about twenty-four hours longer than her usual ten minutes to gain back her sea legs. It might have happened that way in any case, since the weather was bad enough out of New York. Minerva didn't emerge from her stateroom for the entire first day and night. When she finally did, the ship was smoothly under way. She felt better than she had in years.

At odd moments, when the breeze teased her a certain way as it wafted off the water, or the light angled toward her just so in the late afternoon, memories as sharp and insistent as chapel bells would clang across her field of vision, and carry her right back to the day she first laid eyes on Saint Kathareen's from the hills above. She seemed to be recapturing every bit of the giddy anticipation, the boundless hope, that had energized her through that buoyant adventure. This time she had a better sense of where she was going geographically, but the rest lay before her in the same sort of splendid mystery.

Claire, Tasha, and Baba met her at the Customs House. She had not anticipated their appearing, but when she saw them, she wondered why she had adhered to the scrupulous ritual of arriving and departing in solitude over all the years. Their smiling faces fell over her like an eiderdown in the dreary fog of early morning.

"Oh, Minerva," Tasha greeted her, "Mummy says you've come to have a baby! Is that really true? May I see your tummy?"

Claire, an honest woman, made no attempt to silence the child or to squelch her loving concern. Besides, she could see Minerva beaming all the way from the inside of her soul.

"It's true, Tasha. I've come to England to have a baby. I can hardly believe it myself!" The latter was no surprise. In more than five months, Minerva had never uttered those words out loud to anyone, even herself. The baby was an active little creature by that time, fluttering occasionally like a hummingbird on the wing, or else sparring like a punch-drunk kangaroo, on the move almost incessantly. Minerva was never unconscious of her unborn traveling companion, yet, until that rendezvous, the baby had remained a joy unshared. Uttering the truth of it aloud to Tasha made it real. With the deep pleasure of the revelation bathing her in a luminescence, Minerva settled into England to thrive and gestate and enjoy the rest of her pregnancy.

They had all assumed that the baby would be born at home. Baba had indeed delivered Claire of Tasha in fine style. No one anticipated any problems whatsoever with Minerva. Minerva, herself feeling sturdy, invincible, and quite female, thought that she could surely handle the entire process by herself. She deigned to allow the others along for the ride as a courtesy. They, after all, were allowing her to stay with them for all these months.

It started simply enough, on an ordinary evening in Indian summer. Minerva, distantly nostalgic, was trying to convey what the phrase "Indian summer" meant to her. Suddenly her eyes went wide and her breath caught somewhere in the back of her throat. She didn't want to appear too anxious, so she just went right on talking, or trying to. Claire and Baba both saw what had happened. Pointedly they eyed each other, then Minerva. In quiet wisdom, neither of them said a word. Both, however, took careful note of the time according to the corner clock which had seen Baba's own mother and grandmother through moments like these.

They went on to speak of autumn in Russia, how the birch forests blazed gold, then how the leaves withered overnight and raced the first snowflakes down for possession of the ground. Baba's eyes grew misty as she recalled the frigid winters, the sparkle of a pallid sun on frosted windows, the comfort of a samovar. Minerva thought that probably the old woman's mind was wandering. The truth was that she kept a portion of her thoughts firmly affixed to Minerva and another portion to the minute hand of that clock. The memories, like the birch leaves, were nothing but ground cover.

Suddenly Minerva went rigid. Baba arrested what she was saying in mid-sentence.

"Baba, dear, please excuse me." Minerva tried to keep her voice within normal registers, but her eyes shouted a beseeching cry. "I think I feel a little peculiar." And she headed, staggering slightly, toward the lavatory. Claire bounded right up after her, but Minerva, by instinct or reflex, had flung the door shut. Claire decided to wait it out tactfully. She didn't budge from the doorway, however, against the moment when Minerva would need her.

It arrived almost instantly. "Oh, my God!"

Claire tapped lightly on the door, opening it at the same time with the other hand.

"Claire, what's happened? I'm frightened." Minerva stood shivering in a puddle on the tiled floor. She couldn't have been shivering with cold, because the room was sweltering.

"Poor dearest"—Claire smiled–"there's nothing at all to be frightened of. Your water has broken. That's the first sure sign."

"What do we do?" Minerva, being a maiden lady in the collective consciousness of Saint Kathareen's, had actually never heard of such a thing. She had been "spared" the less, and even the more, romantic discussions of childbirth and the attendant woes that occupied many a back-fence or tea-table conversation, on the grounds that she couldn't possibly have any interest in such matters, and had no business being concerned with them if by some off-chance she happened to be. Since Minerva had accepted the rather irregular pregnancy with a combination of bovine contentment and irrepressible glee, Claire assumed that she knew exactly what to expect. For all Claire knew, this might not even have been Minerva's first child. Not that Claire didn't care enough to ask. It was simply that neither she nor Minerva ever asked of the other a shred more of anything than that which was freely given. If Minerva had anything she needed to forget, that was all right with Claire.

The only thing that Minerva probably should have forgotten at that juncture, and couldn't, therefore, erase from her mind to save her very sanity, was the image of Emmaline and her miscarried mess on the bathroom floor at Foothill House, all those years and three live babies ago. The sensation of fluid pouring, unbidden, from between her legs, swept clean out of her reckoning the fact that she had carried a lively, kicking baby to term, and that there was more to the birth process than what had happened to Emmaline and her unformed fetus that morning.

"Hush, Minnie," Claire soothed, brushing damp hair from Minerva's forehead. The freckles seemed to have deepened by many shades in the moments just passed. Actually it was the skin around them that had turned ashen. "What we shall do is exactly what every normal woman does when the waters break. We shall brew some fresh tea and settle down for a long evening ahead. Before too long, I daresay we shall be preparing for a birthday party."

"Am I all right, then?"

"As all right as you can be, luv. Come. I'll dust up a bit in here, while you change into something more comfortable. Baba will get the bed ready."

"Oh." It came out in a massively relieved sigh. "Then let me clean up in here, at least. After all, I'm the culprit," with wry apology in her tone.

Claire was about to say that, Nonsense, it wasn't Minerva's job to be worrying about housekeeping at a time like this, when Minerva's face changed again.

"All right, dear. Steady, now. We'll have you settled down in two shakes. Can you breathe deeply with me?"

Talons of pain gripped Minerva from the small of her back all the way around to her middle, overlapped, went around again. Years later she remembered thinking, with freshly minted reverence for her gender, Is this what it's like? My God, how do we survive?

Then, before she had time to find a tolerable position for herself, a way to mitigate the tightening, it drained away. She realized to her astonishment that except for the few beads of sweat standing out on her forehead like untimely dew, nothing else had changed. She had neither been rent asunder nor even, indeed, lost her footing.

"I'm sorry for being a bit panicky, Claire. I've never done this before, you know. I'll be all right now."

The assurance in Claire's voice had eased Minerva through the first portal. In getting there, she felt a sense of small but significant triumph. She was ready for the pain, because she knew with an unformed but instinctive certainty that anything on earth was endurable if fear was not one of the components. Whatever other emotions had coursed through her in the cyclonic moments she had just survived, she felt them giving way to an unprecedented excitement, a joyous urge to get on with the business at hand. She thought lovingly of Karraman, of Foothill House, of the factory. The next few hours were shaping up into the long slide home. She rested in the interval before the next pain caught her up, and thought that from now on everything was going to be that old piece of cake of hers. They packed Tasha off to bed with the hopeful assurance that by morning she would be awakened by the lusty wail of a newborn.

"May I be the fairy godmother, Mummy? Please?"

Minerva answered for Claire. "You may be just about anything you choose to be in this world, Tasha dear, including a fairy godmother," before the next wave of agony tore at her. Then Claire shooed the child from the room. She must have lingered just within earshot, for as soon as Minerva eased back into a clammy semblance of relaxation, Tasha's head popped back in the doorway.

"Minerva?"

"Yes, darling," she panted, trying to ease herself back into control.

"You will give me some pointers, won't you?"

"What kind of pointers could I possibly give you, Tasha?"

"Pointers about being a godmother, of course. You're absolutely the best one a girl could hope for."

"Bless you, Tasha." Minerva laughed. "I'll do what I can. Just get along to bed now, because no one can be a proper godmother without a proper night's rest." Tasha blew her a kiss and slipped out. Minerva vowed: Just get me through this, dear Lord, and I'll crown her Queen of the May.

Through the night Minerva labored. Baba and Claire took turns crooning, consoling, brewing endless cups of tea. Toward dawn Claire went out somewhere and returned with a huge block of ice wrapped in newspaper. With a hammer and pick she dissected the thing. After rewrapping one of the halves carefully in newspaper and storing it in the pie chest, she made a horrendous din crushing the other half. She scraped the slivers into a pitcher and began to feed them to Minerva by small teaspoonfuls. Minerva thought it was a miracle.

The crash and clatter of breaking ice awakened Tasha, who wanted to see the baby. Claire told her that the baby hadn't come yet and that there was still plenty of time to go back to sleep. Tasha started to say that she wasn't sure she was prepared to do that, especially if Minerva had any god-motherly services she wished to have rendered, but she fell back asleep before she had formulated her argument. Claire tucked a sheet lightly around her, and kissed her gently. As she walked back to the room where Minerva lay and waited, Claire tried to remember what Tasha had been like as an infant, and how it had been for her when she had given birth. Mercifully, she couldn't.

Minerva lay still and pale. Her eyes were closed. In the kindly censorship of the gas lamp, Claire could see that Minerva was exhausted already.

"Has it been only twelve hours, Baba? It seems so much longer."

"She has spanned the longest hours of the clock, the little one." Minerva, who stood almost a full foot taller in stocking feet than the diminutive Baba, qualified as one of the "little ones" by virtue of a suffering that was beyond Baba's powers to alleviate.

"For a first child, that isn't terribly extraordinary, do you think?"

"No, Katchkale. It isn't the duration that causes me concern now. Look at her."

"She's pale, but she's resting. I think she needs all the respite she can find."

"Respite, yes, Claire. But this has been so for"—she squinted back at the clock—"for nearly three-quarters of an hour now."

Claire laid a hand across Minerva's brow. "At least she's not quite so clammy, Baba. Besides"—she shrugged—"the labor starts, the labor stops. These things happen. Sometimes a woman may labor falsely for a week, two weeks, even, before her time. I shouldn't worry so, if I were you. Would you like me to pour some nice tea, then?"

"I shouldn't worry, you shouldn't worry, all I know is that somebody should worry. The labor stops, yes, and then it starts again. But when this happens, the waters don't break. The baby still has a cushion to rest its head. When the water comes, the baby comes. She was having the pains every eight minutes, maybe seven. Now, nothing. Claire—"

Claire was galvanized. "My God, Baba. I can't imagine why I've lost track, but it seems that I have. Watch her carefully. Wait here. I'll be back as fast as I can."

[223]

"So where would I go," mused Baba, but Claire was already beyond her hearing.

Baba expected Claire to come back with an authentic midwife. Claire half-expected that that was what she would do herself. Still, something told her that, in all of London in 1915, there probably wasn't a midwife whose instincts and skills were as good as hers and Baba's combined. Something was wrong, clearly wrong, with Minerva. Claire would never forgive herself if any kind of disaster were to be laid at the feet of her own lack of thoroughness or caution.

In the placid hours of the city coming alive, finding a taxi and hailing it proved ridiculously simple. The problem now was what to do with it once she found herself inside. Harley Street made no sense at all. No surgery could possibly have been open at that hour. Claire couldn't make sense of starting to ring night bells at random. She nearly cursed the rich lode of experience and folklore that had kept them in London all these years without the need to consult a physician even once, never even placing a name in reserve. She ransacked her brain to come up with a customer whose husband was a doctor, but only produced one mysterious old memory of a fellow who spent his days in laboratories and came home smelling of formaldehyde. Or so his wife said while dissipating his income and her energies buying hats and clothes and anything else the shops had to offer.

Finally Claire remembered meeting at a client's party a physician by the name of Lawrence, Patrick Lawrence, she thought. He ran a private clinic not too far from where the irate taxi driver sat, gunning his engine and doubtless wondering about the sanity of his distraught, oddly clad passenger. She didn't know the street address, but she was certain that she could find it when they got to the proper square. The driver waited in an increasingly voluble state of pique while Claire confidently wakened the innocent residents of two pristine-looking households. With a weak, pleading gesture at the driver to wait a moment longer, Claire jangled the bell on a third, promising door. And received no answer at all.

The driver wrestled with the problem of staying or going. His reputation, even his license as a London cabbie, depended upon his fulfilling the requests of his passenger within any reasonable limits. He didn't mind a bit the handsome fare she was running up in the process. Trouble was, from all the lunatic activity, he wondered if he'd have a chance of trying to collect. He and his conscience wrestled. Before either of them had a chance to declare victory, a door opened just across the street from where Claire was disconsolately trying to decide what to do next. A liveried servant emerged leading two corgis on chains that looked like jewelry.

"I beg your pardon," she hailed. The old fellow, full of self-importance and responsibility, probably would never have looked in her direction, but for the cabdriver, who couldn't stand the suspense a moment longer. He leaned on the auto horn for all he was worth. The dogs responded immediately with complaining, high-pitched barks. Whatever peace might have been left before Claire's cavalier arrival on the street had finally been effectively shattered. The old servant stared at her, shaping his prim lips into a disapproving line. She approached.

"I beg your pardon," she repeated loudly, so that there would be no mistake. "I'm looking for Mr. Lawrence's clinic."

"Mr. Lawrence does not have a clinic," and turned in the opposite direction. He tried to be graceful and suave about tugging the dogs, who were far more interested in Claire.

She didn't know what to make of the way in which he had couched his terse response. "I meant Mr. Patrick Lawrence. That Mr. Lawrence."

He turned far enough toward her so that she could scarcely catch the words he parsimoniously scattered. "That Mr. Lawrence has no clinic."

"But," she stammered, "I know he did a very short while ago. That is, do we mean the same Mr. Patrick Lawrence?"

"Mr. Lawrence, madam, has gone to the Front," implying that any patriotic Englishwoman not only ought to have realized as much, but probably should have been there herself, doing hospital turn, rather than disturbing elderly citizens who were doing all they could to keep the home fires burning and the dogs comfortably walked. "If you have need of a physician's services, madam, I suggest that you ring up the Public Subscription Hospital after twelve this afternoon. They will refer you."

To the driver: "Do you know the hospital he's talking about?"

"I believe I do, missus."

"Then let's go."

"Missus, he said this afternoon."

"Driver, the baby isn't going to wait until this afternoon." She had said it calculatedly, knowing full well that although she couldn't pass for pregnant on close scrutiny, her smock and trousers were sufficiently ambiguous to give him real pause.

"Hang on, then, missus. We'll have you there in no time at all. Why didn't you say so at the beginnin'?"

Claire was too exhausted to reply.

When they raced up to the entrance of the hospital, he surely thought she had lost her reason altogether, because she asked him to wait.

"Lady, this could take days," he pleaded.

She almost laughed, but didn't dare to lose the advantage she had established. "I'll just be a few moments. I promise." He was thoroughly bewildered, but by now too closely drawn into the events of this strange drama to do anything but comply. Besides, he still hadn't been paid.

It took longer than a few minutes. Like every hospital in Europe, that one

[225]

was short-staffed and overburdened. Finally Claire cornered a young doctor who was preparing to leave the building. He had been on duty for nearly forty-eight consecutive hours, and he didn't care if he ever saw another patient. He had been deferred from military duty, Claire was to learn during the intense hours of their association, because a childhood fracture had left him with one leg considerably shorter than the other. He thought he knew about pain, about disappointment, about injuries whose effects endure long after the wounds are closed and the infections healed. But the jagged amputations, the filthy holes, the wretchedly disfigured human skeletons coming out of Belgium and points south drew upon every skill he had acquired, and siphoned out of him more compassion than he thought he'd possessed.

He wanted to go home and sleep for three days.

"Please, madam. Your friend will do best if she's brought here straight-away. Women have babies every day of the year in London. She'll survive the taxi ride, I assure you." His tether was within snapping range.

"Yes, well, Mr. . . . ." She left him a gap to fill. When she saw how easily he leaped at the bait, she knew she had him in the net.

"Gilbert."

"Yes. Mr. Gilbert, have you ever gone through childbirth yourself?"

"I've delivered over a hundred babies this year, madam."

Softly: "That wasn't my question . . . sir."

There followed a long pause, in which Claire placidly watched Mr. Gilbert wrestle guilt and fatigue to the ground.

"Very well, Miss . . ."

"Nikolai."

"Nikolai. I'll ring for a taxi."

"I have a taxi."

A wry smile metamorphosed his features, stripping off hours of armor. "You would."

Minerva was still sleeping when they returned to Bloomsbury. Baba said that she had moaned in her sleep several times but that she could as easily have been dreaming as experiencing pain. Claire had outlined the situation to Mr. Gilbert in the taxi. The driver had hung on every word. As they tried to awaken Minerva in the bedroom, the driver sat in the parlor with Tasha drinking tea out of a glass. He was too deeply invested by that time to think of leaving before the final curtain.

Minerva responded stuporously as Mr. Gilbert prodded and checked her. He discerned the problem easily enough. The challenge lay in deciding how to go about solving it without endangering the mother or the baby.

"The infant is turned the wrong way, Miss Nikolai. It's trying to emerge feet first. I fear that the umbilical cord is wrapped around the neck in such a way that it will strangle if labor continues naturally."

Claire paled. "Is the baby . . . ?"

"The baby is all right at the moment, although the heartbeat isn't what I'd like it to be."

"What are you going to do?"

"The best thing would be to take her to hospital and deliver the child surgically."

Minerva, hovering on the brink of comprehension, said, "No." Softly, firmly, irrefutably. Just, "No." No surgery.

Gilbert was forced to admit that he wanted to agree. The technique, though an ancient one, presented far too many risks. Even the advent of such effective anesthetics as scopolamine and morphine couldn't ward off the fatal sepsis that often overtook mother, or child, or both, after such procedures. Having involved himself in it this far, the doctor, like the driver, had no stomach for a procedure that might end up like a battlefield casualty rather than a blessed event. He would try whatever else he could before resorting to what he considered the drastic ultimate.

Minerva's reasoning had not proceeded as far as Gilbert's had in terms of risk and mortality. All she wanted was to go home free of any scars that she would have to explain to Karraman. She could justify stretch marks. He would consider them a charming concomitant of maturity, no questions asked. To Minerva, it was as simple as that.

Claire saw more dire complications. Her insides were beginning to knot into a hard fist of uncertainty. "Perhaps she ought to be in hospital in any case."

"Yes. I think so. Not necessarily for surgery, but as a precaution. I believe that we can bring the little fellow around without dealing in last resorts. We've an X-ray apparatus that will enable us to see exactly what can be done without moving into extreme measures. Yes." He was undertaking confident action. Thank God the driver had stayed. "Miss Nikolai, I'll take her on ahead."

"No!"

"Beg pardon?"

"I mean, there's no need to go on ahead. If you and Mother will get her out to the taxi, I'll throw some belongings together and be ready at once." She wanted to hang on to every minute. Gilbert shrugged and said that if that was the way Miss Nikolai wanted it, he supposed it couldn't do any harm.

They made a queer party, the driver, the doctor, Baba, Tasha, and Claire, along with the half-conscious Minerva, who was wrapped, shivering, in a feathery comforter on a morning already growing unusually warm and humid for London at that time of year. Minerva was so weakened and dazed that she had no clear idea who was with her, where they were going, or exactly what was happening. All she knew, all she later remembered, was that she had a sense of being borne away on clouds of deep and enduring concern, and that she never doubted for a moment that everything was going to be just fine.

For critical hours, no one shared her confidence. Mr. Gilbert's plan was to manipulate the baby's position with obstetrical forceps until the normal birth procedure could take place without impediment. The progress in such an effort takes place by millimeters. Each millimeter takes time upon time. With each increment upon the clock, Minerva weakened a little. As she flagged, the infant's heartbeat reflected her condition. Gilbert knew that he could not rely too heavily upon the morphine, because Minerva's debilitated system might at any moment abandon the good fight and give itself over to irresistible, permanent rest. He was walking a tightrope, and knew it.

Claire was walking the floors. The day dragged her into a well of fatigue beyond her most haunting memories.

"Claire, close your eyes for a few minutes."

"I'm all right, Baba. The doctor should be back with news anytime now."

"That's what you've been telling me since early this morning. You'll drag yourself into a sickness if you're not careful. Then who will be the friend to Minerva when she needs it most?"

"Babatchka, I know. But I can't rest just now. I'm too anxious." With that, she sank into the coarse armchair next to Baba's, and fell asleep without even putting her head back. Baba started to place the folded comforter behind her daughter's head, when the door opened behind her. She didn't even bother to turn around, there had been so many false alarms during the course of the day. But Claire, alert to the slightest sound, roused herself immediately. And saw Mr. Gilbert, bloodied, exhausted, his surgical mask hanging limply around his neck like something discarded for good.

"It's all right, Miss Nikolai. Mother and child are doing beautifully."

Claire stood there gulping air as if it were something she thought she'd never breathe again. Then she started to weep soft, grateful tears as the others who had shared the vigil bestowed joyous congratulations upon Mr. Gilbert.

"What about the marks on her face?" Minerva asked Mr. Gilbert later that evening.

"Why, you're an American!" he replied.

"Of course I'm an American. What about the marks on her face?" She felt as if she'd known him forever. He had accompanied her on the journey to the edges of her mortality and back, and he hadn't even known that she was an American.

"They're forceps marks. They'll fade rapidly. You're fortunate. Sometimes a delivery like yours causes the infant permanent disfigurement. That won't be the case with your daughter. By the time you take her home to the States, there won't be a trace of a mark."

Minerva looked into the wistful distance. "I'm afraid that won't be for a long, long time."

"Nonsense, Minerva," said Gilbert, who was too tired to puzzle out implications and question them. "The war will be over in no time. We'll all be gadding about across the ocean as safely as if nothing had ever happened."

The war will end, Minerva mused, but that doesn't mean that there will be any gadding across any oceans for this baby. God only knows what kind of life it is I'm letting her in for. Pray for us now. . . .

Minerva named the baby Claire Kathareen Bolton, but in all her life no one, absolutely no one, ever called her anything but Kate.

THREE

XIII

Cara has said "I can't believe it" twenty-five times or more in the three hours that have passed since they left Foothill House with Minerva's identification of Cara's mother ringing in their ears. Perhaps if they had stayed a little longer they would have come away with more of the solid data, more of the hard facts of Kate's exiled existence. Cara would be saying "I can't believe it" a little less often, and trying to assimilate what she has learned into the body of what she has wished, hoped, feared, and utilized for psychic self-defense through the years of her life. But Minerva has succumbed to a wave of utter exhaustion, and asked them if they would mind excusing her so that she can nap. Hawk has had to put to rest an old, cherished fantasy that she never sleeps, is always watchful, always vigilant, somebody's motto personified.

Hawk and Cara have taken turns excusing her to each other, because each is in truth deeply disappointed to have had to cut the session short, but neither can admit it. Moreover, "cut short" is hardly the phrase to apply to a visit that lasted for more than three hours, but neither of them can help seeing it that way in the light of the rest of the story yet to be told.

"She couldn't help it, Cara. For her it must have been like being on the couch for three solid months, dredging her life up after all those years."

Cara agrees. "Being on the rack."

"Really? Did you have a feeling that it was a negative thing? Excruciating, yes, but it had to be exhilarating, too."

"No, not negative. It's just that after all the years of defenses she'd built up, going back into it must be like trying to open an old shipwrecked porthole that's all barnacled over. There's an incredible amount of scraping away to be done, and you're really lucky if you don't mangle your hands in the process. It couldn't have been exactly effortless."

"Yeah, I see what you mean. But it wasn't as if she didn't want to."

"Of course she wanted to. How many times do you get to look your own destiny in the face like that, when you never thought you'd have the chance?"

"Cara?" Tentatively.

"What." Edging toward snappishness, hearing what's coming.

"There still could be elements of coincidence."

"Are you kidding? You must be out of your mind." Cara gets up from her nest of pillows, marches to the window, wheels around because she is practically at a loss for words. "Her name was *Kate,* for Christ's sake. How much more proof do you need?"

"How much more proof have you got," he mutters, walking into the kitchen, "because whatever you've got, it's still circumstantial."

She follows him, fuming. "What on earth is the matter with you? You've spent a hell of a long time accusing me of being frightened to face the truth. Now, when it turns up and stares you in the face, you're not willing to accept it for what it is. Are you out of your mind? Do you want everybody to go through life the way you do, wandering up and down empty highways proclaiming rootlessness as if it were a trophy?" Accelerating. "Sometimes I'm surprised to look down and remember that you have a bellybutton, Hawk. You spend half your time disowning everything you have, and the other half moaning because you haven't got anything. Then, if somebody else happens to come up a winner, you can't stand that, either."

Hawk flames up, then pulls it back in. She is missing the point, in his opinion. He wants more than anything to speak to it rationally. Besides, he always lowers his voice automatically when Radiant is asleep on the kitchen floor, even though months of conditioning have enabled Radiant to sleep through the domestic equivalent of World War III, if he puts his mind to it.

"Cara . . . Hell, I don't even know where to begin."

"Too bad. If you did, maybe you'd have a better idea of where to quit." Caustic as lye.

"Quit what?" He hasn't anticipated the stabbing jolt that crosses his gut at what she has just said.

"For starters, cut out this charitable effort on your part to Help Cara Get Hold of Herself." She opens the ancient refrigerator and pulls out a jar of tomato juice. The fan on top starts to whir as the door opens. Cara slams it shut with a glare at the offending motor. She pours the remaining contents of the jar into a large glass, which she does not offer to share with Hawk. "End your tenure as the exclusive keeper of Minerva's flame and all of her memories. Maybe somebody else has a legitimate interest, too. Ever consider that? Even someone who might have a vital interest. And I mean vital. Necessary to life."

"I know what vital means, Cara."

"That's right. You would, wouldn't you. You're the Writer in the crowd. I'm only the humble nurse." Her voice is hard; then it breaks. Hawk wonders whether the rupture marks the place where rancor ends and pain begins. Or vice versa. He feels himself sliding over into conciliation, pleading, sorry, truly contrite.

"Cara, I'm sorry. I told you. I could have bitten my tongue for saying that."

"I know how you feel," she snaps, "because I could have bitten your brain for thinking it."

"Please, Cara—"

"No, I'll not please, Hawk. We've only managed to be together for this long because our arrangement is no arrangement. When you think you have the right to regulate my existence, then things have gone a damn sight too far. I don't have to deal with that."

Hawk is stunned. He can scarcely handle the roaring collapse of his defenses around him. He feels cold, damaged.

Out of nowhere the telephone rings.

"Shit," Hawk proclaims.

"You're outdoing yourself again."

"That may be, but so are you. In stubbornness. You just plain refuse to use any common sense at all these days. Just because all of a sudden you've decided that you have a grandmother—"

The telephone doesn't let up. Its strident jangle seems to Hawk to be accelerating its meter.

"Shit, Cara. You may never see the woman again."

"What do you mean, never see her again? Are you planning to cut me off or something?"

"No, goddammit. I didn't mean that, and you know it. She's past ninety years old. How long do you think she's going to be able to conduct salons for selected orphans who want to buy into her legend, just like that?"

Cara narrows her eyes and her field of response simultaneously. "Why don't you just answer the phone, Hawk? I have better things to do." She pours the tomato juice, of which she has not tasted more than a drop, into the sink. Hawk watches, disbelieving the profligate waste, listening to the insistent page of his least favorite household appliance. After about twelve rings, it stops.

[235]

Cara has clomped off to their bedroom, which Hawk interprets hopefully as a small signal that she is getting ready for a reconciliation, or at least a change in the mode of argument. He regroups in the merciful sixty seconds of silence which the telephone has provided, when the ringing resumes. This time he decides, superstitiously, that it must be something important.

"Hello," he barks into the receiver.

"Owen?"

Oh, Christ. "Hello, Mother."

"Well, hello there," she coos. "I tried to call a minute ago, but no one answered. I must have reached a wrong number."

"It wasn't a wrong number, Mother. I couldn't get to the phone fast enough." Lying makes him sullen.

Pause. "Oh. I'm sorry, dear. I really just called to say hello and ask how you are. Our last conversation wasn't exactly . . . enlightening, was it?" Guilt transfers itself to the ear of the beholder, and places Hawk immediately on the defensive.

"I've been busy, Mother." Period. A simple sentence, uttered with an icy neutrality that, in turn, provokes Margo into a position that she probably hadn't wanted to occupy.

"Busy, Hawk? How busy can you be? It's not as if you were studying for finals, or anything like that."

"Correct, Mother. It's not as if I were studying for finals, or anything like that."

"All right, Owen," wearily. "I hadn't meant to get off on this foot. I just wanted to hear your voice and see how you're coming along."

Well, he's glad that someone does. He can hear Cara banging around ominously in the bedroom, and wants with all his might to find out what's going on in there. He tries to stretch the telephone cord into viewing range at the bottom of the stairs, but it falls short.

"I'm getting along all right, Mother." She gives him a beat or two, which he decides he'd better fill. "Uh, how are you?"

"Oh, just super, Hawk. Working away at my embroidery."

"I can't think of anything worse than a sarcastic mother, Margo."

"Unless it's an emotionally absent son."

"There you go, Margo. You're really hitting your stride today."

"Hawk, for heaven's sake, let's just start from the beginning and pretend this never happened."

Silence.

"How's Cara?" As the subject slams a closet door shut, and crashes into the bathroom.

"She's super."

"And Radiant?"

"He's super too."

"And old Lucy?"

"Lucy's super too, but he's dead."

"And . . . What did you say?"

"I said Lucy's dead."

"Oh, Hawk, I'm really sorry," sounding as if she means it. "What happened?"

"He died of the twentieth century."

"What do you mean?"

"What can I mean? We're all dying of the twentieth century. Lucy just got an early acceptance."

"Poor Hawk." Which is the last, absolutely last thing that Poor Hawk wants to hear in this world, because it is exactly the way he feels about himself right this minute. Poor Hawk. Poor misbegotten Hawk. Poor, poor, pitiful Hawk.

"Don't 'poor Hawk' me, Margo. Everything's coming down just fine." Cara is struggling across the living room with two huge canvas bags and a backpack. Hawk has always resented her habit of storing most of her gear as if she wants to be ready to leave at the drop of a disagreement. Now she's actually doing it. He expects to see her blazing the trail with an Army-surplus light stick, but the only other item of miscellany she has cradled against her chest is a stunningly lush jade plant in a terra-cotta pot. It must weigh a ton.

"You hardly sound fine, dear. I wish there were something I could say to let you know that I really am on your side."

"It's okay. Really. Don't worry. I really have to go now, Mother." Cara is on her way to the reclaimed Corvair.

"Wait, Hawk. Don't hang up just yet. Let me tell you about an idea I've had."

"Not now, Mother. I'll call you back sometime." Cara is unlocking the trunk of the car.

"It really won't take a minute, and you might find that you like what I have to say."

"I'm sure I will, but not right now, Mother. Okay?"

The trunk slams shut, and Cara marches to the driver's side. Nothing about the car is in alignment, so she has trouble getting the door unstuck.

"It won't take a minute. What do you think of my taking a cottage at the lake again this summer—"

"I think it's a nifty idea, Mother, but I have to go. I can write to you there. Let me know when you're leaving. You'll hear from me. Okay?"

"That isn't what I had in mind, Owen. I thought—"

"Well, you can tell me about it the next time. Thanks a lot for calling. Give my love to everybody."

"Owen! Hawk—"

He clamps the receiver to its base and runs for the door just in time to see Cara peel into a dusty start and screech down the hill.

Slowly he trudges back into the bedroom and looks around. He expects disarray, the poignant symbols of The End of the Affair, but they are all absent. The bed is still made. The closets and drawers are neatly closed. Nothing of Cara's seems to be missing, because there was never that much in visible evidence. The sweet, houndstooth fragrance of Miss Dior lingers, a broken promise. He knows that the jade plant is gone from the huge, old-fashioned bathroom, but he doesn't have the heart to open the door and examine the vacancy it has left. He sits down at the edge of the bed, and realizes that the funny feeling in the middle of his chest and throat is the beginning of a sob. He has never felt so bereft in living memory.

Finally he falls asleep, a feat which he has never been able to accomplish in broad daylight since he was a little kid and got sent to his room for infractions whose burden he didn't understand and didn't know how else to bear but by escaping into slumber. He sleeps restlessly, but without a dream that he can remember. A little later Radiant slips in, tucks an afghan around Hawk, and pulls down the shade. Hawk murmurs "Thank you," and Radiant wonders who it is he thinks he's talking to.

Hawk awakens around midnight. For a moment he is disoriented. Then the clawing emptiness reoccupies a place in his viscera somewhere between gut and soul. He begins to piece everything together. Cara's perfume still lingers on the air, but the car is gone, she is gone, and the place where the jade plant stood in the bathroom is glaringly forsaken. If he had remembered all at once, he would have gone outside into the trees to relieve himself, instead of opening the bathroom door. The absent plant epitomizes the desertion he is feeling. He wanders through the house, looking for something to fill the lacunae that, taken together, seem to be bigger than all of whatever is left of the rest of his person.

Some unshelled walnuts occupy a hubcap on a table in front of the sofa. He picks one up, hunts for the nutcracker, and decides before he finds it that he doesn't have the stomach for anything that he has to work to possess. He roams into the kitchen, setting up a calculated clatter in the hope that Radiant might awaken and be there for him. Just be there. But it appears that Radiant is in the middle of one of his deeper slumbers. He looks as peaceful as a kitten. Hawk's anger at Radiant's unresponsiveness actually consists of hugely piteous envy; envy for the rest into which only Radiant has been able to settle himself this night, for the neutrality which is absolutely real in Hawk's mind's eye.

Fatigued, aimless, tense as a catgut string, Hawk finally goes out the front door. In the distance a dog is barking. Hawk thinks of Lucy, and feels worse. He rolls a joint on an old magazine he has brought out with him, careless in the moonlight of the seeds, even the weed itself. If something germinates beside the front door, and he gets busted and sent to the slammer for the rest of his born days, who will care? Who in hell is going to be around to give a damn?

He sits, toking deeply, until his head begins to lift and then to sway toward a middle ground where he can find the resources to cope. The hunger, the vacuum in the core of his being, doesn't go away. They simply reach a place where he thinks he might be able to manage them. In the morning. Sometime. The compulsive desire for something to eat, something crunchy, salty, noisy, and palpable, begins to course through his consciousness, but he's incredibly drowsy, too, all of a sudden. He realizes with a peculiar self-pride that he'd rather sleep than eat. Hawk doesn't quite know why he's enjoying this merry wave of self-satisfaction, but he welcomes it unreservedly. With a ragged little smile he gets up, goes quietly through the screen door, and puts himself back to bed.

Radiant, who has been alert through most of the evening, is relieved that he can settle finally into what Hawk assumed he was doing all along. He takes leave of the formless terror that some further abandonment is going to take place this night, and falls asleep almost instantly.

When Hawk awakens in the morning, he doesn't need any time to reorient himself to what has happened. He knows. Lucy is dead, Cara is gone, Margo is alienated, Minerva is God knows where. His entire outlook has deteriorated into a Bizarro universe. Nothing there is comfortable or right, but the persistence of memory locks him painfully to his remnants. He is almost shocked to see that the plants are still growing, Paul the Parrot is scratching around under his cage cover, the kittens still frolicking around the dormant heating grid in the hall. Radiant is still sleeping on the kitchen floor. He doesn't know what he has expected, but a line of poetry out of his ancient days courses through his head like a catechism: *Life must go on, I forget just why.*

Radiant pads up behind him. "I could make breakfast," he offers. Hawk jumps a mile. "I didn't mean to startle you."

"You didn't startle me." I'm fine, he shrieked.

"Well, I could make breakfast." Radiant's offer is extraordinary. He cooks other meals sometimes, but it is his practice never to eat breakfast and therefore to be absolved from its preparation.

Hawk is touched. Also vaguely nauseated. "No thanks, Radiant. I'm really not hungry." Radiant means well, but to Hawk he is only underscoring an already intolerable situation.

"Well, if you want anything . . ."

"Knock it off, Radiant. Please."

Crestfallen, Radiant moves back toward his bag. He regards it carefully, and begins to roll it up for the first time in Hawk's memory. Unreasonable panic shoots through Hawk like a flash. "What're you doing?"

"Just rolling my bag."

"What for? You never rolled it before."

"Nothin'. Just looks messy."

Hawk doesn't know what to say, because he understands completely. Radiant is looking at the whole setup through someone else's eyes. Namely, Cara's. If she were to wander back up the gravel drive, what is it about this living arrangement that could possibly entice her to stay? Radiant thinks that cleaning up a little might do the job. Or hopes so. Hawk doesn't want to tell Radiant, doesn't want to believe himself that, number one, she isn't coming back. And, number two, even if she did, a bag-free expanse of shining clean kitchen floor, no matter how attractive, wouldn't turn the trick for her. In fact, she'd probably feel more at home the old way. He sighs, decides to go along with it. Let someone, at least, feel better.

"Okay, Radiant. Just don't knock yourself out. Okay?"

Radiant understands the hopelessness in Hawk's statement, but opts for housekeeping anyway. "I won't, Hawk. I guess I could take a little responsibility, is all."

Hawk nods.

"Hawk, I should have done it when she was still here. I should have, Hawk." He is on the verge of tears, so all of a sudden Hawk is thrust into the role of consoler.

"It's really okay, Radiant." He doesn't add that it wouldn't have made any difference, because he is at last beginning to understand that he has more constructive things to do with his pain than simply to pass it on. "Maybe we ought to get everything scrubbed up a little bit this morning."

Eagerly Radiant takes up the banner. "Yeah. I'll get some stuff together." He heads off toward the caked relics of Spic 'n Span and the ratty broom and mop collection, which have seen little use in their triumvirate tenure.

Hawk concludes that Radiant hasn't had a half-bad idea, that at least the activity will give him something to do for a while. Radiant ties some kind of cowboy bandana round his head, and they dig in.

The hours do not pass swiftly, but at least they pass. The house looks only fairly decent. Most of the accumulated clutter has merely been dusted and replaced. It has a clean feel about it, however. Hawk and Radiant share the satisfaction of having done something necessary. They both feel sweaty but okay. They consume a startling amount of peanut butter, and Hawk retires to the shower. By the time he feels clean and ready, Radiant has fallen asleep again. Hawk doesn't have any idea how one human being can sleep away so many hours of his life, but in this case neither does he know the length or the intensity of Radiant's vigil the previous night.

The housecleaning campaign has been more for Hawk than a simple measure to structure the time. It also has something to do with reclaiming the place. Hawk is going to go out this afternoon. Inevitably he is going to go out. He fears keenly the returning, the coming back to a place where Cara is neither present nor scheduled to return. He has felt that by touching some new corners, by entering a new mode of operation which he has always avoided in the past, he will expand his frame of reference, that he will create for himself a geography whose every contour does not smother him with unbearable memory. Before they cleaned the house, polished the kitchen, glass-waxed everything, Hawk couldn't think of a single thing he had ever done in the house of which Cara was not somehow an integral part. He couldn't believe that he had once been the one who thought that the parting would be as easy as falling off a hollow log. Why hadn't he been able to see the copperhead hidden in the hollow?

So, finally, when he leaves he is able to write Radiant a note saying that he'll be home in time for dinner. Funny, he has never done that before, either. The three of them, or at least Cara and Hawk, had just come and gone. I'll see you when I see you. But then, in those days, everybody's clothes had been safely stashed somewhere or other, and the jade was thriving on the steamy tile and plaster of the bathroom. Now Hawk obeys the compassionate impulse to protect Radiant in a way in which he himself has not been protected.

He arrives at Minerva's just as she is finishing her lunch. A mighty disappointment wells in his throat because Cara's car is not parked in the driveway. He stifles curdling sorrow, telling himself that it was an unrealistic expectation.

"So, Hawk. It frightened her as much as it frightened me. And there she was, thinking that *she* was the one who held all the cards. What a ghastly turn of fate."

Hawk is in a quandary. Cara's precipitate departure was far more complex in motivation than Minerva can realize. Yet Hawk knows that to try to go into any of that would be to do great disservice to the gravity of Minerva's concerns, the import of her entire life. She is keeping her balance, Hawk can plainly see. Assuming that she feels at least some measure of satisfaction at having called Cara's shots with accuracy, Hawk can't bring himself to upset her delicate balance with a contradiction. On the other hand, he is suffering too profoundly to maintain total silence. The fact that he no longer feels free to speak openly in this house depresses him still further. It completes his sense that the refuge is violated, that he is truly cast adrift.

"I don't know, Miss Minerva. I think she was upset about a lot of things, but I just don't know." The despair that he has tried all morning to sweep, polish, and scour out of sight comes swarming back like fruit flies.

Minerva wants to talk about it in her way. Hawk cannot rally up an alternative to listening. "She had her own version of the truth embedded for so long that she couldn't bear to have it any other way, could she? She was almost ready to hear the whole cloth—whether her mother was a bastard, whether she really left her because Cara was a monstrous person, or whether Kate was just a forlorn bungler in her own right . . . Cara was just about to go for the brass ring, and when she started to hear the answers, somehow they didn't satisfy her. Did they? Oh, Hawk, what happened?"

Hawk has never seen Minerva in this mood, given over to the same kinds of insecurities as mortals. He wants to console her, but, as with Radiant, he fears that his very words of consolation will denigrate the role Minerva has chosen to play, minimize her centrality in this drama, aggrandize himself gratuitously.

"It couldn't have been your fault," he begins slowly. "I think she was prepared to believe you long before you knew what you were going to say yourself." He lowers his head, tries to retain his grip. He is nearly at a whisper. "I'm afraid it was my fault."

"You and she argued."

"Yes."

"Not for the first time, surely."

"Oh, no. We've been arguing since the first night we met. You have to argue, sometimes. This was different."

She wanders. "Karraman and I never argue."

Oblivious of her curious locution, Hawk drives on. "I mean, the words were no more vicious, less, if anything. It was just that it went in a different direction."

Minerva is back on the track, clear as a bell. "You told *her* not to move too fast, didn't you?"

"Yes," ashamed, not for the caution, but for the censorship. There it is again.

"What were you afraid of, Hawk?"

He pauses to think.

Minerva watches. She gives him his time, and he accepts it gratefully.

"It's really strange, Miss Minerva. There I was, with Cara on one side and Margo on the other."

She does not know that his statement is literal, but she can well visualize the struggle in a figurative sense.

"I've been telling them both, screaming at them, to leave me alone. Let me be free. Don't crowd me. I guess that's what it was mostly about with Cara. Crowding. I don't think I was actually afraid that you'd take her away from me or that she'd take me away from you, although that's what I had myself believing for a while. What I really couldn't face, I think, was the possibility that the existence of either one of you would *crowd* my relationship with the other. That must be it. I wanted the whole thing on my terms, didn't I? *My terms.*"

Minerva smiles. "Did you, Hawk?"

Hawk relaxes into a grin, too. "You sound just like Cara. Answering me like some goddamn clinician she studied with." He says it affectionately. "Used to irritate the hell out of me. But she was really giving me time, and my own head, wasn't she? She wasn't the one who ever did any crowding at all. It was me."

Minerva barely nods. Waits.

"She and Margo were both after me about censorship. I thought I was supposed to be the enlightened one in the crowd. I was even paranoid enough to think that they were ganging up on me." Quizzically. "I don't even know if Margo knows her last name, and I had them all organized in a sinister league. Anyway, that was so stupid. The reason that they both nailed me on censorship was that they each caught me in the act. My God, Miss Minerva, where was I when the lights went out?"

"Now, Hawk, don't make it so black and white. I imagine you did come down hard on both of them. But it probably couldn't have been helped. That's one of the things I've always liked about you: conviction—even when you're wrong."

"Conviction!"

"Don't interrupt. Don't be too hasty about laying all the blame at your own door. You may have been heavy-handed, but I wouldn't accuse Cara of fielding your tosses with too much agility, either. Nobody can say that she was particularly forthcoming about her motives for ingratiating herself over here. I can't imagine that there have been any engraved apologies for that."

Minerva's reservoirs of language never cease to engage Hawk. He remembers his tape recorder in that connection, and is shocked to realize that, for the first time since he began the Oral History project, he has left it at home.

"True." He smiles sadly. "But what now? She's gone. She might never find out the rest of what you have to tell her." Guilt, which has been vying with pain since yesterday, threatens to gain control of Hawk's entire head. "Who knows if you'll ever see her again. She's so erratic—"

"Don't be tactful, Hawk. It isn't her being erratic that's bothering you.

I'm an old woman. She might not see me again if she takes ten minutes out to go to the store for a loaf of bread. Perhaps you're too young to accept that kind of thinking, but I'm not."

"Yeah. Maybe. But none of this had to happen this way. To any of us. I—"

"You nothing, dear Hawk." She invests it with such tenderness that Hawk can imagine himself as Karraman Robley, falling in love with this woman at the sound of a voice. He wants to crawl into her lap while she smooths his whiskers and tells him he can do no wrong. "What is meant to happen will happen. Perhaps Cara will come back."

"To you, maybe. To hear the end of the fairy tale. Not to me."

Minerva hears the plea, but refuses to commit to anything. "Be that as it may, Hawk. You have a responsibility to get this story finished for yourself. And where's that tape recorder of yours, anyway?" She is chiding him gently, and he understands that she is as much concerned with his interests as with her own or Cara's.

She continues. "The story will be told. Cara will hear it, from one of us or from the other."

"And that's what I have to do, isn't it?" He isn't asking anybody but himself, and he already knows the answer. She has leached the tension out of him so expertly that he cannot imagine what kind of source it is from which she draws her magic or her strength.

"You know, it isn't over yet." She means Cara's life with Hawk, the resolution of their problems. He interprets it differently, because he doesn't yet have the heart to entertain the thought of having Cara back and then run the risk of disappointment. He feels an even keel of understanding bobbing around him from the last few minutes of conversation. He wants to hold it steady as he goes, to steer clear of any impulsive surges of optimism that might leave him in the end completely rudderless, worse off than he was when he started.

"I know. I left the recorder at home, and I really feel bad about that. This is the first time ever, too, in . . . how many times? Even in the early days, when I was scared silly you'd misunderstand, I always brought it anyway." She smiles indulgently. His version of "early days" he reckons in months, fortnights, possibly. Yet she understands minutely the intense communion which has swollen the center of their relationship into grandiosity, and catapulted its beginnings into history.

"Forget the recorder, Hawk. You don't need it. You won't forget any of what I'm going to tell you today. I suppose we ought to be systematic, somehow. What have I left out, Hawk? What do *you* want to know?"

"Her name."

"Whose name?"

Surprised. "Cara's name." Who else is there whose name we don't all know by now?

"Oh. Of course. Well, Hawk, her father's name really probably was Funk, but her legal name is Caravelle Bolton."

"My God. You're kidding."

"Absolutely not. Not a question of a doubt."

"That's it? No middle name? Nothing else?"

"No. Just Caravelle Bolton. After her grandfather and me. I don't imagine Kate intended to make it easy for her to find a way out, in the beginning, at least, before some other impulse led her to stow away the Bolton and add the Funk."

"But you're saying that it's been a game all along. Cara's known from the beginning."

"No, Hawk. I don't think so at all. I think that Kate dropped enough hints along the road that it became an enticing and mysterious game for the child. Enticing, mysterious, and cruel. But I think that some private, self-protective urge led her to get rid of that Bolton name early on. I'm sure that it was long before Cara had reason to recognize it as her own when she heard it."

"Surely she went looking for her identity years ago, especially right after her mother died. She's even told me about the poking around she did when Kate was still alive and well in Cuba."

"Of course she did. What do you think she's doing here?"

"*Was* doing here," Hawk, mournfully.

"In any case. She was searching."

"But we're going around in circles. I meant more than that. How could she have *avoided* coming up with the facts, after poking around in documents, birth certificates, whatever she could lay her hands on?"

"Yes, but it's terribly hard to come up with a document when you really don't know what name to look for, and the only person who might lead you even to the right city gives you a different wrong answer every time."

Hawk winces. "What would cause a woman to treat her own child so heartlessly? That's gruesome." Then he realizes that it's Minerva's own child he's just indicted. He flushes deeply beneath his beard. "I'm sorry. I didn't mean it the way it sounded."

"Nonsense, Hawk. What other way was there for you to have meant it?" Rhetorical, she plows on. "She did monstrous things. To Cara, to herself, to me. For years I couldn't believe that my act of loving Karraman would have yielded up such a bitter fruit. Kate seemed to represent a perversion of all the truths I had ever stood for.

"Do you know, once, when I hadn't seen her for some time, and I was having difficulty taking the time to get out of the country, she made arrangements to meet me in New York. She had been so bitter, so distant from me during my last visits to London, that I prayed, literally got down on my knees and prayed, that she would come to some kind of understanding that would allow her to be at peace with herself, if not with me. I took her gesture as a symbol—her wanting to meet me there meant, I thought, that she'd come at least a part of the way. God knows I'd gone more than half—I'd gone every way I could.

"Well, she wanted to meet me at a certain Russian restaurant I knew. I loved the place, but I wondered at the choice. It was hardly a serene and quiet setting for the intimate rendezvous I'd so looked forward to. On the other hand, I told myself that perhaps she needed the cover of the noise, the crowds, the waiters. All that bustle."

Minerva patted her brow with a hankie.

"I arrived first. When Kate walked in, I have to admit that if she had been a stranger I would have stared."

"She was that beautiful?" Hawk wants to know.

"She was that beautiful. She combined the best of the features from all sides of her various families. And she was petite, like most of the Robley women. I felt like a gangling teenager next to her. She was perfect miniaturization. I could see some of myself in her, I have to admit, but mostly I could see, revealed, what I had loved most in the private, underside of Karraman. My God!"

"That must have been quite a meeting."

"Hawk, you don't know how right you are. But not in the way I'd dreamed."

"What happened?"

"Well, she offered her cheek, conveyed greetings from the Nikolais, and we sat down. In the crush of the luncheon crowd, I could barely hear her cultured little British voice. Finally I said, 'Kate, dear, since the din is so overpowering here at this hour, perhaps you'd like to have a cocktail now, and come back to my hotel for a quiet little lunch. Then we can talk.'"

"What did she say?"

"She looked at me, and her eyes were opaque. She said, 'Oh, really, Minerva? I'd thought you'd be right at home here. It is so . . . Russian, after all.'

"I was confused. I must have stared at her. She virtually jeered at me. She said, 'You know, dear? Russian? Like Claire's? I thought that would appeal.'

"She was like the devil's breath: frozen, capable of freezing solid anything within her range. I said, 'Kate, dear, it isn't Claire's Russianness that draws me—or anybody—in. It's the love, the warmth. The appearances don't mean a thing.'

"In the thousands of times I've reviewed it through the years, I don't think I really gave her an opening to do what she did next. I think she knew what she was going to say, and what she was going to do, and she would have done it one way or another, no matter what I had come up with. She just stared me straight in the eye and said, 'Well, sorry, Minerva, but the appearance is the best I can do. It's certainly all you ever gave me, and I thought I could return the favor. If not, well, perhaps we'll meet again someday.' And with that she rose from the table and swept out of the restaurant before I could even compose myself and ask where she was going, or where she was staying, or anything. Not that she would have told me. That was the last time I ever saw her."

Minerva manages her composure like a veteran actress who has played out this scene often enough that she knows she can make it through without cracking. It is Hawk who has tears in his eyes and a burning in his chest that he fears will burst out into the room in the form of sobs or screams or blood.

"It's all right, Hawk. Go ahead. But if I seem merciless, it's because you need to know. You need to be able to tell Cara and you need to know for yourself what kind of fashioning she must have had for all those defenses that she's trying to get around."

"Jesus."

"Yes. Jesus. But that wasn't the end. I still kept track of her, still tried to do my part, such as it was. She kept gravitating back to Claire and Tasha, and I always stayed in touch. Of course, she made it her business never to be in residence when I was in London again, but hopes die hard. She was so beautiful, so willful, so brilliant. And such an emotional cripple.

"But it wasn't until she gave up Cara, literally gave her away, that I began to feel real terror for the child's sake. I suppose I had always assumed that the maternal instinct would win out. I mean, she certainly had all the resources behind her. She could have found any number of ways to provide the tools for the child to use on her own. She didn't, though. She abandoned Cara. She stripped her of her commission in the human race. She turned Cara's life into the deadliest scavenger hunt I've ever seen or heard of."

"Wait, Miss Minerva," Hawk pleads. "It isn't that Cara's not surviving, or anything. Look at it this way: she's even managed to find her way to you. That's pretty remarkable, I'd say."

"You might say that." Minerva nods. "Yes, you might. But this is not an exclusively heroic bedtime story, Hawk. In for a penny, in for a pound. The hour for self-congratulation is not yet here."

"I know," mollified. "Please go on."

"Not much further to go. After Kate gave up Cara, I think I finally understood the heart of the saga at last. In Kate's mind, she wasn't the one doing the abandoning; I was. The fact that I'd adored my daughter, that I'd longed to see her every minute of every single day, didn't cut a single cube of ice with her. She only knew what she experienced. And what she experienced was a mother who sailed in every year or so with kisses and compliments and presents, then sailed out again. The real horror of it is that throughout every moment of those years, I thought I was doing the most unselfish and courageous thing I could have done.

"I did what I did," Minerva is concluding, "because it seemed the absolutely right thing for me to do at the time. I've never excused myself on any other basis."

"If you saw it that way, Miss Minerva, then that's the way it was. Nobody can hold you responsible for sins of inadvertency." Hawk has reached for the nearest method of absolution, praying that perhaps it will work for both of them. He needs it as much as she does. He is the one who realizes that, out of his own paltry needs for reassurance, he has been stonewalling her bravest efforts to clear her own accounts.

"Not good enough," she snaps. "Ignorance of the law is no excuse. No excuse," Minerva underscores.

"You're blaming yourself," blames Hawk, "and you can't do that. There wasn't any choice, based on what you knew at the time."

"How do you know?" Bitterly. "How do I?" She reaches for the lace handkerchief and absently blots her lips. Her hands again conjure visions of Cara, and something leaden creeps back into the empty places. He doesn't know how long he can sustain this.

"I'm sorry, Miss Minerva. You're right. It's not my business to try to tell you what to feel. I'm just doing the same old rotten thing all over again."

"It's all right, Hawk. Psychology changes, viewpoints change. I'm grateful to you for yours. Thank you."

What colossal grace she has, he thinks. "Oh, Miss Minerva. I don't even know what to say."

"Don't say a word, Hawk. Just listen."

"I'm sorry. I didn't like it when you wanted to make excuses on my behalf for something that I saw as my own folly, and now I'm trying to do the same thing to you."

"I know it, Hawk."

"You understand everything."

"Not quite. I've just had a year or two longer than you have to think things out."

He rallies, comes up swinging great arcs of false heartiness. "Well, I'll tell you one thing, Miss Minerva. The years certainly don't show!"

"And I'm supposed to believe that?" she parries.

"The trouble is," Hawk replies slowly to some other question, "it's so

[248]

goddamn hard for human beings to get their words and their feelings pointed in the same direction."

Minerva's answering silence makes him feel first brilliant, then oafish, then, somehow, equal. Then Hawk measures the torment in her eyes and understands that she really has been on his side all the way.

XIV

Minerva wondered why everybody always seems to reserve sympathy when loved ones part for those who happen to be left behind. She let them accompany her to the pier for the first time, wondering why they looked so forlorn standing in a small cluster when she stationed herself on the promenade deck to wave good-bye. Why would anyone assume that they had cornered the market on suffering? They, after all was said and done, still had each other.

Tasha held the baby, who was swaddled contentedly in a downy bunting. Minerva could hardly bear to look at them. Her arms strained to go back and nestle little Kate in her own arms, to stay, to be everything at once: the milliner, the traveler, the mother, stirring up formula (which of course wouldn't have to be stirred at all if Minerva stayed). She wondered if Claire and Baba could see her tears from that distance. She supposed she didn't mind if they did.

The infant she left behind was beginning to resemble the child Peter Robley, as she remembered him, except that the striking blue Robley eyes, which Karraman apparently passed on only to a selected few of his children, looked clearly ahead. They showed already, Minerva would have sworn, a touch of gentle mirth. They didn't keep heading for the nose, no matter what the head intended, as Peter's had once done. Little Kate had, from almost the moment of her perilous birth, seemed to be a child of sweet nature and placid patience. Minerva thought years later that she must have been warehousing the nastiness for use in a prolonged tantrum that lasted from her late teenage until her death around the age of forty-five. Standing on board the liner that day, Minerva mused that if she had known babies could evoke such loving tenderness, awaken such billowing instincts toward protection, she might have thought it out differently. She might have taken Kate home with her. She might have stayed in England permanently, allowing Felder to do what he was already more than groomed to do, with herself as European agent. She might have opened her eyes to the rest of the universe of possibilities for herself and her daughter.

But she couldn't, wasn't ready. Couldn't see her way.

She stood at a polished railing, watching blurrily, with barely the energy to wave. The small family on the shore dwindled and dwindled and finally was gone. "I'll write to you," she whispered to the distance. "I'll be back soon. Please take care of each other. Please . . ."

She returned from New York to Saint Kathareen's via Wheeling by river steamer. When Karraman received the cable to that effect, he seethed. After all the months she'd been away, he would have thought she'd take the most rapid and efficient form of overland transportation out of New York, not the most dismally archaic. He could only conclude that she was postponing their reunion. He thought, then tried not to think, that she would come back with an announcement of the most devastating sort, with a husband, with a lover. He foresaw the worst, and couldn't bring himself to dwell on what the worst could possibly be. He needed her more than ever, and spent more cumulative time than he ever had before or would again experiencing the coward's little deaths.

He was right on one count. She did want to postpone their reunion. She wanted the fullest possible recuperation for her entire self. She wanted the edge of weariness to melt away along with the increments of flesh at her breasts and belly. She counted on the careful pace of the sternwheeler to finish the job that the salt air had started, bringing color and strength back to her face and body, restoring open clarity to her eye. She didn't want to greet Karraman blanketed in several days' worth of train soot, her fatigue underscored by the rhythm of iron wheels in the restless nights. If she had had it her way, those silly little flying machines that were dropping explosives and firing guns all over Europe would be commandeered to peaceful purposes, carrying weary travelers across oceans in a trice. Then she'd drop down in a grassy field somewhere near Foothill House, say howdy-do, and live happily ever after. Since the long days of the ocean liner were enforced, and the decadent fruits of her wishful fantasies couldn't possibly come to pass, she gave herself over to the entire distance, river steamer included. That was that.

Karraman stood on the levee, nervous as a rodent. To add insult to his imagined injuries, he was fuming because he would have to greet her in full view of half the population of Saint Kathareen's. In cabling him just prior to embarking on the last leg of her journey, she had effectively cut off his margin for response. He couldn't arrange to meet her in New York, or anywhere else upstream. Nor could he fail to meet her at all. Therefore, whatever shattering news she had saved up to drop on him would have to be dropped in public. The whole town would bear witness. From half a mile away, Minerva could see him in his white-rage posture.

It had never taken longer to drop an anchor, set a gangplank, lash a boat into port at Saint Kathareen's. Crewmen had never moved so slowly or so inefficiently. He had to fight the impulse to take his forty-nine-year-old body down to the water's edge and handle the ropes and buoys himself. He did not recognize that in the deepening cold, which he himself did not feel, everyone was already moving at double time, without any help from any dockside superintendents. The captain of the vessel stood at the wheelhouse, stopwatch in hand, preparing to take effusive credit for the efficiency with which his men were putting into port.

For Karraman, the interminable agony finally ended. Minerva was the first passenger down the gangway. She wore a felt cloche against the bitter river wind. It camouflaged her russet curls, covered her brow, changed the contour of her face, but Karraman would have known her anywhere. His senses had memorized her carriage, her gait, the rhythm of her persona. If she had been draped and veiled like an Arab woman, he would have known the pattern of her step and the angle of her head.

Minerva had been watching him from the window of the grand saloon long before he had spotted her. She waited behind a slender veneer of calm. For a second her psyche screamed: My God, what have I done? The question was supplanted instantly by the pragmatic Minerva asking with all her usual forthrightness, and a steady eye on the main chance: *My God, what am I going to do?*

"You're really back."

"Yes"—she smiled—"it would seem that I am."

"Minerva, sometimes I think that you could walk through the middle of the battlefield itself, with the bombs dropping right and left, and not only emerge unscathed, but bring an acceptable peace treaty out with you."

"Don't exaggerate, dear heart. I wasn't anywhere near any war, and you know it."

"Ah, my sweet innocent. Some things never change, do they? We're all of us near a war. Too near for comfort, I'd say. If this country isn't in the middle of it before another year is out, I'll eat one of your gorgeous creations, apple blossoms and all." Karraman had said "apple blossoms" deliberately. He had calculated it to rekindle certain memories for Minerva's sake, even though she hadn't worn anything of the sort for years. He was reestablishing the ground. Making sure.

Minerva smiled the signal that it was all right, it was there. He could go on.

"Don't worry about the bags, Min," he announced casually. "The boys will get them."

"Good. And thank you. You do see to everything, don't you, Karraman? That's a pleasant feeling, after having been on my own for so long. Please just ask that they put everything in the room, not the studio."

"Uh, Min, before they do that, uh, there's something I'd like to talk to you about."

Minerva experienced a surge of trepidation so unfamiliar that she couldn't recognize it as alarm. Had she been somehow caught out, rendered vulnerable? An instinctive armadillo, she tugged at her carapace and rallied to buy time. There opposite her stood Karraman, her beloved Karraman, but who was he? What suffocating secrets was he waiting to release into the atmosphere?

She stared at him. He looked shorter than she remembered, but only because of her higher-heeled European slippers, played off against his accumulating rotundity. His sparse eyelashes had whitened and virtually disappeared behind the spectacles he had newly acquired. His nose, small but previously quite acceptable in the boyish planes of his face, dwindled into an absurd comma beneath the pretentiously gilded rims. The eyeglasses, which Karraman relished for the purpose of seeing his beloved in new and precious detail, Minerva was perceiving as a symbolic barrier against approaching him intimately ever again.

He looked, to her, absurd, a carnival Kewpie all bespectacled and costumed up as a businessman. She couldn't imagine what she had ever seen in him. Yet, as he stood silently and authoritatively conveying directions to everyone in terse pantomime, her mind's eye saw the raw, casual, accustomed power, the square stolidity embodied in his bones tempered by the silken tenderness of an increasingly hairless pate, the sweet vulnerability of a translucent temple where the veins pulsed out the betrayal of his soul.

Abstracted out of time and space, he cut a ridiculous figure. Standing there on the wharf, master of far more than he could survey in a sweeping glance, new spectacles or no, Karraman Robley was a magnet to Minerva's every sensibility. Her eyes widened suddenly with wanting him. Failing all other possibilities, she was seized with the urgent impulse to sit down somewhere and cross her legs. Tightly.

His voice washed over her like a balm. "Please, Min. Quite a bit has happened. There's something I have to discuss with you immediately."

The eternal seduction of his voice wheedled into the crevasses of her body and wrapped around all the bleeding edges of her fears. Minerva could feel her very breasts swell out to meet his touch. What could be more important than that? Yet caution persisted.

"What's the matter with my settling down, first? Then we can sit and talk for as long as you can spend with me. I haven't even asked you about Em and the children."

"That's just it, Min. There's something about Emmaline that you don't know. I'm going to need every last measure of your understanding."

A long pause. Eyes met, implored, became so deeply ensnared in questions that they almost forgot how to read answers.

"Yes, Karraman. I suppose I'm ready." She spoke with coolness, an attempt at insulation. It was as phony as a cigar-store Indian.

Karraman, dreading the conversation ahead for all of his own reasons, gulped the last vestige of pride down his gullet like a bitter tonic. "Min, I don't want you to settle back in at the hotel."

She thought calmly: I am learning the meaning of "dumbstruck."

He continued. "I want you to come and stay at Foothill House. I need you there."

"You must be joking. The last thing Emmaline needs at Foothill House is to have me back again. She couldn't see me off to Europe fast enough, and I was hardly staying at the house at all right before I left."

"That's just it, Min. Emmaline isn't there."

"Isn't there? But where is she?"

"She's in Pennsylvania. In the mountains." He was working up to it.

"In the mountains? At this time of year?" Minerva was completely bewildered. "It's winter. Why would anybody in her right mind want to go to Pennsylvania in the winter? It's bad enough here in tropical Ohio."

Karraman couldn't help smiling. "I'm afraid you've touched on all the truths at one time, Min. She didn't want to go to Pennsylvania, not one little bit. And she's not in her right mind. That's why she's there."

"What are you talking about? You never wrote, you never . . ." She stopped, words froze as she anticipated her own accusation turned back upon her.

But Karraman, reliable as always, led her out of her own ambush. "Writing was out, Min. Putting it all to paper would have been so . . . firm. I wanted—I still want—to talk it over with you. To hear your voice, Min." He paused, closed his eyes, seemed to draw himself into a more solid package. "Besides," he snapped accusingly, "who was to know whether mail boats would get through the lines? We've never written before—the middle of a monstrous war seemed to me a hell of a place to start in. Min . . ."

She had more replies than feathers in a wicker chest, but they all snagged at the opening.

"This isn't getting us to the point."

"I know, Karraman. Let's have tea, and talk about what the best course of action is." Easily, as though she had been the sensible one all along.

"I'd rather not talk in a place where we can be overheard. The best thing would be to head right across the river and up to the house." A pleading note had entered his voice.

Minerva wanted to capitulate, but she held firm. "Then we'll go up to my room long enough to talk it over. I simply cannot plunk myself down in Foothill House under the circumstances you're implying without understanding exactly what's going on. We can leave the luggage in the lobby."

It wasn't leaving the luggage in the lobby that led Karraman to agree, but the disclaimer immediately preceding that. She had said "without understanding what's going on." The full implication of her phrasing was that when she understood, she would be prepared to do whatever was necessary. Karraman was enough of a diplomat to recognize giveaway negotiations when he saw them.

"Fine, Min. Good idea." Meanwhile, the bellmen were already loading her luggage onto the ferry.

Karraman had spoken a word to someone on the way through the lobby, so the tea reached the suite almost as soon as they did. He watched her hands as she poured and stirred.

"Now. What happened, Karraman?"

"I wish I knew. Apparently it started soon after the last of the babies was born. She didn't seem to recover her strength."

"It takes time. Especially after having so many so close together."

"Maybe, but the fact is that Emmaline didn't seem to want to recover. She saw the babies less and less. Shunted the responsibilities off on the help. I don't know how long it would have taken me to see the light of day if Maybelle Kennebec hadn't been around."

Minerva couldn't suppress a smile, remembering. "What did she do?"

Karraman, however, was not presiding at an entertainment. "She didn't do a damned thing," he said. "She went on strike. One night I came in, dog-tired as usual, and there was Maybelle, waiting at the front door to greet me. I was filthy and thirsty and lonesome for my children. If there was one thing I needed less than being greeted at the door by one of Emmaline's tirades, it was being greeted by Maybelle Kennebec on a tear."

"She is willful, isn't she?" Minerva chuckled tentatively.

"That's putting it mildly. She went on and on. Seemed like hours. She said that if I thought raising Miss Emmaline Musgrove had been 'a Sunday-school picnic,' I had another 'think' coming, but that was 'a outing in the country' compared to this. At least Emmaline had had a mother to guide her, Maybelle said. I hadn't the faintest idea what she was getting at. Finally she wound down and glared me in the eye. She said, 'Well, Mr. Karraman, just what are you proposin' to do about it?' For the life of me, all I could figure out she was asking me to do was to take Emmaline, and do something to her, and come out with a better product."

Minerva kept silent, but couldn't help thinking prayerfully that Maybelle didn't have such a bad idea at that.

"I must have stammered like a fool," Karraman continued. "Then the phrase 'at least Emmaline had a mother' hit me like a boulder. I asked her what she meant by that. She told me, in no uncertain terms—"

"—as only Maybelle can."

"Yes, with a vengeance, that the way Em was acting she might as well not have any children at all. She was refusing to come out of her room, she was sleeping most of the time when anybody knocked at her door, and when someone did hear her moving around, she was usually singing some sort of gibberish that Maybelle called 'opry.' Of course it was nothing of the kind."

The smile had faded from Minerva's face, leaving only sympathy, perfectly distilled. When Karraman had said that Em was exhausted after childbirth, Minerva had thought that was perfectly natural. Minerva had been a bit drained herself. Considering how often Em had repeated the act, and how much extra energy she expended in the complaint department alone, fatigue was no surprise. As the story progressed, however, Minerva's concern grew. The singing part chilled her sensibilities for good. A dozen Mad Scenes paraded across her memory. In every one, Em was singing, accompanied by a single haunting flute. At the end of each scene, Emmaline fell on a dagger or floated out of sight on a barge. Or went to Pennsylvania for the winter, while her pitiful infants sobbed into the deaf ears of Maybelle Kennebec. Minerva hardly knew what to ask first. "Did you take her to a doctor? What happened?" Encompassing as much as she could.

Karraman made an effort to collect himself. "Not at first. I didn't have any idea how to approach that kind of thing.

"Don't think I didn't brood about it day and night. I didn't know whether it was bad blood, or nerve disease, or what-all. I couldn't get past the thought that my children would be growing up in the same house with a mother who had turned into a raving lunatic. God knows I never thought that could happen in the Robley family," he finally blurted.

Neither did I, thought Minerva vehemently, and wondered what to say next.

Karraman saved her the trouble by surging ahead. "I tried to talk to her. First I acted calm. Then I got tough, pretended I was furious. It didn't make any difference. No matter what I did, I got the same response as everyone else in the house. Either she slept through every attempt I made or she woke up like a zombie and acted like someone from out of this world.

"Then I was really furious," he continued. "It was no act. Oh, I understand now that I was angry at the whole situation as much as I was at Em. It was a mess—with me away all the time, not noticing what was happening to my own wife and family, and then having to hear from Maybelle Kennebec, for Christ's sake." He paused, looked away from Minerva, then back down at his hands. "But I actually thought I could fix it. I assumed everything—that I could have the power to shatter the universe completely for another person, then pick up the pieces and put them together at my will. Can you imagine that kind of vanity?"

"Not vanity, Karraman, honesty. That's what human beings are like."

He was probing her eyes again. "Well, nothing worked, anyway, Min. Whether or not I accomplished the destruction, I sure as hell couldn't do anything about the cure."

"No one expects you to be God, Karraman."

"I did."

"It's a waste of time. I love a man, my love. A man didn't create Emmaline."

"But he created a number of her problems."

"So . . . ?"

"So, finally I decided to consult a doctor. Somewhere else. I couldn't consider talking about it in Saint Kathareen's. You know how—"

"I know."

"Well, I had an old friend at college who's now in New York. I'm sure I've mentioned him to you—teaches at Physicians and Surgeons, has a large practice, very successful?"

Minerva nodded recognition.

"I wrote him and tried to describe everything that was going on. Do you know what he said? He told me that he thought he recognized the answer, all right, but that I was going to have to discuss it with Emmaline's local doctor. He told me to ask about the medicines she'd been taking."

"Did you do it?" asked Minerva, suddenly wide-eyed at the memory of how a potent and unaccustomed medication had temporarily addled her own mental equilibrium in the London hospital.

[257]

"Talk to him? By then I had no choice. The Emmaline we had always known, for good or ill, had departed. There's no other way I can put it. The person she left in her place was out of my reach entirely. I couldn't argue, or cajole, or persuade, so then I'd lose my temper, and that would make things all the worse. I couldn't get anything I needed out of an inconclusive letter from New York. I had to ask the doctor to come up on the hill. I couldn't face going to the office, and I certainly couldn't take Emmaline out anywhere."

"You asked old man Grainger? I thought he was decrepit the first time I saw him, and that was just after the '06 Flood."

"No. I meant his son. The old man finally gave up the practice completely around the time you left for Europe. When Em thought that she was pregnant this time—"

"Pregnant? Now?"

"Damn. You didn't know. I forgot. I always assume you know everything. Min, I didn't mean to break it so abruptly . . ."

"It doesn't matter. I was surprised, that's all. I don't know why I should have been." Minerva didn't make an effort to keep the edge out of her voice. Suddenly she was fatigued with the effort of trying to juggle so many emotional oranges at one time. Why shouldn't Emmaline get pregnant again? Once she had finally gotten down to business, nothing seemed to stop her. Just because Karraman had a daughter named Kate, why should that change anything?

Well, it changed something—Minerva admitted that much to herself. The events he was describing would certainly postpone any announcement she planned to make. Her five and a half months abroad, as far as Karraman was concerned, might never have taken place. It would not comfort Karraman today, Minerva accepted sadly, to learn about a lovely infant daughter rocking cozily in the middle of the War to End All Wars.

For an unprecedented moment, Minerva felt invisible, negated. She didn't know whether to scream with rage or howl with laughter. She concluded with exquisite reason that she was going to do neither. No one was going to hear her anyway, since she didn't exist.

When Karraman saw her trying to fight a sudden well of tears, he was powerless to think beyond the obvious feminine emotions. He thought she was simply jealous of the thought of another Robley baby, conceived under God knew what circumstances in her absence. He thereby proceeded to compound all the conflict already raging in Minerva's head.

"Min," he whispered, "the peace and joy you bring me mean so much more than any child. What there is between us now will last as long as we live. Nothing else matters. A child is something that spends its years between governesses and God until, if it's lucky, it finds a love of its own and forms its own life. Parents have so little to do with it that you can't begin to imagine." He actually thought that she couldn't.

"You're wrong, Karraman," she told him gently, but she didn't tell him why. Instead she willfully drew him back to the explanation he hadn't completed. She wanted nothing more than to touch him, to embrace reassurance into his body. But she had resisted so far. It was imperative that she avoid false resolutions now. If she allowed passion to overtake her now, she risked making hash of everything. And she had come too far for that.

"So," she prompted, "young Grainger came to the house."

"Yes, he did. At first he was sanctimonious as hell. 'The medical profession' this, and 'the medical profession' that. Then he gave me a long lecture about my being too old-fashioned for my own good. He said that if his father hadn't trusted him, he damned well wouldn't be turning over an entire medical practice to him. I didn't know what the hell he was talking about. I hadn't accused him of a damned thing."

"Maybe not, but obviously he guessed that you were going to."

"I don't know. All I can say is that he acted mighty nervous for a first-rate professional man."

"Nervous?"

"Defending himself. He kept talking about this 'new-techniques' business until finally I asked him what new techniques had him so worked up, since I hadn't noticed that he'd used any to help Emmaline."

"He must have squirmed."

Karraman chuckled. "I thought he'd wear the seat off his trousers. But it got worse. He pounded his fist on an end table, and upset a snifter of brandy right onto the wood, and from there onto the rug. It was only a mediocre brandy, but the girls had a devil of a time getting the stain out of the table."

Minerva was not amused. She was beginning to lose patience with Karraman and his digressions. Where was he leading? "That doesn't sound like the new breed. What made him so angry?"

"I sure as hell couldn't follow him. He said that it wasn't my affair, so I carefully pointed out to him that it was *my* wife whose health and welfare were at stake. Then, all of a sudden he started accusing me of criminal behavior because I didn't know *enough* of what was going on."

"What on earth did you say to that?"

Sheepishly, "Just what you think I said."

"You called him a son of a few things . . . ?"

"Yes, for starters. I would have gone on, and he probably would have grabbed his gloves and his cane and walked out, when all of a sudden, who should waltz down the stairs and into the library but Emmaline. She hadn't been out of her room in weeks."

"Good Lord. How was she?"

"How she was, was that I would have said she was drunk as a lord, except that I know she never touches a drop. She didn't have anything on her breath but a hint of onion."

Something that started as a compassionate sigh, Minerva's nerves turned into a snicker.

Karraman went right on. "She walked straight past me, and fell all over Grainger as if he were the evangelist who had saved her soul. She said that she had just been about to have Doremus drive over to his office, because she was running out of that marvelous 'tonic.' She wanted to get some more before she emptied the bottle. She said she knew what people meant when they said that something was a lifesaver, because this had certainly changed her outlook.

"Min, I damn well remembered what my friend in New York had said about checking the medicines thoroughly. But I had thought he meant to make sure that she was getting enough of what she needed. It finally hit me like a shot what had happened. Old Man Grainger had given her a preparation of some kind to make her feel better after the very first baby. His bloody fair-haired boy followed suit, only he upped the dosage a little each time. Without anybody noticing it, my wife had developed a full-fledged addiction to opiates. No wonder she slept all the time. And no wonder she didn't know who the hell she was when she woke up. The doctor at the clinic told me it was a good thing she was too stubborn to nurse the babies, because they probably had some of the effects of laudanum in their systems already at birth. Peter had a good old Robley colic, and that was bad enough. If Em had done anything so normal as to nurse her babies, she would have passed the drug on through her milk as soon as she started taking it again each time. We would have had the only houseful of infant drug fiends on the North American continent. Min, can't you see what it's been like?"

"How can I not see, Karraman?" Finally she tried to settle his turbulence with her touch. Her trembling voice betrayed her. "It must have been hell," she whispered.

"For her, too, don't forget. Before I mastered the nerve to call Grainger, she already knew that she was pregnant again. But she was trying to keep it a secret, because she knew he'd tell her to put the stuff away, and she couldn't face that. God knows what damage she did this baby in the interim."

"So it all came out during Grainger's visit?"

"Then and there. It was horrible. I should have spared her the humiliation, but—"

"Don't think of it that way, Karraman. It was for her benefit, don't forget. And the baby's. And that means everybody's." She sounded convincing.

"Well, at the time it was brutal. Just brutal. First she tried to deny everything. The drugs, her dependency, how she spent her days. The whole business."

"But surely Grainger knew? He was providing the laudanum, wasn't he?"

"Of course he was providing it, the son of a bitch. When we finally got down to cases, he mumbled a good bit about how the stuff affects different people differently, and how little is known about it. He even suggested that she managed to get an additional amount from somebody else. That's ridiculous. And worse than that, he had the colossal nerve to chuckle and tell me that 'these people,' as he called them, do learn to be very sly in their habits.

"My God, Min, he says he doesn't know anything about opium, so it can't be his fault. Whose fault is it, then? He gave her the goddamn stuff. And kept giving it to her until she was only a few steps from turning into a blithering idiot."

Minerva couldn't tell whether the emotion firing Karraman was grief or rage or guilt or a ghastly combination in which the whole was infinitely greater than the sum of the parts. She opened her mouth to try to quiet him, but thought better of it. He probably hadn't had a chance to get any of his frustrations out of his system since she'd been gone. She sat forward, reaching toward his pain with her eyes.

He drew a deep breath, trying to go on. Instead, his look softened, and he inhaled again. "I haven't held you for a long time, Min."

"I know."

"I've dreamed it, though. Often."

"I know that, too, Karraman. I was willing myself to be there."

"I wish you had been there in the flesh. The will doesn't warm a bed."

"I couldn't have stopped anything from happening the way it did, Karraman."

"No, but it would have been easier to bear."

"But we have to clear it up now, Karraman," she said slowly. "You must tell me what happened next."

"She was wild. So do you know what the son of a bitch Grainger did? He turned around and gave her an injection of more of the same. I wanted to kill him, but he said that he had to do it to get her under control. I told him that it seemed to me that if she had to have more and more of the stuff to get under control, then she was a hopeless addict already and he might as well throw her life away with the evening's table scraps. I might sound calm about it now, but believe me, Min, I was far from calm when it happened.

"I imagine you know who I really wanted to throw out with the table scraps. But not until I had finished picking the flesh from his bones. Well, of course it didn't happen that way. He told me that it was standard procedure to sedate her in order to make arrangements to get her cured, and frankly, I would have gone along with anything that held out a hope. Doing it at home was out of the question, because it would make her a virtual prisoner in her own house. Her own room, actually."

"Mrs. Rochester."

"What?"

"Nothing. The wrong person's been in the tower anyway. Go on."

Karraman sailed on. "He told me about the place where she is now. A rest home. Specializes in cases similar to hers."

"How long will she have to stay?"

"Until sometime after the child is born."

"Which will be?"

"In late February or early March, probably," he said. "In any case, once we got her there, the first problem was to wean her from the drug, and at the same time to restore her to some semblance of physical health. The second will be to keep her in a stable condition through the rest of the pregnancy, so that the baby will at least have a fighting chance."

"You mean there's still a doubt?"

"We hope not, but who knows? Grainger was honest enough about that. All they can do is to build her up, keep her away from the medicine chest, and hope for the best."

"And afterward?"

"She'll stay for a while. She'll be recovering from her fourth confinement in as many years, don't forget, and she's not as young as she used to be."

"Who is?" Dryly.

"Ah, Min. You're springtime."

"You're sidetracking, Karraman," she chided.

"Indeed I am," he shot back, "and only because you asked for it, Minnie."

She smiled. "I suppose I did. But I didn't really mean to. This isn't nearly the end of the story, is it?"

"No, it isn't," he admitted. "I didn't get to the third problem."

"Which is?"

"After the baby's born. We have to get her back to normal somehow. And then the hardest part of all: to keep her that way."

"But I'm not sure I—"

"There's a pattern. At the rest home, it's much easier to keep things on the up-and-up. The major obstacle to complete recovery, they say, seems to occur when the patient goes home. Right now she has no decisions to make, no lives to feel responsible for. Not even her own. It's entirely possible that the simple fact of walking through the front door of Foothill House will send her running back to the medicine bottle."

"But surely you'll have removed it long ago, Karraman."

"Of course. But if her need is that desperate, there's no telling which would be the worse prospect: for her to find it there, or find it missing. It was the drug that made her into a madwoman, not a hidden strain of family lunacy that suddenly cropped up. What we have to remember is that there's some kind of inclination to weakness there. It can happen again at any time. Some people go to church when they feel despondent. Others write poetry. Emmaline took laudanum. That's her way. We'll have to guard against it forever. Period."

"You make it sound like an indictment."

"What do you want? A defense?" He jolted to his feet. "What good can that do?"

"I'm not defending her—I don't think. But if I were, it wouldn't mean that I'm automatically attacking you. This is no time to line up and choose sides. A terrible thing has happened to Emmaline—"

"And to me. Don't leave that out."

"Of course I'm not leaving that out. She happens to be your wife. Whatever affects her affects you. Do you think I ever forget that for one instant of my life?" Her voice had circled the long way around, and come back to the verge of breaking. Her effort at self-control drew Karraman back like a magnet.

"I know you never forget, Min. Forgive me. I've been so distraught. Em in such despair, you completely out of reach, bombs bursting all around you day and night . . ."

"Damn you, Karraman, every time I get myself all in position for a good cry, you start me laughing all over again," she said. "Please, please forget your bombs. I'm here now. And of course I'll go back to Foothill House. Whatever needs to be done, we'll do. When Em gets ready to come home, with any luck at all we'll have the place running well enough that she'll be able to feel as relaxed as she did at the rest home. With any luck at all," she prayed, "she'll never need to think of laudanum again."

"God bless, Minerva." Then he looked at her critically for a moment. "You know, Minerva, you're one hell of a woman. In all these years, I've brought you crisis after crisis. You started life at Foothill House in a multiple disaster that bowled strong men over. Now, here you are, going back again, into something that even the doctors aren't sure how to handle. When I stop to think about it, the bombs in Europe are probably a welcome relief after your daily existence in Saint Kathareen's."

"Karraman, I swear, you have bombs on the brain. If I ever have any bombshells to drop on you, I promise that they'll be something far different than just gunpowder and mortar."

He chuckled affectionately and pulled her into his arms. Of course he knew that she was only trying to protect him from the most alarming details of what she must have experienced in England.

[263]

It was incredible that he could be so right, and still miss the mark by so much. It was also incredible that, for all the tears and scars and shocks and days they bore, they made love to one another like two frolicking, carefree explorers, better than ever. And he never even noticed the stretch marks.

XV

"And you never left after that?"

Minerva answers him from out of a dreamlike distance. "That's right, Hawk. I never left again. At least, not for more than a little while. I would go to England, or supervise the opening of another boutique. But never with the idea that I wasn't coming back."

He frames the next question carefully. "Then is that the way you think it works, Miss Minerva? Do people always end up in the places where they're supposed to be?"

"Don't put words in my mouth, Hawk," she retorts. He catches a brand-new glimpse of her stern underpinning.

"Miss Minerva, I didn't—"

"Oh yes you did, Hawk. Don't sneak in my back door wearing disguises that make you look like Edward R. Murrow when what you're really acting like is a mooning schoolgirl."

"Edward R. who?"

"Never mind. Don't ask me questions about whether you're going to live happily ever after with Caravelle, and try to couch them in grand universals to trap me into saying what you want to hear. I'm far too old for that kind of nonsense."

"Zap."

"I beg your pardon?"

"You got me, Miss Minerva."

Hawk is wondering what it will feel like if he bursts into tears right here in this very room. Her soul would give him sympathy on its inmost levels, he is sure, but in her present mood she doesn't seem inclined to let any of the soul's tendencies slop over into her behavior or her comments.

"I know, Hawk dear. I know *you*. You don't fool me for a minute. You didn't want to talk half as much today about Cara's past as you did about her future, and, most notably, her present. You thought she'd come here first, didn't you?"

"Yes." It is almost inaudible, curiously guilty. Minerva is certain that she knows exactly what Hawk looked like as a little tad of a boy, caught with his hand in the cookie jar.

"I know, Hawk. But she hasn't been here at all. And do you know something? I was as disappointed when you showed up at the door without her as you were when you got here and found that I was by myself."

He hasn't expected such a confession from Minerva, doesn't know what to do with it.

She fills his silence for him. "But I do admire you, Hawk." She chuckles. "You scarcely let it show."

"Scarcely let it show? Miss Minerva, if we keep up this conversation for another thirty seconds, I'm going to dissolve into a Victorian vapor on the horsehair."

She laughs outright. "No you're not, my friend. Not as long as you can keep talking that way."

"Oh, Miss Minerva, those are just words. That's the whole problem. It's always words that get me into trouble. With Margo, with Howard, everybody. Now Cara." He knows better than to follow this well-marked trail into the kingdom of self-pity, but plunges right in again despite himself. "You don't really think she's going to come back, do you?"

"Now, Hawk, you can't go about it that way either. No matter how you try to disguise it, you're still asking the same question. I can tell you the answers to a lot of things, but the fact that one-quarter of her genetic complement belongs to me doesn't mean that I can read her mind. I never laid eyes on her until yesterday. I can't begin to guess how her mind works."

"But, Miss Minerva," Hawk is pleading, "you practically came out and said you knew she'd turn up sooner or later. How do you account for that?"

"Now, don't get all het up about that, Hawk. It was a little bit of drama to liven up an old woman's day. You'll notice that my prophetic soul didn't drop any hints to that effect *before* she arrived. I could have meant that I knew my dear friend Hawk would introduce me to his lady sooner or later, no matter whose family tree she had sprouted from."

"But you know there's more to it than that."

"There is now," Minerva agrees. "Imagine my position: opening the door, looking my own history straight in the eye. Could be my sole posterity, too."

"Come on, Miss Minerva. Your life is your posterity."

"Not in the same sense, Hawk. Books can be eternal," she says pointedly to him, "but I've never heard of an immortal hat."

He opens his mouth to protest, but she isn't having any.

"Naturally I was enchanted when I saw her, Hawk. Who wouldn't be? But my feeling has another component, too. You never knew Minerva Bolton at twenty or thirty, so how can you see it? But I *am* Minerva Bolton at twenty or thirty—dreams and emotions don't end up with estrogen deficiencies. They abide, Hawk. They never stop hoping. When that child turned up at this door, it was the Kate that should have been. It was my most hopeful fantasy fulfilled—that Kate might really have been a fluke, and that Karraman's and my legacy might, just might, have turned out to be something fine and worthy after all.

"You do understand, Hawk," she adds confidentially, "that however romantic it might be to say that being with Karraman was its own reward, there was always a feeling that I wanted to have something extraordinary to show on earth for the extraordinary years we had spent together. You can't imagine what the silences were like—the years of silence. It isn't even that I've wanted to make any loud verbal claims about anything, including Cara. Privacy is privacy. I respect hers, because I respect the interests of anybody who's still involved."

"Like Howard?"

"Yes, like Howard, the poor son of a bitch."

Hawk, thinking precisely the same words, is delighted that Minerva has voiced them.

She continues. "But just knowing that my beautiful granddaughter has a home in the world, that she knows the truth about her secret heritage—that would be enough for me to die happily. She can do with the knowledge whatever she pleases. Transmitting it—that would do for me."

"Miss Minerva, this talk about dying is silly. With your energy—"

"Hawk, all this denial, this refusal of yours to face the facts of life *and* death—it's unbecoming. Let's work with what we have. We can only pray for the best."

"Okay, your Honor. I plead not quite innocent"—but not exactly guilty, either. He has what he considers a lifetime investment in Minerva. He isn't ready, not old enough, not sufficiently philosophical to allow her to any eternities beyond those he can comprehend all by himself. "Anyway, I really didn't mean to make you digress. Tell me what you were going to say."

"I think I already have, Hawk. It boils down to the fact that there really isn't a great deal more I *can* say. I can no more speak for Caravelle than walk a tightrope. At this stage of the game in what seems to be her current mood, I'm not even sure which of the two activities would be more dangerous. Don't ask me for any more second-guessing, please, Hawk."

"I really am sorry, Miss Minerva. Really."

"No—I wasn't eliciting apologies. But there's one more thing I must say."

"Yes?" Warily.

"Hawk, I think you're an awfully nice person. I don't think I've ever said that to you before. You've spent a good many hours listening to an old lady ramble when you could have been doing any of a number of other things. Even today, here you are, sorting through my problems, when you could have been out enjoying the luxury of feeling sorry for yourself in peace and quiet, and cultivating your suntan at the same time."

"Don't worry about it, Miss Minerva." There is a bit of the old Hawkish twinkle in his eye as he mischievously says, "I can't think of a better place in the world to feel sorry for myself than Foothill House." He truly cannot. Her purview feels to him the only perfect repository for his shredded soul.

"I see your point, Hawk," she shoots back. "Intended or not, you certainly do fall into an endless tradition of believers."

Emmaline was the first to perfect the art, but not the last. Karraman went to fetch her before the new baby was three months old, and the surfaces of life resumed much of their former character. The infant squalled and belched and broke out in cradle cap, but so had all the others. That would pass.

It was Emmaline everybody worried about, but the worries all turned out to be, if not groundless, at least misdirected. If she ever thought about reverting to laudanum again after her extended tenure in Pennsylvania, she gave no sign. Of course, she rarely exhibited much in the way of a sign that she thought about anything at all, so it was part of the whole picture. She never again appeared suspiciously groggy or mentally intoxicated. Not to Karraman, not to Minerva, not to the legions of servants who dutifully reported to Karraman all the confidences and intimacies of Emmaline's days and nights. She simply absented herself in a nearly imperceptible way. She received all the overt respect one would expect to see accorded to the lady of the manor. Hardly a soul dared smirk behind her back about any of the obvious peculiarities she displayed, such as her practice of apologizing to inanimate objects for any and all slights she might have committed over the last twenty-four hours. She was engaged in active verbal relationships with the potted palms decades before it occurred to most people that speaking to them was an existential necessity for the peaceful coexistence of both parties. If only her household had fared as well with her as the plants.

If a callow new servant dared suggest Em's eccentricities aloud, word got to Maybelle Kennebec the Elder faster than telephone Central got across town. Maybelle was, in turn, a more accurate conduit to Karraman than any oil-field spy he paid handsomely for the same service. The offending party was usually headed down Calvin-and-Levi, personal effects in hand, by noon of the selfsame day. Emmaline was protected, adulated, dressed in nothing but the finest. She presided over her household like the Queen of England. And she had precisely as much power, which is to say, she reigned, but did not rule. Everyone in the house deferred to her left and right, day and night, yet she had no function in the running of things. The Emmaline who sat enthroned at dinner, or at tea, or in the formal parlor, prowled the corridors during the mundane remainder of each day·like an imperious visitor, nosing into everything, taking responsibility for nothing. If her emotional repertoire was limited, she kept petulant resentments forever poised for action, hauling them out at frequent and erratic cues recognizable only to herself. Thus no one was ever sufficiently girded for her onslaughts. If Emmaline ever did perfect an art in her life, it was that of the stunning gratuitous insult.

No wonder that the children grew up with varying numbers of screws loose or missing altogether. She took displeasure in acts they hadn't even realized they had committed. If she managed to find a word of praise for anybody, it covered some category she had incorrectly attributed to the wrong child, one who wasn't remotely capable of accomplishing what she told him he was doing rather well. Therefore, on top of insecurity and the devastating inability to get through a single day without some sort of entirely irrelevant reprimand, each child was further endowed with a set of expectations which it would have been impossible for any mere mortal to fill. Everybody in the house knew to a fine art what would please her majesty. Trouble was, every last unfortunate knew bleakly that it was only some other person who was capable of delivering the goods.

Emmaline padded blithely through it all, entering rooms without knocking, conversing volubly with people who wanted to be alone, denying her presence to a flock of children who would have prospered by any touch of their mother's hand and affection, however minuscule. They would have subsisted gladly on castoffs. She denied them the bare threads.

Minerva was torn. She chose deliberately not to become deeply involved with any of the four children. She knew that the convoluted forms of Emmaline's vindictiveness might fall heavily enough to snap the greenest, most resilient twig. Minerva didn't fear so much for herself as for the children.

Mustering what patience she had left, she talked to Emmaline exactly as if Em had been a sane person. It couldn't do any harm. Besides, Minerva admittedly feared for the destiny of the entire establishment if Em were to throw her out once and for all. It was still Minerva's organizational sense that held the place together. All those lives banked on it.

She needn't have worried. Emmaline would never turn on Minerva. Through some hybrid variety of the Providence that protects fools and children, Emmaline kept sight of the fact that Minerva was somehow essential to everybody's survival. She never let on by word or gesture that she actually needed Min. She simply stayed within the boundaries of what conventional people understand as human relationships at all times, where Minerva was concerned. The long and short of it was that she had turned Minerva into the only demilitarized zone in the family.

Minerva never wanted to know what went on behind the closed doors of Karraman and Emmaline's marriage chamber. Not that Karraman was home often enough to provide the occasion of curiosity. When he was, he retired at night with the woman he had married, just as the bulk of society would have expected him to do. In every other respect, Minerva was his wife, his heart. Thus she kept her balance, and thus she managed to cope with the various distances that she and fate placed between her and those she loved, prepared always to live with ghastly separations and wrenching farewells. One would almost have said she thrived on it.

"Min, how can anybody with a forehead and cheekbone full of felt dye look so beautiful?"

She had remotely heard someone enter the office behind her, but the whirring undertone of machinery from the rooms beyond, the rhythmic theme of over three hundred people at harmonious work in her factory, had masked the sound and kept her concentration intact. She grinned, unabashed, without taking her hands from the wig form where she was pinning and shaping, thinking aloud with her hands.

"Oh, that. I didn't realize it hadn't dried until I already had it all over me. Something has to be done about those forms. They're supposed to be a clever approximation of everybody's head, so they end up being just right for absolutely nobody."

"So you decided to become the universal woman and do it on your own head, did you?"

"I suppose so," she admitted cheerfully. "Well, better me than an eggplant, don't you think?"

"Better you than anything, Min." He started toward her, and checked himself.

"Karraman—"

"I know, Min, I know. But I've never seen your face covered with cordovan dye before. I want to immortalize you with my lips in case you turn to leather."

"Seems to me," chiding, wishing that she could simply draw the blinds on obligation and take him into her arms right then and there, "seems to me that Mr. Robley of Saint Kathareen's ought to have a few more pressing matters on his mind right now than immortalizing anything." She glanced up, hoping to pry his intent loose from her warming desire. Karraman retreated a step, pulled out her swivel chair, and sat down with a heaviness that surprised her.

"As a matter of fact, Min, you're right."

"Mmmm."

"What's that mean?"

"Mnnn." Pause. "It means that I wanted to say something, but I had just put four straight pins into my mouth, which you didn't see because you were too busy fumbling about for that cigar, which means that you really are concerned about something. What is it?" Her fingers, pinning, patient, did not betray the alert that flooded through her torso like molten lead. "Is it Em? Something at the house?"

She waited out the beats of Karraman's first long breath, wondering if people ever used Clydesdales for transportation anymore. It seemed to her that a lot more streamlining could be done, if people put their minds to it.

"The damned census came out."

"What census?"

"What census? The only kind of census that's been ordained and taken since the day this country was born. The *Census*."

"Karraman, you're getting all exercised." She stuck a few more pins around at random, shoving them at awkward angles to the meticulous work she had been doing moments before. She put down the hat form, walked to the door, and shut it. Then she pulled down the green windowshade on its glass upper half. Generally she adhered to a strict open-door policy on the premises. When she deviated, everybody in the vicinity knew that she meant business.

Minerva Bolton was a benefactress as well as an employer. She gave turkeys at Thanksgiving and bonuses at Christmas. Her orders went forth in friendly accents. But a closed door, in the genteel codes of La Vallée, was a command to keep out.

So was Mr. Karraman's presence. Rumors flew incessantly: he was her silent partner; he was the brains behind the business; they were lovers; she was the brains behind *his* business; they were friends. It was, all of it, obviously false; also, according to those whose instincts were best, infallibly true. In any case, when Minerva closed the office door, her employees considered it inviolate.

Once or twice she had conferred with Felder in such closeted conditions, usually when personnel problems arose. They worked well together at spotting the germs of trouble and defusing them. The staff welcomed their "conferences," since an easing of tensions around the workshops invariably followed.

With Karraman, it was another story. Minerva had always tried to avoid the occasion of gossip. She reassured herself that their personal crises fared better at the Inn, where the possible forms of reconciliation enjoyed a broader range. On the day that Karraman came in raging about the matter of the census, however, something in his mood, and the subject matter, reordered Minerva's thinking.

She perched on an unoccupied corner of her worktable. "All right, Karraman, what about the census? Don't tell me we're going to have to go to Bethlehem?" Aiming toward proportion.

"What? Oh, of course not." A small rueful smile.

"Well, then?" As if to say: What can be so bad? Urging: Tell me, my love. I'll kiss it and send it packing.

"But don't underestimate, Min. It's not good."

"How so?"

"The figures are down from all our estimates for the entire county, and down most of all for Saint Kathareen's. We know that the figures we've been giving for the town proper were right, within a margin of less than a percent, because of the church rolls."

"Counting churchgoers in *this* county? Don't make me laugh!"

"No, they did it the old way—modeled it after the Renaissance in Italy. House-to-house. You know. The upshot of it was that Saint Kath's came out looking pretty damn stable. Rosy future. But the last one was five years ago. And this federal-census thing—oh, Min, what a comedown. In fact, a few of the outer townships in the county are up a bit, but that just makes the picture in town average out all the more bleakly."

"Karraman, that's impossible. Have you seen the tax duplicates? We're practically drowning in our own prosperity. Have you seen La Vallée's last annual report? It's practically embarrassing to be grossing so much money. Felder's arguing for diversification far beyond the boutiques and accessory stores. I'm beginning to think I'm going to have to start listening to him. If my little vanity enterprise is growing like a beanstalk, I can't even imagine what the Robley Enterprises ledger looks like."

"I know, Minnie, I know, but that isn't the point. We're all selling everything we can produce as fast as we can produce it. No question about that. But where are we selling it?—to the outside market. The tourists love the place. The Inn needs another expansion, and the plaster's hardly dry in the last one—except for one major problem."

"What?"

"Have you seen the reservation book for May and June?"

"Of course not, Karraman. Why would I?"

"Well, don't bother. There's nothing in it to look at, to speak of. Hasn't been for years. Probably won't be for years to come, and for exactly the same reason that the population's down."

"What are you talking about?"

"Ha!" Karraman popped out of the chair, pointed the cigar at Minerva, and started to stalk around the room like something caged. "*You* forget, because you've lived it, and you know that you survive it, maybe even learn a little, keep on going, tougher than you were in the first place. No one on the outside can forget it, though, because they've imagined it up into a monstrous, insurmountable specter. They stay away in droves."

Softly, comprehendingly: "The Flood."

"Not the Flood. The FLOOD. It screams at them. We haven't had a real flood worth crowing about since nineteen hundred and six. That's years ago, and we still can't get a convention or a party to book in here in the spring no matter what we do. Can't get an industry to settle, can't get a substantial segment of the populace to sit still. Can't get a single business concern that hasn't been here since great-grandfather's day to take us seriously enough to move in and establish itself."

Minerva started to interject something, to ask, what did he consider La Vallée, anyway, an idle-hours hobby? But she resigned herself to hearing out the rest of the forming tirade when she saw that Karraman's pause was for breath, not polite interchange.

"Shipbuilding," he complained. "We thought we'd always have the shipbuilding. Then what happens? One ill-tended floating hazard of a sternwheeler burns out of Cincinnati, and all of a sudden the government steps in and tells us that we can't build ships anymore the way we've always built good, proper ships. So we don't build sternwheelers. Okay, I admit that there are more efficient ways to get upstream than in one of those tinderboxes of a tub. I'm all for change. I'm simply asking," he pleaded, "why we can't go on with the new kind of shipbuilding right here in Saint Kathareen's, the way we always have?"

"I'll tell you why," he answered himself, floating on his own swift downstream current. "We don't have the materials, is why. And why don't

[273]

we have the materials? Because there are no steel mills in Saint Kathareen's. And there will be no steel mills in Saint Kathareen's."

"Karraman, aren't you being unduly pessimistic," interrupted Minerva.

"Ha! I wish I were. But you mark my words, Min, there won't be a new steel mill or anything else in Saint Kath's, because every two-bit manufacturer in the nation is scared blind of us. Oh, the Valley's lovely, all right, but the rivers have this nasty habit. Occasionally, mind you, not too often, they overflow the banks, and all of a sudden lovely old Saint Kathareen's is the nation's pariah." His sarcasm was the measure of his pique. It was considerable.

"What about Pittsburgh?" Minerva interjected. "What about Cincinnati? Homestead? Those places are on rivers." She knew the answers as well as he did, but she wanted to erect a structure in which he might calm himself. She watched carefully the percussive accent of that small bellwether vein at his temple.

He sighed. "Yes, what about them. Of course they're all on rivers. Can't have a goddamn steel mill without a goddamn river, for Christ's sake. And you can't have a river without an occasional flood."

"So it would seem."

" 'So it would seem.' " He mimicked her irony, then worked straight back up the decibel scale without warning. "Then what in the holy hell is the matter with Saint Kathareen's? At Marietta they've jumped from six thousand souls to almost eleven in ten years. *They* have floods. Great God, the Muskingum River half the time doesn't even know that it's supposed to have boundaries. Just try getting down there from Zanesville in any eight given months of the year. You have just as even a chance of ending up underwater as making it all the way down by road. But up there, they can't develop fast enough to fit the new population. Here—nothing."

He sat back down wearily in the swivel. "How do we get ourselves out of this spiral, Min? Do you know how many families are going to be affected when the yard closes down for good? After all, it's not as if an operation that turns out timbered riverboats splinter by splinter can suddenly switch to a fabricating yard for battleships. Do you know what the impression will be on everybody who sees a ghost shipyard sitting in the effective middle of downtown Saint Kathareen's? Devastating. Death on the hoof."

Minerva slid from her perch on the worktable and walked toward him. She leaned over from behind the chair, nuzzling what was left of the familiar bristle of his hair. "Now, tell me the whole story, Karraman. This isn't really just a matter of shipyards and populations, is it? No one can convince me that this cloudburst has to do with a simple case of being jealous of Marietta. What's going on?"

He gave out a choking snort of a laugh. "Can't get past you, can I, Min?"

"Not hardly," she answered softly, mimicking the vernacular.

"Not at all. Well, I can't say I came in here in order *not* to talk to you, now, can I, Min?"

"No, Karraman," she agreed softly, waiting for him to find his tempo.

"I've made some heavy investments on spec, Min," he began.

"Speculation?"

"Yes."

"And? After all, it isn't as though you haven't done anything like that before."

"In a way, it's very different from anything I've even considered before. In the first place, I've taken considerable acreage where there are already two working wells, and one ready to be fractured at any minute."

"That means the prices are already sky-high."

"Yes. And on top of that, I'm collateralized up to my eyes."

She raised a questioning eyebrow.

"Everything. The Inn, Foothill House, everything that wasn't already mortgaged to the teeth, with the exception of the rest of the oil lands."

"That's a considerable exception, I daresay."

"But they have to be producing, for starters. And the oil economy has to stabilize itself in this part of the country. No one lives in an oil field, or uses it to draw the tourist trade. I've risked damn near every stable holding my family took over a century to build up, because that godforsaken acreage north of town looked appealing to one of the largest banks in the country for real-estate development. A whole new idea in living, they called it. Suburban community. Oh, Christ." He snuffed the cigar, smothering it the way he would have liked to put an end to the complexities of bad judgment that had landed him in as deep a despair as Minerva had ever seen.

"And so," she continued for him, "with the population down, the birth rate down, a major industry pulling out, and the general picture looking bleaker by the minute, the bank wants to pull out too. Is that what you're trying to tell me?"

"They don't just want to pull out," he responded heatedly, taking her perspicacious understanding for granted, "they already have pulled out. Not that they were ever in it for more than a handshake," he added, "but somewhere along the line I was brought up to think that that meant something."

"Well, Karraman," she began slowly, "it certainly does appear gloomy, doesn't it?"

"If the understatement of the century is what you're after, Minerva, yes, it certainly does."

She chuckled. "But," she continued, "I'm not sure that 'gloomy' means the same thing as 'defeated.' I think the situation needs to be turned around, and I think I have an idea or two that might just have found the ideal place to sprout."

"Just like that." Ironic, dubious.

"No, silly, not just like that. It's something I've been thinking about at the outside edge of things for quite a while. I think I just might see some ways that we could make it apply. Now, this is long-range, mind you—"

"I don't care what range it is, Min. I'm listening."

"Good," briskly. "Let's talk while we have lunch."

"All right," he agreed readily, picking up the telephone. "I'll just phone over to the Inn and have something sent up to the suite."

"No, Karraman. We're going to eat in the dining room today." He looked at her as though she'd taken temporary leave of her senses, which was, of course, the farthest thing from the truth. She wanted nothing more fervently than to spend the afternoon consoling him among the endless unfoldings of her body, but business was business. She was not going to let him hide out in bed from facing a potential, but avoidable, catastrophe. Staring it right in the eye was the only way she saw to get it taken care of. By the wily expedient of outright visibility, she was going to endow this undertaking not only with energetic optimism but also with respectability. She was going to have a full-fledged business meeting with Karraman Robley, in plain sight of any citizen who wanted to take a careful gander. Since a heavy investment of her time and energy was about to go into this little plan, she was going to provide for herself the added fillip of offering every curious old biddy of either sex in Saint Kathareen's a wide-open field day to speculate on just what in hell was going on between Karraman and Minerva this time.

"Let's go, Karraman! I want to be sure to get a good table."

By the time they had finished dessert, Minerva had outlined the aggressive blueprint for the Saint Kathareen's Valley Municipal Chamber of Commerce in brilliant detail. As she talked, she warmed to her subject, unfolding profuse details of her plan to turn the Valley on its mercantile ear.

"Min, it's exotic, it's creative, and I don't know where you found the time to develop it down to the last cross of the T—"

"Thank you, Karraman," demurely, knowing full well what was coming next.

"—but of course it'll never work."

Having expected it, she held poise and temper, but not without effort. "That's where you're wrong, Karraman. I told you it was long-range. You have to give it a chance." Coolly.

"Min, I just don't see where a printed prospectus and a few dozen free lunches are going to change the course of my fortune. Or of this community."

"In no particular order, of course."

"Of course. Oh, come on, Min. Don't be bitter just because I'm not going to go along with your idea. It's a good idea. Really it is. I'm sure that the community will latch on to something very much like it someday. Right now, you simply must see that I need to devote everything I have to pulling out of this mess with my person still in one piece."

"Don't start patronizing me now, Karraman. We've come much too far for that."

"I—"

"We're not talking about a few brochures and a few free lunches. Just ask Felder, if you want an idea of how to get things like this across. We're talking about the entire attitude that this community has about itself. I'm not suggesting an overnight miracle, either, just a simple but full-fledged advertising campaign. A communal expression. I wish I could think of a better word for it, but I'm talking about the kind of thinking that symbolizes the difference between Nikolai and La Vallée, just for one for-instance."

"What do you mean?"

"You know perfectly well what I mean. You're the one who made it an issue in the first place."

"What?"

"Well, self-promotion would be one way to put it."

"That's beside the point, Minerva, you're the biggest and the best in the world and you know it."

"Be that as it may, Karraman, it didn't happen by wishing. She's more innovative than I am, more daring. Sounder. She's a better designer, and she always has been. But I'm the one with a factory, a salon, a New York outlet, and twenty-two boutiques, not counting the two that are under construction—an empire, practically. She still has one steamy little room in Bloomsbury with a mannequin and a samovar. Oh, granted, she wants it that way, but granted, that's also the way it stays, willy-nilly. She's exclusive, exotic, and has a mile-high reputation. But she hasn't moved an inch, in the business. No progress."

"If she'd rather be exclusive than practical, I'd say that's her lookout. At least that's what you've always told me. Seems as if I'm finally starting to agree—but I imagine it's not so easy to feed herself on her clever little reputation."

Minerva ignored miles of waiting detours, and pounced directly on what he said. "Exactly, Karraman! That's precisely the point I'm making about Saint Kathareen's. I don't want to see this Valley turn into a wretched octopus, but I don't want to see it sink into oblivion, either. There's a time and a place for blowing one's own horn, and I think that this is exactly where we start tuning up."

"Do you really believe, Minerva, that the best attempts of a little provincial town to impress a bunch of inbred bankers from New York are going to make any difference? It'll be amateur night from the start. Then what? They'll laugh all the way to the sheriff's sale."

"No, Karraman. Because we'll go about it carefully, that's what. First, I think, we actually form the Chamber of Commerce, and print the prospectus. Then we circulate it here and there. *Then* we use it, but not to impress the bankers with our artificial urbanity. We're *not* New York. That's the idea. We *show* them, quite confidentially—and confidently—how we're going to use it to impress everybody else. Don't you see? We set up an alliance that way, not an adversary. And at the same time, we incidentally let them know the myriad advantages of investing in this kind of community."

Minerva knew that she was right. In Karraman's slowly altering expression, she could read that he might be beginning to believe so too. "Look at it this way," she pressed. "If we, as a community, present a systematic approach to new industry that might be interested in moving to a prime river location like Saint Kathareen's, we accomplish a double purpose. On one hand, we can actually succeed in bringing interested parties in to look things over. Once they get here, I think we can do all the convincing that needs to be done. At the same time, we can show the bigger fish that we're developing quite a promising community on our own. Most of all, we'll show them that we know how to handle it ourselves." She was ready to start, ready to organize the first meeting. She wanted to get on with it yesterday at the latest, but, still cool, she swallowed her exuberance in a sip of cooling tea.

"How will you handle the flooding?" Karraman asked tentatively.

Ready for him: "Treat it as colorful ancient history. Romanticize it. Turn it into a challenge. Ever hear of Noah?"

"It's a daydream of an idea, Min."

"I know, and a hell of a good one, don't you think?"

"It'll never fool a New York City banker."

"Not supposed to. No fooling intended."

"You're going to be the laughingstock of a number of people around here."

"I know that, too. So was Columbus, and he was out discovering a new world. All I want to do is a little promotional booklet about the one I've discovered."

"I could lose everything."

"You won't."

"How long do you think it'll take you to design a pamphlet?"

Minerva could imagine Hammond Bolton's fatuous outrage. He naturally would have thought it was vulgar. He considered vulgar all human activities that weren't private, and most that were. He had always kept up with the millinery business in the trade papers, and he surely followed the progress of the Saint Kathareen's Valley Municipal Chamber of Commerce in the *New York Times*. The newly organized Chamber had sent one of its artful and informative brochures to the business editor as a matter of course. The fact that so remote and apparently entrenched a community had undertaken such a project attracted notice secondarily to the fact that the entire undertaking had been developed and designed by a woman. A note from Felder reminding all interested parties that this was the same woman who had single-handedly laid waste to abusive child-labor practices in the Valley more than five years earlier sent reporters scurrying in and out of newspaper morgues and interview files. Minerva was a hot item again. If Karraman, belatedly, beamed, Hammond must have shivered.

He took up his pen, dipped it in acid, and wrote to Minerva:

The name of Bolton has never lent itself in the past to such blatant self-advertisement. It is to be assumed that you will withdraw from this unbecoming limelight and refrain in the future from any such ill-considered undertaking as that in which you are currently engaged.

He signed it simply "Hammond Bolton," folded it neatly, sealed it into an envelope, left it unaddressed and unresolved, in the dead center of his desk blotter for nine days from the date of the heading to the date of the postmark.

The decision not to do something can always be amended. Inaction readily secures the status quo. The decision to do something is a different order of beast. Hammond Bolton had the fortitude to go so far, and no farther. In his cramped little hand he finally affixed an address to the envelope. He placed it at the corner of his desk where the outgoing mail usually waited. Then he left his office for the day, heading toward the sullen routines of evening.

In the morning, he noted with grim pleasure that the envelope had disappeared. He sought out his secretary and asked if he knew the whereabouts of the envelope.

"Yes, sir, Mr. Bolton," replied the poor fellow from beneath his eyeshade. "I saw it waiting when I brought in yesterday afternoon's mail, so I posted it myself."

"I see. Thank you," minced Hammond Bolton. Then he had the poor bastard fired for having done exactly what he had been hired to do.

Minerva blanched when she saw the envelope. At least she had the advantage of opening it alone in her office. Her heart raced. It might have been anything. For years she had never been sure that he knew where she was, but neither did she doubt that he would find her when he was ready. She was almost relieved. At least she wouldn't have to wonder about it anymore.

Karraman walked in just as she had finished digesting the contents.

"Look," she commanded.

"What?" Scanning. "Good Lord," omitting "what an idiot," which Minerva quite expected and believed would have been a perfectly appropriate comment. She understood Karraman's restraint, however, because through the years they had developed a scrupulous ritual of avoiding recriminations regarding one another's unfortunate bonds of marriage.

"Do you s'pose he means anything by it?"

"Oh, I suppose he thinks he does, Karraman, but what can he do? Issue an injunction?"

Minerva spoke calmly, but she felt an ugly, insistent chill welling up from her depths. For the first time in years Minerva began to realize that Hammond Bolton actually did harbor the vicious potential for putting a stop to anything, if he wanted to badly enough. He had only to work up the gumption to free himself from his obsessive daily routines. She shivered when she realized at last that he had probably had that potential all along. Her imagination, optimistically dormant in this particular arena for many long years, suddenly went back to work overtime. She felt as if her entire person had been invaded by something unclean.

The Saint Kathareen's Chamber, as it became quickly and widely known, did not work out exactly as planned. Instead, it took unexpected turn after turn for the better. Before eighteen months had passed, Saint Kathareen's had ended up with two new major industries. Substantial population recovery showed up both in new residents and in a rising birth rate. The New York bank never did buy the land to the north, because they never had the chance. Before they could take action to renew the options which they had casually allowed to expire the first time around, Karraman Robley, sole owner of several thousand previously wasted acres of township soil, enjoyed the rare pleasure of being roused from sound sleep five nights in two weeks to learn that unpromising wells had come in after all. On the last of the five nights, if Karraman had gone to sleep after the first time, he would have experienced the perhaps unique thrill of being awakened for the second time, courtesy of the sixth well.

The bank, by that time eager to remain in the picture, offered its full range of financial services to Karraman, but he declined, taking the opportunity to be as selective as he pleased in his affiliations. He decided, prudently, to keep as many of his dealings as he could where he could retain a close eye on them. He stuck to a local bank, slightly more than half of whose ownership his New York backers helped him acquire. The arrangement satisfied everybody. The oil business, consolidated as Midvale Oil, went onto the big board in record time, and split three times before it settled into a range that never even saluted when the Depression marched by.

Karraman credited Minerva with saving his business, his empire, and his face. Minerva tried to make him understand that the credit circled right back to Felder, who was a genius at organizing anything, but Minerva knew that Karraman would heap the praises on her as usual.

Confidentially, she told Felder that Karraman was indebted to him for life. She neglected to mention that Karraman was not exactly aware of that fact, but Felder understood, and didn't see it as any skin off his small and classic nose.

For herself, Minerva was content to feel further welded into a partnership that embraced all the complex strata of her life. Karraman told her convincingly that, with one another's help, they could accomplish anything they set out to do. Minerva, content, leaned across the pillow and agreed with him. And felt that she was more than ready to move along into whatever was coming.

XVI

Which was, as usual, absolutely unanticipated.

As time passed, Minerva had almost completely stopped wondering how they would all cope with another pregnancy if Emmaline happened to break out in one. La Vallée had undergone a period of breathtaking expansion. The business occupied Minerva more than ever. The Robley family seemed to have stabilized, if such a word can be applied to so murky a tangle of relationships, at four children. Karraman was no longer a man in his prime. Minerva had the impression that he contemplated the prospect of eventual grandfatherhood with more relish than he did an expansion of fatherly responsibilities.

In some ways he had always appeared middle-aged to Minerva. Although the accumulation of years did not loosen the firmness of his grip or the tautness of his flesh, he was broadening into an unmistakable Older Man. He took elaborate, successful pains to keep from growing slack. Still, Minerva hardly saw him as a dashing young buck. In fact, she didn't recall that she ever had. He had started old—magnetic, but old.

Minerva knew that the passion he spent with her, at his age, represented more than floor samples. She realized that, to her good fortune, she was participating in a considerable portion of the inventory. Still, she assumed that he continued to sleep in Emmaline's bed from time to time, although she couldn't understand why a woman who had been driven to the far reaches of her mental equilibrium by her previous pregnancies would ever want to do anything that might connect to a similar possibility in the future.

As it turned out, Minerva was dead wrong. Just as her first crop of offspring were ready, one by one, to enter gawky and troublesome adolescence, Emmaline announced triumphantly to Minerva that she was expecting another child. Minerva felt as if someone had kicked her soundly in the solar plexus.

For months they all existed on tenterhooks. Minerva elected to stay home from England for the first time in nine years. Not even the missiles and artifacts of war had prevented her booking some kind of passage, no matter how unconventional, when she was determined to go. When international conflicts did not suit her purposes, she ignored them. The Valley, to which news of everything came tardily and with diminished impact, always conspired to help her realize her intentions. Now, with the brand-new emotional conflagration threatening Foothill House, she knew where her unequivocal duty lay. Claire Nikolai's household certainly didn't need Minerva to oversee its management and sustain itself in peace.

Not that the decision weighed upon her lightly. She developed an upset stomach that matched Emmaline's, day for day. Nothing like that had ever happened to her before. When Em settled into a kvetching but healthy fifth month, Minerva's nausea subsided into a continuous fist that refused to release its grip at the center of her rib cage. Her lusty appetite dwindled. When her plate arrived each evening at the dinner table with more china showing than food, Karraman expressed concern.

"What's the matter, Min? Surely the kitchen can do better than ᴕat. That's no nourishment for a grown woman."

If Maybelle Younger happened to be serving, she simply walked out, leaving Minerva to field Karraman's wild pitches however she could. One evening when Minerva was already furiously impatient with the abnormal state of everything, herself included, Maybelle Elder happened to be doing the honors. In usual fettle, Maybelle decided to take on the situation herself.

"She don't eat nothin', so I don't serve nothin'," she told Karraman. "If she wants to nose around the kitchen complainin' about the waste a-goin' on there, she kin keep her own kettle from turnin' black at the same time."

"That will *do*," Karraman underscored, but Maybelle had already disappeared, trailing self-righteous malevolence behind her.

Minerva tried to avert attention from the problem by tackling her portion with feigned gusto. Indeed, life imitated art, and her appetite gradually improved. Karraman did not know that easing the rest of her general discomfiture was far more complicated. He could not have suspected its source.

Minerva thought about her daughter every day. When the season of her annual visit approached, every cell in her body perked up, conditioned to the exquisite thrill of anticipation. Unfulfilled, the energies funneled into her gut and turned it into a battleground. She was losing weight, losing heart, finding niggling little tasks to perform daily in a factory that was just as attuned to her annual absences as she was herself. What La Vallée required of her was heart and mind. She had only muscle left. Small delegations approached Felder, told him that they hated to see a lady like Miss Minerva sweeping up, and had they missed something? Felder, with no information but perfect insight, told them not to worry, it was Miss Minerva's way of thinking something through, it would blow over. The worrying he hoarded for himself, as Minerva kept sweeping.

Each evening, if she didn't stay to work late or be with Karraman, she hurried back to Foothill House and addressed herself to an array of social tasks that most women complained they didn't have time to perform in a week. Several nights a month, long after the carpets of silence rolled in over Saint Kathareen's and only dim streetlights speckled the darkness beyond the black stripe of the river, she wrote long letters to Kate and the others. Only the thoroughness of her chronicles betrayed the depth of her longing to those who could read between the lines.

Something had to give. Minerva weighed the alternatives time after time. Invariably she reached the same conclusion. There was no phase of her activity that she willingly could—would—forfeit. Something would fall apart if she did. If it wasn't the household or the factory, it would probably be herself. She felt like a wind-up toy that stayed erect just as long as it kept the momentum of ceaseless motion.

She could relieve the pressure only by talking to Karraman about it, she finally decided. They had always worked things out, hadn't they? No matter how overwhelming the obstacles seemed, they always weathered the onslaught, survived the deluge. They would do no less this time, would they?

So she tried. But she couldn't do it. Her loyalties had so much geography separating them that she couldn't imagine how she would. She felt like a sailor with a girl in every port. She felt like a metamorphic character out of Grimm, tough, efficient-but-always-lovable Minerva by day, anguished, duplicitous mother-in-absentia by night, a Janus figure, headed always east as well as west.

She wasn't afraid that Karraman would reject her when he discovered all the years of pretense, or love her any less for having failed to confide in him all along. She knew him well enough. He would always find sufficient purity of motive in her actions to end up loving her more than he had before. No, it wasn't her own security that she saw as jeopardized. It was his.

Karraman bore the burden of Emmaline, too. He lived daily with the knowledge that some essential fastening in her reason had unsnapped so long ago that no one could actually remember how or when it had happened. He didn't know what to do about her.

There was no longer a question of putting her away. She was no longer dramatically mad. People came to dinner or to tea, for Karraman and Minerva agreed that to stop social intercourse would be tantamount to incarcerating them all in a gargoyled torture chamber. Invariably guests went away thinking that Em was a little talky, perhaps, but no more eccentric than a dozen other ladies well-known in Saint Kathareen's. The Valley bred them as easily as it bred tomatoes or alfalfa. What the genteel visitors missed was the emotional destruction that Emmaline was capable of wreaking on a nominally harmonious household in the course of a few short minutes.

How could Minerva increase the onus, add to what Karraman already had to bear? Yet, she was moving closer to something. . . . Perhaps, perhaps it would bring him more pleasure than it would pain. . . .

Then, one night several weeks before what anyone had calculated as the proper time, and before Minerva had gotten around to belling her own particular cat, Emmaline went into labor. They had planned for Maybelle the Elder to take up residence in a bedroom closer to Emmaline's in case Karraman happened to be absent when the time drew near, but nobody thought it would happen so soon. Maybelle, of course, had declined to give up her rightful room until she absolutely had to. As it happened, Karraman was in the oil fields that night, a place where he enjoyed the nostalgic camaraderie of the old-timey oilmen and their apprentice sons as much again by half as any other section of local society. Minerva thought he was entitled.

She had retreated to her loft, writing to Kate by the flickering light of the student lamp, losing herself occasionally in the sweet remembrance of simpler times. The caress of moist evening air wafting through the window bore the flawless imprint of other days. If not peace, Minerva at least had respite there.

When Emmaline felt the first pain, the first minor foreboding of a twinge, she did precisely what Minerva would have expected her to do. She bellowed: *"Minerva!"* But Minerva was centuries out of earshot, as were all the other responsible adults in the house.

All four children, whose bedrooms Emmaline insisted be located within shouting proximity to hers, awoke immediately. The younger ones simply burrowed and scudded more deeply into their beds, ardently trying to look peacefully undisturbed.

Peter, the eldest, heard it differently. Although his mother's pregnancy was never discussed in front of any of the children, Peter, as always, knew exactly what was going on. He was not exactly a sly child, slyness implying more of both cruelty and intelligence than Peter had the fortune, good or ill, to possess. Nevertheless, his genes carried the ingredients of a born eavesdropper, trespasser, meddler. He usually knew more about everything in his immediate vicinity than was good for him, in Minerva's opinion. Peter didn't quite know, at nearly fifteen, what he wanted out of life. He did know he wasn't going to let any of the possibilities slide by without examination. So he listened. To everything.

Consequently, when Emmaline issued forth her first summons of the night, Peter was abreast of what was happening. Her cry, while notable as ordinary cries went, was hardly Best of Breed for his mother. She had done better when she merely popped a garter, or wanted Maybelle to bring her a glass of lemonade.

Nevertheless, Peter climbed out of bed and slipped into his shoes. He always slept in his clothes in case of fire or anything else that might put more interesting demands on his time than getting dressed. He changed every morning, and carefully rumpled a fresh pair of pajamas before consigning them, unworn, to the laundry chute. His mother was grimly satisfied because he always looked like he had stepped right out of a bandbox. Maybelle One thought it was a waste of good laundry. Minerva wondered whom he was trying to impress with the turnover of linens. Perhaps he secretly wet his bed? All three of them would have come within various perilous degrees of tanning his hide, had they known what he was really doing.

He didn't run to his mother's room at all when he heard her howl. Only God and Emmaline knew what kind of havoc he'd have encountered or created if he'd done that. Maybelle was also out of the question. Peter acted as if he knew exactly what he was doing when he ran for Minerva.

He beat a hasty path to the wing of the house where she slept. As he rounded the corner near her door, he slowed to a casual walk. He puckered his lips into a silent, nonchalant whistle. He tapped on Minerva's door, and waited. Nothing. A little louder, but nothing still. Finally he pounded, and tried the knob at the same time. It turned. In the silent room one small light stood sentinel. No other presence was in sight. "Horsefeathers," Peter muttered.

Minerva, in the tower, had pulled the ladder up behind her. With the trapdoor thus blocked off, and two opposite windows open in the loft, more of the gentle night air circulated about her. With the ladder down, at that time of the year, every breeze entangled itself in detours, accomplishing nothing. She created her own damper system, and partially, at least, controlled the situation.

A sound below had attracted her ear. At first she attributed it to any one of the thousands of things that go bump in the night throughout the lifespans of vast broad-plank-floor houses. When the sound became more insistent, it was curiosity, not fear, that led her to release the ladder. At the precise instant that the trapdoor began its creaking descent, Peter was electing to pull at the dangling chain to see what unsuspected eccentricities might turn up on the level above. Neither Peter nor Minerva expected to find a pair of investigating eyes staring back at the other end of the ladder.

Minerva was as startled at the sight of a large male figure making his way stealthily toward her in the middle of the night as he was to encounter a female clad in fluttering layers of sea-green chiffon descending from somewhere in the vicinity of heaven on a ladder that he hadn't known for sure was there. Emmaline in her unfathomable wisdom had seen to it that certain regions of their own house remained unplumbed and virgin to her children. When Minerva was in residence, she tried to bid everybody welcome, but Emmaline's attitude made it clear that Minerva's quarters remained off-limits. When Minerva stayed away for the night or longer, Emmaline kept the door to the vacated room sealed like a tomb.

Hence Peter's amazement. Veterans of the carnival aspects of Foothill House, both he and Minerva got their bearings and recovered themselves in relatively short order.

"You gave me rather a start, Peter. What brings you here at this hour of the night? Or should I say morning?"

The golden opportunity to parade his nonchalance in full regalia allowed Peter to digress from the true purpose of his visit. "Oh, I guess you could call me something of a night owl, Aunt Minerva. I rather enjoy these wee small hours. Don't you? No noisy children to impose upon one's thoughts, that sort of thing."

Minerva allowed a smile. She studied the noisy, imposing child standing before her. "I suppose so, Peter. The cares of the hours that people think of as 'sensible' certainly do seem very far away, don't they?"

"Yes. As a matter of fact, that's exactly what I was going to say."

"Really?"

"Oh, yes," he assured her. "Really."

"Do you make unexpected visits like this to anyone else, may I ask?"

Whereupon Peter recovered himself. "Oh, I do my share," he lied hopefully. "But actually there was another reason I came to find you, Aunt Minerva." Elaborately casual, he was fairly bursting with the magnitude of the news he was about to deliver.

"Yes?" Anticipating an adolescent confidence, a tale of calf-love, perhaps. She wondered whether she was going to be able to say the right thing. After all . . . "What is it, dear?"

"It's, uh, Mother, Aunt Minerva. She seems to be having some sort of difficulty."

"Oh, my God, Peter. Why didn't you say so?" She tore out of the room so fast that he had no opportunity whatsoever to read the expression of shock, terror, pain—whatever it was that he had tried so artfully to manipulate.

"Come with me. I'm going to need your help," she threw back over her shoulder.

She spoke with such quiet, decisive authority that Peter found himself scuttling along like a kid, trying to keep up with her before he had a chance to figure out why he was doing it. Her technique was disarmingly simple. She turned her back, plowed ahead, brooked no argument. It was a lot more effective than standing around sneering and smirking, waiting to see how thoroughly you had bested a victim. Peter was beginning to realize that you had to do a lot more than sleep with your clothes on to get up ahead of good old innocent Aunt Minerva.

Who entered Emmaline's room after the flimsiest pretense of a knock. Emmaline was sitting in bed, as nearly upright as she could manage. What held her up, Minerva thought at first glance, was more the rigidity of her fear than the mechanical efficiency of her structure.

"Is it bad, Em?" Minerva spoke out of an instinct to reassure Emmaline that help was near at hand more than out of any conviction that accurate information was going to be forthcoming.

Em's eyes stared blankly at a point just over Minerva's left shoulder, toward the door.

"Em?"

No reply. The intensity of Emmaline's fixed focus unnerved Minerva to the point where she had to turn around, to glance to see if a specter had frozen Emmaline into virtual paralysis. Nothing. Nothing was there. Even Peter had absented himself.

There was no one in sight, no sound in the murky hallways of Foothill House. Minerva realized that Emmaline was staring, immobilized, straight into the vastness of her own memories. They had washed over her like a floodtide at the trigger of the first real pain. Her physical distress didn't seem to be especially acute, but Minerva had no way of knowing whether her mental state had somehow robbed her of the ability to respond appropriately to bodily pain or even, indeed, to understand it.

"All right, Em. We're going to get you taken care of. Try to relax for a few minutes, won't you?" Minerva felt as if the clock had jumped back to the desperate nights during the Flood, when Emmaline had been so constantly, wretchedly ill. The difference was that that time there had been nowhere to go for help. If she had been able to try swimming for it, everyone would have been too busy to come back with her. Well, things were going to be different this time.

"Just wait here, Em. I'll be right back." As if there were anywhere she would go.

The hall was empty. "Peter." Silence.

"Peter?" Not more than a stage whisper, but penetrating. She knew it was all she needed.

[288]

"Peter. *Peter.*" She managed to wheedle the command into her voice without changing the decibel level. "Peter, you get over here right away. I know you can hear me, because I know that you wouldn't miss this for the world. You don't fool me for a minute."

The door to the room Minerva had occupied during her very first weeks with Emmaline at Foothill House creaked and whispered, and Peter slunk out from behind it. A hybrid strain of contrition and defiance mottled his face with the irregular suggestions of a blush.

"Peter, your mother is going to have to go to the hospital."

Minerva thought she saw his skin rear up and start to crawl. "What's wrong?" he pleaded.

"Nothing's wrong, as yet. And nothing's going to be wrong, if I can help it. That's why she's going to a hospital."

"What for? Robley babies have never been born in hospitals."

"Be that as it may, Peter, this is the year of Our Lord 1925, and this Robley is going to be born where the conditions are safest and best for your mother and her new baby both."

"Well, you can have all the newfangled notions you want, Aunt Minerva, but you'll have the devil's own time getting her there. The ferry won't run again until dawn, and if you want to take the new bridge as far as it goes and then swim the last two hundred yards, that's your business. My mother certainly isn't going with you."

"The point is not arguable, Peter. Your mother is going to the hospital, and I need your help immediately." She didn't give him the flick of an eyelash in which to reply. "Who keeps boats on this side of the river?"

"Aunt Minerva," suddenly childish and fearful, all pretense gone, "you can't get her across in anything that anybody keeps docked over here. There's nothing much better than a dinghy moored in any direction ten miles or more up and down the banks."

"I don't intend for her to go in it, Peter," straining now to keep her patience in check somehow.

"You're right, then," he affirmed, "because only a lunatic would take one of those things out in the middle of the night."

"Not only a lunatic, Peter. Also a young man who considers himself grown-up enough to patrol his own house fully dressed at all hours of the night, giving trouble a place to come home to roost."

"Me?" Peter was livid.

"Nobody else, my friend. Get down there to the wharf and borrow anything you can get your hands on, as long as it's reasonably safe. Wake up anybody you have to in order to get it done. Then get across that river in double time, and find Perley Stevens. I need to have him fire up that ferry of his and get over to this side just as soon as he can. No delays."

"But . . . but what if he won't do it, Aunt Minerva?"

"Then ask him if he'd rather pilot his boat over here tonight with all his running lights keeping him safe and sound, or deliver a baby on board tomorrow morning while I try to handle the wheel."

Peter's eyes went wide enough to let every one of the implications sink in. "What if the current's too strong for the dinghy?"

"Then swim. I don't care how you get there, Peter. Just get there. Now, make tracks."

He almost reared up and saluted. "Yes, ma'am. I mean, okay. If you say so, but my father would never—"

"Just leave your father out of this, Peter, and get moving. *Now.*" Peter glared a last plea for reassurance into her eyes. "Now."

He turned to flee. "And, Peter . . ." she called after him.

"What now?" Skidding to a halt.

"God bless."

Everybody else always believed that Emmaline's fifth was the first Robley child to see the first light of day in a hospital. Minerva didn't disabuse anybody of that notion. Karraman decided immediately upon returning home that afternoon, to find that he had become a father still again and that everything was smooth as whipped butter in spite of it, that he liked the idea of the hospital very, very much. Saved on linen, too.

Emmaline was apparently fairly enamored of the idea herself. At least that was what she led everyone to believe, signing on for a return engagement in the maternity section approximately once a year until Howard was born at last. Despite her incessant complaining, despite her perpetual dissatisfaction with everything and everyone in sight, she kept bringing along further human beings to share her lot in life. And despite whatever inconsistencies she harbored, despite the fact that she couldn't stick to a single project long enough to bring it to completion—even a single woven pot holder, a letter to a friend, anything—it could always be said of Emmaline: Yessir, she went right on having babies until the very day she died.

Hawk has barely heard the last of what Minerva has been telling him, because he has been carefully mulling over something she let go several concepts back.

"But what if you had been right in the first place?"

"About what, Hawk?" It hasn't occurred to her that she'd been wrong.

"About telling him. Just think—what if he had known that there was this beautiful love child out there somewhere, making it, doing well. . . . Maybe it would have helped him to know that he had a serious role in the creation of some neat stuff, too." At least until Kate B. Neat-Stuff turned sour, he thinks, but does not add that to the conversation. He doesn't think it would advance matters.

Minerva's nod is barely perceptible. "Yes. Don't think that I don't wonder about that every day of my life. I seem to be preoccupied more with my child and her fate after her death than I was while she was still alive and sniping. What you're suggesting is undoubtedly valid, logical, right, and true. I know. But don't you see, that wasn't how it seemed at the time. It was a different story entirely."

Hawk does see. That's the trouble. He sees that his perfectly well-meaning comment has come out in a way that can only hurt her more. He fumbles for still another apology, then aborts. He realizes mutely that there is something more important going on. On her face he reads more relief than anything else. She is actually saying it, after all these years. For several of Hawk's lifetimes her thoughts have done nothing but echo through the silent chambers of her solitude. On a desert island she might have found some kind of solace talking to the sea grapes and sand dollars. At Foothill House, always surrounded by something, somebody hostile or loveless or disconnected, her silence has been total. Hawk is her only confessional, and absolution is irrelevant. The release is worth everything. She sighs, straightens, and goes on. He listens.

"Em was pregnant for eternities, Hawk. It sometimes seemed that there wasn't a single day when she wasn't pregnant, recovering from a pregnancy, or getting ready for the next one. In the off-seasons, we tiptoed quietly around the hot coals of her illness. She could have gone off her rocker at the slightest provocation, and everybody knew it.

"One day, Hawk, she sent a little housemaid off across the river to get her a new dressing gown. Oh, she could have had all the dressing gowns in the Valley if it had made her happy. But the point was that the child went off, came back with some hideous thing that Em never wore after all, and was back about her chores before anybody even missed her. That was when I realized that there was real danger in the house. Em could have accomplished anything she wanted to, through an innocent proxy. There was always somebody around to enlist as an inadvertent accomplice. I had never realized just how fine the line was that Karraman was walking. Who was I to do anything that might upset the balance?"

"But knowing about Kate would have made it different," Hawk muses, emboldened by his growing comprehension. "It would have changed his space. You never know what people are going to do when their space is changed." He is talking about Karraman, but he might as easily be talking

[291]

about Cara. He never would have believed that things would turn out to be so much of a piece.

"I know what you're trying to say, Hawk. And I think I felt somewhat the same way off and on for years. But there was more to it than that."

"As if that isn't enough."

"It's all ironic. The biggest irony of all was that when Emmaline finally did die, Karraman and I were master and mistress of the big house, free to live according to what we had daydreamed for years—and we ended up not moving an inch to make a single change in the status quo. And what's more, by that time, nothing on earth could have moved me to tell him about Kate. There simply wasn't a force strong enough."

"That's hard to understand."

"It wouldn't be if you had been there," she assures him. "Karraman was working like a demon. He would go to bed at mid-evening, then get up at two or three in the morning to go out to the fields again. I have the feeling that he was working away the memories of all his absent offspring the way some people drink away their guilts. I was his total confidante otherwise, I think, except for that one secret place. It was almost as if he had to hoard it, just to show how stoic he was. And I could read him like a letter. He saved his mightiest grandstanding for the times when I was sure he was suffering the most. I could always tell, because he would start to talk about how much worse off other people were than we could imagine."

"People are like that, Miss Minerva," says Hawk, singing a transparent variation on precisely the theme Minerva has just described.

"But they don't have to be! He never understood that. When he was most vulnerable, he saw it as weakness. *I* saw it as humanity, and I loved him all the more. But he wouldn't have it. It was as though he was trying to absorb all the misery of the world, and atone for it all by himself. How could I spring Kate on him in the middle of that?"

"Yeah, Miss Minerva. I guess I see what you mean," but he is disconsolate nonetheless. It is Kate's daughter that he is thinking about, wanting to talk about, just plain wanting. He wishes Minerva would keep on talking. He knows that if, somehow, he can just get to the bottom of the whole story, hear it out, the healing will somehow begin. He feels like a gigantic abscess of a person, waiting for the surgeon to hone up the scalpel. Only, the doctor is Minerva.

He prods her on. "Did you ever change your mind about telling him? While he was still alive, I mean? Didn't you ever come around to thinking that you might begin to regret it after it was too late?"

"What an incisive interviewer you've turned out to be, Hawk." If she weren't broadcasting such affection, he'd have sworn she was bitter. "Yes. Of course. I not only thought that I wanted to tell him. I made up my mind that I would. After twenty years of rationalizing myself out of it in every conceivable way, I finally decided that I was actually going to do it.

"The time seemed right. Peter, after slinking around the house for a long time, and, I think, spending most of his days telling dirty secrets to Baby Howard, finally decided to go out and seek another fortune. The one that Emmaline had settled on him apparently failed to meet his needs," she sniffed, then continued, as if enumerating. "Howard wasn't actually a baby anymore, but a terribly bright, if not terribly lovable, child on the verge of entering school. Karraman had decided that one harmless little Howard wouldn't be a detriment to gracious living in the house, so he arranged for him to attend day school here in Saint Kathareen's. Overall, things were shaping up relatively serenely, for the first time in over a quarter of a century. Imagine!"

"I hardly can," Hawk reassures her. "I'm not even that old yet."

"I know." She smiles. "That's why I said it. I thought it would impress you."

Hawk laughs in spite of himself. "Right on, Miss Minerva." She bobs her head in wry acknowledgment.

"I could almost close my eyes and foresee a Golden Sunset for Karraman and me," she says dreamily. "I sensed a new period in our lives. All the growing pains were behind us—the children's, the businesses', Em's, ours, everybody's. For years, while I was trying to run Em's concerns as well as my own, without letting her know it, without seeming like a usurper, I used to scurry from one segment of my existence to another, saying, 'Remember, Min, it isn't always going to be like this.' Then, all of a sudden, one day it really happened. I felt that the future was an open book. It felt wonderful. Really wonderful."

Hawk remembers feeling wonderful once upon a time. He has no conviction that it will ever happen to him again.

"Then, almost as if it had been preplanned, Kate thrust herself front and center of my preoccupations. She was almost twenty-one years old, ornery as a mustang, and on her own. Against all the advice Claire and Tasha could give her, she decided to come to the United States."

"This was the time you met her in New York?"

"No. This was long before that. She apparently hadn't decided at that point to make the big break yet. She just wanted to have her life story spelled out for her once and for all. Oh, she already knew most of it anyway. Heaven only knows what her real motives were."

"My God, weren't you horrified?" Hawk wants to know.

"Yes, Hawk, of course I was. But do you know, I finally realized what mystery writers mean when they allude to a 'thrill' of terror. Part of me was frightened, there's no doubt about that. But another part of me, some rakehell character that I hadn't even known I was carrying around inside, couldn't wait for it to come to pass. It had taken Kate's initiative to shine the light on me, as they say. But finally, finally, I realized that I had wasted an entire lifetime second-guessing and making up stories to protect myself from realizing whom I really wanted to protect. All of a sudden I couldn't wait for the moment to come when I could introduce my daughter to her father."

Hawk knows from everything she has said in the past that the grand reunion never took place, but he doesn't know why. He is so caught up in the threads of her narrative that he speaks before he thinks. "What happened?" And regrets the words before they escape his lips, because he can see the shadows that cross Minerva's features as abruptly as a one-two punch. It turns her for the first time in his memory into a weak and weary woman.

"Nothing happened," she says emptily. "Kate decided at the last minute that she didn't want to see Saint Kathareen's after all. I always resented that she didn't even bother with a meaty excuse. Something spiteful, she was. But even if she had gotten here as planned, by that time it wouldn't have made any difference. By that time, Karraman was dead.

"I've thought about it up and down and all around, Hawk. I can picture it—there's no question but that it's true. Yet, to this very day, I have a sense of wild disbelief whenever I have to say out loud that he's dead." She pauses, rolls it around on her tongue, then says it again. In repeating it, she seems perceptibly to age, but at the same time she jacks herself up with the prideful ego of complete responsibility. It is as if she is bestowing a precious confidence upon Hawk, beseeching him to guard it with his life.

"It's true, Hawk. Karraman was dead."

XVII

It wasn't that Minerva was a bad judge of things, or that she had been unrealistic about Karraman's advancing years. True, he was no longer young, but he had no immediate plans to depart the vale, nor did his body seem to have any imminent plans to betray him. On the contrary.

"Karraman," she told him, "when you touch me that way, I'm younger than I was the day we met. Thirty years ago, Karraman, and you still make me feel like a girl."

"Ah, Min," he countered smartly, "when you touch *me* that way, no—ah, yes, *that* way—I'm as young as *I* was thirty years ago. And if you didn't have your eyes closed, you'd notice that mine are wide open. Looks like you're the one paying a price for sticking with an Ancient Mariner like me."

"Oh, Karraman, you didn't used to have to resort to that kind of nonsense." She laughed.

"Nonsense, is it? Not on your life, Min. With my eyes wide open, I see a woman far more beautiful than I ever dreamed she'd become, and I don't mind telling you I had some fantastic dreams!"

"We both did. Most of them have come true."

"One hasn't, Min."

"Which one was that, pray tell?" She was still bantering, but thought was turning Karraman solemn.

"The big one, Min. You and I. We've . . . never married."

"Each other," she amended quickly. "We've never married each other."

"That's what I meant."

"Oh," at a loss for another reply.

"And I can't think why," he pressed. "It isn't that I'm a fortune-hunter—"

Karraman, whose great wealth can still buy Minerva's spectacular success many times over, was so solemnly sincere that Minerva couldn't help smiling. "No, my love," she reassured him, "I don't think I've ever seen you in that light."

"Then why?"

"Haven't we married? Because of Em, I suppose," recovering.

"She's been dead a long time, Minnie. I'd have left her in a minute if—"

"Now, Karraman . . ."

"Well, maybe not that fast. Obligation, and all. But she's been cold in her grave for quite a while."

"And I'm hot in your bed." Minerva giggled wickedly.

"That's exactly what I mean. Thirty years, and I can't think of two people better suited."

"We've been through a lot together, Karraman."

"That's my very point, Min. We ought to be married."

"Karraman?"

"Hmmm?"

"I think you've just proposed to me!"

"So I have." Pause. "Well?"

"Oh, Karraman . . . no. We mustn't do that."

Exasperated: "Why in hell not, Minerva? I'm not joking."

"Neither am I, Karraman. That's what governs my answer, I suppose: the very seriousness of it."

"Minerva, good Christ! Change has been your middle name for thirty goddamn years. You're a bloody pioneer. What do you think pioneers are, anyway? They're changers, that's what. I've never seen a challenge trip you in your entire career, and now you're sprawling spread-eagled over a goddamn technicality. What the hell's the matter with you?"

She hadn't seen that kind of fire in him since God knew when. It ignited her. She ran her hand along the places where she knew it would do the most good. Karraman didn't mention marriage again that day, but Minerva was sure she hadn't heard the end of it.

Actually, he had hit the nail right on a head, but not the one he presumably imagined. When he said, "middle name," that was what it all boiled down to. Minerva Bolton he knew inside out. She had created herself in Saint Kathareen's as deftly as she had constructed a visionary symbol out of velvet and apple blossoms thirty years ago.

Minerva Kathareen Robley Niesenwandering, mother of Kate, descendant of Robleys—Karraman didn't have a passing acquaintance with those people. Between Karraman Robley and Minerva Bolton there were no secrets. Between Karraman and the rest of the others there lay only questions, dubiety, disbelief.

Minerva, queen of risk, would not risk that much. Minerva, queen of the high rollers, would not roll herself into an irreversible tailspin. Between lovers, every mystery is an enticement. Between husband and wife, every kindness by omission is a lie. In her heart, Minerva Bolton believed that she had never once lied to Karraman. By her own standards, doubtless she hadn't, and she certainly wasn't going to start now.

She wanted Karraman as she had always wanted him. She ignored the fact of her husband in Massachusetts, because Hammond Bolton's chief function was to remind her that marriage isn't in the document; it's in the bonding. The bonding resided forever with Karraman. She wanted to cherish him, her effervescent hero, for all the time they had left together. The last thing she wanted was to bog down in the technicalities.

Always, she cultivated optimism. She read his propitious future as easily, and as often, as she inhaled his sweet, clean, youthful breath. The problem was that while Minerva had spent a lifetime expanding her vision in almost every conceivable direction, she had effectively foreclosed a few of the areas that proved to be vitally significant in the end.

It is improbable that she could have done anything to alter the course of events no matter what she had attempted. To have married Karraman would only have compounded the situation. A sequence fell into place the day she left Massachusetts, and everything had followed that as the night the day. Nevertheless, for the rest of her life her grief for Karraman bore the ugly tincture of her guilt. She never ceased to assume the ultimate responsibility, even though the jury is eternally out on the scanty evidence in the case, and the coroner ruled quite differently long, long ago. God does not need to bother judging Minerva Bolton. Her own self-indictment is so strong that there isn't a thing a higher court can do to make it worse.

During all the engaging accruals of her experience, she rarely thought about Massachusetts. It lingered in the deepest recesses of her memory like a vignette borrowed from someone else's life. If anything ever happened there that might have been of serious interest to her, no well-wisher had bothered to convey the news by visit or post for many years. Minerva easily understood how the Saint Kathareen legend had been heightened into a virtual beatification in less than a generation. She could almost believe anything she heard about what was going on all those distances away, and she was living in an age which possessed weapons of communication of which nobody's forebears had ever dreamed.

She had stopped actively wondering what had become of Hammond

Bolton, although alone in the office at night she occasionally turned with a start, surprised to find that he was not behind her, eyeing her procedures with jaundice, indicting her very presence in an arena where he thought no woman would dare to venture. She didn't need to waste her time wondering about *his* practices and procedures. He was such a creature of ingrained habit that she knew, absolutely knew, how he spent every waking hour. Bothering to think about it would have been, in addition to all other kinds of folly, a groaning bore.

Minerva knew that if Hammond had had any legal or quasi-legal reason to be in touch with her, she would have been notified with all due ruffles, flourishes, and pomposity. She didn't go so far as to hope that he had dropped from the face of the earth after his single angry communication, but for all practical purposes she assumed as much. When images cropped up, unbidden, she fought them down with a vengeance.

But of course Hammond Bolton hadn't dropped from the face of the earth at all. He had lived the years through, amassing money in his own nit-picking fashion, taking profit where he could, taking pleasure in nothing. If Minerva had remained with him, he might have developed into some semblance of a man. When she fled, the scope of his ambition went with her. Every retentive urge, every covetous impulse, every sorry little trait he owned, magnified to become the definition of his character.

The folks around town had always said that he was so reliable a man that you could set your clock by him. They were right. The added implication of such a statement was that he was absolutely incapable of creative thinking, of the willingness to take risks, of the breadth of imagination, of the composure in the face of the unforeseen, that mark a man of strength and power.

Although everyone who knew Hammond Bolton knew that he had inherited money and had been making more of it for himself hand over fist for years, no one ever visualized him as a man of means. It wasn't his miserliness that created the impression, although he suffered from that affliction as well. It was simply that his thoughts were small, his gestures were small, his range of activity was small, his sphere of influence was minuscule. He was a man absolutely incapable of largess. If he had any emotions billowing around inside his person, he had never made anybody aware of that, either. Only his physique conveyed a strangely ambiguous impression of reckonable size; yet, because of the unfortunate way in which he had taken on weight over the years, he continued to give the impression of a rather small man who had accidentally wandered into the middle of many layers of soft, puffy, ill-fitting flesh. Minerva would have had trouble recognizing him in a crowd. Nor would she have bothered with such a specimen.

Hammond saw things differently. If Minerva thought of his segment of her life as an abstracted portion of very ancient history, he thought of her as his lawfully wedded wife who had, incidentally, left him one day. Not that he actually envisioned her coming back to him, or would have known what to do about it if she had done so. It was simply that, in his bewildered frame of reference, marriage was the condition in which he understood himself to be living. The fact that he had no apparent wife to perform in the roles similar to those of other wives he knew about was a matter of little or no apparent concern to him. The fact that he was a married man, in his own eyes as well as those he presumed to be the eyes of God and the Commonwealth of Massachusetts, served perfectly well to fortress him against precisely the kind of damage he had suffered at Minerva's departure. He was invincible.

He never mentioned her name, but Minerva obsessed him. He had finally evolved a fairly reliable method of keeping tabs on her. The buying offices in New York teemed with drummers, agents, all manner of busybodies for whom gossip was a consuming avocation. Displaying cursory interest, Hammond had tracked Minerva's activities—all kinds of activities—for years, ever since La Vallée had placed her squarely on the map of fashion. Once she had acquired the crude habit of calling public attention to herself and her scandalous libertarian business practices, even the newspapers joined the conspiracy of information.

Figuring out where she had been headed in the first place was mere child's play. Even as a bride who was volubly happy to be quit of her maternal nomenclature, she had poked about the ashes of those infamous and distant Robley relatives until he knew she was going to end up filthied by it all. Blood told. Hammond was repelled—but only by half. Some other, baser part of him kept an eye on the Saint Kathareen's Valley the way a stockbroker keeps his eye on a new but suspect issue.

When Hats of La Vallée had begun to attain a measure of status outside of their own province, Bolton Dry Goods had become immediately interested in the area of millinery. Hammond himself took care of the buying end through New York. He casually befriended the young man who traveled to Saint Kathareen's and dealt with Minerva and her Jew cohort, informing the fellow that Mrs. Bolton was some kind of a connection by marriage. The families, Hammond overexplained, had suffered what appeared to be an irreparable rift, but Hammond was nonetheless concerned for the welfare of his young, courageous distant relative. If it wasn't too much trouble, could discreet inquiries be made . . . ? Completely confidential, of course.

Those discreet inquiries consumed every moment of Hammond Bolton's private life, and numberless pages of his dull, meticulous journal, for thirty years. What no one told him, he pieced together for himself. If he had put that much effort into the management of his own fortune, he could have become the King of England or the reigning Lama of the Hindu Kush. Instead, he moved by leaps and bounds, or so his recorded thought processes reveal it, into the dead center of a classic involutional psychosis. To put it another way, Minerva had slowly driven him nuts.

If anyone had known that he planned to leave town, someone might have engaged him in passing chitchat about his plans and destinations. Forced into utterance, he might have reflected differently upon things, perhaps been embarrassed or intimidated or self-ridiculed out of his determination. Hammond Bolton did not, however, indulge in neighborly interchanges with anybody. He was a different sort of man.

He never told a soul any of his plans, because he thought that if he ever let go of anything that was his for even a split second, he would be Taken. Robbed. Cheated. Set upon by thieves. Embezzled from. Mismanaged. Falsely inventoried. Bamboozled. Swindled. Highjacked at the loading dock. He thought that if he let go of anything, he stood to lose it all. He truly believed that if he left Massachusetts for an unprecedented length of time (meaning anything longer than the overnight that it usually took him to go to New York, swing through the wholesalers, buy essentially the same styles as last year, and check up on matters in the Valley), the multimillion-dollar business that had taken four generations of Boltons to build and stabilize would be set upon by vandals and disintegrate overnight. He also believed that his house, which hadn't been entered by a soul besides himself and the meter reader for two decades, and hadn't been refurbished since Minerva had left, would be plundered for its irresistible booty. He thought that if he simply went to wherever he had to go with no fanfare, matters would progress, business as usual, with the specter of his vigilance keeping everything under strict control. It was the only absolutely foolproof way he knew to keep treachery from befalling his domain. Daily, anew, he compensated for the loss of his garnets.

Hammond Bolton was sufficiently in touch to understand that he couldn't say an incantation, finger an amulet, and be invisible in the real world. With uncharacteristic foresight, he reserved a room at the Saint Kathareen's Inn under the name B. Hammond. When the train chugged up alongside the tile-roofed depot in the middle of downtown Saint Kathareen's, a limousine driver was paging at the modulated top of his discreet lungs a Mr. Hammond from Massachusetts. Even though he had been informed along with the written confirmation of the reservation that he would be duly collected at the terminal, Hammond was so disoriented that he could not recognize the sound of his pseudonym.

He was actually standing directly opposite the driver from the Inn, not six feet away, failing to register that the name being called was his own. Suddenly, as the porters began to roll carts full of luggage past his vantage point and toward waiting vehicles, Hammond Bolton came to his senses. He realized that he had to get himself transported. It was then that a semiexasperated call for a Mr. Hammond wheedled its way into his senses. He presented himself, slightly abashed, to the fellow doing the paging. It came as a mild surprise to anyone who happened to be listening to hear so meek a tremolo issuing from so corpulently layered a body. On the other hand, nothing about Hammond's weak little face or drably attired frame commanded anything in the way of attention. The rest of him simply followed negative suit.

The driver was satisfied to write him off as another strange character in a community where strange characters were rather the rule than the exception anyway. After working for Karraman Robley and dealing with his ideas and fancies day and night, one became perfectly inured to the unexpected.

Hammond Bolton checked in and settled down. When he caught sight of the elegant little shops in the lower lobby, he put a pudgy hand to his face immediately to avoid detection. Not that the hand would have begun to hide the expanse of jowl and blubber, and not that he would have been recognized on sight by anyone who had not seen him for thirty years. During that span of time, the germs of what sprouted as sensitivity had come to full blossom as effete and prissy decadence. He needn't have bothered to shield his nervous countenance in any case, since the La Vallée salon operated several floors above, out of the same genteel and withdrawn headquarters as ever. But such was Hammond Bolton's flavor of delusion that he did what he did.

He took all his meals in his room. Cyril Cybele, whom anyone could have recognized after thirty or more years, since he had become a shade gray and a fraction stooped around the dowager's hump, but otherwise had neither changed nor matured nor learned anything beyond the lateral accumulation of detail, couldn't figure out what the mysterious Mr. B. Hammond was all about. He claimed no business, no friendship, no particular activity in Saint Kathareen's. It worried Cyril Cybele. He would have loved to envision the Inn as a fashionable spa where people would alight to rest, regroup, reinvigorate themselves among swaying trees or in sulfurous steam baths, but alas, such was not the case. No one had ever, in Cybele's memory, turned up at the Inn for the sole purpose of lying around by himself.

Apparently Mr. Hammond, whoever he was, did go out once or twice during the several days in which Cybele's inquisitiveness germinated into

something carnivorous. Twice Cybele quietly observed Hammond returning, walking up the grand staircase in a small, tiptoeing way. He never
seemed to pause in the lobby long enough to wait for the elevator, let alone
to pass the time of day. Cybele couldn't stand not having a clear sense about
what was going on. He fidgeted behind his desk like a nervous sentry,
passing off to the nearest competent person any task that demanded serious
attention. He himself sat and watched. And waited. And watched some
more.

Until the morning of B. Hammond's fifth day in Saint Kathareen's, when
he came stealthily down the stairs shortly after midmorning. Normally Cyril
would have been immersed in the paperwork necessary to order the events
of each day and to ensure that the smallest whim of each guest received the
attention that kept the Inn's reputation as a hostelry among outstanding
hostelries alive. Amid the nagging protocols of that morning, Cybele's
preoccupation centered only on the peculiarities of that one lone guest. He
was thus completely off his guard when Hammond nodded to him
abbreviatedly.

"Ah, Mr. Hammond," he recovered, "it's nice to see you on this brisk
morning." Cybele was trying on the hail-fellow mantle for perhaps the first
time in his life. It didn't fit quite like a glove, but Cyril held fast to it.

Meanwhile Hammond muttered something that sounded vaguely like
accord, so Cyril pressed on.

"We hope that you're finding everything comfortable here at the Inn,
sir?"

It didn't seem to be a hostile encounter. Hammond didn't quite warm to
it, but after sitting around and talking to no one for all those days, he had
begun to realize that he needed to say something to somebody. Otherwise
he'd go back to Massachusetts having accomplished nothing beyond
spending a large block of idle time in yet another friendless land. Even if he
was befuddled about what it was he wanted to accomplish, Hammond's
buried motive popped to his surface like a cork when Cybele addressed him
in such a comradely way.

"Yes. Thank you. Yes. That is, I . . . yes."

Cybele noted that the man was lingering, obviously searching for a
comfortable route along which to guide conversation. Despite all his years
as professional quasi-host, however, he was no more adept at pulling clever
riposte out of the conversational bag than was a recluse like Hammond.

"Perhaps there's some additional service we might provide for you," he
essayed. "I have here a map of some of the interesting landmarks in and
around the Valley. The Inn can secure the services of a car and driver, if
you wish."

Hammond's expression remained lifeless, but Cybele observed that his
posture had undergone a subtle change.

"The Inn seems to be quite competently managed, to provide such detailed services," Hammond ventured formally.

"Thank you, sir," replied Cybele, inflating under the flattery like a pouter pigeon.

"Then it's you who are responsible for such innovations as the chauffeur service, and the personal valets, and such amenities?" Hammond continued, with purpose.

Cybele was annoyed. Just as he had been about to receive, and accept, for once, credit where he thought it was due, this character had to go on and start into specifics. "Well, sir, as a matter of fact, all of us here in the Inn's little family contribute what we can." He wanted to let it go modestly at that, but guilt spawned honesty, which forced Cybele into the breach. "Actually, Mr. Hammond, a great deal of what we have to offer here at the Inn comes as a result of the ingenuity of our owner, Mr. Karraman Robley."

Aha! "Seems to me," Hammond offered with a great tugging at his left ear, his symbolic gesture of careful consideration, "that I've heard that name in some other connection." Hammond Bolton knew more about all manner of Robley connections than the silly little man behind the desk could conjure in his wildest fictive moments. "Oil, was it?"

"Oil is one of Mr. Robley's many interests, I believe," said Cybele with resentful discretion. "He is a man of many parts." The latter was an interesting choice of words, since Cybele had no way of knowing that one of Hammond's concerns was Karraman Robley's most private one. He wanted to sever and embalm it.

"I've heard as much. It would certainly be a pleasure to meet as fine and successful a man as Mr. Robley. I do believe I've made the acquaintance of some of his relatives in my travels." The last statement, at least, was the genuine truth.

"I'm sure it would be Mr. Robley's pleasure, sir. The trouble is, he's a hard man to pin down. The oil fields have claimed a lion's share of his time lately."

Suddenly a dawn awoke upon Hammond. Suddenly he knew what his life had been fixed for. He felt like nine kinds of mastermind as he prepared to make the single most confident decision of his entire career. His confidence lay in his duplicity. He knew dead to rights that he would never, could never, be caught out. He was about to utter a few polite, innocent phrases soliciting the respect of the man facing him across the desk, and he would be revealing nothing (Nothing!) of the plans taking over his mind like marsh marigolds overrunning a spring garden. Hammond Bolton, who had survived abandonment, war, the Depression, and who knows how many of the other indignities that gods and people visit upon each other, was about to manipulate something into his own charge for the first conscious time.

"Ah. Perhaps I might leave a message, then." Simple!

"Certainly, sir." Cybele reached for a pad and a fountain pen.

"Please convey to Mr. Robley that I should like very much to meet him for a bit of a talk, at his convenience. I'll be in my room after, shall we say, four o'clock."

"Excellent, sir." Cybele prepared to bid the odd duck a good day, but Hammond was just beginning to warm to his purpose.

"Now. Between now and then, I think I'd like to have the use of an automobile, after all."

"Certainly, Mr. Hammond. We have a fine driver available to be at your service for as long as—"

"No, not a driver. I think I'd enjoy a little spin around the countryside myself, with the assistance of one of those fine maps, of course."

"Very good, Mr. Hammond. Occasionally our guests do prefer such an arrangement. We have a splendid 1936 Packard which is . . . let me see . . ." He riffled through a small stack of filing cards. "Yes, it's available for you right away. It will just take a moment or two to have it brought around."

"Yes. Excellent. I'll just run upstairs and get my overcoat. And remember, I'll be back by four. I hope Mr. Robley will be able to see me sometime after that." Yessir.

Hammond Bolton had chosen four o'clock because he had learned from his observations that Cyril Cybele left the front desk just at about that time on most days. His plans were beginning to take shape. His heart raced. Its flutter played in circles at the base of his throat.

Hammond had made a few careful inferences from the terrain he had observed and the well-crafted maps he had studied. He knew where the oil fields did not lie. Oh, he was aware that in oil-rich country like this Valley every farmer and squatter was bound to have a working well or two in the middle of cornfield or lawn, but he didn't seriously think that a man like Karraman Robley would be investing his resources in such lonesome schemes. Hammond deduced where he thought the bulk of the paydirt lay, and headed toward the new bridge across the Saint Kathareen's.

At home, Hammond Bolton drove an eight-cylinder 1923 Apperson Jackrabbit. Although he could have afforded anything that chugged down the Massachusetts toll road, he had governed his selection by the wish to remain as inconspicuous as possible. It probably had worked at first, but as the car entered its second decade under his negligent stewardship, the rattletrap sound of it alone, not to mention its antiquity, singled it out in any of its rare forays.

Abroad, which was where he considered himself to be in Saint Kathareen's, he warmed quickly to the leather-padded luxury of the Packard. He smugly scraped into high gear, scanning the roadway for any sign of skeletal rigs.

They loomed around a bend in the road almost before he was ready for them. Among the crack-frozen memorabilia of last fall's corn harvest, they rose like antisocial guests in a reception room, charged to the gills with potential, but standing isolated and proud. Hammond eyed them with fascination. He slowed to a speed a gear or two lower than where he had been cruising, noisily shearing valuable slivers of ratchet off into the gearbox.

A dirt road led off the highway at an acute angle into the field. Hammond slowed even more. He lost sight of the narrow and primitive path at a slight rise in the cornfield, but immediately became aware of the direction it had taken. Marking the spot as surely as a bull's-eye on a target, there sat a small conclave of elderly jalopies and two pickup trucks. One of the latter Hammond Bolton would have recognized anywhere. He had been attending its comings and goings for several days now, noting with interest the attention and deference paid to it amid the limousines and touring cars and far glossier monuments to ingenuity that graced the parking lots at the Saint Kathareen's Inn.

Hammond also registered the fact that the truck in question often returned to the Inn many hours after the men in the fields would have gone home from a weary day shift. Moreover, it never crossed the river by bridge or by ferry at night, whether its owner did or not. When the gentleman, and he always dressed like a gentleman, truck or no, did leave the Inn at night, he drove a different car; one, in fact, far more luxurious than the Packard in which Hammond sat entertaining his malign thoughts.

He was satisfied. He had no feeling of clairvoyance, no sense of heavy omen. He simply knew that he was satisfied with the place to which the road had thus far led.

It was close to four o'clock when Hammond stepped conspicuously into the lobby of the Saint Kathareen's Inn. He affected much hearty stamping of feet and flailing of arms, a calculated pantomime of coming in from the cold. He was actually far too fevered with intent to feel a trace of chill. At the desk he stopped to inform the management that he had enjoyed his foray and would like to have the lease on the car extended. Cybele was still at his post to accept the request.

Next Hammond inquired deliberately whether Mr. Robley had received his message yet. Cybele regretted. Hammond took pains to appear disappointed but hopeful. "Perhaps later," he lied. "Oh, and also, Mr. Cybele . . ."

"Sir?"

"I'll be dining in tonight. Will you kindly have a menu card sent up at, say, seven?"

[305]

"Yes, sir, with pleasure. I'll be off duty by then," he admitted, "but please rest assured that it will be done. Have a pleasant evening."

"Yes. Oh, and Cybele . . ."

"Yes, sir?"

"Please ask the boy to slide it under the door if I'm showering when he knocks."

"Of course, sir. I'll leave the notation right here."

"Thank you."

"Yes, sir." Cybele made the appropriate notations in his precise little script, and prepared to bring the rest of the desk up-to-date for the next shift. Allowing for the few minutes of overlap, he thought that he could be off and gone by 4:30. Not bad, Cybele thought, for a traditional drill that used to take several hours and keep him puttering and fussing about until late in the evening. Cybele wasn't ready to be put out to pasture yet, but he'd be damned in hell if he'd give Karraman Robley one penny's worth more than he paid for. The way he figured it, Robley owed him a decade's worth of salary in overtime for sheer zeal. Cyril Cybele had no compunctions whatsoever about beginning to collect his debt.

Hammond Bolton, like a chameleon, edged down the grand stairway as drably as he could. Verifying with a quick glance that Cybele had given over the keys to the kingdom for the evening, Hammond scurried past the front desk without a nod. He had managed so far to avoid attracting so much as a sidelong glance from anyone other than Cybele, and he had no intention of changing the status quo at that late hour. He headed straight for the car that he had parked inconspicuously at the tree-lined end of the Inn's main car park.

And took off, in the cold brilliance of lowering day, toward the site where he had found the silvery pickup earlier in the afternoon. When he got there, as he had hopefully anticipated, all the other vehicles had gone off to roost. In precise conformity to what he had rapidly recognized as Karraman Robley's habits and practices, the truck remained.

Hammond had memorized the precise location of the dirt road. He slowed in preparation for his approach. The landmark he followed was a cluster of purple martin houses poking forlornly into the bitter sky. He assumed that some stalwart and compassionate soul had once erected the birdhouses on the near property of a farmhouse which had long ago crumbled into eternity. Only the tiny aerial apartments remained, leaving poets and historians to their conjecture. As for Hammond, he thought they were a damned convenient signpost, period.

No human figure was visible anywhere across the three hundred and sixty degrees of Hammond's scan. He was not careless, however. He knew that the slight protuberances of hills, barely noticeable to anyone who had never attempted to walk briskly up one, were nonetheless of sufficient dimension to hide a man's approach. Besides, there was that abomination of an ungentlemanly truck. Hammond reasoned correctly that its owner could not have strayed too far afield of that.

The hoarfrost, long embedded in the dirt road, had obviated any possibility that Hammond might get himself stuck in the mud or, equally damaging, leave behind a tire track. He drove cautiously, alertly, up to where the truck rested.

Hammond Bolton has left to posterity absolutely no evidence that he had in any way planned the vis-à-vis of which he was in such hot pursuit. It never seemed to Minerva that he would have been capable actually of constructing a conscious alibi or intending to keep his navigations sheathed in the mufti of a solidly frozen dirt road. The operant factor in the courses he took, minute by minute, was surely more a function of the inherent retentiveness and secrecy he wore like chain mail about himself. Metaphorically, Hammond Bolton had probably always wanted to kill Karraman Robley for all the real or imagined dishonor he had visited upon Minerva, and thence, according to perverse logic, upon Hammond himself.

Those sentiments he left, unalloyed, in the journals whose crabbed little hand would so neatly have matched B. Hammond's signature in the register at the Inn, had anyone but Minerva been inspired to make the comparison. To take up an actual weapon, to toy with the humanity residing within another human being, was something outside the mild-mannered Hammond Bolton's imagination. He had spent more than thirty years as martyr, victim rather than villain, reluctant even to swat flies. Murder in the literal sense resided so far away from his functional routines that he never read a dime mystery novel even when they were the rage. He couldn't stand that kind of disorder.

Yet to Minerva the conclusion seemed inescapable as the pieces of the puzzle filtered in, and seems inescapable still: murderer Hammond Bolton was about to become. Minerva's own construct of the events is so clear to her that she can still tell it as if she had been along for the ride inside Hammond's head.

He pulled alongside the truck and sat for a minute or so. Then he clambered out of the Packard, impelled by an insatiable, nerve-racking inquisitiveness. He circled the truck, examining every speck of dust or rust it bore, as if by so doing he could learn the secret of Karraman Robley: what made him tick, what sort of man was this who, sight unseen, had turned Hammond's entire life into an upside-down facsimile of what he had always thought he was going to be.

With no one visible as far as the eye could see, Hammond Bolton decided to take matters a step further. He peered into the truck, looking through the windshield, which was impeded by a combination of heavy condensation and building frost. Although not quite able to realize that it was he, himself, Hammond Bolton of Massachusetts, getting this deeply involved, he tried the door on the driver's side. It was open, of course. People in the Saint Kathareen's Valley had not begun to fortress themselves or their possessions against intruders, nor have they yet.

Hammond, the long-ago rider who yearned to be a huntsman and never quite managed, noted the guns first. Suspended in carrying racks above the windshield, they shone with the spit and polish endowed by hunters who take solid personal pride in all the impedimenta of the sport. Hammond was not surprised to see that the vehicle was armed. After all, didn't he fancy that he knew the hunter's mentality? And didn't he know that coyotes and wolves and who knows what other manner of beast roamed this Godless wilderness at will? After all.

A variety of firearms made up the arsenal. Standard racks held conventional long-guns. Hammond dismissed them as ordinary. A twelve-gauge weapon lying across the seat captured his attention immediately. It was without a doubt the most elegant instrument of its kind that Hammond had ever seen. If the stock wasn't crafted of rosewood, it might as well have been, for all its warm richness. Every bit of metal had been lovingly, ornately carved so that the entire impact was more of artistry than craft. Hammond reached in and picked it up. He fondled it more tenderly than he had fondled any person or thing in all the years since Minerva had left him. Having momentarily forgotten everything else that had motivated this bizarre, joyless ride into a bleak and deserted countryside, Hammond knew that he had to heft that gun into shooting position, sight along its barrel, savor the sensation of holding the masterly piece of workmanship in his hands and arms and on his shoulder. He could barely believe that such a piece of work could deliver performance commensurate with its beauty. On the other hand, he knew deep down that a man of Karraman Robley's stature would never settle for anything less than the all-around best. He never had.

Hammond hoisted the gun and found the sight. He was lost in a reverie, dreamily cocking the mechanism, drawing a bead along the horizon. Slowly he scanned the distance through the hairline hatching of the gun's lens. He rotated a shade faster as he met with the slight rise that impeded his view, almost losing his footing as he moved. No dervish Hammond, the vertigo he suddenly felt came as much from the heady throbbing of the pulse inside his skull as from the actual ground speed of his movement. His chest felt heavy. His ears were filled with something besides the roar of the wind. To Hammond it sounded like an ovation.

He had moved almost back to the place where he had started his circumnavigation. His bearings were far from true, as a direct result of both his unfamiliarity with the terrain and also his insistence upon keeping his eye peeled to a telescopic lens, which would have added to anyone's sense of distortion. Suddenly the roar that he had perceived earlier was coming, without warning, from another place. At first he failed to realize that it was his own mouth, throat, larynx, the cavernous pit of his chest. He was screaming, reflexively, because into the sight of the gun had loomed the hideously distorted upper-right quadrant of a human face. Hammond's trigger finger contracted in the same seizure as his heart and his expression. What had been a man, approaching fearlessly to challenge, had become a corpse fallen in the frigid winter shadow of his own truck. Hammond Bolton knew even before thought could enter the process that he had murdered Karraman Robley.

He stood paralyzed. He had only wanted to talk about everything. . . .

And knew before he had ventured a step down that mental path that there was no more talking to be done. Although his limbs felt leaden, and although he felt an unfamiliar lethargic fatigue ooze into him like something viscous and inescapable, he was calculating enough to know that nothing could be served by standing around in a desolated oil field in the company of the most prominent corpse in the Valley. He began to muster his thoughts as he ran for the Packard, noting, with meaningful satisfaction this time, that the ground was solid. It hadn't turned to mud under the fevered rise of his nervous processes. Like Karraman Robley, it would tell no tales.

By the time he got back to the Inn, he had worked it all out. It had come as naturally as the act of leaving the gun lying casually on the ground next to Karraman Robley. (Whom Hammond could not possibly have identified as "the body," being bonded to him now forever, far beyond the hateful affinities he had felt during the decades that the man had shared Minerva with him.) Both men had been gloved. The gun bore no traces of Hammond's handling. In his haste to get clear of the scene, Hammond made no attempt to fabricate a suicide attempt on Karraman's part—who would want to kill himself with a shotgun, in the middle of an open field, even if he did have arms like King Kong which, to Hammond's mild surprise, Karraman didn't.

No, it did not belong to Hammond's style to create an exotic act from scratch. He found quite sufficient satisfaction in knowing that when the body was found, everyone concerned would have one hell of a time figuring out exactly what had happened. And by that time, there would be no earthly way for anybody to learn anything at all from Hammond.

He checked the tires and the mudguards for traces of identifiable mud or cornstalks or anything that might link the Packard to the time and place of Karraman's untimely demise. Nothing betrayed him, at least as far as his eyes could detect. Hammond felt satisfied on that score. If he was incapable of outward vision, at least no one had ever accused him of lacking a fine eye for detail, even to a point beyond most people's tolerance.

Hammond's breath was coming heavily, although he had drawn no more on his actual physical reserves than he might have by reaching out the front door to get the Sunday paper. He attributed the strangeness in his chest to the river air around Saint Kathareen's. Never in his life had he experienced such infernal bone-rattling dampness. He wondered how long it would take for the Valley people to feel the warmth ooze into the marrow after a winter like this one. He remembered with detachment that he had been perspiring fiercely only minutes earlier. It did not occur to him that the chill he was experiencing had as much to do with the sodden condition of his personal linens as with the temperature of the outside air.

He drew his collar higher around his neck and crossed the short distance to the Inn's entryway. One step at a time, that's all. One step at a time.

Cybele's evening counterpart stood watch at the desk. Hammond felt mild disappointment. Now that he knew with confident precision what he was about, now that the deed was done and he was firmly maintaining his rhythm at one step at a time, he would have relished playing to as full a house as possible. That included Cybele. What settled his nerves was the compensatory realization that the fellow before him would little note the hour of Hammond's return, nor have any reason to connect it to the events of the afternoon, when they came before public notice.

Then, for the first time in a lifelong career of having been dealt with by fate rather than doing the dealing, Hammond decided upon a more daring course of action than he would have believed himself capable of just hours earlier. He decided to follow through to its conclusion his earlier conversation with Cybele. In that way, he would construct for himself not exactly an alibi, but at least a casual declaration of innocence.

"'Evening."

"Good evening, sir. May I help you?"

"Yes, I think so. Has Mr. Robley come in yet?"

"No, sir, he hasn't. We have no definite word that he'll be in at all tonight, although of course anything's possible. I believe he's in the fields today, sir. May I take a message?"

"Ah, the oil fields, you mean," with an elaborate and spurious dawning of comprehension. "Then that's why he hasn't answered my earlier message."

"Oh, you have a message waiting for Mr. Robley? Perhaps I can help you."

"No, no. Not at all. I'm Hammond. Guest here. Looked forward to meeting Robley while I'm still in town, but I'm afraid that if it isn't tonight, it's going to have to be on my next visit. Business matters pressing right now. I'm going to have to be checking out in the morning."

"I see. Well, I'll be sure to give Mr. Robley the word if he does come in, sir."

"I'd appreciate it."

"Not at all, Mr. Hammond. Now, if you'll be taking the morning train— that would be westbound or eastbound?"

"Eastbound."

"Eastbound. Yes. In that case, you ought to be at the station a few minutes before seven. If you'd like to make the arrangements for checking out tonight, Mr. Hammond, we can hasten the procedure in the morning so that you can sleep a little later and arrive at the station in our limousine in plenty of time."

"Excellent. But please don't forget about Mr. Robley," he insisted.. "It would be a most peculiar feeling to return home without having exchanged a word or two with the gentleman."

"Of course, sir. Very good."

"Yes. Now. I'll be ordering dinner in my room very shortly, if that's all right."

"At your service, sir." Hammond had relapsed into his bland diffidence, but the man at the desk didn't detect the shift.

It didn't matter. Hammond Bolton had done all right for himself. Nothing about him, not a hint of a telltale gesture or clue, would have identified him as what he couldn't quite believe he had, in the frozen Valley afternoon, become: a cold-blooded, conscienceless murderer. He just plain didn't look as if he had the nerve for it.

Hammond enjoyed a hearty dinner and an unbroken night's sleep. He awoke in the morning to the sound of the telephone jangling. Momentarily disoriented, he thought the same thoughts he had been experiencing every day and every night throughout the years since people had come to have the gadgets installed routinely in all the public and private buildings in creation: maybe it was Minerva calling to say that she was on the way home. Then, dismissing the thought with his customary alacrity, he jumped to the next natural connective: what he had done, and who was coming to get him for it. He picked up the receiver, denial at the grand entryway of his lips, waiting to hear whatever it was that would accomplish the ribbon-cutting and turn loose his explanations.

"Yes?"

"Good morning, Mr. Hammond. The time is now five-forty-five."

"Oh. Yes. Thank you."

"You're welcome, sir. Will it be all right if we send a bellman for your bags in approximately one hour?"

"Yes. Fine. Perfect. Yes. Well. Thank you for calling."

"You're welcome, sir."

He replaced the receiver in the cradle, wondering at the absurdity of having worked his way into an unnecessary frenzy over an invention as miraculous as the telephone. He set about the details of dressing and finishing packing, wishing only that he could do something to quiet the infernal festival of thudding going on inside his chest.

Nothing worked, not the gently rolling countryside, not the hypnotic rhythm of the train, not the familiar hissing of steam radiators or the lovely glasses of Portuguese rosé he decided to drink instead of taking meals, hoping it would quiet the turbulence inside. Nothing worked to keep his pulse contained inside his rib cage, where any sensible pulse ought to be confined. It was still hammering away when he arrived at Grand Central and dismounted the train with his luggage and his redcap. Nothing worked until he had walked from the long concourse into the middle of the main waiting room. It was there, finally, that he collapsed clumsily of what was later called a massive coronary thrombosis. He didn't die of it, but he didn't feel anything, either, for days and days afterward, except a strangely menacing pain that possessed every attribute of belonging to somebody else.

Because he carried no identification on that trip, nothing whatsoever to connect him with his identity or his origins, they normally would have taken him to Bellevue right away. If he didn't quite resemble a fugitive from Skid Row, neither was he the picture of prosperous security. The policeman who happened to be passing when he fell searched his wallet and found therein a momentous amount of cash. Somehow the incongruous coupling of those substantial moneys with an otherwise undocumented person did not arouse undue suspicion. Minerva never accepted that the chap who rescued him hadn't inferred indefensible chicanery regarding the money, hadn't bellowed, "Take 'im to the station house and book 'im," when help arrived, thereby setting the stage for a full confession to that other crime, of which Hammond was never to be accused. Perhaps the explanation was simply that Hammond looked so bland and bloated and guileless that the policeman reacted accordingly. In any case, the sixth or seventh sense of a city cop told him that the fallen man, who had by that time begun to turn blue and breathe in bubbly, uneven gulps, belonged in a discreet private hospital. Consequently, when the ambulance arrived, a discreet private hospital was exactly where they carted the patient.

The decision had been fortuitously proper. As Hammond began to recover his health and his senses, he communicated to his offices in Massachusetts concerning where he was and what had happened to him. He led the people at home to believe that he had been checking out new buying offices. He implied heavily that it would in no way bolster relations with any of the firm's usual New York associates were they to find out that he had been shopping around. Mum became the solid word.

To the New York people, the explanation of Hammond's sudden unfortunate illness was more than sufficient. It also unleashed a whole new barrage of chocolate candy in fancy boxes, get-well wishes, and roses done up into wreaths of the sort that horses wear when the race is mercifully over. Hammond's lonely affliction probably even helped the New York end of the business a little bit in the peculiar way that the resident of the host city tends to feel guilty and compensatory when somebody gets sick while visiting.

There was no reason to connect Karraman Robley's death with Hammond Bolton's physical breakdown. Neither event garnered much publicity. Nothing attested to Hammond's presence in the vicinity of Saint Kathareen's at any time, ever, let alone on the day in question.

Strangely enough, two people in Saint Kathareen's thought of Mr. Hammond—and they had no cause to think of him as anyone else—quite independently and with a degree of pity, when the Robley tragedy was discovered several hours after Hammond's train had chugged into its own future. Cybele, whose lifelong resentment of Karraman had instantaneously transmogrified into guilt-laden grief, wished that he had been able to engineer the introduction between Robley and the stranger from the East. That way, Cybele reasoned glumly, Mr. Hammond would have known that there was more than one power running things in Saint Kathareen's. He, Cyril Cybele, might have been the arranger for once. Then he, Cyril Cybele, would have been the one that Mr. Hammond, and all the Mr. Hammonds, would ask to see the next time. And he had muffed it.

The night clerk, on the other hand, felt a genuine regret. He had pegged Mr. Hammond for a lonely man at the outset, and felt himself in Hammond's corner, so to speak. By failing to produce Mr. Robley upon request, he felt that he had somehow let down both men in an abstruse hour of need. Of the two, naturally he felt sorrier for Mr. Hammond. When you got right down to it, Mr. Robley didn't seem to have missed out on too many of the good things in life. Even his death had been merciful.

Not often are so many so wrong about so much, unless one begins to consider nations and battles and political philosophy. This was just two millionaires in an oil field, and nobody ever got it quite right. One person actually was making all the proper connections, but she, of course, was shackled hand and foot when it came to the problem of trying to verify. She heard about Hammond long afterward. When he finally died, in the early 1950s, it was mere anticlimax. A law firm in Boston notified Minerva that she was the sole heir of record, after his alma mater. The lawyer seemed to think that the gesture was touching, but Minerva thought it diabolically vengeful: Hammond doing his utmost to pester her from beyond the grave. The university got the assets, a more-than-handsome endowment to the school of business administration. Minerva received the several composition books which comprised Hammond's journal. They verified her suspicions, more or less, about what had happened that day among the derricks and the stubble. Hammond's prose was elliptical, but she fancied that she saw through his paltry little codes, all right. The tragedy was that at the time when she had most bitterly needed any reassurance whatsoever, there had been absolutely nothing for it.

She accepted the sheriff's embarrassed condolences along with his verdict of death by misadventure, and wished that she could stop feeling like an accessory before, during, and after the fact. Piecing it together, she simply knew what she knew. And who, especially at the merciful remove of history, can judge with pinpoint accuracy exactly what constitutes the blind spot of another and what does not?

Saint Kathareen's loved a funeral. The gentlefolk did it up brown, defying time and place. Horses led the cortege, wailing trumpets followed. The same fashionable ladies who waited like nervous fillies for next season's hats to appear attended funerals in black contraptions of faille and organza that looked as if they had been designed for a previous generation. A Saint Kathareen's funeral was as stylized as a wedding, and Minerva thought it was preposterous. When Karraman died, she chose her only natural course of action: she refused to go. Since her position was equivocal to begin with, nobody knew what to do about her. In the end they stayed away, too. Not from the festivities. Only from Minerva.

She repaired to her private room at the Inn, dressed in understated mourning, and sat, erect, tearless, vigilant. She expected no one, wanted no one. She needed the fearful silence in which to try to put the pieces of her life together.

When the knock came to the door, she knew reflexively who it was. "Come in, Felder. It's open."

"How'd you know who it was, Min?" opening the door.

"Who else would it be, Felder?" she countered sadly.

"How are you, Min?" Tender.

"Fine, Felder." She looked older by many years than yesterday, but she was telling a truth, in her fashion.

"I'll have lunch sent up."

"Thank you." She wanted food as much as she wanted hives, but knew she needed to normalize something. "Did you go, Felder?"

"To the funeral? I went."

"What did they say?"

"Too much by half." She nodded. He was telling her that no one's words could gild the reality of Karraman himself.

"Was it crowded?"

"Broadway would have loved it. Standing room only. Of course," he added, "your absence was larger than everyone else's presence."

She nodded, and pondered as he phoned down to room service.

Then he leaned back in his chair.

"What are you going to do, Min?"

"Why, what I've always done, I suppose. Run the business, go to Europe, manage the house." Her eyes clouded, but she fought for control, and won. "It isn't that I was his dependent, you know."

"I know."

"And I've always wanted to do some research, Felder. I've never really had time for that. You know: genealogy, geography, geology."

"The three G's." He chuckled.

"Well, it's always seemed to me that those are the variables that direct the fortunes of this Valley. The tidbits of data fascinate me. I'd like to try to put it all together, somehow."

"That's a life's work. For posterity?"

"No," she told him, "nothing like that. For pride, perhaps. For peace." She hesitated. "For filling the hours."

Then she did cry. Felder rose and crossed to her side. He placed a hand on her shoulder. Minerva neither yielded nor resisted. He was an anchor. One needs anchors, she thought, relies on them. But does not necessarily embrace them.

It was so easy, so incorruptible. She had always read that such moments establish entire futures. The heroine either betakes herself to his bed or resoundingly slaps his face, and so the plot turns. But the moment with Felder did not demand that kind of decision, and Minerva was unready to make one of her own.

"You know," he ventured after her composure began its long voyage back into place, "I'm here whenever you need me."

She put her arms around him then, but it was a mother's gesture, a sister's, a friend's. That was how he accepted it.

"You've always been here when I've needed you, Felder, from the very first day. No matter how loath I was to admit it at first," she added contritely. That brought the crinkles of humor back to the corners of his eyes.

"Just so you know," he insisted as he rose to answer the waiter's knock at the door.

"Oh, Felder, I know," she assured him. "I've always needed you. I assume I always will."

The problem was, she thought, as she tried to see beyond her awful bereavement, that she'd never need him in any of the ways that he wanted to be needed by her. What a faithful adulteress I've turned out to be, she mused, and was not dissatisfied with her outlook toward the future.

Her vision of the ensuing years was accurate, largely because she chose to create herself that way. She delved seriously into history, no mere hobbyist. Simultaneously, she remained the working chief of La Vallée, never missing a new season, until she was past eighty. Her boutiques blossomed into chic department-store franchises, setting their standards of excellence by her unerring instincts.

Felder stayed by her side, the next thing to a full partner. Why he never pressed for the title or the honorifics, she never quite understood, but she was relieved. She was fully partnered for life anyway. The fact that the consort in question had died in an oil field struck her as entirely beside the point. Privately she thought that Felder's complacency indicated a *goyische kopf*. He himself had explained that, given the opportunity, the gentile would invest most of his savings in a secure company, while the Jew would go into debt to buy the company for himself. Not that Minerva believed him. But she sometimes wondered why he was spending a lifetime in contradiction to his own adage. After Karraman died, she was too busy for idle psychological conjecture about why Felder chose to keep things as they were. If all else ever hit a lull, there was always something new to contend with over on Calvin-and-Levi.

XVIII

"Karraman did leave the house to me, you realized."

"I kind of expected that."

"Oh, my dear, how I wish I had. Not only didn't I expect it, but even less could I accept it at first. I tried to refuse the legacy, until Karraman's dusty old lawyers convinced me the will was unchallengeable." In the reliving, her composure falters. Hawk, reluctant inquisitor, wants to change his roles, play shepherd to her.

"I think I know how you must have felt, Miss Minerva. Accepting the house meant first you had to accept his death. You—"

"No, Hawk." His staff is too green. She'll make her own way. "That's overly analytical. I was too deeply wounded to venture anywhere near my elementals. I trapped myself in perhaps the most superficial aspects of the problem."

"You never—"

"Hush. I'm getting there. It was the Robley house, you see. To make it the Bolton house was to change everything. That would have obliterated Karraman. I couldn't have borne that and survived."

"But, Miss Minerva, you're a—"

"I said hush, Hawk. Of course. I'm a Robley too. And as soon as I was capable of working that fact back into my reckoning, it was all right.

Karraman had intended to leave Foothill House to his beloved: me. He never did learn that his beloved was his posterity as well, not just through Kate but in the blood. I had spent so many years . . . abrogating, I suppose is the word, that I actually saw certain aspects of myself exactly as I had created them. I was my own Henry Higgins. As soon as I was able to identify myself as an inheritor in double trust—a lover and a Robley—it was all right."

"But you never did present yourself publicly that way, did you?"

"True. Didn't need to. Everyone in town rather expected things to work out just as they did. It was my own guilty doubt I needed to assuage." She fixes her gaze out somewhere in the middle distance of her life. "And of course there was Peter. Poor Peter. He was outraged." Minerva is admitting this fact aloud for the first time in her life. In the heavy afternoon, she knows that if Cara is to learn any of these facts, it is certainly, finally, Hawk who will be the vehicle. If not he, then no one at all. And he is, thank heavens, keenly encouraging her, even as her fatigue mounts and threatens to overtake her.

"What right did Peter have to be outraged? He had left, hadn't he?"

"Oh, Hawk, he had left, in a sense. But in another sense, no one ever really leaves a place like Foothill House. Peter decided Foothill House was his manger, and I was the dog in it. Female dog, to be exact. He was too enamored of New York to want to come here and live. But he didn't want me to have the pleasure, either."

"Did you offer to sell it to him, or what?"

"Hawk. I'm surprised at you," she chides. "Of course I didn't offer to sell it to him. Money was never an issue. Even if it had been, how could I have asked the boy to pay for what I thought he rightfully owned, regardless of Karraman's will. That damned document was the silliest testament to thoughtless largess and at the same time the most tenderhearted legal instrument I've ever heard read. Just imagine all the disgruntled non-heirs. You should have been there! There was a good book in that day alone." Minerva has thrown in that last offhand statement with an intonation that suggests—no, demands—that a book is what this exercise is all about.

Hawk has been feeling the earliest flutters of the same intent for a number of days now. Suddenly he can't remember a time before he knew that the book was writing itself in his head. He senses that his restlessness has as much to do with wanting to seat himself at the old Olympia portable, No. 2 pencils anally lined up before him, reams of twenty-weight manuscript bond at the ready, as it has to do with Cara's departure and their problematic future. Now Minerva's matter-of-fact utterance has fired all his burners into white-hot life. He wants to get going. But so many questions tumble into the vanguard of his thoughts that he has to breathe deeply, settle them, select the balance.

"Let's back up, Miss Minerva, okay?"

"Is that a good practice when time is running out?"

He hears the fearsome implications of her question, but presses on. "Yes, I think we have to do it. We can't assume that there's a single drop of dross."

She nods assent.

"Tell me about Peter."

"It was simple, really. He had already gone east, to New York. I believe you know most of that. He really didn't want to live in the house, so that part of it was moot at the outset. He just wanted it to be here, awaiting his whim, in case he ever came back to the Valley."

"He did come back, didn't he?"

"Not really. Not in his lifetime."

"That's a strange way to put it."

"Strange, but true. I'll get to that. If you want to go back over the whole thing, at least let me give it to you in order."

"No censorship, right?" Hawk shoots back a wry grin.

"My boy, you may be a slow learner, but you do learn with a vengeance when you finally get around to it."

"Touché."

"Never mind, Hawk. I'm teasing you."

"I know it, Miss Minerva. Please don't stop."

"No, I'm not stopping. It would have done no good, you see, for me to have tried to convince Peter of anything. The house, lived in, was a far better investment than the house empty. That's pure economics, but he would have called that line of reasoning self-serving. It was in every way to Peter's advantage to have the house maintained exactly as it always had been, and with me in it. And there was little Howard to think of, too. I wanted to see one of Karraman's children escape early incarceration. Remember, the babies who weren't already at some kind of school or somewhere by the time Emmaline died ended up back with the Musgroves. I shudder to think which was the worse fate. In any case, it was sealed by then."

"So, aside from Howard, that left just Peter," Hawk reiterates.

"Yes, just Peter. I deeded the house over to him, with two provisos. The first was that I could stay on here, if I chose, for my lifetime. Obviously he wasn't going to come back. If he did, I could always add a codicil. The second was that Howard would receive commensurate compensation, when the time came, for what would have been half-interest in the property. What the legal papers didn't spell out, but what I made sure I had written and notarized and sealed in my vault at the factory, was my intention to vacate the premises completely if Peter ever decided to return home and truly did find me in the way. Of course, I never needed to make use of that provision."

"The next question is a hard one," Hawk warns.

"I already know the answer. No, I don't think he would have come back if I had let him know about that clause, or even if I had actually moved out and left it to him. He had suddenly discovered another world out there. As far as he was concerned, the sun rose over the East River and set over the Hudson."

New waves of incredulity sweep over Hawk. She has gone and read his mind again.

"But," she continues, "when he made it abundantly clear that he had no intention of taking up residence here, I did make one small alteration in my own will. For years afterward I bore the guilt of thinking that I was probably committing an act that would match the best of the Musgrove-Robleys in matters of spite, but I don't feel that way anymore. Truly, I don't."

Hawk believes her. He also thinks that, tit for tat, he knows what she's getting at. He prods her to verify. "What do you mean?"

"I mean, I included the provision that upon Peter's death or mine, whichever occurred later, the property would revert, not to his heirs and assigns, but my own."

Hawk thinks: *Wow.* The implications settle over him like a cloak. "What about Howard?" he asks.

"Nothing changes in that regard. He is still to be compensated for his share in the property. My estate will take care of that. Besides, Karraman left the vast majority of his cash, his properties, his securities—every single bit of negotiable paper that he had, plus most of the open shares of San Diego Light and Power—to Howard. Poor Howard, he never would have had to work a day in his life, if he hadn't been so obsessive."

Hawk is duly impressed, but he would rather nudge Minerva gently back to her lost place than continue in this vein. "And you said that Peter was back in New York by then?"

"Yes, New York. And that was what led back to the beginning of the cycle, if you will."

"Something to do with Cara?"

"My word, no, Hawk," as if it is his memory that is being taxed, and somehow coming up short. "It was Gossamer."

"Gossamer Fitzmorris Waldron," Hawk embellishes.

"Not quite. What you should have said is 'Gossamer Fitzmorris Waldron Robley.'"

"You're kidding."

"Not at this stage of the game, Hawk."

"Then who is she?" Hawk has always known that an ineradicable proprietorship exists between Minerva and Gossamer, but he has never been able to make head or tail of it. He has always assumed that Minerva is, as usual, the giver. He does not believe that Gossamer is any more a key to the past than he has already observed, yet he feels an inner pitch of excitement rising. He anticipates fitting another corner piece in a puzzle whose solution he had once assumed was far beyond his ken.

"Peter did marry her." Hawk is astonished that he has missed that fact all along, but realizes quickly that he would actually have had no way of knowing. "She was a New York girl, of course. Gossamer was almost the fulfillment of a dream for Peter. Not only was she born on the island of Manhattan, but both the Waldron and the Fitzmorris families had been entrenched in the *Social Register* forever. In fact, they probably had to *invent* the *Social Register* just to cover families like those. Gossamer was educated, cultivated, stylish, and very, very expensive. She was also meaner than a tomcat, but Peter was purblind. Peter might have even figured that out for himself, if he had lived with her for more than ten minutes."

"What do you mean? Did she divorce him? Is that why she doesn't use his name?"

"On the contrary. She used his name for quite a long time after he was killed. It belonged to a genuine war hero, you see. In those days, that was a profound asset. Besides, it got her into Saint Kathareen's on precisely the terms she wanted. She resumed her maiden name, or should I say names, when she had no more use for the Robley."

"Sounds charming." Minerva's expression tells him that he doesn't know the half of it. "But tell me about the war-hero business. He's always sounded pretty craven to me. Are you saying that he was one of those characters who suddenly grow up under fire, then come back to the old neighborhood to make all the bullies eat their fighting words?"

"Not quite. If growing up under fire had been his destiny, there was plenty of that around here when Em was alive to provide him with all the experience he needed. If the War Department had seen the contortions he tried to devise to avoid being drafted, especially since he was already thirty years old and a newlywed when he got his greetings, they probably would have farmed him out to the enemy as a gift. No, Hawk, as it happened, he occupied a reasonably comfortable Codes and Ciphers desk in Mayfair for nearly four years. Oh, I mustn't be unfair: surely it was harrowing beyond my ken, at times. But you have to admit that there's a certain elegance to it. Especially compared to sleeping in the trenches and lining up for K rations on a tin tray. At least he had his powdered eggs on bone china." She seeks Hawk's concurrence, but he is simply listening.

"Well, shortly before the end of the war, he was playing poker in an air-raid shelter one evening. Suddenly a live grenade rolled down the staircase from nowhere. It had been a quiet evening, they said, almost a normal London night—except for one live grenade that happened to land right smack in the middle of that room. As far as I know, nobody ever even determined that it had belonged to the enemy.

[321]

"Everybody inside fled as fast as they could shove each other out of the way, including Peter. What happened—and precisely because of the kind of coincidence that only happens in wars and murder mysteries, one of my best customers was working as a correspondent in Europe, and happened to be in that very shelter at the time—what happened, as I was saying, was that everybody waited for what seemed like eternities, and the charge never did go off.

"Well, Peter had been the high man in the game that they were playing, and the stakes, I gather, were staggering. He must have been fired by wartime insanity—so many of us were—because God knows he didn't need the money. But he couldn't stand it; he decided that he had to go back and collect the pot. Coincidentally, there was an infant sleeping in a corner inside. Its mother had slipped out before the grenade arrived, most likely to try to scare up some food or something. No one noticed the baby in the bunker, or its absence in the exodus. Just as Peter ran in to collect his booty, the mother came back, hysterical. The baby started to squall, and Peter lost his footing. He fell onto the grenade, and everything went up in smoke. The baby survived, because Peter absorbed most of the blast. There wasn't anything identifiable left of him except his dog tags."

Minerva's voice acquires a quaver. She is, after all, talking about Karraman's firstborn son. But she raises a hand to hush Hawk's condolence. She has more to say. He still attends.

"That poor mother. From the first gruesome panic to the ultimate revelation that her baby was safe, no one could tell her that the rescue had actually been an accident. And in a sense, I suppose Peter did save the child. At least, he gave his life for it. And that, my dear Hawk, constitutes the entire sum and substance of how Peter Robley became an accidental hero.

"I know I'm not being fair. Who knows what he might have done that night if he had actually known that the baby was inside the bunker? And, I keep reminding myself, it was Peter who really did row the river the night that Emmaline went into labor when there was no bridge and the ferry was closed. I doubt whether even Karraman would have been capable of that. But Peter was."

"I'm . . . I don't know what I am," Hawk stammers. "What an incredible story."

"Just an anecdote," Minerva reminds. "There's more."

"Gossamer."

"Yes, Gossamer. She was a pistol, that one. She collected Peter's medals, accepted the tributes, and even went to England right after the war. She said she wanted to visit the scene of Peter's apocalypse. She played it for all it was worth. I don't know when I've ever seen such a flair for drama," said the lady who had blasted her way into the Saint Kathareen's Inn a Diamond Age previously on the wings of a carriage horn's song.

"Her wedding must have been something."

"It must have been. I, to my eternal indifference, was not invited."

Hawk doesn't know whether she's protesting too much or not, so he blurts out the first thing that comes to his mind. And instantly regrets it, in case he has added insult to injury. "My God! Then who made the hats?"

It's all right as far as Minerva is concerned. "Oh, Hawk, thereby hangs the rest of the tale. You should know," gently chiding, "that nothing in the world could have induced Gossamer to buy *anything* in the blighted Valley of Saint Kathareen's, before her marriage, or for many years afterward. I think she even tried to have her groceries imported for a while! Well, in the process of planning the most spectacular wedding New York had ever seen, even New York itself wasn't good enough for Gossamer."

"Uh-oh. I think I know what's coming."

"Of course you do. She did it. She went to London, to the most exclusive milliner she had ever happened to hear of."

"Claire."

"Claire. Naturally, while she was there, she met my daughter, who happened to have chosen to be in residence for the season. Dear Kate, always managing to be at the unfortunate nexus. It seems to have been her most consistent gift. And according to what Claire, who was absolutely aghast, told me, those two played each other like a game of Ping-Pong. The advantage kept going back and forth so fast that no one could keep track of who was winning. Claire always said," she adds, "that the only way they could have kept it up was that each one always thought the other was losing."

"What were they trying to do to each other?" asks Hawk, still smarting for Minerva, who had been so involved, so central, so far away. She must have suffered unutterably. He can't imagine why her skin is still smooth, rather than plated like an armadillo or a Brink's truck.

"I think Kate's motive was to cast enough vengeance into the air about me that life would be brutally uncomfortable, without quite allowing a scandal large enough for me to get out into the open and proceed successfully to live down. Gossamer apparently wanted to store information like a time bomb, and pull it out when she thought it could do her the most good."

"Which is to say, the most damage."

"Yes," Minerva agrees evenly, "one might say that."

"Apparently it didn't work that way on either side."

"You're quite right, Hawk. Not that Gossamer didn't give it the old college try."

"What about Kate?"

"Oh, Kate never stopped trying to hurt me. Her sense of injustice was the backbone of her benighted life." She gives Kate a small wave of dismissal, then pauses to look back at the memory. "She did succeed, you know," she finally amends, "but not in any of the ways she intended. And not"—Minerva takes a deep breath, as if to inhale the basic ingredients of strength—"not permanently. She never reckoned with the possibility of you, Hawk Simon."

Hawk thinks she means because he has been the agent of bringing Cara into both of their lives. "Or Cara."

"Yes, or Cara," but that has not been Minerva's meaning at all. Cara is almost a postscript now.

"But Gossamer, oh, that foolish old Gossamer." Hawk isn't worrying seriously about whether the subject is in a position to eavesdrop, because E. Power Biggs creates as much white noise as any saboteur could hope for. Then his mind's eye harks back to the phenomenon of Minerva standing two rooms away under similar circumstances, responding heartily to his stage whisper about lemon squares, and he wonders. Minerva follows his glance, and tells him not to mind, that Gossamer is as deaf as cardboard. Hawk, who doesn't even realize that his eyes have wandered Gossamer-ward, attributes Minerva's reassuring comment to further clairvoyance, and doesn't know where to look.

"I had never met Gossamer," Minerva tells him, "nor even corresponded with her in a meaningful way. She wrote a very proper thank-you note for my very proper wedding gift, but she ignored all of my other attempts in the direction of family solidarity, or even common courtesy. I assume she was biding her time."

"What for?"

"Well, I don't know what her original plans could have been, but after Peter's death, she consolidated herself in a hurry. I doubt that his body was even cold, or what was left of his body, before she wrote her first unsolicited letter to me. She implied heavily that she had matters to discuss that would affect my entire future, and that of those nearest and dearest to me as well. I suppose she thought that she had me over several barrels, but she didn't know that I had two aces of my own in the hole. The first was that she had not been nearly as subtle with Claire and Kate as she had imagined. Claire was able to perceive perfectly and communicate very clearly what she was leading up to. Forewarned is forearmed, as they used to say."

"They still do," Hawk solemnly assures her.

"Hmmm. Well. The second thing was that I was not only legally secure in everything I owned for as long as I wanted it, but I no longer had a solitary thing—possession, relationship, anything in this world—that I couldn't have borne to lose, except Claire and the family, and I was perfectly secure that I'd never lose them anyway. I was invincible, because I didn't care. I had been in Saint Kathareen's for so long that I almost wished someone *would* come along and reveal everything about Karraman and Kate and me, just to liven things up."

"But," Hawk tries to puzzle, "she never did exactly do that, did she?"

"No, she didn't."

"Why not, after all that buildup?"

"Not because she didn't want to, I assure you. She actually came all the way out here in a chauffeured Daimler just to give me fair warning. But something gave way instead."

"What do you mean?"

"I don't know exactly what it was myself. Perhaps it was the covetousness in her coming to the surface. In Saint Kathareen's she was meeting the big-fish principle face to face for the first time. I think she liked what she saw."

"You mean she was recognizing what it meant to be a Robley right here down home in Robleyville? With all the rights and privileges, and everything?"

"Yes, I think so. Also, perhaps she knew something more about her own mean streak than Peter had understood when he married her. She hadn't been young, you know. Perhaps she had been on the postdebutante circuit for too many years in New York, and she knew that not too many Peter Robleys would come wandering down the pike just dying to marry a locale and the pedigree. He didn't care how stiff the neck was, as long as the credentials were hanging on it.

"All I do know," she continues, "is that our first encounter began with her supercilious announcement that she knew Kate, and ended with a feeble thrust at my reputation in the form that she would be pleased to introduce my daughter to polite society for me if we couldn't agree on the manner in which things were to be handled."

"In other words, you're saying that she tried to blackmail you?"

"I suppose so, although it does seem absurd to call it that. Not only did I have nothing to hide, but there was the proposed victim, me, actually anxious to help the process of revelation along its way."

"You boggle my mind, Miss Minerva."

"I boggle my own, sometimes, Hawk. I keep thinking that I'm talking about some other, distant person."

"I know. Well, don't leave Gossamer hanging. . . ."

"There was a time when that's exactly what I would have wanted to do, you know." She laughs.

"Yeah, but I mean, how did she end up here, in the house? Peaceful coexistence and all?"

"I suppose you'd prefer a more dramatic answer, but the fact is that it was a matter of course. We were two women of a certain age. She was bereft of a husband she had scarcely loved, and I of a beloved I had never married. We were related as closely to each other through the history and eccentricities of all the Robleys as either of us could have been to anybody at the time. She was a poor little rich girl looking for a roost, and I was the sole legal possessor of the henhouse. She undoubtedly thought at the beginning that she'd be able to get it away from me without a whimper, but in the final analysis, I truly believe that she never would have stayed if I had actually gone. It was Emmaline all over again. After all"—she chuckles—"who would have been left to lord things over with her incessant claims to legitimacy? Maybelle Junior? Or the Third? None of those gutsy old Maybelles has ever been impressed by *anybody*. What a lesson we could learn. Ah, well . . ."

Hawk can feel Minerva's relief at having delivered herself of this much this afternoon. He not only perceives, but intuits, that she is suddenly fatigued beyond her prior mortal experience.

"Miss Minerva, I think I'm going to go home now. I think I have a lot of organizing to do, so that I can come back tomorrow with the tape recorder. If it's okay."

Minerva understands that he is tactfully skirting the reality of her exhaustion but that there is indeed truth in his protests about his own. He looks worn out. She has placed the burden of her entire existence squarely on his young shoulders. She prays that he isn't going to buckle.

"Of course you can come back, Hawk. Since when do we act so formal?"

He wants to tell her that it is since he has begun to perceive the grandeur of all the dimensions of her life, but he just smiles engagingly. "I never meant not to be polite, Miss Minerva. I guess my tongue is getting all caught up in my lack of sleep."

"Well, dear, you go on home and do some catching up. I'll look for you sometime tomorrow."

Each one of them wants to implore the other please to call if Cara turns up, to come running, to send up flares or light sticks. But both remain silent, not only because each hesitates to tax the other at a time like this but also because there exists between them now a new, scarcely perceived but palpable level of trust. What will be, they will handle.

FOUR

XIX

Maybelle Three Kennebec answers the door.

"She ain't a-feelin' good, and I don't think you oughtta see her today. I don't know what ya told her yestiddy, but she ain't a-feelin' good about it." Surly as ever.

Hawk has never known how to respond to Maybelle, so he asks politely if he might just pay his respects for a minute. What he would really like to do is shake her by the shoulders and tell her that he didn't tell Minerva anything yesterday. She did all the telling. What was probably bothering her was the temporary aftereffect of a simple surgical procedure for the excision of a lifetime of memory.

"Maybelle, just get yourself out of Hawk's way and send him in here," comes Minerva's voice, decisive and clear. He can't tell much about its vitality or lack thereof, over the eternal din of Gossamer's playthings.

Minerva looks drawn, somehow. Hawk has the momentary illusion that she is leaning back with her feet propped up on cushions, but she is actually sitting erect on the davenport. Something in her face has given him the phantom vision of another kind of repose.

Maybelle stalks away. "Just like her mother and her gramma before her," Minerva observes. "She owns it all."

"Yes, well," says the recovering Hawk, "I've seen pride of ownership handled a little more delicately."

"I suppose so," she consoles. "You have the recorder today, I see?"

"Yes," brandishing the microphone.

"Good. I think the ends are tied up now, but I suppose I do have some final comments for posterity. After all, this did start out as an oral history." She looks dreamy.

"Are you sure you're up to this today, Miss Minerva? Yesterday was pretty exhausting." Something deep inside him is suddenly wary. "Tomorrow—"

"Forget tomorrow," she snaps.

"Are you sure?"

"Hawk, this is Minerva you're talking to. Would I say so if I weren't?" Of course not. With a smile, he gives himself back to her, feeling like a child who tried to sneak off without asking to be excused. Minerva gazes off into the distance, her hands wandering idly over the opal-and-diamond lavaliere hanging elegantly at the base of her throat.

"But before we begin," she tells him, "I'm parched. Will you be a dear and scout up Maybelle? She can make some lemonade, if Gossamer has already finished what was in the refrigerator."

"Sure. I won't be a minute."

Hawk checks the kitchen, but Maybelle isn't there. He shouts down the basement stairs, but only darkness lies beneath. Gossamer's door is slightly ajar. He tiptoes up to it and sees that she is apparently sleeping like a mammoth, opaque jellyfish. For some reason she has converted the output of the stereo to Piston's *Incredible Flutist*, whose dirgelike opening processional is entertaining at full blast. The lemonade pitcher emptily reflects a pinpoint of light from a tiny moth hole in the velvet drapes which Gossamer insists upon keeping perpetually drawn.

Maybelle Three is nowhere in sight. She could be anywhere in either of the rambling wings of the second floor, or up in one of the towers. She might have gone on one of her mysterious unchronicled errands, or she might just be hiding out, refusing to acknowledge any claim upon her time made by someone other than a certified member of the household.

Hawk won't traffic with that. He feels certified, anyway, to do some independent acting of his own. He tiptoes to Gossamer's bedside and takes up the pitcher. Feeling like a combination of trespasser and king, he steals back to the kitchen, finds the lemons, and starts to measure sugar out of one of the incongruously Bauhaus collection of canisters arranged precisely on the counter of the ancient four-legged sink.

In a few triumphant minutes Hawk has made the lemonade, taken out the ice, and found two of the crystal tumblers that Minerva is fond of using to serve everything from vichyssoise to beer. She says that they grip well. He even finds a tray, and walks out with a final glance around the kitchen to make sure he has restored everything to the order in which he has found it. It's the least he can do. It's high time he started doing everything in his power to begin to repay Minerva.

"Miss Minerva?"

She has dozed off, another unsurprising elderly behavior which surprises Hawk, because he has never seen her do anything elderly before.

"Miss Minerva?"

He looks at her closely. Oh, God. He reaches out to touch her forehead, although he doesn't quite know what that locality will tell him, then her hands, which somehow seem more to the point. Then he realizes that he can't because of the lemonade things in his hand. He sets them down with a crash, trembling in a place that starts in the middle of his stomach and radiates out to every extremity.

He touches her brow, finds with momentary elation that it is warm, human, fleshly. Hope dies in an instant, as he removes his hand and her head lolls improbably to the side.

"Oh God." This time he says it aloud, because he understands fully that she isn't breathing, and he can't think of anybody else to call on. Then he stands up in a jerky reflex and heads for the stairs, shouting for Maybelle Three at the top of his lungs. She emerges from the kitchen, wiping her hands on her skirt, as if she had never been anywhere else all day. Coming from that direction, she startles Hawk like a ghost.

"Stop yer shoutin'. There's old people in this house." As if he didn't know. He is too panicky to be angry or repressed.

"Maybelle, it's Minerva."

"What's Minerva?" In the phlegmatic Valley rhythm, just at the time when her staccato sharpness would have been welcome, familiar.

"In there." Hawk points, and starts to hurry back to the parlor. Maybelle follows in her own good time. "Please, can't you hurry?"

Maybelle has already begun to assume that things are past hurrying. She is right, but Hawk has not yet faced up.

Maybelle looks sharply at Minerva's lifeless frame. Her hand is still somehow attached to the opal pendant, having clenched the chain like a grapple when the final spasm overtook her. Maybelle lifts her eyelid, closes it again, and without a word or a glance at Hawk, she leaves the room.

He thinks he is roaring. On the *Incredible Flutist,* the sixth-movement crowds have begun to cheer. Where was the ovation when I should have been giving it to her? he flagellates himself.

"Where are you going?"

She turns around and answers matter-of-factly. "To call Heidekker's."

[331]

"Why Heidekker's?"

Still nonchalant: "Because the Robleys always get buried out of the Heidekker's." And marches sullenly off to do what must be done.

Hawk is both astounded and grateful. Maybelle hasn't been in this house all her life, woman and child, without acquiring a sense of the rightness of things. In his relief, Hawk stares back down at Minerva, tottering at the edges of his pain and grief. He takes up her hand, still warm, still dead, and can't believe that he hears, issuing from his own lips in a tuneless whisper, the ancient Hebrew mourners' chant. He couldn't even rally it for his father when Margo needed it so badly, and here it is, unsought.

Yisgadol v'yisgadash sh'may rabo, he tells Minerva and God. Then he is unable to remember what comes next. In frustration, in pain, and with the full and overwhelming sense that at this moment there is not a single thing left for him to do, Hawk begins to weep. He falls to his knees, puts his head on Minerva's lap, and does that: begins to weep.

As Cara tiptoes, like something ethereal, through the front door.

"Hawk?"

He looks up, but cannot muster the words for her.

"Hawk? What happened? What's wrong?"

She starts to approach, but he leaps to his feet and holds her off with the barrier of his palm and his expression. She is still many yards away, but she flinches as if she has been touched by something hot and stinging.

Hawk finds his voice. It is the low, perilous thunder he has not used since he took leave of Howard Robley's class a thousand years ago. He is at the limit of his control, and Cara knows it the minute she hears him.

"You're too late, Caravelle."

"What do you mean, Hawk?"

"She's dead, that's all."

"She's dead? No—I can't believe it. What do you mean, she's dead? She can't be!"

"She's really most sincerely dead, your grandmother is. And guess what, Caravelle? I didn't even need you for the postmortem. You might as well stick to farm hounds, baby, because we can handle this kind of thing just as well without you." He betrays the truth behind the bitter, hateful words with the tears which continue to etch salty scars into his cheeks. Cara understands the mechanism, doesn't push.

"I'm sorry, Hawk."

"You're sorry, you cold bitch? How can you say you're sorry? She's your grandmother, not mine, and you were too bloody egotistical to come back here where you should have been."

Cara isn't going to defend herself now. "I'm sorry I wasn't here, Hawk," a nice, all-purpose, temporary cover. "I'm sorry you had to be alone when this happened. . . ."

"Yeah, well, you're the one who's going to be alone with her now. Give me a ring when you're leaving. I'll come back and be here."

"Hawk . . . this can't be what you really want. . . ."

"Oh, yeah? Well, be that as it may, it's what I'm really going to do. Since when have you been paying attention to anything anybody wants, with the extravagant exception of one Caravelle Bolton Funk, fire-breathing dragon?"

With a sharp intake of breath, she lets that go, too. Blood or no, Hawk is so much further into this than she is that he needs to be allowed the irrationality of his shock. He snatches up the tape recorder and makes his way toward the door.

"Hawk . . . one more thing."

"What is it?" he snarls, wiping his eyes with his fists. Cara's heart goes out to that.

"Has anyone been called?"

He won't even give that to her. "Ask Maybelle," and storms out the door. Cara hears the Healey start with a grind and a lurch, and flashes on some malign specter sitting in the driver's seat where Hawk is supposed to be. The real Hawk Simon, she knows, is absent. She breathes a prayer for his safety, uncurls Minerva's hand from the necklace in order to fold it into her lap, and goes to find Maybelle. Cara has placed her tears on hold, but she has no idea how long they will agree to stay there.

Hawk gets back to the farm without incident, but he can never, from that day forward, remember having driven the route. He pulls up beside the chickenhouse by reflex, then begins to wonder how the simple routines of a brilliant day can go on undiminished when the entire world has changed its contour. For the moment, he can't face the house, can't face Radiant, can't surmount the obstacles of pain. He wanders around to the back of the house, aimlessly at first. Before long he understands that he is moving in the direction of Lucy's grave.

"Lucky dog," he mutters. "You missed the worst of it."

Although he didn't mark the grave, the spot is unmistakable. Of course the freshly turned earth will signal the place for some time. Even when the seasons weather the newness away, the sheltering trees will stand monument. Hawk was careful when he chose the site.

But as he approaches, he sees a tangle of rubble in place of the lovingly mounded soil. He sees great clods of earth scattered, and shreds of green plastic flickering to the tune of the breezes which aren't quite powerful enough to swirl them cleanly away. He stands, mutely paralyzed, afraid to peer over the edge into the depths, for fear that he'll find Lucy, decomposing and maggoty. His imagination does a better job on the image than his eyes would have done, because Lucy's body is gone.

Without warning Hawk finds that he is vomiting into the grass more contents than he thought his stomach could hold. Finally, depleted and exhausted, he sinks to the ground at the base of a tree, where he can stare at the grave without seeing into it. He cannot imagine what vile marauders would rob a grave—a dog's grave, no less. Every time he thinks of Lucy, stolen from him both in life and now in symbol, he can't help thinking of Minerva. His mind asks: How can they do this to me? Over and over again. At last it turns into a numbing litany, shutting out the present agonies that are too much and too complicated for him to bear.

The sun is low when Hawk finally pulls himself to his feet and walks back to the house. Radiant, who was sleeping when Hawk pulled up in the Healey, has assumed that he has gone off in somebody else's car somehow. He sees nothing amiss. He is answering the telephone as Hawk comes through the back door.

"Oh. Wait. He just came in." He hands it over. Hawk wants to talk to no one, but has no fighting strength left, either.

"Hello. This is Hawk."

"Hello, Simon. Sorry to be bothering you at a time like this." It takes Hawk a second to realize that he is talking to Howard Robley. It takes a little longer for him to assimilate the understanding that dumb old insensitive Howard is actually extending condolences to him, Hawk.

"It's okay, Mr. Robley. I should be extending my sympathy to you. I do, I mean. You meant a lot to her."

"Thank you, Hawk." There is silence while Howard decides to go on with the script. Meanwhile Hawk is trying to decide how to say, "Well, 'bye," without sounding too rude under the circumstances. Robley picks it up.

"Uh, Hawk, I guess you wonder why I called."

"Well, at first, Mr. Robley. But I guess you realize that she meant a lot to me, too."

"Well, yes. I do realize that."

"Thanks."

"Yes. You're welcome. But there's something else, too."

"Something I can do for Miss Minerva? I mean, for the family? Anything at all, Mr. Robley. All you need to do is ask."

"Thank you, Hawk. You see, this is a little awkward for me."

"Don't worry about it. Just ask."

"Well." He fumbles some more. "It's not customary in our family to ask immediate relatives to serve as pallbearers, Hawk . . . That is, I feel that you're almost *too* close to ask to do this favor for us, Simon. You've become as much a part of Minerva's family as anyone could have. Yet," he continues, at last warming to his assignment, "I know that she would have wanted it this way."

Hawk, unsure of exactly what Howard has almost said, hesitates.

"Please say yes, Hawk. We'll be most grateful. The family and I," Howard amends. "We want you to be a pallbearer."

Hawk swallows hard. "It would be an honor," he tells Howard, trying to keep his voice from blowing into smithereens along with his entire future. "Just tell me what to do."

"Be at the church twenty minutes early. Someone from Heidekker's will tell you then."

"I'll be there." Hawk, in the new intimacy of his situation, can't bring himself to say "Howard"; yet he has long since bypassed "Mr. Robley." He lets it go at nothing.

"Thanks, Hawk. It means a lot."

"Welcome." And hangs up. Then realizes that he has ascertained neither the day nor the time of the funeral. He almost lifts his hand to call back, but doesn't have left that much initiative or conversation. He'll read it in the paper.

The stated time was two o'clock the following day. That was a shockingly speedy arrangement for the good folk of Saint Kathareen's, who chattered their resentment at being deprived of the usual festival of mourning. But Minerva had had no intention of losing control of this one. Karraman's had been more than enough. Efficient to the last, she left a letter detailing the efficient dispatch of her body, and the conduct of the surrounding ceremonies.

Hawk felt at home with her plans. He couldn't wait for the public mourning to be over and done. He needed desperately to get home to the farm and start to work things out for himself. As long as Minerva lay unburied, he felt unsettled, unable to rest in peace until he felt assured that Minerva was going to do so, too. Everything that was sane and rational in him said that a silly burial ritual had nothing to do with it, but he couldn't help the way he felt. He was restless, edgy, close to hysteria.

He didn't think he'd ever forget a moment of the funeral. All through the service he kept asking himself how people ever manage to set themselves free of haunting events like this, which sear straight through the forehead into the cells of the brain. Mercifully he had forgotten even that thought process before the week was out. He could have sworn, however, that someone had sprayed the church with lavender and apple blossoms that day. For the rest of his life, whenever he encountered that aroma again, he recalled, not Foothill House, but the stifling, hard-backed first pew on the left.

Hawk has driven his own car, alone, to the cemetery. It wasn't bad on the way out, when he had a solid sense of direction and purpose. He feels sentimental about funeral processions and parades, and doesn't particularly feel like sharing the feeling, or thinning it out. Now, the formalities over, he feels bad. He feels especially bad about Radiant, whom he hasn't even told about his agenda for this day. Radiant never met Minerva, but he would have come anyway, Hawk is certain. Radiant would have come along just to make sure. Make sure of what, Hawk doesn't quite know, and probably Radiant doesn't know either. But since Cara walked out, Radiant has Taken Responsibility. He wants things to be sturdy, the way they used to be. He hasn't said anything, but Hawk sees him watching. Hawk totters around between annoyance and gratitude. He should have told Radiant.

The cars ahead of Hawk's on the narrow cemetery road are starting to pull slowly away, but one or two ahead of him are still unoccupied. He leaves his door open against the heat, since he has left the top up out of a deference he realizes Minerva probably would have chortled over. Wearily he puts his head down on the steering wheel and closes his eyes.

"Hawk?"

Whatever gave his heart the right to put up that kind of clamor? Can she hear it?

"Hello, Cara." He looks up squinting, partly because the sun is behind her, and partly because he doesn't want her to read what might have crept into his eyes to ambush any emotions that he'd left lying around.

"I'm sorry, Hawk. I really am." He doesn't know whether she's apologizing or offering condolences, but he's too burnt-out to take it at anything but face value.

"So am I, Cara. So am I." That's as far as he can go.

"Hawk?"

"Yeah?"

"Could you drive me back?"

"How'd you get here?" Not contrary, but curious.

"I came in the limousine."

"Don't you want to go back with them?"

"No. Howard keeps crying in a snotty old Kleenex, and Maybelle keeps telling him in no uncertain terms that cryin' don't profit the dead nothin'. I feel too crummy to deal with how hilariously funny both of them really are. They're—I don't know—readable."

"But not today."

"That's right. Maybe not for a long time."

Hawk notices that the limousine has departed, as have all but one of the cars in front. The other car contains some elderly strangers who have stared down Hawk and Cara separately but uttered no greeting. She leaves him precious few options, that Cara.

"Well, I guess you better get in. We're holding up the line in back."

"Thanks, Hawk." She hurries around to the passenger side of the car. When did she last sit there? Hawk can't quite remember.

For a while he drives in silence. Then he clenches his fists and firms up his resolve in one stroke. "Where did you go?"

"I went downriver," she answers softly.

"I can't believe this," he shouts. "What kind of answer is 'I went downriver'? You sound like some kind of river rat. What does 'downriver' mean?"

"Downriver means downriver." She says it more casually than she is feeling. Emotion is welling in her for many reasons. Not the least of these is the fear that something has permanently scarred Hawk, that she will never be able to cut through the veneer of his dispassion again. But now, somehow, she thinks that maybe it's going to be all right: here he is, flailing away inches from his own surface, and she hasn't half-tried to get through. She feels the first optimism in what seems like centuries.

Until he gets to the bottom of the cemetery road, and begins to turn left.

"Where are you going, Hawk?"

"I'm driving you home. Isn't that what you wanted?"

"The farm is the other way."

"Who said anything about the farm? Your home is Foothill House. You might have missed the main event, but you certainly got back in time to cash in at the window." He is seething.

She looks like a forlorn shuttlecock, battered between anger and pain and humiliation and incredulity at the crass motive Hawk has just attributed to her. Caravelle What's-her-name, cool in a crisis and vulnerable only as the schedule permits, bursts into plaintive, gasping sobs that issue from a place in her being that neither Hawk nor probably anyone else has ever seen before. It undoes Hawk.

"Cara . . don't." He shifts into neutral, jams on the brakes, reaches out to her with his arms and his sorrow and his regret and his ambition and the encapsulated histories of his past, present, and future. The cars behind him begin an impatient clamor, to which he responds with a soft curse, a gentle pulling back from Cara, and a shift into reverse. He backs up straight into the bumper of the car behind him, curses again, and peels away with a screech, turning right, toward the farm. Cara is crying and crying, Hawk grinding relentlessly through the gears until he reaches a place where he can free his right arm to hold her again.

"It was just more than I could handle all at once," she sobs.

"I know," he answers, from the center of his own pain, "but I would have helped you."

"I didn't know that," she confesses. "No one ever did that for me before."

"You never had a family before."

"Don't say that, Hawk," she tells him. "I had Kate. I really did. And I always knew that I was going to find something special waiting for me. I wouldn't have kept looking if I hadn't known that."

"Baby, baby, come back from Oz. Maybe Minerva was right. It was the quest itself that became your family, not the people who were there at the end of the story. But this is the last reel. All the identities have been revealed. The question is, what are you going to do now that the lights are going up again? People have to go home—if they can decide where that is."

Silence. She doesn't answer. Hawk knows she needs more time than this, so he doesn't press. He cradles her as gently as he can, with the gearshift as the bundling board between them, and thus they arrive home.

Hawk doesn't want to let the moment escape. There's more that needs to be settled. But Radiant is shouting from the kitchen.

"That you, Hawk?"

"Yeah, Ray. What's happenin'?"

"I'm cleaning up."

"Congratulations, old buddy. I'm proud of you."

"Yeah. Well, what do you think I ought to do with the rest of this groundhog stew?"

"For Christ's sake, Radiant, what's that stuff still doing around here?"

"Honest, Hawk, my mom always said you could keep stuff a week. Cara hasn't been gone even half that long." He's pleading a case. Hawk can't imagine that Radiant can be right about that. They all seem to have been hurtled through eternities; but Radiant is, for once, absolutely correct.

"Well, it doesn't matter. Toss it."

"Hawk, Cara doesn't like to waste stuff," shouts Radiant with a hint of admonition, as though he really wanted the vile mess in his icebox, as though Cara has been standing guard all along to make sure that things have been going just right. As though everything might be jeopardized once and for all by this final defiance.

Hawk opens his mouth to punctuate the throwaway order with further profanity for emphasis, when Cara wipes her eyes, smiles faintly, silences Hawk with a gesture, and shouts, "It's okay, Radiant. Groundhog doesn't keep for more than a lifespan or two. We've been through several."

Radiant comes crashing out of the kitchen, his ponytail flying, and crushes Cara in a breathtaking squeeze. Hawk wonders belatedly what it is about himself that has prevented him from entering into that kind of uncomplicated reunion.

"Hey, Cara! You're back!" He looks so irrepressible behind his grin and his apron that Cara has to laugh.

"Not so fast, kid. There are a few things to settle first."

"I rolled up the sleeping bag, Cara, and I didn't even know you were coming. I roll it up every day. Come on in and look. You'll see. . . ."

There's so much more to it than that that Cara doesn't know how to refuse. She follows along. She is newly touched at the massiveness of human guilt, which so often allows everybody to take responsibility for everything.

"Super, Radiant," she tells him, looking around at the nearly unrecognizable orderliness. "You've done an incredible job."

"Hawk helped a lot," Radiant offers shyly.

"I know, baby. I know."

And thus the late afternoon passes, with support and praise and tentative self-congratulation being passed around the house like wishes.

Radiant has proudly constructed an eccentric lasagna out of some of the usual ingredients, plus some leftover matzo which Margo sent Hawk from New Jersey a Passover or two ago. Radiant read somewhere that you could soak the sheets and squeeze them, and create a facsimile of noodles that are no harder to handle than the real item. The resultant concoction is really pretty good, Radiant thinks, and he doesn't understand why nobody is eating much. With no Lucy around for Leftover Management, Radiant is more conscious of such things than anyone would have dreamed possible. Besides, his ego is involved.

What he doesn't understand is that the lack of appetite which is epidemic at the table has nothing to do with the food on it, or even with the funeral. Hawk and Cara, each in a separate way, are simply too filled up with everything to have room for one more commodity or emotion or demand on their personalities. Hawk realizes suddenly that people vomit when they grieve for more reasons than uncomplicated rejection of the loss. There is also the bitter alloy that he is now experiencing for the first time—the sense of being replete, tested beyond capacity, glutted with an unselective measure of brutal living. Queasy again, he has to leave the table.

"Don't you want any frozen yogurt?" Radiant calls sadly after him. "They had natural banana."

"Don't worry, Radiant. He'll be okay."

"Yeah. I guess he's been through a lot."

"You've helped him get through it."

"Nah, not really." Embarrassed but not ungrateful, Radiant starts to clear the table. He decides to keep the leftovers next to the groundhog stew, which he has saved after all. In memoriam of something.

Cara trails Hawk out to the front steps. "I need to go over to the big house, Hawk," she announces gently.

"So that's the way it's going to be, is it? I had to wait all day, and sit through that godawful ethnic folk festival of Radiant's, and listen to you heaping all kinds of kudos on him on top of that, just so you could tell me that you're leaving after all? What happened to all that righteous indignation in the car after the funeral? Or was that just another part of the old act?"

He expects an outburst in kind, and girds for it. Cara surprises him. Her posture, her voice, are full of equanimity now. She reminds him so much of her grandmother at this moment that he wants to reach out and enfold both of them, all of their shared and unshared coding and being, and cherish them forever. Package deal.

"Hawk, please. My car is at the big house. My things are at the big house. I stayed there last night—remember?"

"Then you saw Howard?"

"Yes."

"Did you tell him?"

"That she left the house to me? Of course."

"That must have been one hell of a bomb."

"You'd be surprised."

"I would?"

"Yes, because he wasn't. Surprised, I mean. I think he expected a revelation of some sort all along. I think he was a little disappointed that it was as long as it was in coming. He wanted to join the party as early as he could."

"Really? Is that what he said? I thought he'd be infuriated."

"No, Hawk, dear." In her attempt to reassure him, Hawk still hears Minerva, loud and clear. "It was funny, though. His major regret seems to be that he didn't know more about Minerva's whole story, and mine, and everything, when he was, as he puts it, 'in a more *feck*-und phase.'"

"I always did wonder how to pronounce that word," Hawk interjects. "Leave it to Howard actually to use it. King Anachronism."

Cara nods solemnly. "Anyway, he told me that he thinks the story has to be written, but he's going to leave it to someone a little better up to the task."

"Ha. Do you think that was a hint or anything? Too bad he couldn't have suggested someone who could fill the bill."

"Are you being bitter, Hawk? Because, please don't. Just think about it, okay?"

"Cara, I've thought about it until I can't remember when I wasn't thinking about it. But what am I supposed to do when my whole world turns upside down at one time? I'm just not that disciplined. I feel like I don't have a stable place to dig in and rest my bones. Listen. I want to tell you something. You know how people say that genius responds to tragedy, and great work comes out of great suffering? Well, I'm here to tell you different. Real people respond to tragedy by wallowing in it."

"Like you're doing now, right?" she challenges.

"Right. No, dammit, wrong. Like I'm doing everything in my power not to do, but it isn't that easy. I can handle all the turbulence outside the frame, Cara, if the foundation's solid. Right now I don't feel like i have any foundation at all." Hawk knows that he is being theatrical. But so what?

Cara sees him warming to his role, goes along anyway. "I'll tell you what," she proposes. "I'll take the Healey over to the big house myself, if you'll let me drive it, and you can stay here and settle your head. That way you won't have to deal with Howard or anything. You'll feel better when I get back, and we'll talk."

"What about your car?" He doesn't know whether he's being contentious or practical.

"We can get it another day. Or Radiant can come with me and drive it back, if you want."

The latter idea galvanizes Hawk. "No, that's okay. I'll go. That way we won't have to worry." About whatever vague Radiant things there are to worry about.

"You know," she introduces tentatively, "it will be Howard's house now."

He didn't know, didn't even think of it that way. "You do know that it belongs to you? That's what you said."

"It did. Yes, no one wasted any time getting that information disseminated. My grandmother's last few days must have been busy ones, Hawk. Imagine! Finding me, figuring out that I was who I was—taking it on faith, actually, and getting the legalities all straightened out, with one foot virtually in the grave. Well, anyway, it isn't right for me, and it is for Howard. We'll be friends, Howard and I, and the door will stay open between us. And Gossamer can stay put. Let *him* manage her and Maybelle," comes the twinkling afterthought.

Hawk is surprised to find that he isn't disappointed, but he hasn't identified the source of his relief. It's he for whom Foothill House isn't right, and he has been fearing that he would have to hassle that aspect out with Cara if she ever came back. Now she seems to have come back, and the hassle doesn't have to happen.

"Okay, Cara. I'm glad. And I think I'll stay here after all, while you run over there. We can pick up the other car tomorrow."

[341]

"I'll be back soon," she promises.

"Okay."

"You all right?"

"Sure. You?"

She pauses, and looks at him squarely. The flecks dance in her amber eyes, and she smiles. "Sure. Keys?" Takes them, and heads out the door.

Hawk watches the Healey wind down the hill, past the beans as they scale the poles, past the bushy tomatoes, toward the stand of sassafras, not so unfriendly in the perspective of other healthy things growing. Cara has said she'll be back soon. Howard Robley is ensconced where Hawk can easily find him to tell him what he's going to do, ask his assistance, make his amends. Radiant is in the kitchen, and Paul the Parrot is in his cage. Hawk doesn't need to go hunting for Lucy's body any more than he needs to check out the cemetery to make sure that Minerva hasn't gone out wandering among the spooks in the Valley night.

He crawls into the house through Radiant's window, then goes to the typewriter and pulls a stack of twenty-weight paper out of the library drawer underneath it. The pencils are already in place. He must have done that the other night in some kind of daze.

Hawk seats himself at the table, just as Radiant strolls out of the kitchen with his mouth open, all ready to start a conversation. As soon as he realizes that Hawk is really, at long last, going to work, Radiant smiles, puts on his brakes, and gives Hawk a silent God-bless. Paul tweaks his feathery head in the direction of first one and then the other.

Hawk, determined, ignores both of them. What's past is prologue. Now it is Minerva's turn.

The text of this book is set in 10 point Baskerville No. 2.